**Passions caught up in a poignant conflict
between violence and peace . . . hate and desire**

Blair Tyler—Loyalty to the South burned in her blood until she met Matthew Harwell and discovered in a Yankee's arms a greater fire.

Matthew Harwell—Weary of battle and death, he wanted to believe in Blair and her love, yet he no longer knew how to trust.

Callie Tyler—Full of youthful energy and innocence, this child on the verge of womanhood would witness events to test the strongest heart.

Samuel Tyler—An old man left to defend his family, he stood straight as a ramrod before the enemy's guns aimed at his land.

Anna Mary Tyler—No matter what their uniform, the wounded were precious boys she would care for, never forgetting the son and husband who rode away clad in Confederate gray.

KATHERINE KILGORE

THE SABER AND THE ROSE

A DELL BOOK

Published by
Dell Publishing
a division of
Bantam Doubleday Dell Publishing Group, Inc.
666 Fifth Avenue
New York, New York 10103

ISBN: 0-440-20917-X

Printed in the United States of America

Published simultaneously in Canada

December 1991

10 9 8 7 6 5 4 3 2 1

OPM

For Gerry, who keeps getting better

*And in memory of my lean and fierce
Confederate grandfathers:*

*Private Samuel Brentz Turk,
4th Kentucky Infantry*

*Private Joshua Jasper Cobb,
5th Georgia Cavalry*

Author's Note

All military references in *The Saber and the Rose* are historically accurate with one exception. I have taken the literary liberty of replacing the 7th Illinois Cavalry in Grierson's Raid with the 2nd Illinois Cavalry, my hero's regiment.

1

It was a beautiful morning for mid-November in northern Mississippi. The warmth that beat on Callie's back had a crisp feel to it, with a hint of hard frosts to come. The sun was so bright she had to squint her eyes against it to see the crimson of sourwood and sumac across her grandpa's pasture where the trees of White Oak swamp began.

As Callie leaned against the snake-rail fence, she was unaware that the sunshine lit her hair with a brilliance to vie with the sourwood and sumac. Callie's flyaway red hair was the bane of her twelve-year-old existence, eliciting cries of "gingersnap!" from the wretched boys that she wanted to impress. Callie hated it! And now she'd gone out again without her bonnet and could all but feel the freckles popping out across her face. Tomato-colored pigtails and freckles were a cross to bear!

Scuffing her toe in the dirt, she tried not to think about the hideousness of her personal appearance as she continued talking to Eli Spence and Willie Carr. Eli and Willie, privates in Company K of the 6th Mississippi Infantry, were on picket, guarding the northern outposts on the road to Holly Springs. Anna Mary Tyler, Callie's mother, had said she shouldn't talk to the men while they were on picket, but Anna Mary had gone into town for her weekly duty at the hospital. The picket stand was right in front of Waverley, the Tyler house.

Callie was now in the middle of a detailed description of a Grand Exhibition put on in the Masonic Hall for the benefit of the soldiers. Callie's older sister, Blair, had had a prominent role in one of the *tableaux vivants*, but Eli Spence and Willie Carr had been unable to attend.

"Smilax in her hair?" Willie was saying with interest. He propped one hip against the fence, hands wrapped casually about his musket barrel.

"Yes," Callie said. "And she had on Isabella Kendall's black velvet opera cloak and chains on her wrists that we painted with gilt so they'd look like gold, and her hair long, down her back, and the wreath of smilax on her brow—"

"Lordy!" Private Willie Carr breathed in appreciation. "What I wouldn'a give to see it!"

"And she was kneeling in front of Lieutenant Phillips —he was King Cotton—and he was holding the Confederate flag, and—"

"What'd they have her chained up for?" Eli Spence said.

Private Spence did not look first-rate military, Callie thought. His linsey blouse and butternut-brown Confederate britches hung on his lank, angular frame as if flapping about a skeleton, while his wispy black beard dangled past his Adam's apple.

"Blair represented Maryland," she said. "That's why she was chained."

Eli considered this for a time in silence. Then he apparently decided the effort of further contemplation would require more energy than he was disposed to devote to it. Turning his head to one side, he spat a rich stream of tobacco juice into the dust of the road.

Callie started to explain about Maryland lying beneath the Yankee despot's heel, but decided she'd rather go on with her description of the Exhibition. She'd not yet told them about *her* role in the entertainment, and that was really the most thrilling part of all.

"What I wouldn'a give to see it!" Private Willie Carr said again, with obvious sincerity, looking hopefully toward the Tyler house.

"I recited a poem in the Exhibition," Callie said quickly. "I stood up on the stage all by myself."

Willie Carr kept staring dreamily in the same direction and gave no sign of having heard her. Eli Spence, masticating slowly, looked as if he were in a trance.

"Everybody said it was real good," Callie continued.

And Private Willie Carr could just give up trying to catch a glimpse of Miss Blair Tyler, because if he but knew it, she was awaiting the arrival of Lieutenant Phillips. When Callie'd left the house about twenty minutes ago, Blair was getting into her riding habit and saying that it was almost warm enough for a picnic.

"Would y'all like to hear it?" Callie felt a tight, sour sensation rising in her throat. Tossing her head, she slung a bright red pigtail behind her shoulder. Lieutenant Phillips, resplendent in plumed slouch hat and collar bars, should be riding up any minute. If she was lucky, he would say, "Heartbreaker!" and wink at her as he passed.

" 'Oh yes, I am a Southern girl and glory in the name!' " Callie almost shouted. Eli blinked and Willie turned and looked at her. "That's the first line," she said quickly. "Now I'll recite the rest of it."

She was already feeling better. The stirring words of the poem buoyed her spirits, enabling her to forget for a moment the terrible affliction of being twelve years old, freckled, and flat-chested, while forever languishing in the shadow of a dazzling older sister. Callie set her mind on higher things.

" 'And boast of it with greater pride than glittering wealth and fame!' "

Her delivery last night had been inspired. All the ladies had said as much to her mother. Yet how could she have helped but be, when the poem had wrapped her in trumpets and drum rolls of patriotic fervor, making her feel the same as when she'd watched the Grand Review and seen her brother Preston pass the stands in a mock cavalry charge with his company: solid squadrons of yelling horsemen going by at a thundering gallop, sabers flashing, hooves pounding, regimental colors streaming. It had left her breathless, trembling with pride at the invincibility of those reckless warriors.

The next verse was her favorite.

" 'The Southland is a glorious land, and hers a glorious Cause!' " she recited to Eli and Willie. " 'And here's three cheers for Southern rights! And for the Southern boys!' "

Should she go on and actually give the cheers? Of course! Callie opened her mouth. "Hurrah! Hu—"

"CAA–LEE!" a voice called impatiently from an open window in the house. "You come on in now! You hear me? Come on!"

"—rah," Callie finished. "I'm comin' in a minute."

Slam! went the window.

Blair didn't repeat her summons. Callie supposed Olivia had put her up to it. Olivia was their oldest brother Robert's wife, and very picky about proprieties. Hanging on fence rails and talking to soldiers were not considered proper by Olivia, but neither was hollering out windows. Callie could just hear Olivia nagging! "Didn't Mama Tyler tell Callie not to bother the soldiers on picket? Well, she's out there right now, Blair. You'd better go and get her."

Callie knew she could stretch the "in a minute" indefinitely. As a matter of fact, when Lieutenant Phillips arrived, Blair would probably forget all about her. Moving back a little from the fence, she dragged her hand across the top rail, to make it look as if she was thinking about leaving.

* * *

"I don't see what it hurts to have her out there," Blair said, turning from the window and going past Olivia to a small gilt-framed mirror. That morning she'd decided to coil her heavy honey-colored hair into a chignon. As she stood before the mirror, she was pleased with the result. The severity of the style, drawn back from her face, accentuated the classic oval of its structure, with its high cheekbones, wide-set blue-green eyes, and proud lift of the chin.

Olivia, seated on a sagging couch between the windows, was busy knitting. "You'd better hurry," she said. "Aren't you and the lieutenant supposed to meet Preston and Isabella at ten o'clock?"

Isabella! Blair made a face. She loathed Isabella Kendall. But Blair's brother Preston, who reveled in his role as a dashing cavalry officer, had decided that the four of them would go riding together this morning. He'd gone into Holly Springs to meet Isabella at an early hour.

After adjusting her chignon a trifle, Blair went to the kitchen in search of provisions for a picnic basket.

The kitchen at Waverley was connected to the house by a short covered passageway. Four wooden steps led from the back veranda to the passage, and beyond the kitchen various structures dotted the commodious backyard. They included a smokehouse, a dairy, a henhouse, and a woodshed. Farther out across the barn lot, behind a Cherokee rose hedge, more outbuildings clustered around the Waverley barn. Blair, accustomed to the cluttered view since childhood, hardly gave the backyard a glance.

In the kitchen Telithia, a tall rawboned Negro woman, was frying chicken on the cast-iron stove. Blair's great-aunt Sophie sat at the scrubbed-oak table slicing squash. A plump and pious old lady, Aunt Sophie had lived at Waverley ever since Blair could remember.

Aunt Sophie paused in her slicing. "You are revealing the shape of your body," she said accusingly. "Where is your modesty, child?"

Blair stepped over Olivia's two-year-old son, Robbie —the grubby child was rolling on the floor—and opened the pie cupboard. "It's a riding habit. You don't expect me to go riding in a hoop, do you?" she said rudely, with a tone she'd never have used in her venerable relative's presence had her mother, Anna Mary, been there. "Telithia, what happened to the ham? I know there was some left over from dinner yesterday."

Mahogany face shiny with sweat, Telithia poked at the frying chicken with a turning fork. "Yo' maw done took it to the hospital when she left to nurse this mornin'. She took the leftover Sally Lunn, too."

Thunderation! Blair thought. Her mother was worse than a swarm of locusts. You couldn't put down your coffee cup without her snatching it off the table and giving it to the soldiers.

"That jacket is indecent," Aunt Sophie went on. "It fits so tight around your bosom and hips that it is certain to provoke thoughts of carnal lust. The thought is tantamount to the deed, child. Consider their immortal souls—"

Great jumping Jehoshaphat! To hear Aunt Sophie, you'd think I was one of the harlots of Sodom! What would the old lady say if she knew her niece had allowed Lieutenant Phillips to sneak a kiss?

Was that a horse she heard coming?

He was early. But who was Dan Phillips trying to impress? He was making enough racket galloping up the driveway for a whole troop of cavalry.

Blair moved toward the kitchen window.

The sharp report of a pistol shot cracked across the bright sunshine of the November morning. As she froze in her footsteps, another shot rang out.

Telithia looked up, startled, from the stove. Aunt Sophie, holding an onion, opened her mouth to say something.

"Shootin'!" Telithia cried suddenly. "Somebody shootin'!"

The loud bark of a musket almost sent Blair out of her skin. Telithia dropped her fork and cried out, covering her ears. A regular fusillade of shots erupted— like firecrackers going off, Blair thought inanely as she leaped toward the window.

Heart hammering, she strained her eyes toward the road. For a split second she couldn't see anything out of the ordinary. Just the crape myrtles, golden-leafed, along the driveway, and the brightness of sunshine, and the trees of White Oak swamp across the pasture.

Then she saw a strangely miniature, faraway figure, running, running, its long legs churning across the brown stubble of her grandpa's pasture, a moving blur of loose, flapping butternut trousers and black beard— *Oh, God!* Blair raised icy fingers to her mouth.

The pickets! The pickets in front of the house!

As if in a bad dream she saw the blue-uniformed men on their horses milling about in a cloud of dust at the end of the driveway. Some of them were aiming their pistols once again, pointing them toward the fleeing butternut figure. Telithia's fingers dug deep into her arm. "Jesus!" she moaned. "Miss Blair—ain't them—them's Yankees!"

A huge rock of guilt and terror went plummeting through Blair's stomach. There was something she'd forgotten; something she'd neglected. She twisted away from Telithia's pinching fingers, running for the door leading to the yard. *Oh, Lord!* the blood pounded in her head. *Callie!*

2

Callie hung on the snake-rail fence as if nailed to it. Her eyes felt red and itchy from the dust of milling horses swirling around her. Her eardrums were still ringing from the crack of bullets being fired. They seemed to have sailed past her very nose. The smell of gunpowder hung heavy in the air. Yet, through it all, she struggled with a single all-encompassing emotion.

Utter amazement that Private Eli Spence could run so fast!

The blue-coated riders had been upon them so quickly that by the time they realized what was happening, the Yankees were close enough to use their side arms. Unwisely Eli had headed for the open pasture. Only Grandpa's fence rails, separating the road from the pasture, saved him from pursuit on horseback, for the Yankees' horses drew up at the fence and refused to take it.

The fence proved no such hindrance to Eli, who dived beneath it and came up on the other side without —as far as Callie could tell—breaking stride. There were no trees in the open field to offer protection, and he presented an unobstructed—albeit swiftly moving— target.

Amid pistol shots and shouts of "Get him! Gee-yet

him!'' Eli miraculously made it to the shelter of White Oak swamp.

Things were happening so fast that Callie scarcely had time to register them. While she was trying to watch Eli and his pursuers, she realized that Private Willie Carr had fled in a more prudent direction—toward the pecan grove on the south side of the Tyler house.

A pack of mounted Yankees cut out from the others and took off through the pecan grove after him, their horses' hooves spraying pellets of dirt against Callie's fence rail as they passed.

Back on the road, the main body was drawing rein and discussing Eli. Callie heard several exclamations of profanity that would've turned Olivia green! Some of them seemed to think Eli was going to carry the alarm of their arrival back to the troops in Holly Springs. ''Hell!'' another cried. ''He's headed in the opposite direction! That damned runnin' Johnny's halfway up to Tennessee by now!''

She suddenly realized that Blair was beside her, sobbing, ''Callie! Callie!'' and trying to peel her from the fence.

As she struggled with her little sister, Blair felt as if she were moving in a nightmare. What was *wrong* with Callie? Why wouldn't she turn loose of that fence? Rude remarks began to issue from the group of mounted Yankees, and she became aware of the tight fit of the riding habit's jacket around her breasts and hips. She recalled Aunt Sophie's words of warning concerning carnal lust. *Oh, God, what if they*—one of them was coming toward them, moving his horse at a gentle trot. *Oh, God! Just let me die! Aunt Sophie and Telithia must be having spasms in the kitchen, watching out the window—why don't they come out and help me? Sweet Father in heaven!*

Here he is!

What's going to happen to us now?

"Ma'am? You'd better get that little girl back in the house."

Blair looked up to see muddy boots resting in hooded stirrups, a belt buckle with an eagle on it, a short evil-looking carbine, and somewhere far above, against the blueness of the sky, a sunburned face, chestnut-brown moustache, and a dark-blue forage cap.

"You needn't think Eli and Willie ran because they were scared!" Callie cried.

"Hey, Cap'n!" one of the men in the roadway shouted. "Maybe the Rebs oughta' conscript the little redhead and issue her a musket! Looks like she might put up a better fight than the last two we come up against!"

To Blair's mortification Callie shouted back. "We can beat you fightin'! We can beat you at anything we try, 'cause we just beat you runnin', too!"

The officer with the chestnut-brown moustache up above them laughed. "It'll be fine with me if they out-run us all the way to Vicksburg." He wheeled his horse, looking out toward the pecan grove. "Evans!" he shouted. "Got him? Bring him up!" Turning back to Blair, he said, "I'd advise you to keep her off the picket stands from now on, miss. We may be paying you another call."

All the way to Vicksburg? A little chill moved across her heart. But that was ridiculous! General Van Dorn's Confederate Army was between here and there!

As she jerked Callie toward the house, a wicked inspiration occurred to Blair. Impulsively, she gave way to it.

"Oh, do call again, Captain!" she cried over her shoulder. "We'll be so glad to see you when our troops are chasing you back from Vicksburg! That is, if you have time to stop!"

Callie, twisting her neck around, still couldn't see any sign of Willie as Blair, assisted by Olivia, who'd run out to meet them on the veranda, pulled her into the house.

Blair slammed the door.

Olivia's dark eyes were round with disbelief. Her left arm supported Robbie, who was balanced on her hip. "Where did they *come* from?" she cried in a trembling voice.

Now that she and Callie were at last inside the house, Blair's knees were suddenly weak. She remembered her sarcastic parting comment to the Yankee captain, and her heart began to pound so rapidly that for a moment she felt faint. What if he forced his way into the house and took his revenge? What if he ravished her—

"Thojahs!" Robbie said happily and aimed a chubby finger. "Bang! Bang!"

Someday, Blair thought, Olivia was going to have to take that child in hand. And where was Callie? She'd disappeared from the hall. "Callie!" she called, leaning limply against the door.

"I'm in the office!" Callie's voice answered. "I'm trying to see if there're any more Yankees comin'!"

Any more! Blair's heart twisted in renewed terror. Speechless, she and Olivia stared at each other.

"More?" Olivia's lips formed the word soundlessly, her olive complexion turning pale.

"No, Olivia, I don't think so!" Blair answered quickly, searching for a reason why this should be so. "It must—it must be just a raid! A—a cavalry raid!"

Yes, that must be what it was! From listening to Preston she was vaguely familiar with cavalry raids. The logistics involved in advancing large bodies of soldiers were unknown to her. Hazily she thought it must necessitate the dull booming of artillery and the burning of bridges, none of which seemed to have occurred.

"Blair!" Aunt Sophie screamed from the kitchen. "Here come your grandpa and Austin!"

Olivia and Blair hurried from the hallway, both of

them aware of a pleasant relaxing of tension. For now, even though their grandfather was nearing seventy, and Austin, being a colored man, was not allowed to shoot Yankees, there would be males in the house.

Grandpa, upon entering the kitchen, was immediately surrounded by a swarm of his female relations, all talking at once.

Samuel Tyler wore his usual working clothes: Kentucky jeans supported by a single gallus, calico shirt, rough boots, and a tattered straw hat. He loomed above his womenfolk like a rough-barked Mississippi pine, tall, lean, and white-haired.

Grandpa heard out their chattering with enough sharp questions of his own to ascertain that in spite of their guinea-hen cackling, none of them were hurt. Samuel Tyler had little patience with the gabbling of womenfolk, and especially did his sister Sophie exasperate him. Staring down at her plump flushed face and rapidly working mouth, he thought she looked like a hooked catfish, and was making about as much sense.

"Every one of you shut your mouths," he said, "and let me rest for a minute."

A sudden silence descended. Wearily Grandpa moved over to the scrubbed-oak table, pulled out a chair, and eased himself down. Though he hated to admit it, the hurried trip back from the cornfield when he and Austin heard the gunfire had about worn him out. He reached up and removed his straw hat. A new hole was in the crown and he held it up and wiggled his finger through it.

"That pack of blue-coated Hessians took a shot at me," he remarked thoughtfully. "Came damn near hittin' me, too."

The remark was a mistake. A fresh chorus of wails arose.

Grandpa slammed the hat on the table amid the hastily deserted squash and onions. On the stove something was boiling; it looked to be boiling over. He and

Austin had been coming out from the cornfield, running toward the pasture, when the Yankee cavalry had suddenly passed just ahead of them on the Holly Springs road. One of the Yanks had seen them and turned in his saddle, firing his pistol in their direction as the troop galloped past.

The bastard had been a pretty fair shot, Grandpa admitted, looking down at his hat.

"One of you go over and take care of that mess on the stove," he said grimly. "And when that's done, I want you to tell me where them bluecoats was heading." He fixed his older granddaughter with a gimlet eye. "Mary Blair? You was out there. Any of 'em let it slip?"

Olivia hurried to the stove and Blair flushed and bit her lip. "Grandpa, he said—he said they were going all the way to Vicksburg!"

Samuel Tyler snorted. "It's likely they're goin' into Holly Springs. Or make a crack at it, in any case." He stood up. "An' that means I got to ride in and see to Anna Mary. You-all finish up dinner and I'll be back soon as I can."

Their protests were immediate and voluble. The Yankees might be coming back at any moment! He might be shot at again! He might run smack into the 1st Mississippi Cavalry and get caught in the crossfire. He might get *killed!*

Patiently Grandpa explained that he'd keep off the main roads and cut through the swamp. Anna Mary had gone into town in the buggy with Little Austin driving. He didn't think there'd be fighting in the vicinity of the hospital. He didn't think the Yanks would get that far, but he couldn't take the chance. In any case, he wasn't going to have his daughter-in-law driven home by some young fool darky who would be terrified out of his wits. The horse might bolt and the buggy overturn.

"Brother—" His sister Sophie had begun to quaver again, her fat chin working against the second chin beneath. "We shall be without male protection. We shall—"

"Austin'll be here," Grandpa said shortly. "He'll keep a lookout while I'm gone."

Before he reached the Confederate armory, just north of town, Grandpa heard the ominous crack of carbine fire and the answering bark of musketry. So the armory was their target, he thought. He swung his mare through the swamp, circling around the armory and coming out on a wooded ridge behind it.

Clouds of smoke were rising from the main building, while beside the flanking wings he could see Yankee incendiaries, busy as ants. The Confederate guards had already surrendered. Muskets stacked, they sat in a dejected huddle. In the prisoners' midst Grandpa caught a glimpse of a familiar cavalry officer: Lieutenant Dan Phillips, resplendent in plumed slouch hat and collar bars.

Shit! Grandpa thought.

He left the ridge and turned his horse toward Holly Springs. If he left the swamp and rode hard down the road, there might still be time to get help from the troops south of town.

But as he neared the road, he was forced to change his plans. The telltale approach of hoofbeats gave evidence that not all of the Yankees had stayed to fire the armory. Their scouts were still advancing. As he cautiously guided the mare back into the trees, Grandpa saw a sight that made his breath whistle through his teeth.

Riding leisurely down the road was his grandson Preston, accompanied by Miss Isabella Kendall. As Grandpa shouted a warning, the point riders of the Yankee cavalry came into view.

Preston abruptly reined in his horse. With a whoop the scouts spurred to meet him. Isabella, fetching in a forest-green riding habit, watched openmouthed at their approach. "Run!" Preston shouted, maneuvering his horse between her and the Yankees. "Ride back to town, dammit!"

Isabella sat in her sidesaddle as if riveted to it, making no move. From the shelter of the trees Grandpa cursed under his breath.

Preston leaned over from his saddle, caught Isabella's reins, jerked them around, and gave her horse a resounding whack on the rump. It took off like a bullet, its mistress clinging to the pommel.

Pistols drawn, the Yankee scouts surrounded Preston with shouts of triumph. He grabbed for his saddle holster, thought better of it, and threw up his hands.

"God damn!" Grandpa said under his breath.

At Waverley the hours of afternoon dragged slowly past. Callie wandered forlornly about downstairs. From the dining room she went through the double doors into the parlor, where an array of black horsehair upholstery, rosewood piano, and dark pine floors emitted a funereal air.

She didn't know whether it was good or bad that they'd seen no more soldiers coming or going past the house. Walking slowly across the hall from the parlor, she went into her father's office, dragging her finger across his rolltop desk.

Her father wasn't there. Dr. Tyler was a regimental surgeon, and his family hadn't seen him since the end of May, when Beauregard's army moved down to Tupelo and Dr. Tyler came in on one of the hospital trains with the sick and wounded. Then Bragg replaced Beauregard, and after the ill-fated Kentucky campaign the army went into camp at Murfreesboro, Tennessee. Callie's father was there now, as was their older brother, Olivia's husband, Robert.

A tight burning sensation closed around Callie's throat. Maybe Grandpa was already in Holly Springs. With Mama in the buggy, they'd have to come home by the main road, wouldn't they? She thought desperately, *My brother and the rest of the 1st Mississippi Cav-*

alry can lick a whole regiment of Yankees! They will make them skedaddle!

She heard the creak of buggy wheels coming up the drive.

Blair met her in the hall, but Callie brushed past her, her cloth-topped Congress gaiters flashing down the steps. Blair waited beside the veranda while Grandpa reined the buggy up, climbed down, and helped his daughter-in-law alight. Anna Mary looked tired.

Callie was all over her mother, hugging her, exclaiming, trying to tell her everything that'd happened, while Blair stood and watched. Her sense of relief was so great she felt almost sick to her stomach. She wanted to be clinging to Anna Mary, too, but Callie was the youngest, the baby. She always came first.

Finally, after a lifetime of waiting for Callie to move, Blair felt her mother's soft cheek touching her own. "You were a brave girl," Anna Mary said gently. "Your grandpa told me how you went out and got Callie."

And not a word about her wretched neglect, without which Callie wouldn't have been on the picket stand in the first place!

Blair hugged her mother quickly. "Oh, Mama! I'm so glad you're home!"

Anna Mary Tyler was a tall woman, and as Blair pressed her head against her mother's shoulder, she realized that beneath the brown basque of her dress her shoulder was thinner than she remembered. *Oh, Lord!* she thought swiftly. *Mama's working herself to the bone!* Anna Mary's blond hair was so frosted with gray now it had a silvery sheen.

Callie was jumping up and down, trying to get her mother's attention. "Mama!" she cried, and when Anna Mary turned patiently to listen, "The Yankees haven't come back! We haven't seen anybody pass the house! Do you think—"

"Did they get into Holly Springs?" Blair interrupted.

"They came as far as the armory," Anna Mary said calmly. "They didn't get anywhere near the hospital."

Grandpa, slinging the reins over the horse's head, said shortly, "Seems they left on the road to Hudsonville. That's why you ain't seen 'em coming back by Waverley, missy."

"Papa Tyler," Anna Mary said firmly, "you must let Little Austin put away the buggy. You must come inside and rest."

"But where was our cavalry?" Blair cried.

Grandpa snorted, his naturally ruddy complexion turning redder. His boots and Kentucky jeans bore the marks of briers and cockleburs from his recent ride through White Oak swamp.

"The cavalry," he said, "was a-callin' on Miss Isabella Kendall."

"Preston?" Blair said, her hand going to her throat. "Is he—"

"The durn fool got himself captured!" Grandpa yelled.

Blair's heart turned over. "Mama?" she said. Anna Mary's face was drawn into tight, unyielding little lines.

"Mama? Is he hurt?"

"No," Anna Mary said quickly.

"By the way, Mary Blair," Grandpa said, "they picked up that popinjay lieutenant that's been hangin' around out here, too. I saw 'im at the armory when the Yanks was a-burnin' it."

Lieutenant Phillips! She had forgotten all about him!

"Was *he* hurt?"

Grandpa shrugged. "Looked healthy to me."

Well, she'd cry about Dan Phillips later. There were simply too many other catastrophes crowding her now. "Mama, what will they *do* to Pres?"

Anna Mary's face looked haggard. She shook her head. "I don't know, Blair. Now let's go inside. I think I hear Olivia. They'll be wanting to know."

3

The next day was a Sunday and, as was their custom, the female members of the Tyler family dressed to attend services at the Methodist church in Holly Springs.

For a time, however, there had been some question of whether they would go at all, for Grandpa had at first refused to allow it. A fool notion for womenfolk to be out on the roads in unsettled times like these, he had said shortly.

"Then," his sister Sophie retorted, "*you* must escort us to services, Samuel."

On this Sunday morning a pall of heartsick worry hung over the inhabitants of Waverley, and in the tenseness of the atmosphere it appeared that Grandpa and Aunt Sophie were going to have a row.

Grandpa had not set foot inside the church in the past ten years, and even before that his attendance had been sporadic. Now Aunt Sophie began reminding him of this lapse. Anna Mary came hurrying in, already dressed in her indigo silk but with her silvery hair hanging loose on her shoulders. She had been in the midst of brushing it when the sounds of the argument drifted upstairs. Now she stepped between them with a look of strain on her face.

"Papa Tyler," she said, "I must attend services this

morning. Please don't refuse to let us go. It would—it would be a great comfort."

Grandpa, looking down at his daughter-in-law, saw dark circles beneath her eyes and tiny wrinkles fanning out from their corners that he had never noticed before. He turned impatiently. "All right, then. I reckon I can mosey over to the lobby at the Magnolia Hotel and find some officers hangin' around. Might pick up some information about what the devil's goin' to happen to Preston. It's worth a try, at any rate."

Aunt Sophie retired in triumph, Anna Mary went back upstairs to put up her hair, and in the bedroom they shared across the hall from their mother's room, Blair and Callie went on to apply the finishing touches to their own costumes.

Callie's didn't take long. What was there to do after you'd been buttoned up in back and managed to get a minute at the mirror to plait your hair?

Besides sharing the big four-poster bed with its plump feather mattresses, the Tyler sisters also shared the massive walnut dresser. The dresser's surface was Blair's exclusive territory. It was strewn with hairpins, cologne bottles, tucking comb and curling papers, coralline lip salve, almond oil, and rosewater hand cream, her glove, handkerchief, and jewelry cases, a little enameled tole box that held her crushed rose sachet, and other indispensable supplies.

Blair stood in front of the chifforobe in ruffled lawn petticoats and embroidered chemise, undecided as to what to wear. The weather was still sunny outside, and it was too late in the season for silks, but too hot for her heavier things.

Shifting impatiently, Callie said to her sister, "I wish you'd hurry up." She couldn't leave until she'd hooked Blair up in back, and it looked as if her sister was never going to make up her mind.

"I guess the merino will have to do," Blair said crossly, pulling a burgundy-colored walking suit from the bulging rack of dresses that filled her half of the chifforobe.

"Come button me up," she said to Callie.

Blair's pink dimity blouse had a long row of tiny crystal buttons in back, and Callie fumbled with them for what seemed hours. Blair's rolled steel hoops beneath the ruffled lawn petticoats were so wide Callie almost had to lean over to reach the buttons. She heard Anna Mary coming out of her room across the hall and knew it was time to go.

When they all descended, Austin was waiting out front with the buggy. A quiet, dark-brown man of slight build, he looked dignified and neat in his own Sunday-go-to-meeting outfit of brown linsey, and Callie noticed he was wearing the gold-chained watch, as usual. Telithia had given him the watch last Christmas. Grandpa allowed her to raise her own chickens, and Telithia had saved her egg money for a solid year to purchase the watch for Austin.

Austin and Telithia attended services at the Cooper plantation, which bordered Waverley on the south. The members of Holly Springs Methodist had so many servants the slave gallery would no longer contain them, and some of the planters had built rough-hewn meeting houses to take up the overflow.

Grandpa climbed into the jump seat and told Austin it was Little Austin's job to bring around the buggy.

Austin replied with his usual serious demeanor that he didn't know where Little Austin was. He reckoned he would refuse to attend church over at Cooper's again, like he'd done last Sunday.

Little Austin was rangy and rawboned, like Telithia, and big for his sixteen years. Lately he'd taken on a sullen expression, as if he were always mad about something. He sassed Telithia when his father wasn't present and moved with deliberate slowness when given an order by anyone but Grandpa. Another thing that puzzled Callie was that Austin and Telithia had expressed concern over Preston's fate at the hands of the Yankees, but Little Austin hadn't.

Grandpa clicked to the mare and flipped the reins, Callie waved good-bye to Austin, and they were off to Holly Springs.

The trip was made in gloomy silence. As the mare trotted by yellowed fields of corn and occasional cotton rows not yet fully picked, each occupant of the buggy seemed lost in his or her individual thoughts.

Blair, sitting well back under the hood to protect her complexion from the sun, was pensive. She was remembering a night six weeks ago, after the battle at Corinth.

They'd known Van Dorn had been defeated, for his army had retreated past Waverley, headed back for the lines on the Coldwater River. Later people said that Van Dorn was reckless and irresponsible and had insisted on the attack without waiting for adequate reinforcements. But Blair had little interest in military rehashings, and nowadays it seemed that some general had always behaved scandalously.

As the buggy drew nearer to Holly Springs, Grandpa slowed the mare to a walk because he always liked to take a good look at the residential section. Every time he left Marshall County, Samuel Tyler told everyone he met that Holly Springs was the capital of north Mississippi, and there wasn't a finer-looking town in all the world.

The rich soil of the Pontotoc Ridge had made many of its citizens wealthy, and the planters had built white-columned Greek revivals, red-brick Georgians, and neat English cottages along Salem Avenue, Chulahoma Avenue, and other pleasantly shaded streets.

Most of the commodious lawns were enclosed by ornamental wrought iron fences cast at Jones, McElwaine and Company, the local foundry. The foundry had recently been converted into an armory and was now engaged in manufacturing small arms for the Confederacy. This was the building that the raiding party had fired yesterday. However, on his way home with Anna Mary, Grandpa had assured himself that the armory suffered little damage. After the Yankees left, the workers had soon extinguished the blaze.

Blair knew some of the older citizens had not been particularly pleased by the addition of the foundry, nor by the headquartering of the Mississippi Central Railroad in Holly Springs. A roundhouse and extensive railway yards now spread about the depot, and many "new" people had moved into that area to work for the Mississippi Central.

As the Tyler buggy approached the red-brick church, the Kendalls' gleaming English phaeton was just coming up with Jonas Kendall at the reins. Isabella sat beside him, her emerald-green skirts filling up the rest of the phaeton. After his wife passed away when Isabella was three, Mr. Kendall had never remarried, and his daughter was the apple of his eye. She was waving frantically in Blair's direction, as if, Callie thought, there was any possibility of anybody's not seeing them.

Mr. Kendall said loudly to Grandpa there was no question but that Preston would be immediately paroled.

Grandpa watched him with barely concealed distaste. Mr. Kendall wore a suit so expensively tailored it looked as if he'd had it run up on Savile Row. He also sported a pleated white shirt of the finest linen, an embroidered waistcoat, and a cravat so flaring it almost obstructed his chin. Grandpa found the garments offensively effeminate. Jonas Kendall's mansion on Salem Avenue might be the showplace of Holly Springs, but to Samuel Tyler, its owner was an insufferable old toad-frog who should have had the sense to realize he was long past the dandy stage.

The appellation of "toad-frog" had come naturally, for Mr. Kendall had a short thick neck, heavy jowls, and pale protruding eyes. "Within ten days!" he said emphatically to Grandpa. "I am willing to assure you that your grandson will be paroled within ten days!"

"Is that so?" Grandpa said without shifting a muscle, his big frame hulking over the reins held loosely in his hands.

"Yes, sir!" Mr. Kendall shouted, making ready to alight. As he climbed down from the phaeton, he went on talking to Grandpa. "I wouldn't concern myself for an instant that Preston will be sent north to prison! The Yanks don't ship every man they take to Johnson's Island—"

Anna Mary, standing in front of the buggy, turned and said sharply, "Johnson's Island?"

Mr. Kendall removed his black beaver top hat. "Mrs. Tyler, I assure you, there is no cause for concern. I merely mentioned it as an—"

"What is it?"

He paused. "It's a prison camp for officers. Located on Lake Erie, in Ohio. It's near Sandusky, I believe."

Johnson's Island, Blair thought numbly. *On Lake Erie. Near Sandusky.*

She had visions of ice-locked, brooding waters, ragged Confederates freezing and starving, and squat northern factories belching forth melancholy clouds of soot. *Oh*, she thought in terror. *Preston will get pneumonia in such a godforsaken place!* He wasn't used to struggling through snow up to his knees! And the Yankees would probably march their prisoners barefoot through it, like—like the Revolutionary War soldiers at Valley Forge! She had a sudden vivid picture of bloody footprints staggering all the way across Ohio, and of Preston collapsing and being bayoneted by his captors when unable to go on.

Someone murmured gently that she was sorry to hear of her brother's capture. Looking blindly to her right, Blair saw the Widow Lockwood, who had four small children and had lost her husband in the battle of Shiloh, the previous spring. Now Mrs. Lockwood struggled to maintain her small farm east of Waverley.

The sight of her struck new terror in Blair's heart.

"Thank you, Mrs. Lockwood," she whispered through lips gone stiff with uncertainty and dread.

Isabella was tugging at her arm and Blair turned, hardly seeing her. "I cried all night," Isabella was saying. "Daddy finally had to make me take some paregoric."

Blair's vision began to clear.

"Oh, I could have died!" Isabella continued. "It was my fault Preston got captured! *It was all my fault!*"

Blair's vision was now clear enough to notice that Isabella was wearing a new bonnet, a dashing green velvet trimmed in blond lace with marabou feathers curling down from the brim. Her tremendous violet eyes did look a little puffy, and her sorrow had given her a pouting, swollen look.

What do men see *in Isabella?* she thought for the thousandth time.

There was no getting around it. She had more beaux than any girl in town. Even more than Blair.

"Don't be silly, darlin'," she said in a voice dripping with sugary reassurance. "It wasn't all your fault."

Isabella managed to look pathetic.

"Oh, it was! If I had just run when Preston *told* me—"

"Don't let's talk about it," Blair said quickly. "Here comes Brother Thackerford. I think he wants to talk to us. I'll see you again after the service."

"Oh, dear!" Isabella moaned. "If you hear *anything* about Preston, please, *please* let me know!"

Great jumping Jehoshaphat! Blair thought as she moved to join the pastor of the church, Henry Thackerford, who was hurrying toward her mother with a look of concern on his plump rosy face. Can it be that Pres and Isabella are getting serious? That would mean I'd have to have her for a sister-in-law!

The church services were a disappointment. Of course, Blair told herself, she appreciated everyone's being so kind to them, but Brother Thackerford's two-hour sermon had been stultifying, and as she sat glassy-eyed in her pew, no handsome young officers were among the congregation to cast admiring glances across the aisle and take her mind off her troubles.

Actually there were no uniforms of any kind in church that morning, and she wondered if they were all at the Magnolia Hotel with Grandpa, rehashing the cavalry raid. The burgundy merino was totally wasted. One would think the soldiers had never seen a Yankee before!

Grandpa didn't have much news when he returned to the church to pick them up. In fact he was stubbornly uncommunicative, and simply said, yes, he reckoned Preston would probably be paroled.

After the service he refused to let them linger and chat, and said bluntly that he wanted to get home. Anna Mary immediately acquiesced to his wishes, and home the Tylers went.

Once dinner was finished, Blair became more despondent by the hour. *Surely*, she thought, *surely someone will call this afternoon.* There was nothing she hated more than a long Sunday afternoon with nothing to entertain her, and out of desperation she kept her hoops and pretty dress on, though as two o'clock drew nearer it appeared that no one was going to come.

She sat down at the piano and began playing "Lorena." The doleful lyrics suited her mood.

> *"The years creep slowly by, Lorena,*
> *The snow is on the grass again;*
> *The sun's low down the sky, Lorena . . ."*

As always the sound of her own voice—a rich, husky contralto—gave her pleasure. She knew that people liked to listen to her play and sing. When she performed at musicales and cotillions, her audience was always enraptured. Dan Phillips had been so bold as to say that she should go on the stage—

"Blair!" Olivia screamed, running into the parlor.

"Where have you been? Oh, come quick! Preston is *home!*"

Blair looked up at her blankly. Olivia's face was flushed, she was laughing and crying, and as far as Blair could tell, she was making no sense.

"What?" she said.

Olivia leaned over and shook her by the shoulder. "He's home! They just rode up! Aunt Sophie saw them through the bedroom window, and now everybody's out on the veranda—oh, Blair, come on!"

Blair's heart began to pound. She got up from the piano as Olivia whirled and started running to the door, unable to wait another second before she went back outside.

"Wait, Liv!" she called frantically. "What happened? Did he escape?"

Turning in the doorway, Olivia hugged herself with joy.

"He's been paroled! Some Yankee soldiers brought him back under a flag of truce!"

Olivia whirled again and disappeared into the hall.

4

Blair stood motionless for a moment, then lifted her skirts and went flying outside in a flurry of burgundy merino, ruffled lawn petticoats, and incoherent cries. Just as Olivia had said, Preston was on the veranda— and his brief confinement seemed not to have affected him at all! He was still the same happy-go-lucky, raff-ish-looking Preston, towering above his family and re-turning their adoration with rib-cracking hugs and what Blair always thought of as his "I'm splendid and here I am, so come and get me, girls" look.

"Preston!" she cried. "Oh—Pres!"

"Blair!" He laughed.

She ran to him and his hug was so massive it swung her off her feet. She reached up and touched her brother's face. Beneath his sweeping blond mous-tache, his face was stubby with golden whiskers.

"You need a shave," she said, smiling.

Preston set her down and ran his hand over his chin. "You don't think I look more interesting this way? Kind of gaunt and mysterious?"

She laughed. How pleasant it was to be able to laugh!

"I've suffered terribly, you know," he said, his eyes sparkling. "At the hands of my captors. And now—"

Preston took Blair's arm and gestured toward the blue-uniformed officer who stood on the veranda. "Allow me to present Captain Matthew Harwell. Captain, meet my sister, Miss Blair Tyler. I believe you've been introduced to everybody else."

Blair beamed her most brilliant smile upon him and held out her hand. In the rose-colored glow that enveloped the afternoon, even the Yankee officer looked downright benign. He could do no wrong in his spick-and-span blue uniform and polished brass buttons, for he had just returned her darling brother to the bosom of his family beneath a flag of truce! In addition to the officer, three Union privates waited a short distance away, near the front gate.

"How nice to meet you, Captain Harwell," she said sincerely. "You were very kind to escort my brother home."

"I was happy to do it, Miss Tyler," he said, returning her smile. "Heading into enemy territory is a risky business, but it's always a pleasure to view the scenery down here."

The captain was a muscular, solid-looking young man in his middle twenties. Not as tall as Preston, but then few people were. He had, of course, removed his hat and his hair was a rich thick brown, curling about his forehead and in sideburns down a face that was deeply tanned. He had a moustache, though it was not as sweeping as Preston's, and brown eyes that had a merry twinkle in them as he bent over her hand. For a moment Blair had the odd feeling that he looked vaguely familiar.

"Goodness!" she said. "I can't imagine why you returned Preston to us so soon! But I'm certainly glad you did!"

"Now, see," Preston interjected quickly. "The Yankees aren't so bad, after all. Are they, sis?"

That seemed a rather tactless remark, considering the circumstances, and she turned to frown at Preston, but was unable to turn all the way, because her hand was still in the grip of Captain Harwell, who was taking his time.

"I—ah, understand you had a fracas with some," Preston added. "Back before they got me. Or at least that's what Callie told me. It must have been pretty upsetting. Weren't you—ah—scared?"

Oh! she thought, her face burning. *How* can *he be so gauche!* The Yankee captain had at last released her hand, and she gave a light little laugh. "How you do carry on, Preston," she said brightly. "Scared? Me?"

"One never knows what one will run into these days," Captain Harwell said with a grin, as if the idea pleased him immensely.

"Unfortunately, one doesn't," she said shortly, beginning to feel annoyed with them both.

"You were not subjected to any insults, I hope?" her brother said sternly.

"Well, if I wasn't," she snapped, "it was no thanks to *you!*" She turned to the Yankee captain and said, "Of course I was frightened. My little sister almost got caught in the crossfire. Have you ever had a brigade of cavalry charging down on you? Evidently not. I assume you're generally behind the lines."

As soon as the words were out, she had a sinking feeling that she had gone much too far. Why was it that she let Preston goad her into behaving like this? He'd always been able to bring out the worst in her, ever since they were children.

"Rough-looking customers, eh?" her brother was saying, with tardy concern for her welfare. Preston reached up and stroked his luxuriant blond moustache. "A whole brigade, you say?"

Anna Mary approached in a rustle of silk. "Preston? Won't you join us in the parlor? Perhaps Captain Harwell would enjoy some refreshments."

Captain Harwell appeared to be enjoying himself right where he was. Blair's slurring implication as to his lack of combat experience seemed to have rolled right off his husky blue back. Bowing slightly in her direction he said, "I apologize for our cavalry," his brown eyes twinkling as merrily as before.

Well! She supposed Yankees must be woefully lacking in gentlemanly sensitivity. Could she say anything she liked and not have him take umbrage?

"We'll be right with you, Mother," Preston said. "On the contrary, sir," he said to the captain. "I would say their performance was exemplary. No apologies needed."

He began guiding Blair toward the hall where their mother stood waiting, a welcoming picture in her wide skirts, her halo of silvery-blond hair and sweet face free of any torment or worry, its gentle features reflecting only a warm glow of happiness and relief. Anna Mary took Captain Harwell's arm as he came through the door. Blair heard her saying, "You'll stay for supper, of course . . ."

As they disappeared into the parlor, Blair turned quickly, pulling Preston aside for a moment of privacy. She pushed him against the mirrored hatrack in the hall. "You embarrassed me to death out on the veranda! And how long is he going to be here? I don't—"

"What are you fussing at *me* for?" he whispered back, sounding injured. "Mama asked him to supper."

"Do you think he'll accept?"

"I don't see why not. I think I'll invite him to spend the night."

With a surge of irritation she thought that he was looking particularly guileless and innocent. All six feet three inches of him in his rumpled gray uniform. She was glad to see him, of course, and she shouldn't be feeling irritated with him, not five minutes after he'd stepped through the door. What exactly had he done?

"Spend the night? Pres, I realize you want to be hospitable, but there must be a limit, even for you! Doesn't he have to get back behind his lines, or something? After all, he is a Yank—"

"Why, Blair!" Preston said accusingly. "I believe you're trying to get rid of our guest!" He grinned and took her arm, forcing her toward the parlor. Just before they passed through the doorway he leaned down and whispered in her ear. "Don't be rude, sis. You were the one who invited Captain Harwell to call again."

It took a moment for the full implication of Preston's words to hit her, and by that time they were already in the parlor. Callie sat hunched on the piano bench, resting her elbows on the piano and watching her mother and Captain Harwell through narrowed eyes. They were seated and appeared to be engaged in amiable conversation. He was leaning forward attentively, smiling and responding to something Anna Mary had said.

Blair, standing frozen a few steps inside the doorway, thought, *It isn't possible!*

Her mind groped back toward that hideous, horrible occasion—yesterday morning. She'd gone flying out to the picket stand to get Callie, convinced each step that took her forward would be the last she'd ever take . . .

Slowly the picture formed. Muddy boots resting in hooded stirrups. A short, evil-looking carbine. A belt buckle with an eagle on it.

And a chestnut-brown moustache!

Oh, Lord! she thought, staring across the room at the neatly tailored blue uniform and the pleasant, smiling face listening to her mother. It was the same man!

Her jaw dropped ungracefully.

Blair recovered hurriedly, praying that no one had noticed, and took a deep breath to regain her composure. Shoulders stiff, she sat down in a lyre-back chair. Preston was moving about the gathering in jaunty good-fellowship. He stopped Telithia with her tray of coffee cups and looked down into them. Due to the Yankee blockade, the "coffee" was made from parched yams. "It looks like iodine," Blair heard him say.

She wished she could jump up and kick him in the shin, as she used to do when they were little.

"Blair?" Her mother was leaning forward, trying to

get her attention. "Blair, Captain Harwell has just told me he is from Springfield, Illinois."

"Really?" Blair answered coldly. "The same place Abe Lincoln comes from." Just yesterday, she'd been terrified that this Yankee might rape her! Her face flamed. What an indelicate thought!

"Yes," Captain Harwell said firmly, ignoring her sarcastic tone. "President Lincoln's home wasn't far from our house."

"How interesting. Is he still splitting rails?"

"Blair—" Anna Mary began reprovingly.

Captain Harwell interrupted. "And is he really the original gorilla? In certain circles it's become fashionable to refer to him as that. No, Miss Tyler, I'm sorry to disappoint you. The President may be a little rough around the edges, but he's been wearing shoes for quite some time."

His voice had a steely edge to it. Remembering how formidable he had looked on his horse, bearing down on her, Blair felt a ripple of danger. The hard body in the blue uniform belonged to an enemy. No matter how civilized he seemed at the moment, yesterday he had been armed to the teeth. Now, incredibly, here he sat in the parlor with everyone fawning over him. Worse yet, by not recognizing him, she had made a complete fool of herself.

A short uncomfortable silence followed the captain's last remark. Anna Mary moved in gracefully with a new line of conversation. Preston suddenly appeared to say, "Don't drink that stuff! You don't know what it's like! Grandpa! Have you got any wine?"

Grandpa, sitting on the horsehair sofa with Aunt Sophie, pretended not to hear him.

"Grandpa!" Preston said loudly. "Wine?"

"It's in the bottom drawer of my highboy," Grandpa growled.

Blair's back began to feel stiff from holding it in its rigid position. Was he going to stay for supper? Had

Preston actually invited him to remain overnight? How long was her torment to continue?

"Blair!" Preston bellowed from the back hallway. "Come help me find the wineglasses!"

For a moment she was almost tempted to ignore him. But that would be impossible. No one had missed hearing him. And if she continued to sit there without responding, Anna Mary would make her do it. Without saying "Excuse me," she got up and swept grandly from the parlor.

Preston was in Grandpa's room rummaging through the highboy. One bottle of peach brandy already sat on top of it. "Did you know he keeps a regular arsenal of bottles mixed in with his underwear? Where does he hide the good stuff? All I can find is homemade peach and apple." Blair noticed that he'd already got the glasses from the dining room. They were sitting on Grandpa's dresser.

"I don't think there is any more of the imported," she said frostily. "Why don't you ask your friend to bring you some from Springfield?"

"Stop sulking," Preston said shortly.

"Sulking?" Blair reached behind her and closed the door to keep from being overheard in the parlor. "You knew it was the same Yankee all the time, you skunk! And you were leading me on deliberately—"

"I've been watching you, sitting there with all the grace and charm of a Chickasaw Indian. For God's sake, Blair! My hide must not mean very much to you! They didn't *have* to parole me, you know. Had you rather they'd shipped me to Johnson's Island?"

The awful words "Johnson's Island" hung like the echo of doom in the air. At the sound of them all the anger drained out of Blair. *Oh,* she thought, twisting her hands together and watching Preston hunting for the wine, *what's the matter with me? Am I so snippy and selfish that I can't think of anything except my own little miffs?* The Widow Lockwood's pale face rose before her and she remembered the thinness of her mother's shoulder beneath the brown basque. She thought of Anna Mary's hours spent nursing the sick and the wounded, and of Olivia, so faithful to Robert, so content to miss all the balls and cotillions.

"No," she said, feeling worthless and wretched. "No, I hadn't rather they'd done that."

"By God, I found one!" Preston cried, holding up a bottle of Madeira and reading the label. "The old tippler probably thought he had it salted away somewhere else!"

"Pres . . ." Blair felt the tears rising to her eyes. "Pres, do you think I'm totally useless?"

He stopped reading the Madeira label and looked at her in surprise.

"I mean, everybody else is always helping the Cause, and I—I don't do anything, Pres!"

"Well, don't bawl about it. And no, I don't think you're *totally* useless. Because if Captain Harwell hadn't decided he wanted another look at you, I might not've gotten my parole."

Blair's heart gave an odd little leap. "What are you talking about?"

Preston put the Madeira on top of the highboy, leaned back against it, and folded his arms across his chest. "Yesterday, after we were safely past Hudsonville, the Yanks were able to relax enough for us to indulge in some chitchat. Captain Harwell happened to be the one I was riding alongside of—suitably disarmed, of course—and I complimented him on the clean sweep they'd made of our pickets. He, in turn, complimented me on the unusual pulchritude of the young ladies out in this neck of the woods."

Preston paused.

"Well?" Blair said. "Go on."

"I thought that would interest you." He smiled. "Anyhow, the captain was moved to remark that although his trip had been hurried, it had been beneficial in more ways than one, because earlier that morning he'd run into the prettiest girl he'd ever seen in his life."

Preston paused again and grinned wickedly.

"Naturally, I assumed he referred to Miss Isabella Kendall, who was my companion at the time of my ignominious surrender. But—imagine my amazement, sis, when further conversation revealed he meant you!"

Blair gave an excited little jump.

"And then you told him you were my brother? But how did you know it was me, Pres?"

"Well—he described you."

"How?" she said quickly.

"Oh, I couldn't tell you," Preston said, smiling. "That would be ungentlemanly, you see."

Blair wanted to stamp her foot. Was he joking again, or what? She felt pleasantly mollified, however. The Yankee captain had preferred her over Isabella, which certainly showed his good sense.

Frowning a little in concentration, she thought rapidly. Maybe he wasn't so dangerous, after all. Actually her first impression of Captain Harwell had been the correct one. He seemed a very pleasant young man. And, she thought, she'd been inexcusably rude. She lifted her chin. Well, it certainly wasn't too late to make amends. She'd go back in the parlor and be her most charming self. After all, he *had* brought Preston home. The least she could do would be to show a little sisterly gratitude.

Preston picked up the wine bottle and gestured with a turn of his head toward the tray of glasses on Grandpa's dresser. "Would you get those? And when we're back in the parlor, how about batting your eyelashes at Captain Harwell? Make the poor Yank's heart ache a little. Come on, sis. Here's your chance to do your bit for the Cause."

Blair got the glasses, and as they were going through the door, he said, "Be nice, sis. I'm serious. It never hurts to have a friend at court."

"What do you mean?"

"Nothing. I'll tell you later. Now come on."

Blair paused at the sideboard in the dining room to pour the wine and plan her strategy. She took a quick glance in the mirror that hung above the sideboard and made minor adjustments to her hair, relieved to see that the recent rapid shift of emotions had done no more than heighten the color in her cheeks and give a brighter sparkle to her long-lashed eyes. Thank goodness she'd decided to keep the burgundy merino on in hopes of callers. Now. How should she handle this?

To go dashing into the parlor and immediately start radiating charm all over her admirer wouldn't do. That would look as if Preston had taken her outside and given her a lecture, then sent her back in on her promise to be a good girl.

Well, no matter. She'd manage as best she could. Blair had no feelings of modesty as to what her best was. She picked up the tray of wineglasses and sailed from the dining room. Captain Matthew Harwell was as good as her captive.

As she entered the parlor, she put on her most fascinating expression and zoomed in on her target.

"Guess what, Captain? We found some Madeira. Preston is simply unbelievable! I'll just put the tray down on the table over there, and let the others serve themselves. There. Now, here's yours."

She sat down and turned to hand him his glass. He had some kind of document in his hands.

Captain Harwell's sun-browned face registered pleasure mixed generously with surprise. Evidently he had forgiven her for her remarks about Lincoln. He shifted the paper, or whatever it was, to his left hand and took the wine with his right.

"What in the world do you have there?" Blair asked brightly, wondering if it could possibly be Preston's parole.

"I'm not sure," he said, looking down at the paper

with a faintly puzzled line between his eyes. "The lady in the black dress—your aunt?—came in a few minutes ago and gave it to me. I had just started glancing over it."

A horrible suspicion began to creep over Blair.

"Oh," she said quickly. "I wouldn't bother to read it. It's—it's probably just one of those funny little tracts."

"Tracts?" he said.

Oh, how *could* Aunt Sophie do this to her! Before the war, her aunt's chief interest in life had been conversion of all the heathen at camp meeting revivals, where she sang "Brother, Will You Meet Us?" in stentorian tones. But when the Confederate Army had gone into camp near Holly Springs, Aunt Sophie's missionary fervor had embarked on rich new fields.

"Just Aunt Sophie's tracts from the Evangelical Tract Society," Blair said, fighting hard for one last shred of fascination. "She always gives them out."

Captain Harwell was turning his tract over and studying it. "Mine has an interesting title. It's headed 'Sinner, You Are Soon to Be Damned.'"

"Aunt Sophie gives them to *everybody!*" Blair insisted, thinking that now it wouldn't matter how charming she was—he'd be convinced he'd descended into a den of lunatics.

However, Matthew Harwell was not thinking that.

Yesterday morning at the picket stand in front of Waverley, he had looked over from Company D and been rewarded with a vision of loveliness. Now he thought he hadn't been mistaken in his original quick impression of a flawless face and long-lashed, blue-green eyes blazing up at him. This girl was as lovely as he'd remembered. In fact, if it were possible, she looked even *better* than he remembered.

Today her golden hair framed her exquisite face like a halo, with random little curls lightly kissing her temples. Delicate, oval-shaped earrings set with amethysts dangled from her ears. But what really fascinated Matthew was the blouse she was wearing. Of a pale pink,

soft material it had full ballooning sleeves and was
gathered all across the bodice in little rows of tucks.
He noted the sleeves because he could catch a glimpse
of white rounded arms through the thin material, and
the tucks on the bodice were arresting because they
covered even rounder curves.

All in all, he had the feeling of being in the presence
of an airy, intoxicating, pink-and-gold-and-white
cloud. And after fifteen months of sharing the company
of the bewhiskered, sweating, tobacco-spewing members of the 2nd Illinois Cavalry, he was enjoying a
pleasant feeling indeed.

Through her agony of embarrassment Blair made an
effort to change the subject. "By the way," she said,
straightening her shoulders, "I was wondering if you
knew anything about what happened to a lieutenant
who was—er—detained at the same time my brother
was. A Lieutenant Phillips?"

"Phillips?" he responded absentmindedly, his eyes
on her blouse. "I don't believe I'm acquainted with
him."

I didn't ask if you were acquainted with him, she
thought impatiently, feeling a little guilty that she
hadn't asked Preston about Dan Phillips before this.
Why was she always forgetting about him? A dashing
young Texan, he had seemed quite smitten with her in
the last few weeks, and it wasn't nice at all of her to
take his capture so lightly.

The Yankee captain put down his Madeira and
seemed to be thinking her question over.

"Ah—yes!" he said. "The officer in the hat!"

This remark was not as pointless as it might have
seemed to the uninitiated, for Blair was well aware of
Lieutenant Phillips's hat: a magnificently wide-
brimmed, black felt slouch affair, with a waving red
plume stuck in the band. When Grandpa had first seen
him wearing it, he had looked on in amazement and
then, ever afterward, referred to Dan Phillips as
"Henry of Navarre."

"You'd better get dressed in a hurry, Mary Blair,"
Grandpa would say with maddening condescension.
"Henry of Navarre is a-comin' up the driveway."

It was useless to point out to Grandpa that Jeb Stu-
art himself wore a plume in his hat, and a fringed yellow silk sash and scarlet-lined cape besides, and that
he could fight rings around the Yankees. None of it did
any good. It only made Grandpa more inventive in his
derision of gaudily bedecked popinjays.

And now—here was this Yankee, also referring to
poor Dan's lovely hat!

"Has he been paroled, too?" she inquired, managing
to keep her voice level.

Captain Harwell took a sip of his Madeira before
responding. Then he looked at her in a rather personal
manner and said, "A friend of yours, ma'am?"

"As a matter of fact, yes."

He smiled. "Unfortunately, the lieutenant was unable to obtain an immediate parole."

At this point Blair looked up to see Preston approaching. Time was passing, he said, and they should
be leaving. Some kind of military protocol was involved in getting him exchanged for Federal prisoners
now held in Holly Springs, and they must be off for the
provost marshal's.

Well, she thought, frankly relieved, they'd never intended to stay for supper. And even though Captain
Harwell had been civilized enough, and his opinion of
her gratifying, conversation with him had proved to be
a strain.

After they left, she felt drained from the day's excitement and thought how nice it was that everything had
gotten back to normal again.

5

That night, after all the womenfolk had gone to bed, Grandpa waited in his room until he heard Preston going down the hall toward the back veranda. Then he rose deliberately, laid aside the *Memphis Appeal*, and followed his grandson to the kitchen.

He found Preston scavenging through the pie cupboard. After his return from accompanying the flag-of-truce party to Holly Springs, he'd put away a hearty supper; but of late every time his grandson set foot in Waverley his appetite had been insatiable.

"Don't the commissary ever issue you any rations, boy?" Grandpa asked, easing down into a chair at the kitchen table.

Preston, who already had a slab of cold cornbread and a thick slice of bacon balanced on his platter, added what was left of the turnip greens, got out a bottle of pepper sauce, and stood inspecting the inside of the pie cupboard.

"Surely, Grandpa. Week before last, I got presented with some pickled beef that had turned the prettiest green you ever saw. The cornbread they gave me as a side dish had the weevils baked right into it. So thick I couldn't pick 'em out. Had to eat the little varmints."

Grandpa leaned back in his chair and watched Preston juggle his platter and the pepper sauce and decide he had all he could carry. "You get fresh beef and pork, don't you?"

Laughing, Preston turned to get the pitcher of milk he'd brought in from the dairy. "Yessir. Five day's worth of it. We eat all we can the first day, and then throw the rest away. Kind of difficult to keep it. They neglect to issue any salt along with it."

"Hard to find salt, nowadays," Grandpa said. "I picked up three sacks in Holly Springs last week. At fifteen dollars the sack. This time last year, it was goin' for a dollar and a quarter."

Preston sat down at the table across from him and began to pour pepper sauce on his turnip greens. "And this time next year, I'll wager you'll be paying a hundred dollars." He broke off a chunk of the cornbread and hesitated. "No, Grandpa, I retract that. Next year, we'll have 'em whipped, and the blockade will be lifted."

Samuel Tyler watched in silence while his grandson loaded his fork with turnip greens and used the cornbread to sop up the pot liquor. He had eaten several hearty mouthfuls before Grandpa broke his silence.

"So," he said slowly. "You're takin' off and leavin' us to the Yankees?"

Preston's cornbread paused in its pushing across the platter. After a few moments he said, "It looks like that's about the size of it."

Grandpa took a deep breath of disgust, tilted back his chair and rammed his fists deep into his trouser pockets. He was recalling the oratory of fire-eaters. The "Cotton Garden of the World," they called this section of Mississippi. Its sacred soil never to be profaned by the vile heel of the invader. The gateway to the delta, where millions of bales of the white gold sat awaiting shipment to the cotton mills of Europe. King Cotton *ru-ools* the world, Grandpa remembered them braying. Rhett and Yancy and Quitman and all the rest of them. And when deprived of it, England will tremble and intervene for the Confederacy! *The damned jack-asses*, he thought contemptuously. *What the hell have they gotten us into?*

"Mind tellin' me where you spent last night?" he said to Preston.

His grandson looked down at his platter and resumed eating his greens and cornbread. "La Grange," he said with his mouth full.

"Sittin' right on the state line, are they?"

"They've got advance cavalry units thrown out ten miles below it."

"You figure they'll be headin' directly south? Not veerin' east to the Mobile and Ohio? Toward Macon and Columbus?"

"They're advancing down the Mississippi Central."

The Mississippi Central Railroad went straight through Holly Springs. Why the hell couldn't they go through Corinth? That ground had been fought across before.

"You lookin' for the army to make a stand anywhere around here?" Grandpa asked. Judging from the atmosphere at the Magnolia Hotel this morning, the civilians were confident that northern Mississippi would be defended.

Preston sopped up the last of his pot liquor and uttered an obscene expletive.

"Is that so?" Grandpa responded. "Wasted a mite of time diggin' all them fortifications on the Coldwater, then, didn't you?"

"Grandpa," Preston said wearily, "there isn't anybody *in* those breastworks. How in the devil do you think that reconnaissance raid got through so easy yesterday? Our lines are so weak around here Robbie could get through them."

"And why ain't there anybody in them? What's the infantry doin'? Sittin' on their butts out south of town?"

Preston wiped the back of his hand across his blond moustache, leaned back in his chair, and looked at his empty platter. "They're not sitting on their butts at the moment. They're pretty damned busy getting ready to fall back. Fall back? Hell, the last time I was down there, it looked like they were getting ready for a god-damned panic!"

Slowly Grandpa crossed his long legs. "So Grant's getting ready to move, is he? And where might he be headin'?"

"Vicksburg, Grandpa. Vicksburg."

"They tried that last summer."

"They steamed past the batteries. You know they didn't get anywhere with that. Now it looks like they've decided to try the overland approach."

"And Earl Van Dorn? He got anything to say in this?"

Preston stood up from the table. "We don't have Van Dorn anymore. We've got a damned-Yankee coward from Philadelphia. Rumor has it he's falling back to the Tallahatchie. Where he may make a stand. Although I wouldn't lay any bets on it." His voice was beginning to shake with anger. "If General Van Dorn was still running this army, we'd fight them here! We could hold them, dammit! I know it!"

Yeah, Grandpa thought. *Dashing Earl would make a stand, all right. Whether he'd be able to hold it is another question.* His contempt grew larger. It swelled to encompass Van Dorn, who had bungled Corinth and left the way open to the fertile fields of Mississippi.

"They say he was drunk as a skunk at Corinth," he said deliberately, watching without expression as his grandson's face turned red with anger. *That's right,* he thought. *Swell up and call me a liar, you young hotspur. The damned fool Van Dorn had let the Yanks send him back from Corinth with his tail between his legs, and what we need here is a Lee of Virginia. Maybe someday it's going to dawn on you and your knothead general that this is more than cavalry charges and swaggering around in fool hats and high-topped boots . . .*

"That rumor was a damned lie," Preston said.

"And went off and left his wounded to the Yankees. And his negligence and his whorin'—"

"You quoting Senator Phelan, Grandpa? That was all in his letter to President Davis, wasn't it? Well, there's a court of inquiry being held in Abbeville tomorrow. And mark my words, Van Dorn's going to be cleared. Of *all* the charges." Angrily Preston massaged the back of his neck. "God! Why can't they quit their yapping! I'm so damned sick of listening to every two-bit politician in this state who thinks he can run the army better than the generals!"

Grandpa sat silently after this outburst. For several moments the only sound in the room was the soft breaking of the last charred log in the kitchen fireplace as it gave way and dropped into the ashes.

"Grandpa," Preston said, staring at the fireplace, "have you still got your cotton stored at the warehouse in town?"

Samuel Tyler looked up sharply. "Where else would it be?"

His whole year's crop was in the warehouse, though he had planted sparingly this spring, heeding the government's request that the planters turn to cereals and grains. The need for food and forage for the armies should take precedence, Richmond had said, appealing to his patriotism. So Samuel Tyler had planted most of his former cotton fields in corn. The rain had been plentiful that summer, the crop was good, and now the Waverley cribs bulged with the bounteous yield.

But his cotton—of course it was still in the warehouse. With Memphis occupied last June, and New Orleans a few weeks earlier, there had been no way to get it to market.

"Grandpa," Preston said quietly. "You're going to have to burn it."

Something inside Samuel Tyler's chest twisted. He felt the sharp taste of bile rising in his throat. "You know what you're sayin', boy? You're tellin' me to take your mother's income, and your sisters', and your father's and brother's—and send it up in smoke! Burn it? You tell me to burn it? And after I do, what in the hell am I supposed to use for money for the rest of the year?''

Preston paced restlessly about the kitchen, rubbing the back of his neck again. "Go down to the bank in town and they'll issue you notes on it. When the war's over, the government will pay you the ruling market value on every bale you burned."

What government? Grandpa thought bitterly. *The one in Richmond? Reckon I'd play hob gettin' the rulin' price from the one in Washington!*

"First they tell me not to plant much," he said. "And now they tell me I got to burn what I *did* plant!"

"The hell with it!" Preston shouted. "Hold on to it, then, and sell it to the Yankees!"

A sharp pain gripped Grandpa's chest. It had been reported that within a month after the fall of Memphis, eight thousand bales of cotton had passed through the market there. The planters were crawling in on their bellies to do business with the Federals. Taking the hated Oath of Allegiance. Selling their souls for the almighty Yankee dollar. The unspeakable Ben Butler, Yankee general commanding at New Orleans, was said to be making a fortune in the illicit cotton trade.

He leaned forward, bringing the legs of his chair to rest on the floor. "No. I ain't sunk so low as that."

Still, there was a burning in his chest. It wasn't right and it never would be. *Truth forever on the scaffold,* he thought, not able to remember who'd written it, nor even where he'd read it. *Wrong forever on the throne. Work your guts out. Stay honest. Think that in your old age, you've made a little something of yourself.*

"I'll put the match to it," he added. The price of cotton was higher than it had been in sixty years. And briefly Samuel Tyler remembered the dark days of the forties, when his crop had gone for five and a quarter cents a pound.

He felt his grandson's hand pressing roughly on his shoulder and heard him saying behind him, "You know if you tried to hide it somewhere, the patrols would find it sooner or later. I'm—sorry, Grandpa."

"Don't waste your pity on me, boy. I don't reckon we're about to starve to death, even without the cotton. Smokehouse is still pretty full."

Preston laughed, squeezed his shoulder, and sat back down at the table. "Not thinking about refugeeing then, are you? I'll admit the idea crossed my mind. Why don't you give it some thought, Grandpa? You could all come back once the Yanks have gone."

"Jesus Christ Almighty! What are you comin' up with next, Preston? You think at my age, I'm goin' to put everything I got in a saratoga an' hit the road?"

Watching him from across the table with an amused sparkle in his eyes, Preston shook his head. "No, sir. On second thought, I guess I can't quite picture you running from anybody. Much less U. S. Grant."

"And what would Waverley look like when we come back to it? After a whole Yankee army had tramped through it? Hell! Without me and Austin to watch out for it, they'd likely burn it to the ground!"

And even if I did agree to refugee—which I ain't, Grandpa thought, *where would I go?* Anna Mary's people, the Carters, lived in Alabama. He wasn't about to accept charity from her folks, though she could take the girls and go there if she wanted to. (He did not believe for a moment that his daughter-in-law would.)

As for his sister Eugenia, and Olivia's family, in Memphis, well, Memphis was occupied already. It would be a fine bit of foolishness to run from one bunch of Yanks straight into another.

"Grandpa?" Preston said. "There's something else I want you to do."

Samuel Tyler looked at him with guarded eyes.

"When the Yanks get here, I want you to remember Company D, Second Illinois Cavalry. That's Harwell's outfit. If you get in any real trouble, I want you to look

him up. Harwell seems like a decent enough fellow.
The cavalry'll probably be coming through first. If they
start burning the house over your head, don't start
shooting 'em, because they'll hang you. Try to find the
Second Illinois and ask Harwell to post a guard."

"Company D," Grandpa said. "Second Illinois."

Preston smiled in an evil kind of way. "Poor old Harwell." His shoulders began shaking with silent laughter. "I sort of hated to do it to him."

"Do what?" Grandpa said.

Preston grinned. "Nothing. Nothing, Grandpa. It's
getting late. And I've got to get to camp early tomorrow. My exchange may be coming through. You sure
you can handle this all right?"

"I can handle it," Grandpa said.

A few days later Callie went into her father's office,
sat down at the rolltop desk and opened one of the
drawers. She took out a black ledger with EDGARS &
THOMPSON, COTTON FACTORS, MEMPHIS embossed in gilt let-
tering across the front.

Opening another drawer, she got out her inkstand,
red chenille penwiper, and Always-Ready pen. Inspecting her inkstand, she saw with satisfaction that it was
over half full. She sat up straight, wiped her hands on
her skirts, opened the ledger, and laid it lovingly on the
desk. Her own printing looked back at her from the
page.

MISS CALLIE EUGENIA TYLER. HER OWN TRUE JOURNAL.

Callie felt a sense of pride in the title, though as always she thought Callie Eugenia was a terrible name.
When she began to write novels, she was going to
change it. No real lady should put her true name to a
novel, anyway. Callie didn't see why her mother and
father couldn't have picked out a more interesting
name in the beginning. Like Morgan le Fay in the King
Arthur stories.

Some day, she thought, looking at the Edgars &
Thompson ledger, *I am going to be as famous as Au-*

gusta Jane Evans and write books just as good as she does. And sign them Morgan le Fay.

Turning to her last entry, she picked up her pen. The most recent pages of the journal were covered with tiny, cramped script. She was using up all the paper, and when the ledger gave out, she wasn't sure where she would find any more. Writing paper cost ten cents a sheet now, when you could get it from Vicksburg. Screwing up her face in concentration, she leaned over her journal and wrote her first line for the day.

The Yankees are coming to kill us.

Callie leaned back, looked at it, and found it satisfactory. She added some more.

Our men are running like quarter horses. They are making railroad time.

Callie leaned back and reread those lines, too. Then, frowning, she crossed them out carefully and wrote:

Our gallant soldiers will defend their homeland, I am sure. They are going into fortifications on the Tallahatchie River first.

She looked at the stuffed pigeonholes in the desk, remembering what the Yankee trooper had shouted on the day of the raid about conscripting the little redhead and issuing her a musket.

Things like that had really happened, she knew, because every so often she'd read about them in the penny papers. The stories would say that some young lady had disguised herself as a man and enlisted in the army. Usually she did this after her sweetheart had enlisted. She would go to camp and drill and everything, and nobody would ever get suspicious. Sometimes her sweetheart would drill right alongside her and even *he* wouldn't know.

The young lady was always unmasked, though, at the end of the story, because she would have to go to the hospital, where—as the writer always said—"her sex was discovered."

Callie wasn't sure what they meant by "her sex." Surely the young lady would not let the army doctors pull down her bloomers? She finally decided they must mean her bosom. She supposed the young lady had flattened herself out some way when she was getting disguised in her uniform. Callie thought glumly that she herself would probably never be discovered, even if she did have to go to the hospital.

She turned back to her journal.

Yesterday Grandpa went into town to get the cotton burned & we went with him & watched the soldiers loading the trains. They are retreating

Callie stopped, scratched out "retreating," and wrote "falling back." Then she frowned and scratched out "falling back." But she couldn't keep scratching out, or she would use up all her paper. Finally she decided on "going" again.

They are going pretty soon now, I guess. Most of them have gone already. Preston is here, but we don't see him much. He has been riding a lot of patrols. Yesterday it was raining pretty hard & we had to run in Levy's Dry Goods. A lot of people were in Levy's. Everybody is pretty excited & some are refugeeing, but Mama & Grandpa say we are not. Mr. Goodman & the rest of them that run the Mississippi Central took their families & went off in a passenger car. They say that will be the railroad headquarters from now on. Our soldiers have been out at the armory moving all the machinery they used to make guns with. They sent it to Macon. Also took all the guns Jones &

McElwaine had already made to keep the Yankees from getting them.

Callie stopped writing, remembering yesterday in Holly Springs. The rain had come down in torrents and the town was in a turmoil, with cavalry splashing through the muddy streets, makeshift ambulances evacuating the convalescents to the depot, and panicky civilians elbowing each other on the sidewalks, demanding to know what was going to happen to them now. Everyone's front porches had been crowded with women, and some of them had been crying.

Callie bent over her journal.

> Aunt Sophie is looking for her Chickasaw Indian tommyhawk but she can not find it any where. Aunt Sophie says we will all be slautered in our beds. Miss Lucy Blaylock has a bottle of some kind of acid that she is going to throw in the Yankees' faces. I do not have anything myself & can not think of what to get. Blair talked about Beast Butler quite a bit.

Callie rummaged through another desk drawer for the clipping she had saved from the *Memphis Appeal*. It told all about General Butler's famous *General Order Number 28*.

Callie found the clipping, perused it carefully, and turned back to her journal.

> Beast Butler said that any lady in New Orleans who insulted a Union soldier would be liable to be treated as a woman of the town, plying her trade.

Callie paused, wondering again what that meant. Something pretty awful, she was sure. In the last few days Blair had talked a lot about the poor defenseless ladies of New Orleans and what was in store for them. Still, it wasn't quite clear to Callie exactly what that was. From listening to Blair, she had a confused impression that the helpless New Orleans ladies were all to be dragged into alleyways by the insulted Union soldiers, where something terrible would then occur. Probably, Callie thought, the ladies would be beaten to a pulp. She went back to her journal.

> President Davis says that if we ever catch him, we are going to hang Beast Butler without a trial. Grandpa talked to a man who had been down that way & he said they were selling chamber pots with Beast's picture painted in the bottom. Grandpa & I thought that was funny but Olivia did not & said I must not tell anybody about it.

Idly Callie examined the point of her Always-Ready pen.

> I told little Benny Lockwood, tho. They all came over a few days ago. That Mr. Hanson the Widow had overseeing for her went off to Baldwyn when he heard the Yankees were coming. It will do him no good because they say there are 50,000 Yanks coming down the Mobile & Ohio. They will get him in Baldwyn for sure. Anyway, the Widow is afraid to stay out there all by herself. She & Mama were in the parlor & I took the children in the kitchen & we played school. I made them all sit down & do their letters on slates. The baby scrabbled lines all over her slate & I pretended like they were really letters & made out like she had done them real good. Benny's letters were disgraceful.

Callie underlined "disgraceful."

> He is 8 & Widow Lockwood had been sending him to the Free School but the headmaster got conscripted & they had to close down. I was going to the Female Institute in Holly Springs until they

changed it to a hospital. When the Yankees come, maybe they will burn the Institute down. I sort of hope they do

Callie thought for a moment and then scratched out the last line.

Mama told Mrs. Lockwood Grandpa would find a man to oversee for her & Grandpa got Mr. Fred Grace to go out there. Mr. Grace is crippled & can not do much work but there is not much to do at this time of year. Mama said the Lockwoods are off the main road & the Yankees would probably not come by her place at all.

Callie paused to flex her fingers.

I am glad we are on the main road, as would hate to miss seeing any Yankees at all. To hear some talk, you would think they are all 3-tailed ogres, but I have seen several, like in the cavalry raid & that one that brought Preston home & they looked fairly normal. Sally Burton in town said folks came to look at the ones our men took prisoners at Corinth & brought through Holly Springs after the battle & some folks from the country actually thought they had horns under their hats.

Sally did not go to see them herself as her mother would not let her, & told her the Yankee prisoners were not animals in a zoo for her to go look at. Of course we did not get to go either as Mama said no & we never get to do anything. Sally heard one old woman from down in the country asked where their horns was, & one Yankee prisoner told her they never showed their horns to the ladies. So she still believes they have them, I guess.

Callie was reminded of another rumor.

They say Bob Sharp is home. I guess now that the army is pulling out, he feels it is safe to show his face again around here. Bob Sharp deserted.

Callie underlined "deserted."

Mr. Jake Sharp got in a fight recently & had his eye gouged out. He wears a black patch over it. Mrs. Pearl Sharp does not come up here much, tho their house is only a mile away from here. Mama is still nice to her, but Grandpa says if Jake ever shows his face around Waverley he is going to kill him. He says he should have gone ahead & killed him that time Jake pulled a knife on him.

Callie paused to remember this episode. She had not been a witness to it, but had heard it discussed many times.

Three years ago Jake Sharp had wanted to hire Austin to do some carpentry work. Grandpa, who said later he would as soon turn Austin over to a rattlesnake as entrust him to Jake, flatly refused.

It was common knowledge that Jake Sharp had killed one of Mr. Cooper's Negroes. The man had been hired out to him and was staying at the Sharp place. Nobody was quite sure what happened, because the only witnesses had been Jake, his son Bob, and another of the Cooper Negroes. The latter, of course, could not testify against a white man in court.

In any case, Jake's side of the story was that Mr. Cooper's Negro attacked him with an ax. While defending himself, Jake beat the Negro so brutally that he never recovered. Mr. Cooper was furious. The other darky had told him Mr. Sharp stayed drunk and mistreated them repeatedly. The night that it happened, he had been hitting the darky he killed with a harness strap.

The man suddenly hit back at Jake Sharp and then tried to run. Jake and his son Bob caught him, tied him up in the barn, and inflicted the beating that resulted in his death.

It was some time after this that Jake approached Grandpa and asked to hire Austin for the carpentry work.

Grandpa refused. When Jake began to give him some lip, Samuel Tyler told him that he was not so big a fool as to turn any darky of his over to a Sharp, and that if there had been justice, both Sharps would have hung.

That was when Jake pulled the knife. He always carried one stuck in his boot top, and Callie had seen some like it on General Price's Missouri troops. They called them Arkansas toothpicks, but Grandpa said they were bowie knives. It gave Callie the shivers just to look at them, and the Missourians said they were going to use them to carve up Kansas jayhawkers.

In any case, Jake didn't get very far with carving up Grandpa, because with a quick swing of his boot Samuel Tyler had kicked him in the groin. Then, as Jake sank howling to his knees, Grandpa reached out, caught him by the wrist, and although Jake was not a small man, almost broke his arm.

Grandpa caught the knife as it fell. While Jake lay clutching his privates and gasping for breath, Grandpa said, "All right, you murdering son of a bitch. Let's see you try pullin' a knife on me again."

Callie sighed and turned again to her journal. She wrote her last line for the day.

> I wish the Yankees would come on & get it over with. I am getting kind of tired of waiting for them.

6

To Blair, the days seemed to pass in a dreamlike succession of pouring gray rain, roads that turned to bottomless mud, and hourly reports of cavalry skirmishing to the north. One after another, heavily loaded boxcars kept pulling dismally out of the depot and rolling south on the Mississippi Central. People said the Confederates were heading for Abbeville, Oxford, Grenada—where they were going to stop, nobody really knew. Rumor said they were falling back to the Tallahatchie. Then that they were falling back to the Yalobusha.

General Pemberton was now in command of the army. People had never heard of him; President Davis had found him somewhere. Van Dorn had been relieved and put in charge of the cavalry. Pemberton was from Philadelphia and had two brothers in the Union Army. *How,* Blair wondered silently, *can a Yankee be at the head of our soldiers?* Was he secretly a traitor, and all this a scheme to lead them to disaster? Why didn't they stay and fight?

She had never realized how quickly an army could leave. Soon the rearguard cavalry was riding out of town—and this was when Preston left them—and suddenly the army was gone. They were abandoned.

The streets of Holly Springs seemed silent and empty and an eerie quiet hung over the countryside. Even the rains stopped.

When the sun came out again it was pale and thin, with a bite of winter in it. The next morning heavy frost rimed the rutted red mud of the road. At 11:00 A.M. Olivia started to the dairy to bring in butter for dinner. Halfway across the backyard she stopped, listened, and then turned and hurried back inside the house. Pausing at the bottom of the stairs, she clutched the newel-post as Blair came running down. "I heard horses," she whispered. "It sounds—like a lot."

Blair leaned over the banister, listening. Her heart seemed to stop beating, as if it were listening, too.

"Do you hear anything?" Olivia whispered.

Blair pattered lightly across the hall and into the parlor. Pulling back the curtain, she looked across the lawn to the roadway. On it, trotting silently from the north, came a group of soldiers on horses. They were wearing the Federal uniform.

She dropped the curtain and turned to Olivia.

"It's them," she said.

A strange humming began in her ears. She had a strong desire to run into her father's office and crawl beneath the sagging couch. "Blair," Olivia whispered, "Grandpa and Mama Tyler are still over at the Lockwoods'."

Early that morning Mr. Fred Grace had ridden up on a mule, his crippled leg sticking out from the stirrup at an awkward angle. He said all four of the Lockwood children were down with the croup and did they have any Ayer's cherry pectoral, or even homemade persimmon cordial? The widow wasn't feeling too good herself, he added. She was about worn out from sitting up at night with the little Lockwoods, and they had run out of cough medicine.

And, of course, Blair thought, her heart sinking within her, nothing would do but Mama must have

Grandpa harness up the mare to the buggy and take her over there.

"Why is it," she whispered to Olivia, "that every time the Yankees come, Mama isn't here?"

"Shouldn't we lock the doors?" Olivia whispered, beginning to twist a little wad of her skirt in her hands.

Why were they whispering?

"I think we ought to get Austin," Blair said, and the sound of her normal speaking voice almost made her jump. "And we should all get together. In one—one place."

Oh, why wasn't Mama *here?* And Grandpa should have had more sense than to go off and leave them! They were neglecting their own! Turning, she looked through the window again. The Yankees were still passing on the road. Some of them were on the other side of the fence rails, riding through the edge of White Oak swamp. How many were there? Twenty? More? No, not that many. They must be advance scouts.

What did they think they needed scouts for? Didn't they know all the Confederates had retreated to the Tallahatchie? *Lord*, she begged silently, *please let them go on past us! Just don't let them stop!* "You go find Austin, Liv," she said, trying to sound calm and reassuring.

After Olivia left, she heard Aunt Sophie puffing down the stairs. She must have looked out her bedroom window and seen them. In tense silence Blair waited in the parlor as Aunt Sophie went breathing heavily down the hall. *I can't cope with her right now,* she thought. *Olivia will have to handle Aunt Sophie. She's better at it than I am.* Blair heard the back door open and close behind her aunt and thought, *She never did find her tomahawk* . . . Running to the front door, she turned the key in the lock. As she put the key in the pocket of her apron, it dawned on her that there was no way of locking the windows. In fact, the Tylers had never locked up in their lives. *We didn't have anything to be afraid of,* she thought, her heart beginning to hammer in panic. *Oh, how could Papa go off and leave us! And Robert! And Pres! Why do men have to run off and join some stupid army and leave their families defenseless? Why didn't our soldiers stay here and* fight?

Blair had the panicky feeling that she was alone in the house. Everyone must be in the kitchen! When she crossed the covered passageway, she looked automatically toward the road in front of the house. There was nothing on it. The mounted Yankees had already passed to the south.

When she entered the kitchen, everyone was crowded around the window. A pot of vegetable soup flavored with beef sat simmering on the stove. The beef smelled rich and spicy, and ordinarily she could eat her weight in vegetable soup. But now the smell of the food made her stomach turn queasy.

The door suddenly opened behind her and Austin and Olivia hurried into the kitchen.

"Pray, Austin!" Aunt Sophie cried.

Austin stood holding his hat in his hands. "You just rest easy, Miss Sophie. Them Yankees rode by didn't look like they's studyin' about comin' up here. Mist' Sam be home in a minute. And he say, if they start botherin' us, we ask that cap'n brought Mist' Preston home to post us a guard."

Captain Harwell! Of course! Blair's knees went weak with relief. Preston had told her the same thing, before the army pulled out. "Now remember," he'd said. "Company D, Second Illinois Cavalry. You must ask for a guard." That was what he'd meant by having a friend at court, she supposed. Well, thank God they had one!

"Look! Look!" Callie hollered from the window. "Here come some more!"

"Thojahs!" Robbie echoed, clapping his hands.

Heart hammering, Blair ran to the window. Austin came, too, and Little Austin ran into the kitchen, for once without his perpetual sullen expression.

Beyond the double line of crape myrtles she could
see blue-uniformed infantry marching down the road.

"Oh, no!" Olivia moaned. "They're coming up the
driveway!" Blair's heart gave a mighty spring and
leaped against her clenched teeth. Austin picked up his
hat and started for the door. "You-all stay inside, Miss
Olivia," he said. "I'll go out and see what they wants."

Telithia protested mightily, but Aunt Sophie grabbed
her and said, "You must let Austin protect us, Telithia!
Call on the Lord!"

"Ohhh—*Jesus!*" Telithia called.

As they watched, a few soldiers entered the front
yard. When Austin emerged from the passageway to
the kitchen, the Yankees stopped and headed toward
him. Paralyzed, Blair saw him meet them between the
back and front yards, at the gate. All of them stood
there for a moment and the soldiers seemed to be saying something to him. Austin turned, pointed, and
started walking across the backyard. The Yankees followed him.

Blair realized he was showing them the well. A little
of the numbness left her body, and she was conscious
of the thumping of her heart.

"They must want a drink of water," Callie said.

Evidently this was so, for Austin stopped at the well
and lifted the rope to lower the bucket. As he was doing it, another group of blue-uniformed soldiers entered the backyard.

In no time at all, a large crowd was waiting around
Austin and it appeared to Blair that he was drawing
another bucket. Would the Tylers be forced to supply
the whole Union Army with water? Two of the Yankees
had begun to look around the backyard in an interested fashion. She saw one of them say something to
his companion and head toward the smokehouse. The
smokehouse was securely locked. Nevertheless she felt
a flicker of unpleasant premonition.

The Yankees had reached the smokehouse now and
were trying the door.

Austin abruptly left the throng of Yankees at the well and went hurrying toward the smokehouse. The two soldiers spoke to him as he came up to the door. Austin made some reply and shook his head. Suddenly one of the troopers gestured toward the other, who reached down and picked up his rifle which he had propped against the side of the smokehouse. Blair whirled around from the window and put her hands over her eyes.

"They're going to shoot him!" she screamed.

A holocaust of sobs and terrified screams erupted around her. With her eyes squeezed shut Blair crouched back against the kitchen wall and waited for the sound of the shot.

It came.

The bottom dropped out of her stomach. Austin was dead!

"Lord! Lord!" Aunt Sophie cried loudly. "Look! Look! Now they are *all* going in!"

Blair whirled around to the window again. Austin stood beside the smokehouse in the same place. Every bluecoat that had been around the well was now converging on it. "What happened?" she said through chattering teeth. "Aunt Sophie? Liv? What are they doing?"

"They shot the lock off," Olivia said in a tiny, weak voice. "They shot it right off the door."

Sounds of shouts and laughter could be heard from the backyard now, and an energetic scuffle started as the Yankees jostled each other to get through the smokehouse door. The one who'd picked up his rifle pushed his way outside through the others. He was carrying a ham.

"They are stealing our ham!" Aunt Sophie said in disbelief.

A few of the soldiers broke off from the group around the smokehouse and headed toward the henhouse. There were more shouts and then a footrace developed for the henhouse. More soldiers began to come through the gate, and they heard shouts and curses that were loud enough to be discernible. "Company A! Detroit Invincibles! Get back, you damn Hoosiers! We seen it first!"

Blair stood and watched in a kind of dumb fascination. So many bluecoats were running back and forth across the yard now that it looked like a circus. They had gone into the dairy, too, for one trooper walked carefully among the throng carrying a pitcher of milk. It was sloshing as the other Yankees bumped against him in their scrambling to get their share of the spoils.

What, she wondered, *will they think of to take next?* Immediately the answer came to her. The house! They would be coming into the house, and they would take the silver, and all of their clothes, and the china, and— oh, God!—the piano!

"Liv!" she cried. "Come back in the house with me! We can't let them in there!"

Olivia stared at her, then, picking up Robbie, went running toward the door. Blair followed close behind. They left the kitchen, went speeding across the passageway and up the back veranda steps, crossed it, ran into the house, and slammed the door.

"Oh, why, why, why," Blair panted in terror. "Why didn't that Yankee who brought Preston home come by! Oh, Liv, if he only had, he could have given us a guard! And at least we might've been able to save something in here!"

"Maybe he still will!" Olivia cried. "I'll watch for him!" She set Robbie down and ran into the parlor.

After a few minutes, Robbie lifted his arms up to Blair and said, "Be up."

She continued to stand and look down at him, but for some reason, she did not respond.

"Be up!" Robbie repeated in a more imperative tone. Reaching down in a rather distracted manner, she picked him up. Robbie settled comfortably on this new hip and put a chubby arm around his aunt's neck. "Go eat," he said.

He had to repeat this remark, too, until she finally looked at him and said, "No, sweetie. You can't have anything to eat now. I'm too busy."

Robbie, who could see she wasn't busy at all, arched his back and gave an impatient kick with both legs. "Go eat!" he cried for the third time.

Abruptly she carried him down the hall and opened the back door.

Just off the veranda in the covered passageway to the kitchen, a red-faced Yankee was saying angrily to Austin, "Well, you'd damned well better remember that, Sambo! You're free now! And if you keep on working for these damned Rebs, we're gonna come back and shoot you!"

Quickly closing the door, Blair stood back against the wall, her stomach writhing in humiliation at this insult to Austin's dignity. She had never heard a darky called "Sambo" except in minstrel shows, and those were not really darkies, but white men in blackface. And this scum had just addressed Austin in this unspeakable manner, right to his face! Opening the door, she stepped trembling onto the veranda with Robbie in her arms. The red-faced Yankee was slouching arrogantly away, and Austin stood there with no change of expression.

Aunt Sophie suddenly emerged from the kitchen and came down the passageway, clutching her skirts. Her face a fiery red, she looked as though she might be in the first stages of stroke. Her gray hair had fallen from its bun and straggled wildly down her neck.

As she passed Austin she said, "Well, I suppose you know they got *your* chickens, too. When Little Austin said they were your chickens, they said to charge them to Uncle Sam!" When she saw Blair standing on the veranda holding Robbie she stopped, dropped her skirts and said, "I told them that the eighth commandment states quite plainly, 'Thou shalt not steal.'"

"Aunt Sophie," Blair said in stunned disbelief. "Have you been outside talking to the Yankees?"

"Outside?" Aunt Sophie said, blowing her hair back from her face. "Indeed no, child. I am not so senseless as to venture out amid that crowd of heathens. They were inside, talking to me."

"They came *inside?*"

"In the kitchen, child. Where are you taking Robbie? You do not intend to take him in the kitchen, do you?"

"Go eat!" Robbie cried.

"He's hungry!" Blair cried. "Do you mean to tell me this baby can't have something to eat because the kitchen is full of Yankees?"

"Yes, and you need not bother to take Robbie there. They stole our dinner, too."

"You mean—you mean they took the vegetable soup? And the cornbread? Off the—off the stove?"

Aunt Sophie nodded. "Telithia is cooking more cornbread now."

Robbie had begun to squirm and whine that he was ready to go eat. Blair had the feeling of being caught in a nightmare. The child would have to make his dinner entirely upon cornbread, which he did not like. Was there any milk left in the dairy? She strongly doubted it. *We shall starve*, she thought.

"They have ordered several batches," Aunt Sophie said.

"Batches?"

"My dear child!" Aunt Sophie replied, sounding pleased. It had always pleased Aunt Sophie to be the first to relate bad news. "Telithia is cooking cornbread for the Yankees! They came in and *ordered* her to do so! She is working like mad!"

Blair felt a stab of pure unreasoning fury. She set Robbie down, said to Aunt Sophie, "Watch him!", and charged down the steps. As she headed for the henhouse, Olivia ran onto the veranda. "Don't go out there!" she cried. Blair ignored her. When she reached the henhouse, a huge blue-coated monster was just emerging from it with a cap full of eggs. Blair came to a quivering halt. "You put those down!" she shouted. "Put them down! You—you thief!"

The monster looked at her in surprise.

Then he grinned. He held the eggs temptingly just out of her reach. "You can have them, honey pie," he cried, "if you'll give me a kiss!"

For a moment Blair was speechless. Then she turned a dark shade of purple. *Kiss* him! He looked like—he looked like a baboon! Oh, how dare he say such a thing! His blue jacket was unbuttoned at the throat, and she could see the top of his underwear above it, and the underwear was *dirty!* In fact, the filthy baboon was dirty all over! Did he never take a bath? No one had ever said such a thing to her! Never!

"Oh!" she cried, not caring if the whole of Grant's army was listening. She was barely conscious that Olivia was almost fainting at her elbow and must have followed her in terror across the backyard. "You— you—" Blair stared at the grinning Yankee, unable to think of anything bad enough to call him. "You pig!"

Other soldiers had been in the henhouse and now they started to come out. Still more troopers paused in their foraging and began to gather round. The Yankee crouched back in mock horror and raised his hand to shield his face.

"My little Rebel darling!" he responded sorrowfully. "Is that any way for you to talk?"

Olivia was clutching at Blair's arm and begging her to come back inside the house. Hoots of merriment greeted the Yankee's second sally. Blair feared that she would explode.

What was the *use?* They would be robbed of everything they had and would starve to death this winter, and if they tried to do anything about it, they would be confronted by some rampaging baboon and invited to —invited to—she couldn't think about it. It was too humiliating. Blair gathered up her skirts and went flying back toward the house. Behind her, she could hear the baboon crying dolefully, "My sweet darling! You're not leaving?"

As she reached the back veranda, she became aware that Olivia was calling for her to wait. She stopped, leaning against the supports of the passageway to the kitchen and struggled to get her breath. She felt as if she were going to strangle.

Olivia came panting toward her, also out of breath. "I *told* you not to go out there! Blair, you've *got* to stay in the house!"

Blair reached out and hit the support with her fist. "I'll kill them!" she said through gritted teeth. "Where's Callie? Do you reckon they insult children, too? You'd better find Robbie. God knows what they'd do to him!"

"Robbie's with Aunt Sophie on the veranda. Blair, please—"

Olivia stopped talking and looked across the yard. Blair didn't bother to look. Whatever new atrocity was being committed, she didn't even want to see. What good would it do? They could do anything they wanted—

"Blair," Olivia said urgently, and Blair supposed she must be losing her mind for Olivia sounded almost happy, and there was nothing in this world to be happy about. "Blair, isn't that Captain Harwell? The one who brought Preston home? Oh, Blair, it is!" Olivia's eyes shone with blessed relief. "Now we can get a guard for the house!"

7

It was small wonder that Olivia had not recognized
their savior right away. Matthew was so begrimed with
mud and dust from the trip down from La Grange that
his own mother would have had difficulty recognizing
him.

For the past two days, Company D had been riding
vedette beyond the infantry pickets. With the Rebel
army retreating at full speed toward the Tallahatchie,
the duty had consisted mainly of keeping an eye out for
roving bands of guerrillas who were notorious for cutting telegraph wires, burning bridges, and ambushing
couriers and foraging parties. The bushwhackers,
often deserters from the regular army, called themselves partisan rangers, but to the Union soldiers they
were guerrillas. And if Matthew hated anything, he
hated a goddamned guerrilla.

The 2nd Illinois had had their first exposure to these
irregular marauders last summer in Corinth. The guerrillas were like hornets, stinging at the edges of the
Federal Army. Lying in wait for the unwary, they
would then melt away, going back to their farming, or
whatever occupation they engaged in. There·was no
way to identify them, for all their neighbors were either rabid Rebels or afraid of reprisals.

The guerrillas had no scruples; they would as soon pick off a lone soldier who'd gone out to attend to a call of nature as ambush a wagon train. Once they caught an infantryman who left the line of march briefly, and—Matthew's stomach turned every time he thought about it—when Company D came across the body, they found it mutilated.

A note had been pinned to the dead man's chest. "Fate of nigger stealers, you Yankee bastards."

Finally in July, Grant had issued an order saying that persons operating without uniforms would not be entitled to the treatment accorded prisoners of war. And, Matthew hoped fervently, that meant every damned one of them captured would be hung.

Now, as his weary horse trotted into the driveway of Waverley, he saw that a company of Michigan troops known as the Detroit Invincibles had arrived before him. This was undoubtedly the reason for the welcome shining so plainly from Olivia's eyes.

She was calling his name and waving with restrained excitement. Miss Tyler, on the other hand, had such an odd expression on her face that it was hard to tell whether she was glad to see him or not.

"Oh, Captain Harwell!" Olivia breathed with marked relief, running out from beside the veranda. For a moment Matthew thought she was going to grab his muddy stirrup. Removing his hat hastily he said, "Mrs. Tyler."

"Oh, we are so glad to see you!" she cried in the same thankful tone.

Miss Tyler advanced to join her, frowning and pushing her hair back from her face. The golden waves had escaped their chignon and tumbled about her forehead. Her face was flushed and an ominous glitter lighted her magnificent eyes. Matthew thought the general disarray in her appearance gave her a rather appealing, wanton look, a long way from the airy perfection of the pink-and-gold-and-white cloud. Evidently there were numerous sides to Miss Tyler's personality. Each more intriguing than the last. He opened his mouth to greet her.

"It's about *time* you got here!" she cried, clutching her apron and glaring up at him. "Look at that!" she continued, making a sweeping gesture to include all of the Detroit Invincibles. "They're robbing us of everything we own! They've been through the smokehouse! And the henhouse! And the dairy! And—"

At this point, a young infantryman chasing a chicken suddenly emerged from the barnyard and bolted among them, causing Matthew's horse to prance back.

"See!" Miss Tyler cried, pointing after him with a shaking finger. "See there! That's what they've been doing all morning! They even—they even came in and stole our dinner off the stove!" She glared up at Matthew in a perfect fury, almost stamping her foot. "You make them stop!"

"Miss Tyler," he began, wondering if she actually believed him to be in command of all the infantry, "things may be a little unsettled at the moment. But I assure you, your family will be as safe with our army here as you were when your own—"

"Army?" she interrupted. Then she did stamp her foot, and gave her apron an angry little shake, as well. "You call that an army? They're a gang of burglars! Look at them! They're—they're—" She paused for breath, seemingly trying to think of another appellation to apply to his comrades-in-arms.

Matthew spoke quickly, hoping to forestall it. "I'll try to arrange a guard for the house. However, I'm afraid you'll have to resign yourself to losing a few chickens. These men have been on marching rations, and when they see something that looks good to eat—"

"A few chickens?" Miss Tyler interrupted again. "They're taking everything that walks! And—"

"We would be so grateful if you could give us a guard, Captain Harwell," Olivia said hurriedly. "It would give us such a feeling of—of safety. You're very kind to stop by." She was looking up at him as if he were Sir Galahad slaying a dragon, and Matthew had to admit it was a pleasant feeling to be the object of such a look. Miss Tyler, beside her, was looking up at him as though she would like to kill him where he sat.

"We're going to starve!" she shouted. Her sister-in-law turned to her with a worried expression and said, "Blair, dear, you are overwrought."

Miss Tyler fixed her companion with a glare of disdain. "*You* heard what that dirty baboon just said to me! How can you say I'm 'overwrought'? If he'd said such a thing to you, I guess you'd have swooned!"

Dirty baboon? For an instant Matthew thought she was referring to him. But no, it seemed to be some incident that had happened previously.

Wringing her hands in an agitated manner, Olivia said, "Our grandfather isn't here at the moment. I'm sure he'd like to see you again. Can't you—could you come in and wait?"

"I'm afraid not," he said, shaking his head. "My company's been ordered on to Holly Springs. But I can ask one of the infantry officers to detail a guard."

"We shall need a regiment," Miss Tyler said tartly. She did not appear to be overwhelmed with gratitude. "If that would be sufficient to protect us from this swarm of locusts. I've never seen such outrageous behavior in my life!"

Matthew felt a flash of impatience. *Why*, he wondered, *does she always refer to us as some type of animal?* She had got in two in the last two minutes— "baboon" and "locusts."

"Ma'am," he said shortly, "if you feel yourself to be in danger of starvation, I'll also request that you be put on the list to draw rations from our commissary. Just ask the guard that's assigned you, and he can tell you how to go about it. We're not in the habit of—"

"Get rations from the Union Army?" Miss Tyler cried in disbelief. "Go begging for a—a crumb from their table? After they've robbed us of everything we

have?'' She shook her apron again. "Oh!'' she added.
"I'd rather starve!''

"Thank you,'' the sister-in-law said, catching Miss
Tyler by the arm and trying to pull her behind her.
"That would be wonderful, Captain Harwell. How
shall we go about getting them?''

Matthew explained that their names would be entered with the provost marshal, and rations would be
issued for each member of the family on a weekly ba-
sis. Probably there would be flour, bacon, coffee, and
sugar. He was unable to keep his glance from drifting
over to Miss Tyler as he talked. She was looking as
belligerent as ever, but, he realized, softening, she had
been terribly frightened by the invasion of the Detroit
Invincibles.

Strict orders had been issued against looting and unnecessary foraging when the march south began, but
enforcement was left up to the individual company officers, and some of them had a tendency to look the
other way. Matthew did not consider dietary supple-
ments from Rebel henhouses to be grounds for a general court-martial, but he did try to keep his own
troopers from getting too far out of hand by utilizing a
system of fines. He docked them fifty cents for an unex-
plained missing cartridge and five dollars for a stolen
hog. Of course, if his men had been subsisting on
mouldy bacon and hardtack for several weeks, he
wasn't going to get overly excited if they requisitioned
a little fresh meat for a clandestine barbecue.

Matthew had almost finished explaining to the
young Mrs. Tyler how she should draw her Federal
rations. And by now, he was staring quite frankly at
Miss Tyler. This was possible because she was looking
haughtily off in a different direction, as if his plans to
save her from starvation were so mundane as to be
beneath her notice.

But she was looking unusually pretty, too, and he
had mixed emotions. He wished that he could leap
down from his horse, sweep her into his arms, and kiss

her soundly. As a matter of fact, he wished he could do more than that. Too bad that the rules of civilized warfare prevented the modern warrior from galloping away with the fair females of the conquered flung across his saddle. How he would like to—

Matthew's lascivious thoughts were interrupted by the sounds of a scuffle from the barnyard. Looking that way, he saw a rawboned black youth being shoved roughly about by a group of troopers. Instead of cowering, the boy was trying to fight back, and some of his tormentors had started punching and cuffing. From experience, Matthew knew that these episodes could turn ugly. Wheeling his horse, he galloped over.

"All right," he barked. "That's enough! Let him go!"

They were slow to do it. "That trifling buck sassed me, Cap'n," a trooper protested. The others echoed agreement.

"That's an order, Private!"

Reluctantly, they turned the boy loose. He gave Matthew a wild, startled look and cut out for the house. As Matthew rode away, he heard the private grumbling. "It's got so if you raise a hand to the insolent boogers, it's six months in the stockade with a ball and chain!"

He ignored it, because as he rejoined the two ladies, Miss Tyler's hostility seemed to have softened a bit. She looked at him with what might be admiration. His attention was distracted from this encouraging sight by a small child, liberally smeared with some kind of red substance, toddling among the foragers and heading toward them. "Is that your little boy?" he asked Mrs. Tyler, nodding in the youngster's direction. Both of the ladies turned immediately, and Miss Tyler pressed her hands to her face and cried, "He's *bleeding!*"

She ran to snatch him up and Olivia stood transfixed with horror. *Good God!* Matthew thought, losing patience again. *Do they think we go around bayoneting infants?*

"It appears," he said shortly, "to be peppermint lozenge."

Olivia wilted in relief. One of the troopers had probably given the candy to the child. Most of it had wound up on his face, but there was still a sticky residue clutched in his dimpled hand. He swung it about against Miss Tyler's hair, pointed it at Matthew, said, "Thojah!" and smiled.

Miss Tyler carried him grandly up the veranda steps and into the house. She did not even say good-bye, although the child did continue to smile at Matthew over her shoulder.

Olivia, apparently also struck by the abruptness of this departure, said nervously, "You must forgive Blair, Captain Harwell, if she's seemed to behave a little—a little strangely. She's been *very* upset. You see, we had hoped you might come, and she's been looking for you all morning."

"She has?" Matthew said, not sure whether or not he believed it.

"Oh, *yes!* In fact, Blair kept saying that as soon as you got here, everything would be all right!"

It occurred to him that any minute now, some pompous colonel was going to ride up and establish his headquarters right here in the house.

"Mrs. Tyler," he said carefully, "I'm not sure how long our army will be here, but it's very likely that officers will be quartered in your home."

Olivia registered dismay and then said what he had hoped she would say. "You mean they would just come in and take it over? But when are you coming back, Captain Harwell? Oh, I wish you could stay!"

"Well," he said, "I imagine I'll be back pretty soon."

Olivia's small face suddenly brightened with a wonderful idea. "Can't you be quartered with us? We would be so delighted if you would!"

Matthew said modestly, "It might be arranged."

And so, with Olivia's expressions of gratitude ringing in his ears, he rode away to find the 77th Illinois Infantry. The 77th had a major from Springfield who was a friend of his. The major would arrange for the guard and the commissary rations, and, hopefully, would keep the house free of squatters until Matthew could return.

On the way, he passed an acquaintance in the 54th Indiana, who with a group of fellow officers had just paid a visit to the Cooper plantation, where they had discovered a large selection of wines stowed away by Mr. Cooper in what he had imagined to be a safe spot. The Indianans were relaxing beneath a large oak away from the road, and as Matthew rode by, the officer hailed him and generously offered to share with the cavalry.

Matthew accepted the bottle, and then, to his consternation, heard the Indiana captain asking him if there were any likely-looking houses back there.

Holly Springs was to be established as an advance supply base, he said, and the town would be garrisoned. It looked as if they might be here for a while, and his colonel was hunting for a roost.

Matthew told him there was only one house, and it had already been taken by the 77th Illinois. The captain, who had a thin little moustache and fancied himself something of a ladies' man, laughed and said, "Well, have they got any Mississippi belles back there? From what I've seen of this godforsaken state, the only thing they've got to puff about is some damned good-looking women."

"I'm afraid not," Matthew said. "They're all old people. And staunch Unionists, as a matter of fact. Had the flag flying when the cavalry came up. Said they'd been harassed by neighbors a lot."

It should have pained him to tell the man such a whopper, after having accepted his wine. But although he had never seen anything wrong with the Indianan before, Matthew now found himself looking at the thin little moustache and thinking, *By God, I don't like your kind!*

Somewhat perturbed—for how long could he keep saying the 77th Illinois had preempted the house?—he rode on and eventually located the major, who agreed to detail the guard. He was a little more hesitant about the commissary rations, however, and Matthew was forced to repeat his story about the staunch Unionists. He wondered what would happen when the Tylers learned of this. But there was no help for it. Hopefully they would not be questioned and asked to take the Oath. He suggested to the major that the private who would be serving guard duty go to the provost marshal's office to draw the rations, too.

Well, the major said, maybe this could be arranged, since the people were elderly and loyal.

God! Matthew thought, sweating a little. *What am I getting myself into?* No matter. If he could just keep the 54th Indiana colonel out of the way and get back to Waverley and not be thrown into the guardhouse for lying to the major, and if Miss Tyler would stop glaring and stamping her foot, it would all be worthwhile.

8

The trip back in the buggy from the Widow Lockwood's had been slow going for Grandpa and Anna Mary.

Although no Yankees had ventured as far off the beaten path as the Lockwoods', the alarm had been given at two o'clock by one of the Cooper Negroes riding up on muleback. Thus the Tylers were aware when they left the widow's that the northern legions had descended.

The main road, by the time the buggy reached it, was clogged with trudging infantry, occasional mounted cavalry, white-topped supply wagons, six-horse-team field artillery, and lumbering caissons. Grandpa, who was heading north, had to draw rein and wait for almost half an hour before he could find an opening and work his way into the southbound traffic.

Once on the road to Waverley, their crawl homeward became interminable. Several times they were forced to come to a complete halt and let more Union wagons and artillery get by. At each stop, Grandpa and Anna Mary bore the silent scrutiny of hundreds of soldiers—none of whom passed by without slowing down to take a look at them—and Grandpa felt his daughter-in-law's hand resting on his arm in tense apprehension.

There were no dwellings on the short stretch of road between the Widow Lockwood's and Waverley, so when Samuel Tyler reached his property, he was not prepared for what awaited him. He had told himself to expect anything. It might be burned to the ground. However, he had refused to believe that the worst could have happened. When he and Anna Mary turned into the driveway between the crape myrtles, he saw that the worst had not happened—the house was still standing—but other than that, he hardly knew what to shoot them for first.

His pasture, his pecan grove, his front yard—every inch of Waverley—swarmed with Yankees.

Across from the house they had pitched their tents in the pasture. Some of them had begun to start campfires, and Grandpa saw that they were methodically tearing down his fence rails to fuel them. His gates had disappeared. The teamsters had not confined their wagons to the road or driveway, and the front lawn of Waverley was a disaster. Turf was plowed up in all directions, shrubs and flower beds trampled. Liberal piles of fresh manure lay in various places.

Anna Mary, of course, had no thought for anything but the safety of her children, and Grandpa knew that she expected him to go immediately into the house. Out across the barn lot he could see wagons pulling up to his bulging corncribs. Where in the hell was Austin?

After following Anna Mary inside and making sure that his womenfolk were all right, he stalked through the hall. Just as he reached the front door, a knock sounded on the other side. Grandpa swung the door open to face another Lincolnite standing on his veranda.

The latest Yankee stretched about four inches over six feet. His bearded face peered out from beneath a forage cap whose leather visor curled up until it almost touched the crown. Apparently the visor had got soaking wet in some rainstorm and then dried in that position. The head on which the forage cap perched was at least three sizes too large for it. It looked like a boulder topped off by a pea.

"Howdy," the leviathan said in dolorous tones. He was carrying a rifle, which was reduced to toy size in his hands.

"Howdy to you, sir," Grandpa responded, fixing his visitor with a stare of thundering disapprobation.

The Yankee did not say anything else, and neither did he wilt before Grandpa's stare. He merely continued to stand and stare back.

After a moment Samuel Tyler had the strange feeling that he was supposed to know something.

"You want to state your business?" he said.

The big Yankee moved his jaw a little, shifting a cud of tobacco in his cheek.

"I'm yur guard," he said sadly.

"You're my what?"

The Yankee chewed again and added, "Name's Weems." Over the man's shoulder, Grandpa again became aware of a leisurely train of wagons winding its way across his barn lot. The melancholy Yankee spoke again. "Sure seems a shame to have a good Union man's fence rails tore down like this."

What the hell did he mean? Grandpa wondered, as he headed toward the barn lot. Apparently Preston's advice had been followed, and the womenfolk had remembered to ask for the guard. Still not having seen hide nor hair of Austin, he shouldered his way through a busy hive of bluecoats around one of his cribs.

They were unloading his corn and putting it into an army wagon. A ferret-faced little Federal stood by with what looked like a checklist in his hands. According to the chevrons on his sleeve, he held the rank of sergeant.

"Would you mind tellin' me what you intend doin' with my corn?" Grandpa said.

Ferret-face looked up from his sheaf of papers. "You

want a voucher? You got to fill out a form, if you do.
Just go down to the provost marshal's and pick it up.
Office'll be open in a couple of days. This is the 37th
Ohio commissary. My name's Sewell. I got it all down
here on my list."

"Is that so?" Grandpa said. "You keepin' track of
how many wagonloads of corn you already took? You
want me to fill out a voucher for them gates and fence
rails, too? And what about my smokehouse? I understand you pretty well ransacked it."

"I ain't responsible for that," Ferret-face said.

"What do you intend to pay me in?" Grandpa asked.
He would not inquire as to the price now. Just the
medium of exchange. There were at least a hundred
different varieties of currency in circulation, including
Confederate and state notes, county notes, and notes
from local banks and mercantile houses, not to mention planters' private bonds.

"Greenbacks," the sergeant said.

"Green—" Grandpa swallowed and counted to ten.
"Why don't you just pick up a bunch of sticks off the
ground and pay me with them?"

"Greenbacks are official U.S. currency," Ferret-face
said, a hint of suspicion creeping over his face. "Say,
what are you, Pap? Union or Secesh?"

Samuel Tyler's complexion throbbed with a scarlet
flush. *Pap?* A sharp pain jabbed at his chest. Careful
now, a voice warned.

"I'm a Whig," Grandpa said.

Ferret-face adjusted his sheaf of papers. "We was
told you people here was Union." He looked at
Grandpa sharply. "Of course, you understand that
when you go down to present your vouchers, you'll be
required to sign the loyalty oath."

"An' if I don't?"

Ferret-face stuck his pencil behind his ear. "No
oath, no greenbacks. It's as simple as that."

"Listen here, you black Republican—"

"Now wait a minute," the Yankee sergeant said,

starting to show a little red himself. "I ain't no god-damned abolitionist, if that's what you mean!"

"Are you tellin' me that if I don't take your damned oath, you ain't goin' to pay me for my corn? What do you expect me to feed my stock on? I've got a drove of twenty mules! Not to mention my—" Grandpa stopped. It began to dawn on him that it might not be politic to mention what else he had on the place.

"By Jupiter!" Ferret-face cried in amazement. "I believe you *are* Secesh!"

"You'd just come in an' take a man's corn, would you? Hell! You've already done it! Man, that is stealin'! What gives you the right to do that?"

"Reb," the sergeant said, beginning to smile. "You ain't *got* any rights! I ain't stealin' your damned corn! I'm confiscating it! You was plannin' on using it to give aid and comfort to the enemies of the United States. And if I hear one more word out of you, you're goin' to end up in the calaboose!"

For a moment Grandpa considered getting his shotgun from the house and blasting Ferret-face squarely between the eyes.

Then, in a cold recognition of reality, he saw the situation as it was. It would serve nothing except as a sop to his manhood to perform such an act. The taste of swallowed pride and outrage was suddenly bilious in his mouth. Already, he reminded himself, the government this man represented had stripped the South of billions of dollars without recompense. The moralistic rantings with which they perfumed their thievery did not obscure to Samuel Tyler that the Emancipation Proclamation did not apply to slave owners outside the Confederate states.

Grandpa had the feeling that before this was over, he was going to stomach a lot worse than Ferret-face.

"All right," he said to the sergeant. "Help yourself."

As he walked away, he added silently: *You needn't waste your time looking for my cotton, though. I've burned it to hell.*

Eventually Grandpa located Austin, and together they tallied up Waverley's losses.

Luckily, Austin said, the milk cows had not come up for the night. When he'd gone down to the south pasture to check, he'd found them all there. He thought that if the cows could be herded safely past the soldiers, it might be a good idea to keep them tethered close by the house.

The smokehouse had been hardest hit, but he and Little Austin had saved a few hams and shoulders. When he saw the seriousness of the situation, Austin had removed one side of the pigpen and allowed the shoats to scatter into the swamp. If they survived there, he could round them up again when hog-killing time came.

The shoats would furnish sufficient pork to carry the Tylers through the rest of the winter, he thought.

The mules—in the north pasture—had fallen into the hands of an army drover. Austin had recognized them as they were being driven past the road in front of the house.

Grandpa, touring his depleted outbuildings as darkness fell, discovered that for some damned reason, the Yankees had also taken his three recently purchased sacks of salt.

Callie sat at the rolltop desk in her father's office, writing in her journal. Yesterday had been so event packed she felt that much material of undoubted historical significance should be recorded while still fresh in her memory.

So much had happened since the Yankees arrived that she had more material than she knew what to do with. The latest entry was getting longer and longer, and she paused to read over what she'd already written.

The 37th Ohio Volunteer Infantry is camped in our pasture. You can look out the front windows &

see the tents. There are rows & rows of them &
they are a new kind called "Dog Tents." They are
not like those big Sibleys & only two Yankees can
get in them. Some Yankees who were in our backyard yesterday told Mr. Weems they had put a sign
in front of their Dog Tent saying SONS OF BITCHES
WITHIN!!! Mr. Weems belongs to the Sons of Tem-
perance & does not cuss. He told them he had better not hear any more of that from them.

He is our guard & does not say much. Sits out
on the porch most of the time & reads tracts that
Aunt Sophie gives him. Today he brought her a
whole bunch of his own tracts which are put out
by the Christian Commission, a Yankee concern.
Aunt Sophie has been reading them all morning &
imagine she was glad to get them, as had about
run out of hers.

This was all Callie had written so far, and after having read over it, she wondered if she would ever get
everything in.

She'd been bursting with nervous excitement since
yesterday in the kitchen, for it was then that she discovered the enemy in confrontation offered unlimited
opportunity for stimulating verbal duels.

"Well, missy!" one Yankee had said to her in the
kitchen. "Where have all your menfolk run off to? We
can't seem to locate any of them around here."

"They're waitin' for you just around that bend in the
road!" Callie cried, rather proud that she'd thought of
it so quickly, although, shamefully, the Confederates
were probably past the Tallahatchie by then. "When
y'all meet them, we'll see how fast *you* can skedaddle!"

"We don't run, missy," her antagonist said.

"I reckon that was an orderly retreat you made at
Manassas!"

Callie felt herself to be on firm ground and well
armed with the facts. This was due to many careful

readings of accounts of glorious Southern victories in the *Memphis Appeal*.

"Oh, that wasn't us," the Yankee trooper said, leaning companionably against the wall. "That was them hoity-toity Easterners. We're all Western men here, missy. We never show our backs to the enemy."

Callie thought for a minute and then fairly outdid herself. "That must have been a sight to see at Pittsburg Landing! All you westerners runnin' backwards!"

"Why, young lady, you are mistaken. I was in the fight at Shiloh, and we didn't run there!"

"So was my brother! And he said you ran as far as you could—and then jumped in the Tennessee River!"

"You are a red-hot little Rebel, ain't you?" the Yankee said, scratching leisurely behind his ear. "Any more here like you?"

"All over the state of Mississippi! You won't find any traitors around here."

Callie bent over her journal again.

> Mrs. Pearl Sharp came up here & said the Yankees had plumb cleaned her out; walked right up the road past all kinds of soldiers. She let it slip that Bob Sharp is home; said her husband & son took off to the swamp.

She stopped to remember this morning, when Mrs. Sharp stopped by Waverley. Callie's mother had listened to her diatribe in silence. Finally Anna Mary said she was sorry Miss Pearl had been robbed of everything, and the Tylers would give her all they could spare.

Then, to Callie's amazement, Miss Pearl said bitterly:

"Yes, we wasn't so fortunate as you nigger owners. We didn't have no Yankee standin' guard at *our* door! Reckon they thought us poor folks wasn't *good* enough for that!"

She had been chewing tobacco, and she suddenly expectorated.

"I hope Jake an' Bob kill ever' one of 'em!" she cried. "I hope they stay out in thet swamp an gut ever' bluecoat they gits their hands on! I hope—"

Anna Mary turned abruptly and went into the house, saying, "I'll look through the things we managed to save, Mrs. Sharp, and see what I can find for you."

Callie began writing again.

> Our upstairs hall is a sight you wouldn't believe. We've got sacks of meal & hams & all kind of junk up there. Mr. Weems told us it'd be better to keep all our eatables inside the house for a while. A few chickens got away yesterday & then came back to the henhouse & I thought for a minute they might end up in here. But last night after we'd all gone to bed we heard a big blast & Mr. Weems had shot out toward the henhouse. When Grandpa went out there, Mr. Weems said some guards will let the troopers get away with anything, but he is not that kind of guard. He keeps calling Grandpa a good Union man & Grandpa said for nobody to tell him any different.

Callie yawned and looked over at the smoldering logs in the fireplace. She hadn't had much sleep because the Yankee buglers blowing reveille this morning woke her up at four o'clock.

The Tyler milk cows, tethered in the barn lot, were also aroused by the Yankee buglers, as were the army mules in a roped-off enclosure south of the pecan grove. The mules brayed, the cows lowed, the buglers blew, and Callie thought she had never heard such a racket in her life.

She turned to her journal.

> The 37th Ohio Volunteers get up awful early. I do not know what they have to do to get up at 4

o'clock. I have never heard so many bugle calls, as
they have one for *every thing*. The first one was for
roll call & some of them came out in their drawers
& dressed while they were standing in line. You
would think they didn't know ladies were present
over here. Altho guess I was about the only one
watching at that hour. Blair would not come to the
window & said if she has to look at one more Yankee she is going to throw up.

After roll call, they had another bugle call for
breakfast, which I heard them refer to as "peas on
a trencher." You see, they are in our yard all the
time so we can hear them talking. They are usually
looking for something to eat—which they *now* offer to pay for!!! Telithia has been making quite a
bit of money selling corn dodgers & buttermilk,
but they are paying her in all kinds of odd-looking
scrip.

Callie couldn't write much more after this. Her fingers felt cramped. She decided to close it.

Would give a dollar to know what is happening
in Holly Springs. We have not seen anybody from
town & when Mr. Fred Grace tried to ride a mule
there, some Yankees took his mule away & he was
forced to turn around & hoof it back home. He
stopped by here & said the Lockwoods are all
right. Have not seen a single Yank out that way.
He was mad about his mule. Of course have not
heard anything about what our army is doing. No
mail comes thru any more & Grandpa said they
would probably hang him if they caught him reading the *Memphis Appeal*.

9

Holly Springs, when the 2nd Illinois Cavalry reached it, had changed considerably. Gone was the drowsy, easygoing atmosphere of a prosperous Southern village. Except for the fine old trees and the stately residences, the place reminded Matthew of pictures of California boomtowns during the gold rush of the forties.

An entire new population had moved in and the streets around the courthouse square were clogged with men in uniform and the civilian flotsam and jetsam that always followed in the wake of the army. The buildings around the north and east sides of the square had been converted into warehouses for the storage of commissary and quartermaster supplies. Hospital flags flew over one building, and already cotton bales were stacked in the courthouse square.

When Matthew reported in at headquarters, he was told that Company D would be camped on the fairgrounds southeast of the business district. He then located the fairgrounds, where he was able to secure tents for the men and assure himself that rations would be issued and that there would be adequate corn and forage for the horses.

By this time, it was almost dark and he decided he'd done all he could for his troopers, short of tucking

them in and hearing their prayers, and now—by damn
—he was going to enjoy the privileges of rank, for
once, and find a place where he could get something
decent to eat and take a bath.

This did not prove easy.

In fact, it proved almost impossible. Matthew
headed for the biggest building in sight, a three-story
brick structure designated by a sign in front as the
Magnolia Hotel.

As he walked down the sidewalk, two ladies approached from the opposite direction. Immediately
they tossed their noses in the air and looked straight
through him. As soon as they drew abreast, the fair
ones jerked aside their skirts as though in danger of
contamination from the vile aura of a Yankee walking
past.

His face reddening, Matthew was unpleasantly reminded of Miss Tyler. He made a sudden decision. Tonight he would stay at the hotel.

The desk clerk, a Rebel civilian, stared at him in
astonishment when he put in his request for accommodations.

They were full up, he said. No vacancies.

The clerk seemed a bit taken aback by Matthew's
appearance. Apparently a three-day growth of beard, a
liberal coating of Mississippi mud, and the aroma of
horse and unwashed cavalryman had aroused suspicion. The damned fool was looking at him as if he were
Attila reincarnated.

Matthew growled that he had the money to pay for
the room, if that was what was worrying him.

"Oh, *no*, sir!" the clerk said. "There just isn't anything available. We've got them four and five to a room
now. They're even sleeping in the hallways."

Further questioning revealed that every place of
public accommodation in town was packed to the raf-
ters. No, the clerk did not know where he might go to
obtain a bath and shave. The barbershops were closed

by now. The hotel dining room, however, was still open for business. And the bar, he added.

Matthew headed for the bar, seeing himself back at the fairgrounds for the evening once again without mattresses and hot water. But halfway across the lobby, his luck took a turn for the better. He heard someone hailing him and turned to see an old friend from Illinois, Captain Stephen Eaton.

Eaton was crossing the lobby in the company of a squat, frog-faced civilian, whom Matthew assumed to be a speculator. The man bore all the marks of success-ful cupidity: beaver hat, watered-silk waistcoat, gold watch chain, and an aura of self-confident acumen. As Matthew waited for Eaton, he thought it was a hell of a situation when a common soldier couldn't get a hotel room because of an influx of bloodsuckers.

"Matt! What the devil!" Eaton said, shaking his hand and slapping him on his crusty shoulder. "I thought you'd be in Vicksburg by now! What happened?"

Eaton and Matthew had spent a fair amount of time together in occupied Memphis, sampling the entertain-ments offered by that metropolis. Steve was hand-some, slim, dapper, and permanently attached to the provost marshal's office. His uniforms were a model of sartorial splendor, and every button gleamed, every crease was razor-sharp, and every insignia impecca-ble. Matthew had never seen a particle of mud any-where on him.

He explained that his company had been assigned to duty in Holly Springs.

"Hey, that's capital news!" Eaton responded, turn-ing to acknowledge the squat civilian's farewell from across the lobby. As the man passed through the crowd, Eaton lowered his voice confidentially. "There goes half the money in Mississippi. Name's Jonas Kendall. Man, if you but *knew* . . ."

In Memphis, Eaton had been involved with half the money in western Tennessee, and Matthew was not sure whether his grandiose associations were actual or a product of his imagination.

Whichever it was, he had wanted no part of it. He had refused Eaton's repeated suggestions that he avail himself of opportunities in contraband cotton—some of which sounded so shadowy as to border on the treasonous—and taken Steve's manipulations with a grain of salt.

He now told him about his inability to find accommodations.

Eaton came through like the entrepreneur he knew him to be. "Hell!" he said. "I've got a room here! A damned fine one! All to myself, too! You're welcome to share it."

Matthew shared it.

Not only that, but Eaton—producing marvels like P. T. Barnum—also secured hot water, soap, towels, laundry service, whiskey, a razor, and his companionship at dinner. Which wasn't very good, considering the prices the Magnolia Hotel was asking.

After dinner, Steve bade Matthew farewell, as he had a previous engagement with Jonas Kendall. "Yes," he said with pleasure, "things are looking up here. If you've got the money to pay for it, you can get about anything you want now. Everything's come in but the whores, and they'll be here shortly."

Matthew, wobbling from his days in the saddle and liberal after-dinner libations from the whiskey bottle, went to bed early.

The next morning he awoke to clean linen, a furry tongue, and a splitting head. When he looked with bleary eyes into the mirror above the washstand, he saw that he was going to have to find a barbershop pretty soon.

A letter from his mother lay next to the basin, where he had emptied his pockets last night. The letter had the usual family news of his two younger brothers and his fourteen-year-old sister, Amelia. Matthew felt responsible for all of them. His father had died when

Matthew was sixteen, and since then he had been head of the family. His father had left them financially well-off, but as the eldest son Matthew had been expected to look after his mother and be the man of the house. The burden had been a heavy one and without his natural sturdiness of character could have crushed him. Instead it had made him stronger. Still, at times he felt as if he were penned in a cell. The bars bore labels like "obligation" and "duty," and he could never break out, like Eaton, and do what he wanted, when he wanted, just because he wanted to do it.

A knock sounded at the door to the hotel room. When he opened it, a grinning Negro was standing in the hallway holding his freshly sponged and pressed uniform.

Matthew tipped him liberally and the Negro thank-you-sahed effusively and did not pause to examine the validity of the currency. He wondered if the man had ever been given money before the Union Army's arrival.

"Those are United States greenbacks," he told him. "Don't let anybody palm anything else off on you."

Nodding, the man thank-you-sahed and grinned again. The Negroes would accept any worthless bit of paper handed to them. In Memphis the cavalry had robbed them of their pitiful belongings by offering payment in green express labels from the depot.

When Matthew had enlisted fifteen months ago, he had felt, along with most of his friends, that he would be fighting to preserve the Union. In the election of 1860 he had voted for Abraham Lincoln and had been among the crowd at the Springfield depot that watched the train bearing the President-elect pull out for Washington. Matthew had been impressed by the somber dedication evident in those gaunt features. He considered Lincoln a moderate, and agreed with him that slavery, although an evil, could not be abolished at the price of tearing the country apart.

But after an atrocity Matthew had seen in Memphis, his opinion had done a dramatic about-face.

An escaped slave had made his way into the Federal lines. As a chronic runaway, the Negro's cheek had been branded. One ear was cut off. Sickened, Matthew saw the healed ridges from old whippings that criss-crossed the man's back.

That such barbarisms could be practiced in modern-day America seemed incredible, and Matthew wondered what manner of savages these Southerners were. At that moment he had become convinced that if the war accomplished nothing else, the abolition of slavery would have made the bloodshed worthwhile.

Now, after putting on his uniform, Matthew descended to the lobby and entered the hotel dining room in an immaculate condition. He did not think the desk clerk recognized him as he passed. Stephen Eaton was already at a table having breakfast, and he lingered over a second cup of coffee while Matthew ate his. Eaton was back on his favorite subject again. He indicated that cotton prices would soon be soaring to an all-time high. After this subject had been exhausted, Eaton expressed poignant regret that he had been forced to abandon his lady friend in Memphis. She had been afraid to accompany him on the trip south.

The lady in question was an uncommonly handsome courtesan whom Eaton had installed as his mistress. Matthew had always been slightly uncomfortable in her presence. After obtaining her, Eaton insisted on taking her almost everywhere they went.

The local Memphis papers had begun to bristle with editorials complaining of this invasion of Northern harlots, who had found slim pickings in their regular bailiwicks and followed the Union armies south. The editorial writers cried that the city's places of entertainment had become so crowded with this riffraff that decent citizens were loath to go out. And, the papers added, the scarlet women were thronging the public conveyances and were out in force on the streets, often —they accused—on the arms of Union officers!

It was all true enough, and Eaton's mistress had been brilliantly stylish—until she opened her mouth. She was from Cincinnati and had a voice like a well-rusted locomotive bearing. Matthew soon found it too grating to remain in its vicinity, and he'd had the puritanical feeling that the Memphis editorial writers had just grounds for complaint. But it was all official. The army even registered the whores.

Now Eaton said that she would probably take up with some general in his absence, and he would lose her services for good. Which galled him considerably, as she had been pretty damned expensive. Costly gifts had been bestowed upon her, and he was beginning to wish he hadn't been so impulsive. But how the hell was he supposed to know the army was about to pull out?

Matthew's head was still throbbing, the conversation bringing back memories of a certain young lady in Springfield, memories that were not particularly pleasant.

When he enlisted, the young lady had wanted them to be married before he left for the South. She was pretty and vivacious, but he was not in love. In a dramatic declaration she declared that since he had spurned her, she would remain a spinster for the rest of her life. Matthew, refusing to be bullied, left with his regiment. Three weeks later she married an infantry major. He had been stunned by the news, not because he loved her, but because she had so blatantly lied.

Matthew was on his third cup of coffee, his head was not getting any better, and for a moment he had the strange feeling that no woman could be trusted and that he wished he were back at the front.

After breakfast, however, his headache began to show some relief. There was no more immediate business pressing, and he thought of paying a call at Waverley.

He should find out whether or not the 77th Illinois major had provided the guard. Matthew did not consider approaching the major himself on this score, as the man might have discovered that the Tylers were not quite as he'd represented them. He wondered if Miss Tyler was still glaring and stamping her foot. Well, he decided, he would ride out and see. And even if she was, what did it matter? Whatever she was doing, she would be a feast for the eyes. He felt fairly confident of a welcome from the rest of the family. The young Mrs. Tyler had been touching in her gratitude and had certainly urged him to come back.

Eaton, who was on his way to the provost marshal's office, accompanied him through the lobby. As they were going down the steps of the hotel, they met an imposing, middle-aged matron. The dowager was dressed in somber, patrician garb: bonnet, mitts, and all the marks of gentility—except for a regiment-size Confederate battle flag that she had pinned and folded across her chest. Her bosom was imposing enough in itself. It jutted before her like the prow of a warship as she came contemptuously up the steps.

Just as she was passing them, Eaton murmured in Matthew's ear, "Are you ready to storm the breastworks, Captain?"

Matthew gave a quick snort of laughter.

At the sound of his laugh the dowager stopped, turned, and looked at them with withering disdain. To his acute embarrassment, she cried in a voice that surely carried back to Memphis, *"Swine!"*

His ears burning, Matthew thought that Rebel females were well aware of the rectitude expected of men toward their sex and were exploiting it to the fullest. He could understand why General Butler had issued his order that New Orleans women who insulted Federal soldiers would be treated as whores. A gentleman could make no reply to shouted epithets from a lady. Matthew wished he were not a gentleman now.

He wondered why he was continuing on to

Waverley. If he expected any better treatment from Miss Tyler, he'd gone soft in the head. Yet on he went.

At Waverley a sad-eyed behemoth in a private's uniform answered his knock.

"Are the Tylers at home?" Matthew snapped.

"Mr. Weems?" a voice called from the hallway. "Who are you talking to out there?" Footsteps approached the doorway, and the elderly aunt who had given Matthew his tract peered around it.

"Oh, my!" she said. "Now let me think for a minute." Pressing one hand against her bosom, she pointed at Matthew and cried, "Harwell! Major Harwell, isn't it? Well, do come in, sir. Olivia tells me you are responsible for Mr. Weems."

She smiled at the behemoth and patted its arm.

"He is a fine Christian gentleman," she added as she escorted Matthew through the door. "Do come into the parlor and sit down. I am in the midst of making peach trifle." She indicated that he should take a seat on the horsehair sofa. When he had done so, she clasped her hands in front of her apron and stood beaming down at him. "Do you like peach trifle, Major? You must join us for supper."

"It's captain, ma'am," Matthew said.

At this point, the young Mrs. Tyler appeared. Olivia seemed delighted to see him. Private Weems was the guard for the house, she said, and the commissary rations had been most adequate. Aunt Sophie cried that she was delighted to have an abundance of white sugar and flour, and they'd been issued real coffee, which Anna Mary enjoyed. "You must promise to stay!" Olivia urged, sitting beside him on the sofa and all but hanging on to his arm.

Impressed by the warmth of his reception, Matthew began mentally retracing the route from Waverley to the fairgrounds. He thought of the tent and his rations of sowbelly and hardtack. From what he'd gathered from listening to Eaton, the base was so secure there wasn't an officer in Holly Springs who hadn't moved into more comfortable quarters.

Why the hell not? Matthew decided.

He had, of course, realized that the vision of loveliness had not put in an appearance, but he assumed she would be present at the supper table. Despite the looks of loathing cast upon him earlier by the ladies of Holly Springs, he found his optimism blooming.

Miss Tyler did join them at supper, but she was in a new mood.

The nearest thing Matthew could think of to compare it with was the frozen Russian steppes. She was barely civil in her greeting to him. Seated on his right at the table, she addressed him abruptly about halfway through the meal.

"Do you by any chance have a newspaper?" she said, in a voice heavy with boredom and brittle with ice.

"Why, no," he answered, turning to look at her. "Not at the moment. Did you have any particular paper in mind?"

"The *Memphis Appeal*."

Matthew said he had not noticed it lying about, but that he would be happy to secure her the latest edition of the *Chicago Tribune*.

Miss Tyler took a contemptuous sip of her Federal commissary coffee and then indicated that perhaps this would be all right.

"It would be better than nothing, I suppose. I'd like to know where our brave soldiers are now."

Matthew dug into his chicken potpie. "At the rate they were retreating, they're probably digging earthworks on the southern tip of Florida."

She looked at him sharply over the rim of her cup. After a moment of ominous silence she said, "Well, at least they're not enjoying all the comforts of home. While you're sitting here at this table, our poor men are out in the mud and the cold."

"Believe it or not, Miss Tyler, I've been known to

swim my horse across a few creeks and camp in the mud on occasion."

She pursed her pretty mouth in disdain. Tonight a chenille net confined her hair, which was coiled on her neck like satin taffy. A faint scent of crushed roses came from her creamy skin. She looked and smelled so delicious that Matthew would have liked to lean over and take a bite.

"Oh, come now, Captain." She arched a delicate eyebrow. "Our men suffer much more deprivation and hardship than you Yankees do. Everyone knows that. When they're defending the sacred soil of their country, they aren't coddled with tents and feather pillows and nice clean cots like your army has."

Matthew silently counted to ten. "If your army loves the sacred soil of Mississippi that much, then they shouldn't mind sleeping on it."

He had the satisfaction of seeing her momentarily stumped for an answer, before Mrs. Tyler, alert and gracious at the foot of the table, intervened to introduce a less controversial topic. With six of them around the table, the talk became lively. Anna Mary expressed interest in Matthew's family, and as he was the newcomer, most of the conversation was directed to him. Miss Tyler fell into a sullen silence and picked at her food. Eating heartily, Matthew thought that Aunt Sophie had surpassed herself with the chicken potpie, which was savory with gravy and rich and crumbly of crust. As the table was being cleared for dessert, he took advantage of the distraction and murmured to his stony companion, "You're being unusually quiet, Miss Tyler. Is something wrong?"

"What could possibly be wrong, Captain Harwell?" she replied sourly, keeping a weather eye on her mother. "I adore being invaded, and then sitting down to supper with the enemy. No, everything's perfectly fine. But how thoughtful of you to ask."

"You're not being a true daughter of Dixie," Matthew said under his breath, pretending to wipe his mouth with his napkin. "If we were on the street, you could insult me with impunity. But I'm a guest at your table. I could be Genghis Khan, and Southern hospitality would require that you be polite."

"Don't tell me how to behave—" she began, before being interrupted by Grandpa, at the head of the table, who inquired of Matthew as to the availability of provisions in Holly Springs. He was about to butcher some of his hogs, he said, and would have need of salt. Matthew told him that necessities were being sold to civilians and that he would be able to obtain the salt. Then Aunt Sophie served the peach trifle, and Matthew knew he'd stumbled into a gourmet's paradise. Praising Aunt Sophie highly, he allowed a second helping of the trifle to be forced upon him. "Ma'am," he said, "what did you put into this?"

Aunt Sophie immediately reeled off her recipe, crying, "I shall copy it off for you, Major. You must enclose it in your next letter to your dear mother. Perhaps she would like to try a trifle, the next time you are home."

They had already learned about his dear mother, as well as his two younger brothers and his dear little sister. In fact, Matthew had given them his entire life history during the chicken potpie.

After supper, Miss Tyler swept from the dining room. Grandpa drew Matthew aside in the hall and said gruffly, "I don't know how you'll feel about this, young fellah, but if you stay here long enough, you're goin' to hear Weems callin' me a Union man." Grandpa fixed him with a gimlet eye and added, "Now, if you want to keep eatin' like you ate tonight, I'd advise you not to disabuse him of the notion. I know I ain't, an' you know I ain't, but what Weems don't know ain't goin' to hurt him. Would you agree with me on that?"

Matthew managed to keep a straight face and nod.

With a satisfied smile, Grandpa invited him into his room to share a brandy. Matthew provided Havana cigars from his baggage, and they remained in good fellowship for quite some time. Then, he heard himself being asked bluntly if he had any idea how long Holly Springs would be occupied.

Matthew said he didn't know.

Looking at him contemplatively through a haze of cigar smoke, Grandpa said, "Well, I don't expect you to give me any vital military information. I'd just like to know when the hell I can get back to my farming."

As he lit his final cigar of the evening, Matthew wondered if the old codger engaged in any activities other than farming. He was of advanced years, to be sure, but looked as tough as a water moccasin. He had a mental picture of Grandpa crawling on his belly through underbrush and taking potshots at foraging parties.

Could it be that here in front of him sat a genuine guerrilla?

He hated to think it of him, but he did not dismiss the possibility. After the genial atmosphere of the supper table, it came as a jolt to be reminded that he was in hostile territory, surrounded by the enemy.

Matthew cautioned himself not to be lulled into false security by an overabundance of hospitality and peach trifle.

"I think we all know what the objective is, sir," he said carefully. "How long we'll be here depends on a lot of different factors. I couldn't begin to go into any of them."

Grandpa continued to regard him through the cigar smoke and said nothing.

Eventually he grunted. "All right. If me an' Austin can round them hogs up out of the swamp, I reckon we'll be pretty well set for the winter. And maybe next spring, when it comes time to plant, things will have calmed down a little."

"I hope so, sir," Matthew said.

10

The Federal wagon trains passed for five days, and in that time Anna Mary didn't let her daughters set foot outside the house. For Blair the confinement was almost unbearable.

The piano was the only thing to save her from madness. During the day, when the family had the house to themselves, she played as much as possible, endless renditions that had become her only source of pleasure.

She was going crazy with boredom!

That was the worst part of it all! One couldn't stay boiling mad for five days, and now her sense of outrage blossomed only momentarily, as she remembered some dreadful occurrence on the day of the invasion. Most of it had turned into a dead, dull resentment.

All the picnics and cotillions were gone. Her entire social life had pulled out with Pemberton's army, and she missed it so desperately she felt like an addict deprived of his opium.

And, to add to her troubles, they had acquired a new Yankee.

Of course, she had absolutely nothing to say about what came into the house nowadays. All her protests thus far had been completely ignored, and Grandpa

and her mother had turned into dictators. Even Aunt
Sophie and Olivia had more say-so than she. She had
considered having her meals in her room, but the pros-
pect of additional solitude was too horrendous. Even
being forced to share the company of a Yankee at table
was preferable to eating alone.

So she had assumed a disdainful expression and ignored Captain Harwell as thoroughly as she'd been ignoring the 37th Ohio camped in the pasture.

Yet even this had proved unsatisfactory, for he
seemed to be more interested in Aunt Sophie's cooking
than in staring at Blair. For some reason, this made
her crosser than ever. He had not yet produced the
Chicago Tribune, and she suspected the neglect had
been deliberate. He was going to make her ask him
again. Well, she wasn't going to. She would rot from
ignorance first. For all she knew, Vicksburg had already surrendered and been burned to the ground.

That first night at the supper table she had learned
that Captain Harwell had two younger brothers and a
fourteen-year-old sister whose name was Amelia.

When she stopped to think about it, it seemed odd
that Yankees came equipped with families. She had
fallen into the habit of thinking they sprang full-grown
in regiments, all outfitted in horrid blue uniforms and
clutching a Springfield rifle in one hand and a southern ham in the other.

But no, there were Yankee women up north, and
Yankee dogs and cats, and even little Yankee babies.

Another disaster occurred soon afterward.

Little Austin disappeared. Blair knew good and well
what had happened. He'd run off to join the abolition-
ists. Telithia was in a continual flood of tears and
wailed that they were sure to put him in a contraband
camp and she'd never see him again. Austin was worried, too, and Grandpa gave him permission to go out
searching for Little Austin. But the search was in vain,
and Austin came home looking graver than ever. And
now, of course, Grandpa and Austin had all the work

to do, and they were going to miss Little Austin's services.

The next day Blair looked out and saw their neighbor, Mr. Cooper, driving up in his hooded chaise. To her delighted amazement his daughter Julie Ann and Louley Burton, who lived in Holly Springs, were with him.

After flying out to greet them, Blair took the girls up to her bedroom. Mr. Weems was on the front porch with Robbie, and she wanted to be able to speak freely.

The three of them sat down on the four-poster bed in a flurry of hoops, and she began to bombard her guests with questions. Louley took off her bonnet and said that the Yankees had taken over every public building around the courthouse square.

Louley was the same age as Blair, and they had been classmates at the Female Institute. Her short brown bangs were fashionably frizzed across her forehead, additional curls bounced indignantly on the back of her neck, and there were more corkscrew curls framing her face. She said that Holly Springs had been turned into a Federal supply depot, with army gear stored everywhere you looked, even in the livery stables. The roundhouse and depot had been preempted, and the second floor of the Masonic Hall was packed with crates of ammunition.

"Our beautiful hall?" Blair cried, remembering all the theatricals and balls she'd attended there, not to mention the graduation exercises of every class at the Female Institute!

"Yes," Louley said. "And that's not the half of it. They've taken over people's houses, too. We have a pile of officers in ours right now! And so does Julie Ann!"

"We've got a big United States flag hanging from our front porch!" Julie Ann breathed in awe.

Julie Ann was sixteen, and sometimes Blair wondered if she had all her faculties. There was nothing lacking physically, for with her glossy auburn curls, round blue eyes, and dainty dimpled hands, she looked like something you would want to pick up and cuddle. Blair had an almost maternal attitude toward Julie Ann.

"Have you seen Lida Coxe?" Blair asked her. "She's in town, isn't she?"

"My dear!" Louley exclaimed. "General Grant is using the Coxe house for headquarters!"

"Is Lida still *in* it?"

"Yes, they let them stay. What do you suppose General Grant thinks of the bathroom? He's probably never seen anything like *that* before!" Louley sniffed. "And I think the *worst* thing that's happened was at Christ Church last Sunday."

"What?" Blair asked.

"There was a crowd of Yankee soldiers at morning prayers, and they *ordered* Dr. Pickett not to pray for Jefferson Davis! They said he'd be shot, if he did!"

"Good Lord, Lou!"

"Blair!" Julie Ann Cooper said in a breathless voice. "Mr. Kendall has taken the Oath!"

Blair turned to stare at her. Her flowerlike face rosy with the import of her news, Julie Ann gave a little jump on the bed, pleased that she'd been able to tell it before Louley.

"No!" Blair gasped.

"He has!" Julie Ann said.

Blair looked at Louley. "But—why, Lou? And—and when?"

Louley's lips tightened. "The day the Yankees got here. The traitor! Blair, he couldn't *wait* to get to the provost marshal's office! And the way he's been acting ever since—it's—it's disgusting! He's been as thick as thieves with the Yankees! And—"

"They got Isabella's fur tippet!" Julie Ann interrupted.

"They did what?" Blair said. Julie Ann's auburn curls, bouncing on either side of her face, were gathered over her ears and tied with pink ribbons. Blair thought the style looked darling on Julie Ann but would be too juvenile for herself.

"That's why he did it!" Louley said. "The first day the Yankees came, they were raiding the Kendalls' smokehouse—just like they did everybody else's—and he went out and ordered them to stop! So that made them mad and they decided to come in his house! Mr. Kendall couldn't find any officers to stop them, and they went swarming all over it! They—"

"They got Isabella's black velvet opera cloak and put *flour* in it! They used it for a *sack!*" Julie Ann cried.

"Yes," Louley said. "And took all the cut glass celery dishes and filled them up with preserves and—"

"And they got all her bonnets and used them for baskets!" Julie Ann cried.

"Isabella's bonnets?" Blair said.

Julie Ann nodded eagerly. "One Yankee put on her green velvet with the marabou feathers and wore it out in the street!"

Her shoulders shaking, Blair put her hand over her mouth and stared at Julie Ann. Watching her uncertainly, Julie Ann emitted a nervous giggle.

Blair collapsed on the bed in a paroxysm of merriment.

Julie Ann joined in enthusiastically, squealing with giggles. "Mr. Kendall ran around trying to get the bonnets away from them! Mr. Charlie Blaylock said he was cussing like *crazy!*"

Blair heard Louley harrumph and remark coldly that she did not find Yankee vandalism amusing.

She sat up, wiped her eyes with a corner of the bedspread, and tried to get a grip on herself. "Oh, Lou. You know what a snit Isabella is, flaunting all those clothes in our faces."

"Well, anyway," Louley said severely, "Mr. Kendall went down that very day and took the Oath. And now they say he's been helping the Yankees get cotton. He had plenty stored away himself, and you can wager he made them pay through the nose for it. He knows about a lot of other folks who have cotton, too. Blair, they're confiscating it! If you won't take the Oath, they just go out and take it! And some folks who refugeed left their cotton still out in the fields, and the Yankees have got darkies out there picking it!"

Lord, Blair thought, her merriment evaporating, replaced by the old dull, dead resentment. "Let's—let's talk about something else. I'm tired of hearing about what the Yankees did. There's not anything we can do about it, and it just makes me mad. Do you know anything about what's happened to our army?"

"Somebody said the Yankees are already to Oxford."

"What about our rearguard cavalry?" Blair asked, thinking of Preston.

"Nobody knows! We heard there was fighting at Oxford, but how can you tell? There's nothing but rumors, and you can't believe anything you hear from the Yankees."

"Lord, I wish I had a newspaper!" Blair said.

"The *Memphis Appeal* has moved to Grenada. Papa calls it the Moving Appeal. That makes the third time it's had to run from the Yankees!"

At least, Blair thought dully, *I should be thankful that I don't have to worry about Papa and Robert. I believe they're going to sit in that camp at Murfreesboro until the end of the war.*

It suddenly occurred to her that with the occupation, the mail service had stopped, and her mother and Olivia had been unable to receive letters. A new foreboding swooped down to perch on her shoulders. Had Bragg's army already moved?

"Let's—let's go down to the parlor and have coffee," she said.

In the parlor Louley commented on the quality of the coffee, and seemed surprised to learn that it had been supplied by the Union Army's commissary department.

"Yes," Blair said. "We have a Yankee captain staying with us. He's been—rather considerate."

She was somewhat surprised to hear herself saying it—in view of the continued absence of the *Chicago Tribune*—and Louley made a wry face. She had not, she said, run into any Yankees of that stripe. The officers staying with the Burtons were rude, impudent, and overbearing, and she would certainly have accepted no favors from *them*.

"It's not a favor," Blair answered coldly. "We consider it rent."

For a moment she thought Louley was going to ask if the Tylers were taking in boarders, and started framing a reply. But Louley didn't say it, and she wondered if she was so on edge that she couldn't stand to be around her own friends.

Mr. Cooper had gone out somewhere with Grandpa, but he soon returned and said it was time they were leaving. He and Grandpa went out to the chaise, and Blair lingered with Louley and Julie Ann on the veranda.

"Do you suppose things are getting back to normal and we can start doing things again?" she said. "What about the Musical Society? Are they planning to meet?"

"I should hope so!" Louley said. "We've got to start rehearsing the Christmas program. You're supposed to play for it, Blair."

"Christmas—do you know, I'd almost forgotten about it?"

"Well, it's December already."

"What kind of Christmas will it be?" Blair could feel the depression washing over her in waves. "We don't know where any of our menfolks are. Or what's going to—"

"Ohhh!" Julie Ann squealed softly. "Are those *your* officers, Blair? They look better than ours!"

Blair looked out toward the driveway and went stiff with dismay. Of all the times—! Now what was she going to do? Stand here and introduce Captain Harwell and whoever that was with him to Louley and

Julie Ann? They were obviously headed for the veranda, and it was too late to sweep disdainfully back into the house. *Thunderation!* she thought. She couldn't even stand on her own front porch and see her friends off, without *them* descending upon her and demanding introductions!

Captain Harwell and his companion had drawn up their horses beside the Cooper chaise. As the unknown Yankee officer looked boldly toward the veranda, Blair felt a flash of instant dislike.

Julie Ann stood on tiptoe and whispered in her ear. "The one with the moustache is sort of handsome, don't you think?"

Blair speared Julie Ann with a glare of reproval. "No, I don't," she said sharply. "And anyway, he is much too old for you, Julie Ann."

Julie Ann went down from her tiptoes with a hurt look on her face. She wasn't used to having Blair speak to her in that manner. Usually her attitude was that of an indulgent older sister.

"Well," she said hastily, "he does look pretty old. He must be about thirty, I guess."

"Don't be ridiculous," Blair snapped. "He's not that old, Julie Ann."

Louley had begun to hiss in Blair's other ear. "See that impudent creature staring at us! *That's* what I mean!"

"Well, for heaven's sake, you-all get down to the chaise! We can't just keep standing here!"

They did not escape the introductions, however, for as they went down the steps, Captain Harwell's friend had already leaped from his saddle and was advancing toward them, sweeping off his hat as he came. He bowed with a flourish.

"Ladies!" he said, straightening up and engulfing them all in his smile.

For a moment Blair considered cutting him dead in his tracks. This proved impossible, because Julie Ann had already started to giggle. Turning to her with an air of suave amusement, the newest Yankee made his own presentation.

"Allow me to introduce myself," he said. "Captain Stephen Eaton." He bowed again to Julie Ann. "Such a charming picture. May I say that when I caught my first glimpse of you on the veranda, I was reminded of a bouquet of beautiful roses? How do you Southern ladies always look so lovely? I am constantly amazed."

Glaring at him, Blair thought that she would like to amaze him further by telling him what she thought of his ridiculous effusions. But Captain Harwell had now dismounted from his horse and was heading toward them with a noncommittal look on his face. "I'm Julie Ann Cooper," Julie Ann said to the elegant Captain Eaton. She actually held out her hand. He seized it and bowed over it, raising it smartly to his lips. Blair had the feeling that her darling innocent was in the grasp of something unclean.

Great jumping Jehoshaphat! This one was the worst yet! She didn't believe she'd like him even if he wasn't a Yankee! What was it about him? He was handsome enough.

Captain Eaton turned to her. She ignored him and began introducing Captain Harwell to Louley and Julie Ann. She had the odd impression that she was glad he had joined them. His noncommittal expression was a relief from the treacle. At least *he* had an honest face.

Louley looked as if she were being forced to swallow a dose of quinine, but Julie Ann was dimpling and widening her eyes. Blair thought she was almost flirting, and noticed that Captain Harwell was smiling down at her as though she were some kind of doll.

"Your father's waiting," she said to Julie Ann. Staring frostily at Captain Harwell, she added, "Miss Cooper and Miss Burton were just leaving."

"How unfortunate," he responded, not returning her stare. "Do you live nearby, Miss Cooper?"

"Yes, sir," Julie Ann breathed. "It's the house with the flag."

Captain Eaton cried immediately that their services were available. If the ladies would but linger a moment —while Matthew went into the house and picked up some papers—the two of them would be delighted to escort the Cooper chaise home. They were going back to Holly Springs anyway, he said.

Louley started to decline, but Julie Ann was fluttering and looking uncertainly toward her father, who sat waiting in the chaise. "Oh—Lou, do you reckon it'd be all right with Papa? I'm not sure—"

To Blair's unbounded amazement it was agreeable to Mr. Cooper, and in no time at all Captain Harwell had gone into the house and come out again with his papers, and they had every one of them ridden away and left her standing on the veranda steps.

Blair had a hideous feeling that she was going to burst into sobs.

Mr. Weems jogged around the corner of the house with Robbie on his shoulders. He greeted her dolefully, eased Robbie off his shoulders, and sat down on the veranda steps. "That's enough horsie fur today, little bub. Horsie's wore out."

Careless of the dust on the steps Blair sank numbly down beside him. "Mr. Weems," she said, looking out across the torn-up front lawn, "have you got a family up north?"

"I got two boys," he said.

"Do you miss them?"

That was a pretty silly question, she realized. But she had to keep on talking. She couldn't go back to her room and she didn't want to play the piano. And anyway, she would really like to know whether Mr. Weems missed his family. Maybe that was why he was so patient with Robbie. Maybe that was why he showed up so faithfully to stand guard—

"I do," Mr. Weems said.

They sat and watched Robbie climb up the steps on all fours and then climb back down again. Eventually he stopped, leaned against Mr. Weems's knee, and put his finger in his mouth. Blair thought he'd grown so much since his father had seen him that Robert wouldn't recognize him when he came home again.

When he came home again.

Shivering a little, she hugged herself. It was too cold to sit on the veranda steps. Robbie was bundled up in a coat, knitted cap, and mittens, but his cheeks were getting chapped and red.

"You have to go inside now," she told him, standing up. "It's too cold to stay out here."

Robbie drew back against Mr. Weems and shook his head.

Blair thought that even Robbie preferred someone else's company to hers. Mr. Weems said dolefully that he would bring him in.

"Oh, all right," she said and went back inside her prison walls.

11

The advance of the Union Army was tied to the Mississippi Central Railroad.

Grant's headquarters were now at Oxford, thirty miles south of Holly Springs. Most of the army was strung out in a slow, tortuous, chaotic crawl of men and animals inching along through intermittent downpours, overloaded freight cars, and rapidly freezing mud.

Sketchy intelligence reports had Pemberton entrenching across the Yalobusha, putting his army behind earthworks near Grenada, some fifty miles below Oxford. His cavalry was reported to be thrown out along the north bank of the river.

Eventually Grant planned to hold the railroad open as far south as Coffeeville, where his cavalry was already reconnoitering. They would probe farther until they had driven the Confederate cavalry back across the river. Then the rest of the army could be brought down on the Mississippi Central for an attack that would force Pemberton to fight at Grenada.

If all went as anticipated, while Pemberton was engaged at Grenada Sherman's army, advancing down from Memphis, would have a clear field to attack the Vicksburg garrison.

The railroad was the key.

As the army moved, the tracks and bridges destroyed by the retreating Confederates had been repaired, and once repaired they must be guarded. Reserves of rations were stacked in the converted warehouses in Holly Springs, but more had to be brought from Memphis, and large stores of supplies waited in Grand Junction, just above the Mississippi line. The Union Army, sprawling out farther and farther southward, now depended for its very sustenance on these fragile miles of rail.

One day a Negro came into the cavalry camp in Holly Springs to report that he had seen a group of armed, mounted men lurking in the vicinity of the railroad north of town. The Negro had recognized two of the men, but the observation had been made at night and had been hurried. The group had ridden away into the thickets of White Oak swamp before he could identify the rest.

A patrol from Company D went out to make a search of the area and give a warning to pickets stationed along the railroad line to exercise extreme vigilance. The countryside along the tracks was heavily wooded and sparsely inhabited, and the Negro, who feared retaliation, declined to serve as guide. But he had given Matthew fairly detailed information as to the lay of the land and the location of the houses. With his help a map had been drawn, and he pointed out the approximate spot where the guerrillas had been seen. He also identified the home of the two men he had recognized. It was less than a mile from Waverley.

When the cavalry patrol approached the house, they found a dilapidated two-room log cabin with an open breezeway running through the center. A slanting porch leaned dismally across the front, where smoke curled from a daubed clay chimney and wooden shutters were drawn tightly over windows. The bare front yard was free of concealing trees or shrubbery, so Matthew sent two privates around the back to block any attempted escape from that direction. A frozen-faced slattern answered his call for anyone inside the cabin to show themselves.

When she opened the door and looked around it, he recognized her. A cold fist knotted inside his stomach. He had seen her at the back door of Waverley, talking to Grandpa.

The woman's pale eyes flickered out toward the mounted troopers in the yard and came back to rest on him. He did not believe he had ever seen such naked hatred on the face of any human being.

"Are you the wife of Jake Sharp?" he asked.

The woman gave a barely perceptible nod.

"You have a son named Bob?"

"They ain't here."

"The house is surrounded. If they're inside, tell them to come out."

"They ain't here!" she shouted. "They're out killin' blue-bellied bastards like you!"

He got down from his horse with his revolver cocked in his hand and motioned for his troopers to follow him. "All right. Search the house."

The search yielded nothing and the slattern stood by the door the whole time and cursed them. When the ordeal had finally ended and they were riding away, Matthew couldn't stop thinking about having seen the woman at Waverley. Suspicion coiled in his mind like a viper.

But at least now they had seen the face of the enemy. Two of the guerrillas had been identified. If the Sharps ever showed themselves, they would be arrested.

And, he hoped to God, hung.

The expedition continued and Company D still unearthed no guerrillas, but from his prior experience on similar manhunts, Matthew had not expected that they would. There was an implicit warning in the presence of Union cavalry, a warning that would be conveyed to the bushwhackers by every white inhabitant who observed the troopers pass.

Last summer in Corinth he had learned that only the Negroes could be trusted. The Southern whites, when questioned, were sullen and devious. They had never seen a guerrilla, had never heard of one, and seemed loath to believe that any such animal existed.

Matthew slept at the fairgrounds with his company that night, in anticipation of a strike at the railroad.

The strike was not made, and it was assumed that the bushwhackers had been scared off by the cavalry reconnaissance. Reluctant to return to Waverley, he spent the next two days in camp attending to paper work. On the following afternoon he abruptly decided to ride back to Waverley, make some excuse to the Tylers, and pack up his gear. He would stay at the fairgrounds with his men.

The weather was gray and dreary, with a weak dilatory sun occasionally peeping through clouds. The temperature was well below freezing, and it looked as if it might be getting ready to snow. When Matthew reached the house, he went in unannounced. There was nobody in the hall and he assumed they were all busy elsewhere.

He had been sleeping in Dr. Tyler's office, and when he entered, the room was as cold as a tomb. The ashes from the last fire were dead in the fireplace. No new fire had been laid.

Cursing silently, Matthew set out for the backyard, where he knew there was a woodshed.

As he was going through the hall, the parlor door opened and Miss Tyler looked out, evidently having heard the sound of his footsteps. By this time he expected her to slam the door immediately upon seeing him, but to his vast surprise, she spoke.

"Oh," she said. "Captain Harwell. What is it? Did Austin forget to lay the fire?"

Matthew stopped.

"It seems he did," he said with caution. He was not, he told himself, about to anticipate any pattern of be-

havior from Miss Tyler. She might respond with
"Wonderful!" and slam the door even yet.

She turned and said to someone who was in the
room behind her, "Go tell Austin to get a fire going in
the office. Hurry, now!" She turned back to Matthew
and smiled. "I'm sorry. It's warm in here. Why don't
you come in and thaw out while you're waiting? It
must be like an icebox out there."

Matthew found it hard to believe he was hearing her
aright. For a moment he almost suspected she had the
guerrillas stashed away in there, waiting to spring
upon him as soon as he entered—but *c'est la guerre!* he
thought. The opportunity was too tempting to pass up.
And besides, with the mercurial Miss Tyler, he might
never be presented with another.

"Why, thank you, ma'am," he said, accepting her
invitation. "That does sound mighty good."

Miss Tyler closed the door behind him and he went
directly to the blazing fire. It did feel good, as the ride
from Holly Springs had about frozen him to the saddle. He turned his back to the fire, clasped his hands
behind him, and while he was soaking up warmth into
his numb backside, allowed his gaze to make a thorough reconnaissance of the room. There seemed to be
nothing out of the ordinary in it.

Except, of course, Miss Tyler, who was wearing a
pale blue dress of some soft woolen material, very full
in the skirt and, he noticed, exceptionally well fitted at
the top. How, he wondered, did they get their waists so
small? He would like to investigate. He imagined the
absorbing interest to be had in unbuttoning the blue
dress, examining the construction of Miss Tyler's corset, and deftly unlacing its stays . . .

She had paused by the piano and now she reached
down and struck an idle chord. Her eyes were lowered
in what appeared to be bemused concentration. "You
must think I'm a perfect ninny," she said.

Matthew—who had told himself he would not be

surprised at anything—was so surprised he almost said
"Yes."

In fact for a moment he did *not* say anything, and his
companion must have taken this silence for assent, for
she moved impatiently away from the piano, walked
over to the horsehair sofa, and clasped the back of it.
"I know I've been behaving badly," she said, looking
off into the distance. "And there's no excuse for it. I *do*
appreciate how kind you've been to us. The guard and
everything—" She looked at him and bit her lip.
"You're not—angry with me? Are you?" There was a
pathetic little quiver in the "Are you?"

"No, you've been the soul of courtesy," he said, pic-
turing her without the corset, or anything else. *Just
come over here*, he thought lasciviously, *and I will show
you how angry I am!*

"Well," Miss Tyler responded demurely, ignoring his
sarcasm and lowering her luxuriant eyelashes, "I'm
glad."

Blair had given way to a sudden impulse to invite
Captain Harwell into the parlor. She simply couldn't
stand the awful boredom a minute longer. She had
heard him go into the office and then come out again—
and what luck it had been to learn that Austin had
neglected his duties and thus provided her with an excuse.

Of course, the fact that he *still* hadn't brought her
that wretched newspaper was a deliberate slap, but
she had overcome even that humiliation, so desperate
had she grown for a little diversion.

She moved gracefully around the sofa and sat down
on it. After a time he would have to sit down, too. And
what would be more natural than that he sit on the
sofa? It was directly facing the fireplace and the obvious spot.

"We haven't seen you for a while, Captain," she
said, folding her hands in her lap. "What in the world
has been keeping you so busy? You never seem to have
a moment to spare."

Except, of course, to escort Miss Julie Ann Cooper back home, she recalled.

Captain Harwell was putting on his noncommittal expression again. "Nothing that would interest you, Miss Tyler. Just the usual army business. You'd probably find it pretty dull."

"At least you're out and about," she said, looking wistfully into the fire. "All I seem to do is sit here. I suppose there're all sorts of opportunities for interesting experiences, nowadays. Why don't you tell me about them?"

After a short silence he said, "I don't see that it's necessary for you to just sit here, Miss Tyler. You had some neighbors calling recently. Perhaps you should get out more. Exchange a few calls."

Why had he referred to that? Was he implying that Julie Ann was more interesting than she? She fluttered her lashes upward and gave Captain Harwell a sharp inventory as she did so, to see if this was the case.

Well, he looked rather bland. But then he always did seem to have such an honest, artless expression about him that it was hard to conceive of his doing anything —underhanded. Again she noticed in what an attractive fashion his chestnut-brown hair curled about his forehead and what lovely brown eyes he had. Actually they weren't all brown, but had little gold flecks in them and—thunderation! Why did he have to be a Yankee? If only he wasn't, what fun she could have!

"You've been neglecting us," she said, smiling. "You must try and stay for supper tonight. I don't know what Aunt Sophie's fixing, but she's already copied off the recipe for peach trifle. She's saving it for you."

"That's very kind of her. I'm sure my mother will be glad to get it. By the way, how is your grandfather, Miss Tyler? Does he ride out much at night? To round his hogs up out of the swamp?"

His hogs? Was she so totally without charm that when in her presence he would think only of *hogs*?

Blair began to be sorry that she'd invited Captain Harwell into the parlor at all.

"I wouldn't know," she snapped. "I suppose he's been out there rummaging around."

"I noticed another neighbor speaking with your grandfather the other day. A Mrs. Sharp."

"She was probably up here begging for something to eat," Blair said with a petulant little droop to her mouth.

He didn't reply.

"Please stay and talk to me for a while," she said, reaching over and patting the horsehair sofa cushion. "I'm so bored I could die!" She smiled up at him in a rather pitiful manner.

At last! Matthew thought as he moved to occupy the sofa. But he had no sooner sat down on it than a great banging erupted from across the hall. A familiar voice shouted, "Hey, Matt! You in there?"

Jesus Christ! It was Eaton!

Why did the damned fool have to show up now, of all times? What did he want? Why couldn't he sequester himself with that whore back in Memphis, where he belonged?

Miss Tyler had turned her head to one side, listening to the racket. "Aren't you going to answer him? He sounds rather impatient."

"Answer who?" Matthew said. "I don't hear anything."

She laughed and shook her head in reproach. "Shame on you, Captain! He may be calling you to duty."

"Not him." Matthew rose wearily as the growing volume of Eaton's hammering indicated he might be breaking down the office door. "Excuse me. I'll be back in a minute."

He opened the parlor door just far enough to edge through it, closed it behind him, and said in a voice low enough to keep Miss Tyler from overhearing, "Steve! Here I am! What the hell do you want?"

Eaton paused in the middle of another bang on the door, a look of interest coming over his face. "Ahhh!" he said, smiling knowingly. "Sneaking about, are you, old fellow?" He tiptoed across the hall toward Matthew. "What've you got in there you don't want me to see?"

"It's none of your business what I've got in there," Matthew said under his breath.

"Ahh-ha!" Eaton responded, looking around Matthew's shoulder as if he thought he could see through the door. "You've been in there with the beautiful Miss Tyler! Haven't you?"

After parting company with the Cooper chaise, Eaton had spent the rest of the ride into town expressing gratitude for the heady helping of femininity that he seemed to credit Matthew with serving up to him. "Three of them!" he had said. "Matt, you devil! You mean you've been out here all this time surrounded by that? And you didn't tell me? What kind of way is that to behave?"

Patiently Matthew explained that he had only just met two of the young ladies himself.

Eaton had thought Miss Tyler to be the pick of the lot. He had also been impressed by the icy force of her glare. It was the best he'd been blasted with by any female Confederate yet. He seemed to regard it as some kind of challenge, which he did not think Matthew would be able to meet. "You're not going to get anywhere with Miss Tyler, old friend," he said.

Then he had gone into further raptures about the charms of Mississippi's belles, which, it turned out, he had already discovered on his own. Eaton described a luscious young lady whose acquaintance he had recently made. Her name was Miss Kendall, and she was even better looking than Miss Tyler, he said. Although she'd been somewhat skittish at first, Eaton believed that Miss Kendall was showing signs of succumbing to his infallible charm. Apparently he would be successful where Matthew would not.

"Steve," Matthew said now, fighting hard for control. "Say what you came for and then get the hell out!"

"You mean she's been in your malodorous company?" Eaton said in disbelief. "Conversing with you? What'd you do? Enlist in the Rebel cavalry? Matt, you can't deprive me of this! I've got to see!"

And then—by damn!—if the door didn't open behind him, and Eaton did get to see. For Miss Tyler was looking around it and saying, "If you're going to be here long, you're welcome to use the parlor. I can leave."

Eaton advanced so quickly that Matthew had the helpless feeling of being caught in a stampede. "Why, ma'am," he cried as he went through the door, "we wouldn't think of discommoding you like that. It's nothing important, anyway. Have you seen the latest issue of the *Memphis Appeal?* One of the young ladies mentioned you'd been without mail service, and when I came across this, I thought I might find someone who'd enjoy it. As a matter of fact, I've got it with me now."

He actually whipped a ragged, single-sheet edition out of his uniform pocket and presented it to Miss Tyler with an elegant bow. As she accepted it, Eaton straightened up, managed to look her over from head to toe, and flashed a cavalier smile.

Matthew slammed the door. Miss Tyler gestured toward the sofa. "Well, now that you're here, Captain, why don't you sit down?"

"After you, ma'am," Eaton said, and bowed again. He moved, Matthew thought, like a windup tin soldier. Turn his key, and he bowed.

Eaton waited until Miss Tyler had sunk gracefully onto the sofa, and then quick as a flash he sat down beside her. Matthew was left to find seating accommodations where he could.

As he was getting settled in the horsehair chair, the double doors into the dining room opened and Callie came through them, saying, "Austin is laying the fire—'' She stopped abruptly, looking at the Federal occupation. "Close the doors, Callie," Miss Tyler said shortly. "You're letting cold air in."

Callie closed the doors and came sullenly around the edge of the room until she reached Matthew's chair. Sighing loudly, she sat down on the floor. She arranged her skirts carefully, paying infinite attention to each blue-checked fold. Matthew could think of no way to get rid of Eaton, short of lifting him bodily and throwing him out; and now if by some unlikely chance Eaton decided to leave by himself, Callie looked as if she were getting settled for the rest of the day. *I knew it was too good to be true*, he thought gloomily.

Echoing his thoughts, Callie said loudly, "We've got enough people in here for a musicale, Blair. Like when you used to do 'When This Cruel War Is Over.' '' She twisted around to look at Matthew. "Do you know that song? I think it's the prettiest one."

Eaton suddenly leaped up from the sofa as if released by a spring. He went to the piano, reached down, and banged a discordant note. "That's a capital idea!" he said jauntily. "Miss Tyler, do you play?"

Miss Tyler looked surprised, then smiled and said with becoming modesty, "Oh, a little. I *try*."

Callie started to say something, but Eaton had the podium again. "Matthew plays," he said, looking wickedly in his direction. "His mother made him take piano lessons until he was twelve."

"Oh?" Miss Tyler said, sounding pleased. "I didn't know you played the piano. Why, I think that's very nice!"

"Actually," Matthew said, "I don't play very well. I haven't touched a piano in years—"

Miss Tyler rose from the sofa. "Oh, now! You're being modest, as usual. Come on! I will if you will!"

How could he refuse her? He got up from his chair with a sinking sensation, knowing quite well that he wasn't going to refuse her anything. Not while she was smiling at him like that.

Eaton made a sweeping gesture toward the piano
bench as Miss Tyler approached it, bowed again, and
pulled it out for her to sit down. She reached up to
open her music book. "Come sit with me," she said to
Matthew. "We'll do a duet."

As he sat down, it was satisfying to note that Eaton
would be regulated to hovering beside the piano. On
the other hand, the bench was short enough so that
Miss Tyler's shoulder was almost touching his own.

"Sally Burton's sister said she'd chop up the piano
with a hatchet when they asked *her* to play," Callie
said, leaning against this piano and not identifying
"they."

"How impetuous of Louley!" Miss Tyler laughed,
flipping through her music book. Any minute now, she
would tell him to play. What? The only thing he felt
reasonably proficient at was "Twinkle, Twinkle, Little
Star."

Mercifully she reprieved him for a while longer, running her fingers lightly over the keys. "Do you like Stephen Foster?"

Matthew nodded. He was so close he could detect a
faint drift of some flowery fragrance and noted that the
pale blue bodice of her gown was rising and falling
softly with her breathing. He wondered if he would be
forced to sit on his hands.

> *"Beautiful dreamer, wake unto me,*
> *Starlight and dewdrop are waiting for thee—"*

That a voice underlaid with such sensuous promise
was emerging from Miss Tyler seemed incredible. She
had miraculously lost all trace of her Southern accent
and enunciated every syllable in crystal-clear tones.
The rich longing voice reached out to cling to each
word lovingly, and then with gentle regret went on to
the next.

"Sounds of the rude world heard in the day,
Lulled by the moonlight have all passed away."

Good God! Matthew thought, conjuring up visions of
being lulled in the moonlight by Miss Tyler with no
rude disturbances. She became aware of his gaze,
leaned softly toward him as her fingers moved across
the keys and gave him an innocent smile. Her sleeve
brushed against his shoulder, and without missing a
beat, she reached up, turned the page of her music
book and sang on.

When the song ended, she clapped her hands together, gave a little bounce on the piano bench, and
said, "Oh, that was fun! I haven't done that one in
ages!"

He said sincerely, "You certainly sing well!"

"I'm glad you liked it," she murmured, turning
pages again.

A knock sounded at the door to the hallway, and
without turning to look, Miss Tyler called, "Come on
in."

Private Weems's sorrowful bearded countenance
peered around it. "Ma'am, there's a bunch from the
Thirty-seventh Ohio out there buyin' eggs. They wants
me to ast if you can open the window."

Miss Tyler turned on the piano bench. "Open the
window?"

Private Weems nodded, but did not add details. He
simply continued to peer sadly into the room.

"Private," Matthew said. "Tell the Thirty-seventh
Ohio that we cannot open the window. If they are outside, and they think about it, they will understand
why."

"Why?"

He felt a strong impulse to curse. "Because it's
about twenty degrees out there, Private!"

"Why do they want us to open the window?" Miss
Tyler asked.

"So they kin hear better."

She looked at Matthew. "Well?"

Could this really be happening? he wondered helplessly. Now, not only was he going to have to share her
with Eaton, her little sister, and Private Weems, but
with a delegation from the 37th Ohio!

"It is your window," he said with irritation. "You
can do what you wish."

This was the wrong response to make, for Miss Tyler
immediately jumped up from the piano bench and
opened the window. Not only that, but she leaned out
and cried, "Do you want some music? All right! You're
going to get some! And I hope you enjoy it!" Then she
marched back and sat down.

Her face was flushed and her blue-green eyes had a
portentous gleam in them as she flipped open a new
song book and set it on the rack. "Callie, you know
these as well as I do. Sing loud, now! You hear?"

> *"Butler and I went out from camp*
> *at Bethel to make battle!*
> *And then the Southrons swept us back*
> *Just like a drove of cattle!*
> *Come throw your swords and muskets down*
> *You do not find them handy!*
> *For tho the Yankees cannot fight,*
> *At running they're the dandy!"*

When the song was finished, the piano keys were
fairly smoking, and a medley of hoots, cheers, and applause poured through the open window from the
Ohio contingent. Matthew would not have been at all
surprised to see them start crawling through the window and into the parlor.

"Very inspiring," he said to Miss Tyler, and rubbed
his hands together in preparation. He was remembering more from the piano lessons than he'd thought.
"Allow me," he said, rudely shouldering her away
from the keyboard. As he whammed into the opening

bars he added, "You'll know this one, Steve. Sing loud
and help me out."

> *"The Union forever, hurrah, boys, hurrah!*
> *Down with the traitor, up with the star.*
> *While we rally round the flag, boys,*
> *Rally once again,*
> *Shouting the battle cry of freedom."*

He included the verse that said, "We'll hurl the Rebel crew from the land we love the best." As he sang it,
he winked at Callie, whose eyes were as big as saucers.

Matthew's contribution ended with a bang. He
turned to Miss Tyler and said, "I hope you enjoyed it."

She was breathing rapidly and shivering, from the
open window, no doubt. She pressed her lips together,
then cried out to the Ohioans, "Don't leave! It's not
over yet!"

Flipping through her book again, she smiled in satisfaction. " 'Our Triumph at Manassas,' Callie!" she
cried to her little sister.

Matthew decided his next rendition would be "We'll
Fight for Uncle Abe."

After that, although the 37th Ohio had gone wild
with applause and was begging for more, he saw that
she was turning blue from the cold and that her teeth
were chattering.

"That's enough now," he said firmly. He went to the
window, pulled it down in the face of jeers and catcalls
from the Ohioans—a goodly crowd, who stood in the
shrubbery—and told them, "It's over. Go back to
camp."

When he turned from the window, he saw that Eaton
was also making his farewells and walking rather carefully around Miss Tyler, who with a stunned expression still sat on the piano bench.

Matthew decided withdrawal to his bivouac across
the hall would probably be his wisest course of action.

Miss Tyler did not look up as he passed by the piano,

but Callie languidly unwound herself from it to make a parting comment.

"That was kind of fun," she said. "We ought to do it again sometime."

"Anytime," he answered as he went through the door. "Just let me know when you're ready."

12

Blair stood over the scrubbed-oak table in the kitchen, rolling biscuit dough. She had never done this before, but Anna Mary looked worn out from the strain of the last few weeks, and Blair wanted to help her mother. She had put on a large bibbed apron and rolled up her sleeves. Mixing the dough had been simple enough, but now, as she attempted to roll it out, great, lumpy gobs stuck to her rolling pin. A lock of hair fell into her eyes. Impatiently, Blair pushed it back with a floury hand.

Outside on the kitchen passageway she heard Callie talking to someone. Blair put down her rolling pin and looked out the window. It was another Yankee, of course, bearded and wearing a sergeant's uniform. She knew this one, because she had seen him before. His name was Evans, and as Captain Harwell's orderly sergeant, he frequently came to Waverley with muster rolls, commissary requisitions, and other papers requiring the captain's attention. Blair didn't reprimand Callie for talking to him, because the sergeant seemed decent enough.

She started back to do battle with the biscuit dough, and then realized that they were discussing Captain Harwell. She stayed by the window to listen. After the duel of songs in the parlor, Callie had developed a schoolgirl crush on the captain. Blair found this annoying, because she thought of Captain Harwell quite often herself. What were they saying now?

"So when you had the early cold snap in Tennessee, what did Captain Harwell do?" Callie asked outside the window.

"Well, little lady," the deep voice of Sergeant Evans replied, "like I said, the quartermaster wasn't prepared for the unseasonable change in the weather. They didn't have enough blankets, and the boys was about ready to freeze. So the cap'n, he takes leave, goes up to Springfield, and rustles up blankets from all over town. Then he has 'em shipped back down to the troopers in his company. All in all, he collected fifteen boxes! Now you name me many officers who'd do that!"

That was a wonderful thing to do, Blair thought. She couldn't imagine Preston doing it. And Pres had also been elected a company captain. He said once that he was the captain because he could beat them all at poker.

"You must all like Captain Harwell a lot," Callie said, with stars in her voice.

As they left, Blair heard the sergeant saying, "He takes care of his men. And here's the acid test. If the army don't pay us on time, he lends us money. And I recollect one time, when they didn't issue no tobacco, the cap'n bought enough for the whole company on credit. Trusted the boys to reimburse him when they got paid. . . ." He and Callie went down the steps of the passageway and his voice trailed off.

Reluctantly Blair went back to her biscuits. When she finally succeeded in getting the dough to adhere to the board instead of to the rolling pin, she floured the biscuit cutter and began cutting out. Maybe she should have learned more about cooking. But before the war, they had plenty of help. And then later, with so many gallant Confederate beaux dancing attendance, she was having too good a time with the balls and cotillions. She thought of Captain Harwell's unselfish concern for his troopers and felt ashamed of herself. No doubt about it, she had been vain and self-centered. Well, now that she had nothing to do but stay in the house, it would be a good time to change. And what better place to start than with the domestic arts. She laboriously cut out a biscuit. So intent was she in separating the tricky white moons of dough from the cutter that she failed to look up when someone entered the kitchen.

"Excuse me," Captain Harwell said. "But Aunt Sophie told me I could find some coffee in here. Since I haven't eaten, she said you might give me a biscuit."

Horrified, Blair thought that she must look like a field hand. Swaddled in the voluminous apron, she had her sleeves rolled up like a washerwoman ready to plunge into the tub, and was up to her elbows in dough. Hurriedly she put down the biscuit cutter and wiped her hands on the apron. She went to the stove. "You can have some coffee," she said. "But the biscuits aren't ready yet." Trying not to show how flustered she was, she got two cups from the shelf. She folded up a dishcloth to protect her hand from the heat, and picked up the coffee pot from the stove. It was cold outside, and Captain Harwell had on a caped overcoat that made his broad shoulders look even wider. He wore a regulation cavalry cap with crossed sabers and the number of his regiment, the 2nd Illinois Cavalry. Blair's mind automatically registered the fact that it was a hated blue overcoat and an enemy regiment. As she poured the coffee, he took off the coat and cap, hung them on a hook by the kitchen door, and made himself comfortable at the scrubbed-oak table.

Blair brought over two cups of coffee. She liked him better without the cap. She could see his hair. However, she noticed that he had had his hair cut, and it was much too short. Some dreadful barber had almost shorn off his curls. Blair set out sugar and cream and, shoving the biscuit pan to one side, sat down at the table with him. *I'm getting as simple-minded as Mama and Olivia*, she thought. *Inviting all comers to share the Waverley hospitality. Sitting here drinking coffee with a Yankee like I don't have good sense.* He viewed the lop-sided lumps of white dough in the biscuit pan but mercifully did not comment upon them.

"Actually, the coffee belongs to you," Blair said, brushing flour from the table. "If it wasn't for you, it wouldn't be here. Or the sugar, either. So you don't really have to ask for a cup."

It occurred to her that not only did they have him to thank for the coffee and sugar, but for whatever else remained in the larder, as well. If Captain Harwell had not provided them with the guard, Lord knew what depredations they might have suffered by now. And not only to their material possessions. With an immense enemy army marching past, the lowest scum might have invaded the house. Blair shivered. She looked at Captain Harwell across the table and thought: *He took care of us like he took care of his troopers.* The feeling of being protected, of relying on his superior strength, gave her a pleasant tingly sensation, as if she were melting inside.

"I wasn't that interested in the coffee," he said with a grin. "I really wanted to see how you were coming along with the biscuits. Aunt Sophie said it was your first attempt."

Blair forced a smile. She had an awful premonition that they would be as hard as tenpenny nails, and thanked heaven that she hadn't yet baked them.

Stretching his booted legs in front of him, he leaned back in his chair, enjoying himself. "Don't let me stop you. I'm eager to taste one." When she made no move, he added, "Don't you have to put them in the oven or something?"

"I'm letting them rise."

"I thought you did that with rolls."

Does he mean yeast? she thought in confusion. "Well, down South we use saleratus," she said brightly, having heard that Yankees called it "baking soda," and hoping that he wouldn't know what she was talking about. "Anyhow, you're not interested in some old dull subject like cooking."

"No," he said, his eyes twinkling. "I'm just interested in teasing. So ignore me. I know you're trying to help out. Aunt Sophie told me you wanted to give your mother a hand. Although she did say your biscuits would probably stop a cannon ball, and we could use them for bomb shelters—"

"If you think you can do any better, I'll give you an apron," Blair snapped.

"I know how to put a flour-and-water dough ball on the end of a ramrod and toast it over a campfire."

"That sounds delicious." But he looked so mischievous that she smiled in spite of herself. His short blue cavalry jacket with its gold shoulder straps made him look dashing. She brushed a few squiggles of dough from her apron. Flirting was difficult in her floury attire, but she tossed him a come-hither glance. "I hope you don't hold those songs in the parlor against me. It's just that I don't usually have a Yankee audience, and a sudden irresistible urge came over me." There, she thought, as she gave him a spirited smile. That was his cue to toss back a compliment. To protest that he could never hold anything against so pretty a girl; or that if she wished she could trample all over his heart. Or some similar gallantry.

"No, I don't hold it against you," he said. "On the contrary, I admire your patriotism. And I also admire your being honest. I'd much rather you said what you're really feeling, instead of pretending you liked me just to protect your property."

Taken aback, Blair thought that he was certainly different from her previous beaux. No one had ever complimented her for her honesty before. Once she got over her surprise, she found this intriguing. To be admired for a character trait was a new experience. As if he saw the real person under the flirtatious facade and liked what he saw. Suddenly she felt more comfortable in her rolled-up sleeves and messy apron. For the first time in her life, looks didn't seem so important. And she sensed that since Captain Harwell put a premium on honesty, this was a high compliment.

"Why—thank you," she said. "You're right. Our Cause is important to me. And I reckon you believe in what you're fighting for too." She stirred sugar into her coffee. "But maybe we can be friends, anyway."

"Maybe we can," he agreed, leaning forward to cradle his coffee cup in his hands and looking relaxed. "One thing for sure, I've enjoyed staying here at Waverley. It's almost like being in a family again."

So Mr. Weems isn't the only one who misses his family, Blair thought. Maybe that was why Captain Harwell put up with her temper. He certainly didn't seem to be knocked off his feet by her charm. However, he did seem to approve of her helping her mother—he reached toward her face. Blair thought he was going to kiss her. Her heart stood still.

"You've got some flour on your nose," he said, gently brushing it off with a calloused thumb.

She felt vaguely disappointed, as they sat there in the warm, cozy kitchen, companionably chatting and drinking their coffee.

Later that afternoon Captain Harwell went back to camp, so he didn't join them for supper. At the table Callie repeated the story Sergeant Evans had told her about the tobacco and blankets.

"Yes," Anna Mary said after she'd finished. "I believe Captain Harwell is a young man with a strong sense of duty. He was only sixteen when his father died, and yet he looked after his family. Now he's doing the same thing for his men."

"And another thing that means," Grandpa grunted from the head of the table, "is that he'll never cut out on a fight. On the battlefield, he's the kind that we need to pick off first."

The ladies looked stunned. Blair's hand went to her throat. "Grandpa!" Callie cried. "That's an awful thing to say!"

"Well, I didn't mean I'm fixing to shoot him myself," Grandpa said, looking irritated. "But have all you females forgotten which side he's on? While you're sitting around admiring his sense of duty, you need to remember that it cuts both ways. In a fight it'll have him leading the charge. So that's the very type of Yankee we need to eliminate."

In deference to his masculine wisdom the ladies were silent, but underneath they were appalled. With a thudding heart Blair thought: *If Captain Harwell met Preston or Robert on the battlefield, would he shoot them?* She couldn't bear to think about it, or to dwell on what Grandpa had said.

A week later Callie sat at a table in her room one evening writing by the light of a candle. Blair had stopped going to bed so early and was downstairs playing the piano. Thus it was possible for Callie to have a little privacy in the evenings to devote to her journal. By an unexpected stroke of good fortune, she had been supplied with a new ledger. And just in time, too, for she was on the last page of Edgars & Thompson.

Grandpa had gone into Holly Springs to buy salt, and she had asked him to bring her some writing paper. But he'd been unable to find any, and upon his return Callie dissolved into tears of disappointment. At supper that night, she'd been mulling over the possibility of using the backs of the pages in her autograph album. It nearly killed her to think about it, because the sentiments from the girls in her class were so beautiful, and their penmanship just perfect, and if she wrote on the backs of them the effect would be spoiled.

She was sitting there brooding over her sweet-potato soufflé when Olivia remarked that she was being awfully quiet and asked her what was the matter.

When Callie told her, nobody said anything, but the

next day Captain Harwell brought her the new ledger.
He'd bought it from a sutler who was peddling his
wares to the 37th Ohio. Callie was almost speechless
with gratitude. She'd insisted on reimbursing him for
it, because of course it wasn't proper to accept gifts of
this type from a gentleman. Captain Harwell hadn't
wanted to take anything, but finally agreed to let her
give him half of a Jeff Davis twenty-cent stamp.

He said the sutlers had all kinds of things in their
wagons. Apples and oranges and ginger cakes and
newspapers and—of all things—yellowback thrillers!

"How much do *they* cost?" Callie asked, practically
drooling. Two dollars Confederate was all the money
she had.

"Does your mother mind your reading them?" Captain Harwell said.

Callie shook her head. *Not if she doesn't know about
it*, she added silently.

"You can have my old ones when I'm through with
them."

She had since been presented with copies of *Red
Rover and the Flying Artillerist*, *Pirate's Son*, and *Dick
Turpin*. They looked brand-new, and Callie thought
Captain Harwell was the neatest reader imaginable;
they hardly seemed handled at all!

Squinting a little in the candlelight, she looked over
her last entry in the journal.

The 37th Ohio has pulled out of our pasture.
They are moving on south. We got some more, tho.
The 28th Iowa. They are pretty religious & have
not stolen anything *yet*. They had a Yankee
preacher over there & Mr. Weems took Aunt Sophie to hear him. The Yankee preacher told Aunt
Sophie that he did not see how people could call
themselves Christians & yet own slaves. Aunt Sophie said he was ill-informed. That Solomon &
David & all the best people in the Bible owned
slaves & what did he think of that. So he said they

all had about 40 wives apiece too & did she approve of that? When Aunt Sophie told Grandpa, he said the preacher forgot to mention the concubines. So now Aunt Sophie is not speaking to Grandpa.

Callie chewed on her Always-Ready pen.

Grandpa only got two sacks of salt as it was so expensive & we have hardly any cash & no way of getting more with the cotton burned. Grandpa & Austin are digging up the dirt from the bottom of the smokehouse & boiling the salt out of it. Little Austin still has not come home. Telithia is scared he is dead.

Callie stopped writing. She thought she heard something besides Blair's piano playing drifting upstairs.

She stood up, closed her journal, and carefully moved the table. Underneath the rug was a knothole in one of the floorboards. She had discovered that when she lay down and put her ear against it, she could hear Captain Harwell's conversations in the office below. She folded back the rug, lay down, and listened for several minutes.

Nothing.

Sighing, she got up, replaced the rug, dragged the table back into position, opened her journal, and sat down to write again.

That conceited Capt. Eaton was over here the other night. He & Capt. Harwell were sitting around & talking in the office. Capt. Eaton said he could work it out so they could both make a little trip to Memphis. He said he was ready for a little horizontal refreshment.

Callie paused. She had heard of liquid refreshment, but horizontal refreshment was a new term. It had sounded like that conceited Captain Eaton was going to lie flat out on the bed and pour his whiskey into his mouth.

After listening to them talk for a while, she had learned another new term at the knothole that evening.

> So Capt. Harwell said Got the Irish toothache, Steve? Do you mean the hoers haven't put in an appearance? Capt. Eaton cussed a little & said no, & he was going to Memphis & get him a hoer there. Then he asked Capt. Harwell if he didn't want to go with him & get one, too.

Callie stopped writing and thought about it.

> I hope he doesn't go.

She sighed. What was a hoer? A Yankee term for dentist? Although she had listened faithfully at the knothole ever since Captain Harwell first moved into the office, no vital military secrets had filtered upward, and she was beginning to think she never *would* get to use her secret code. She had it all worked out, and if she ever did learn anything, she was going to write it all down and smuggle it out to Earl Van Dorn. Callie didn't trust General Pemberton. He was a Yankee himself.

Just exactly how she would get in touch with Van Dorn, she hadn't fully decided. The *Memphis Appeal* Captain Eaton had given Blair said the army was entrenched around Grenada. Maybe Callie could sew the secret messages into her bloomers and cross the lines. She would take the Oath, if necessary. It wouldn't be really taking it; she'd be faking, just so they'd give her a pass to the Yalobusha.

She pictured the glory that would be hers as the savior of Vicksburg. Probably they would have a Grand Review of all the armies, President Davis would come down and pin a medal on her, and all the senators would make speeches. They would refer to her as the Mississippi Joan of Arc. The great Confederate spy and authoress, Morgan le Fay.

Callie squirmed with pleasure and went back to her journal.

One reason I hope Capt. Harwell does not go to Memphis with that conceited Capt. Eaton is that Blair will be mean as a bear. She is mean as a bear every time he goes off somewhere. She was mad at him for singing Battle Cry of Freedom altho I thought he sang it pretty good. She got over it, tho. Now she is down there in the parlor every night & if *he* is not down there too she is snapping everybody's head off. I tell you, I will be glad when the 1st Mississippi Cavalry gets back so she will have something to do. She has been practicing the Christmas program with the Musical Society but they are all girls & Blair gets tired of just girls pretty quick. So now she is down there in the parlor *every* night. I have not had one chance to ask Capt. Harwell how he liked Red Rover and the Flying Artillerist. I thought it was pretty good. He is getting as moonstruck as Lt. Phillips. Will probably soon forget to buy any more thrillers at all.

Blair lived for the evenings in the parlor. She had almost stopped thinking of Captain Harwell as a Yankee at all. Now on the rare occasions when she was reminded of it by the sight of his uniform, it came as something of a surprise. But it didn't matter. Blair had put on a pair of mental blinders and trained herself to ignore this distasteful aspect of his appearance.

This evening, as they sat on the piano bench and he helpfully turned the pages of her sheet music as she played, she found her attention straying. His hand looked so nice! Strong and masculine, it was tanned from his hours on horseback. With a little shiver she imagined how it would be for that hand to caress her.

Just having it firmly on the back of her waist during a waltz would be exciting.

"Do you realize," she said archly, leaning toward him and speaking under the cover of the music, "that I sing like an angel, and that my eyes are like alluring flames? That's what somebody wrote in a poem about me."

"And was the poet like a moth to the flame?" He fought back a smile. "Maybe I'd better draw back before I get singed."

As usual, he refused to flatter her vanity as her previous swains had done. Neither did he pledge undying devotion like Lieutenant Phillips, who had written the poem. Yet Captain Harwell's stubborn forthrightness held a strong appeal. For the first time in her life, flirting wasn't enough. She wanted him to mean whatever he said. As he turned the sheet music, a lock of his curly brown hair fell over his forehead. Without thinking Blair almost reached over and pushed it back. Thank goodness she caught herself in time. Pink with embarrassment, she wondered what his reaction would have been to such an intimate gesture. Not to mention Anna Mary's, who sat knitting on the horsehair sofa.

Blair wondered if Captain Harwell would like to kiss her. But, surely he would. Then why hadn't he tried to? Here again, he was intriguingly different. Dan Phillips was always trying to kiss her when she didn't want to be kissed.

She thought how nice it would be if they were not always surrounded by other people. But she didn't see much chance of their being alone. Until unexpectedly an opportunity arose.

One morning, Grandpa took Anna Mary and Aunt Sophie in the buggy to visit the Lockwoods. Captain Harwell had not yet left the house. Usually he was off for the fairgrounds before Blair got up in the morning. But today he was doing paper work at the rolltop desk in the office, which was more convenient than the field desk in his tent. Blair had an inspiration.

We could go riding together, she thought, her mind working quickly. *I haven't been riding in ages, and it would be heavenly to get out of the house. Olivia is the only one still here who might disapprove, and if I'm careful, I can get away without her seeing me. And why shouldn't I go riding with Matthew? I mean, Captain Harwell. Even if he is a Yankee, Mr. Cooper didn't object when he and Captain Eaton escorted Julie Ann in the chaise. I'll just change into my riding habit without asking Matthew, and when he sees me already dressed, he'll have to take me.*

Blair hurried upstairs and did just that. Her timing was perfect, because when she clattered downstairs in her riding boots, Matthew was just emerging from the office, ready to head back to camp.

He didn't take much persuading, especially when Blair gave him a pleading smile beneath the fetching little veil of her riding hat. She knew that the black broadcloth habit flattered her figure, and as they headed out to the stable, she remembered that she had been wearing it the first time he saw her.

Matthew obligingly saddled her mare. Then he slung his army saddle over his own horse. The saddle had pistol holsters and a ring device for attaching a scabbard for a cavalry saber. Although he didn't have pistols or a saber with him today, he did have his carbine, which snapped on to a sling.

After helping her on to the mare, he swung into his saddle. As she watched him strap on the carbine, Blair felt an unpleasant chill. The sight of all these warlike accoutrements reminded her of what Grandpa had said at the table that night. Armed and mounted, Matthew seemed harder, like a different man from the one she knew in the parlor. If he used that deadly equipment, he would be killing men like her father and brothers.

Resolutely she put the idea out of her mind. She

didn't intend to let anything spoil her day. Matthew wouldn't kill anybody, because there weren't any Confederates within fifty miles. At the moment, Preston was probably impressing the girls in Grenada. And Papa and Robert were in Tennessee.

However, when they rode down the driveway, she began to feel uncomfortable. She still wanted to go riding with Matthew, but she didn't want people to think she was consorting with the enemy. As they turned into the road, the Iowa troops camped in the pasture across from the house stopped dead in their tracks, and gawked as if they had never seen a woman before. Blair felt her face burning. What if someone she knew passed by in a buggy?

She abruptly reined in the mare. "Let's go another way," she said. "The road's so dusty. If we cut through the pecan grove, there's a nice little bridle path to the river."

Matthew gave her a funny look. "Are you sure you want to go that way?"

"Yes." She turned the mare and headed through the pecan grove. He hesitated, and then caught up with her. As they approached the bridle path leading into the woods, she wondered what he had meant by that funny look. Had she sounded brazen? Suggesting that they ride alone into the woods?

As they continued down the bridle path, she noticed that as usual he had jammed his uniform cap over his curls. He seemed determined to cover his most attractive feature. "Where did you go for a haircut last time?" she asked. "They almost skinned you."

"I like it short."

"But your hair looks so nice when it's longer!"

"Not to me. My mother kept me in ringlets down to my shoulders until I was four."

Enchanted, Blair pictured him as a sturdy little boy in long chestnut curls. "I don't blame her. You must have looked adorable. What made her decide to have them cut?"

"She didn't." He grinned. "I got a pair of gardening shears and whacked them off."

"Matthew!" She laughed. Even then he had been determined. She looked about, thinking how glad she was that she had decided to go riding. The woods were so still and quiet, and just the two of them being out together like this was delightful. "We're almost to the river," she said with enthusiasm. When they got there, it would be the perfect excuse to dismount and enjoy the view. And then Matthew might—

The blast of a shotgun ripped through the trees.

The mare shied and Blair struggled to control her, her heart careening into her throat. She looked behind her and saw that Matthew was still on his horse. Her knee, hooked around the sidesaddle and caught in the heavy folds of her riding skirt, started to slip. With a sickening sensation she felt herself beginning to slide from the frightened mare.

Matthew spurred his horse forward. As Blair plunged toward the ground, he leaned from his saddle. His arm clamped around her waist. Gasping for breath, she thought he would cut her in half before he could pull her up onto his horse and get them out of there. Instead, Matthew wheeled his horse and dumped her unceremoniously on the ground. "Take cover!" he barked, as if he were yelling orders to one of his troopers. Dazed and shaken, Blair crawled through dead leaves and underbrush to a fallen log.

As she huddled behind it, she saw Matthew jump from his horse and unsling his carbine. He went down on one knee behind a rotting tree stump and raised the carbine to his shoulder. Aiming in the direction of the shotgun blast, he fired. Blair covered her ears. Then he fired again. And again.

When he was satisfied that whoever had shot at them wasn't there anymore, Matthew got up from behind the stump. Blair struggled to her feet. Her hat had fallen off and dead leaves and twigs clung to her riding habit. Thank God neither one of them had been hurt!

Now that it was over, her knees shook. She wanted to run to Matthew and fall into his arms, so that he could comfort and reassure her. "Who shot at us?" she cried. "Why would anyone—"

"Don't you know?" he said tightly.

She started toward him, and stopped. Something was wrong.

"You mean—our soldiers? But they've all gone! How could they—what do you mean, 'don't I know?' "

"I mean that was a bushwhacker!" he yelled. "A damned sneaking guerrilla that doesn't deserve the title of soldier!"

Was his rage directed at her? His reaction was so different from what she expected that she was stunned.

She said: "A guerrilla?"

His mouth twisted with contempt. "And I suppose that's a new term for you? Some exotic creature you've never heard of before?" He angrily strode over and caught the reins of his horse. "Don't put on that innocent face. Are you disappointed he didn't get me? Well, better luck on the second try!"

Her mouth went dry. "Matthew—what are you saying? You can't think I had anything to do with this!"

"Like hell you didn't! I wondered why you had a sudden impulse to head for the woods. Now I know. It wasn't an impulse, and it wasn't sudden. And I went against my better judgment and followed right along. I must have been out of my mind!"

Her knees gave way. "That isn't true!" She sank down on the fallen log. Trying desperately to think of some way to convince him, she wailed, "He almost shot me, too!"

There was a brief silence from Matthew. Numbly she picked a dead leaf off her skirt. He seemed to be thinking it over. Surely when his anger cooled he would see the logic of what she had said. You couldn't control a shotgun blast. It sprayed shot all over the place. Evidently, Blair thought with a shudder, whoever had tried to kill Matthew wouldn't have cared if he'd gotten her, too.

Finally, Matthew walked over and stood looking down at her. Tears welled in her eyes. "I didn't know anything about it," she said softly, pushing back a strand of her hair. "I don't see how you can think that I did."

He sat down on the log beside her. After a moment he said, "All right. I'm sorry. I guess I'm too jumpy. But I've seen what guerrillas can do to a man."

He didn't sound angry anymore. Blair took a great, sobbing breath of relief. For an awful moment she had thought he would hate her forever. She leaned her forehead against his shoulder and wiped the tears from her eyes. He had almost been killed!

She felt Matthew tense. Then he patted her shoulder. "I was scared to death!" she said in a muffled voice. His arm went around her. Blair's fingers closed on his sleeve. Her heart was still fluttering, but now it took on a different tempo. Pressing against Matthew like this stirred up all manner of unsettling emotions. "It's all right now," he said. His lips brushed her temple, his moustache lightly tickling her skin. She felt warm and safe and at the same time tingling with anticipation right down to her toes. She wasn't sure precisely what she was anticipating, but she had never felt anything this strongly before.

Matthew abruptly removed his arm from around her and straightened up. "We'd better go," he said shortly. "That bas—varmint may still be out there. And anyway, I need to get a squad together and come back and find him."

After she got back to Waverley, Blair didn't see Matthew again for the rest of the day. Since she couldn't tell anyone about sneaking off to go riding with him, she couldn't confide in anyone about the ambush, either. So she suffered alone. Thinking that he would surely join them for supper, she put on one of her prettiest dresses, a rose-colored challis with the bodice worn fashionably open to reveal a dainty white muslin chemisette. But when the family sat down at the table, he still hadn't appeared.

Aunt Sophie started relating the morning's visit to the Lockwoods. The widow had seen very few Yankees, she said. Once or twice, a stray soldier had come nosing around in the night—slipped off from camp, Mr. Grace imagined—but Mr. Grace was a light sleeper and had gone outside with his shotgun and scared them off. The only other unpleasantness occurred about a week ago, when a cavalry patrol came by and searched the house. The widow had rather a bad moment, because her bales of cotton had been hidden in the swamp.

Blair immediately thought of Matthew and wondered what was happening as he rode through the woods with his own cavalry patrol, hunting guerrillas. She worried that he hadn't come back. Surely he was all right? Aunt Sophie's chatter began to grate on her nerves. She tried to get a grip on herself. Of course, she was pleased to learn the Lockwoods were managing so nicely. Anything faintly optimistic was encouraging, these days.

After supper, Blair dragged into the parlor and sat down. At nine o'clock Matthew still hadn't come in and Anna Mary said she was thinking of retiring. The rest of them had already gone.

Anna Mary got up from the horsehair sofa, rolled up her ball of yarn, and put her knitting needles into her sewing basket. "Are you ready to go upstairs, dear?"

"Oh," Blair said, picking idly at a little thread in the rose-colored challis, "I'm just not sleepy yet, Mama. I think I'll stay up awhile longer."

After her mother left, Blair continued to sit on the sofa. As she stared into the fire, an unpleasant memory surfaced. When she'd been at Louley's house practicing the Christmas program, the girls in the Musical

Society said that Isabella had been out driving with Captain Eaton in the phaeton.

At the time, Blair had thought only of how this would affect Preston. She remembered the sick anger that rose inside her as she sat looking through the Christmas carols on the Burtons' piano rack. What was going to happen when Preston found out?

Now, however, she applied it to her own situation, and cringed at the memory of what Louley had said.

Isabella had been seen in Eaton's company before, Louley said. And as far as she was concerned, she never intended to speak to her again. They should all cut her dead, and it was nauseating and disgusting, because even if Mr. Kendall had turned traitor, that was no excuse for Isabella to do the same.

"They were laughing and talking and having a lovely time," Louley said with a sniff.

Blair heard a horse in front of the house.

She felt a stab of relief. She got up and hurried into the hall.

When Matthew opened the door, his boots were muddy, and he looked tired. He had a strained look around the corners of his eyes. Blair's hand went to her throat.

"Did you get him?" she said.

He took off his cap and wearily hung it on the hat rack. "No. But when I do, I'd like to give the slippery scoundrel a good dose of hemp."

"When you didn't come home, I thought something had happened. I've been so worried about you!"

Matthew felt his defenses going up. She looked so pretty in the rose-colored dress. But he still didn't trust her. Nor was he completely convinced that she'd had nothing to do with what happened that morning. Although he kept telling himself that she hadn't. He wasn't sure whether that was because he wanted to believe it, or because he didn't want to admit that he had behaved like a besotted idiot and let her lead him into a trap.

"You look tired," she said gently. The soft glow from the lamp on the table next to the stairs turned her hair to spun gold. "Have you eaten? I can get you something."

"I'm not hungry," Matthew replied, watching her through narrowed eyes.

She swallowed. "You're not still angry at me, are you?" And then, to his undoing, she floated over and put a pleading hand on his sleeve.

"No," Matthew said, and took her into his arms.

Then he kissed her. Long and hard. He didn't think about it. He just did it. He had wanted to for so long. Blair melted against him and didn't protest. She felt so good that she must have addled his brain. It had been months since he had held anything that round and soft.

"Oh—Matthew," she sighed when the kiss ended. She clung to him, burying her face in his chest.

Why did I do that? he wondered. Glumly he rested his chin on her hair. He hadn't meant to fall in love with her, but somehow he had. Now that he had admitted it, her possible duplicity wasn't the only thing bothering him. Of late, a disquieting memory had nagged at his mind. On the day he'd brought her brother home on parole, Blair had asked about another captured Confederate cavalry officer. A strutting young lieutenant with a waving red plume in his hat—

She raised her exquisite face and gave a triumphant smile. "I knew you wanted to kiss me! Why in the world haven't you tried to before?"

"In front of Aunt Sophie?" he said, in a tone so conversational it surprised him.

Blair laughed.

Did she really like him? Matthew wondered. Or was she just a little Southern belle coquette? And what did the ass in the plumed hat mean to her? She hadn't mentioned him again. Dared he hope? Then he remembered the fickle young lady in Springfield, who had married someone else as soon as he was out of her sight.

"You must be exhausted," Blair said, lightly touching his face. "Don't let me keep you. Go on to the office."

Matthew felt fully capable of making passionate and enthusiastic love to her for the rest of the night. Just kissing her had made him rise to the challenge. If she didn't go upstairs pretty soon, he might carry her into the office with him.

"Good night," she whispered, blowing him a kiss as she finally mounted the stairs.

13

Soon after that, Captain Harwell left them again. Callie feared he'd gone to Memphis with that conceited Captain Eaton, but then she heard Blair asking Mr. Weems if he knew where Captain Harwell had gone. Mr. Weems said he thought Captain Harwell was on escort duty up to La Grange.

The next day Grandpa and Austin drove the wagon to the Widow Lockwood's to help butcher her hogs.

When they returned, a dark frightening shadow suddenly fell over Callie's world.

The widow and all four of the little Lockwoods came back with Grandpa and Austin. The baby was wrapped up in Austin's coat and was making a dry, hacking sound. The two middle children huddled on the floor of the wagon beneath Grandpa's coat, and the widow and Benny didn't have on coats at all!

Anna Mary went hurrying out with Callie close on her heels. The pinched faces of the Lockwood children peeped over the side of the wagon at them like terrified, frost-nipped little gnomes.

Anna Mary reached up and Mrs. Lockwood handed the baby to her without saying a word. Austin got down and began lifting out the other little Lockwoods. Grandpa's weathered red face looked like a slab of cement. Callie stood by the wagon and stared at little Benny Lockwood, who was wiping his nose with his sleeve. She tried to open her mouth and ask him what had happened, but her lips had turned into boards.

"Burned it," she heard Grandpa saying in a low voice. "Late yesterday evenin'. Get those young'uns inside. They're about froze stiff."

The Lockwoods had been in the smokehouse when Grandpa and Austin drove up in the wagon. Smoldering ashes were all that remained of the house. The Yankees who'd set fire to it hadn't given the widow time to get their clothes out. They'd barely had time to get out themselves.

Mrs. Lockwood had told Grandpa everything as they were coming back to Waverley in the wagon.

Yesterday morning a foraging party had come out to the Lockwood place. They were a regular detail, and not strays, as the others had been. They told Mr. Fred Grace that they were requisitioning for the 23rd Indiana. Mr. Grace said the widow had nothing to spare. The sergeant in charge looked the place over and then said that since she was a widow woman, they'd not take the provisions she had stored in the house, but that they would have to take the chickens and pigs.

Pretty soon, the troopers were running chickens down and wringing their necks while the little Lockwoods watched openmouthed from behind their mother's skirts. When the Yankees started shooting the pigs with their revolvers, the sow, leaping about in the pen and squealing, knocked the side of the pigpen loose. All of her brood followed her out.

Three of the soldiers took out after them, laughing and firing at them as they ran. The sow went all the way into the woods, and the Yankees followed her there. The Lockwoods could hear them shouting and crashing around through the underbrush, and then there were no more pistol shots, and one of the Yankees still at the house said the durn fools had emptied their revolvers. Now they'd have to catch the sow with their bare hands.

He had no more than finished saying it, when the sharp repeated bark of shotguns echoed from the woods.

Then, Mrs. Lockwood had told Grandpa, she saw the Yankees who'd gone after the sow come running back toward the house. At the edge of the woods behind them a group of mounted men emerged from the trees. They were firing their shotguns at the fleeing Yankees, and as the widow watched, one of the Yankees fell sprawling and she heard him yell, "For God's sake, don't shoot!"

One of the men on horseback galloped up beside him, took aim with his shotgun, and fired a double load of buckshot into the fallen Yankee's face. Then he swung his horse around and shouted to the mounted men behind him. The Yankees in front of the house had started toward the woods, firing their rifles as they ran.

Mrs. Lockwood recognized the black eye patch on the man who shot the Yankee and knew he was Jake Sharp. She'd told Grandpa she thought Bob Sharp had been in the group. But she didn't know who the others were, it had happened so fast.

The guerrillas had ridden quickly away into the woods, and the foraging party, who'd come in wagons, had no means of pursuing them, except on foot. When it was over, the Yankees found another dead comrade out in the woods. The third soldier had crawled under some blackberry bushes and escaped with a wound in the arm. The soldiers were terribly angry, Mrs. Lockwood said, because the dead men had been unarmed. They'd used up all their cartridges shooting at the sow.

The Yankees loaded the two bodies into the forage wagons, bandaged up the wounded man with a towel Mrs. Lockwood gave them, and drove away.

By that time the Lockwood children were hysterical, and the widow spent the rest of the afternoon trying to calm them down.

It was almost dark when the second group of Yankees rode up to the Lockwood place. A captain accompanied them, and he told Mrs. Lockwood to get out. They were going to burn the house.

The captain, a dapper, handsome fellow, said she'd been harboring guerrillas who had made an unwarranted attack on a foraging party. She was in sympathy with the rebellion and had failed to suppress the bushwhackers. As compensation for losses sustained by the occupying forces—and as a warning against future guerrilla attacks—her movable property would be taken and her house destroyed.

In vain the widow protested that she had known nothing of the activities of the guerrillas, that the sudden attack had been as big a surprise to her as to the foraging party.

No, the captain said, they would not give her a few minutes to remove her personal belongings. If the Rebels wanted to raise the black flag, his army would have no choice but to retaliate in kind. Then the troopers under his command came swarming into the house. They opened bureau drawers, threw their contents into the middle of the floors, and poured coal oil from the widow's lamps onto the piles of clothes. Then they ignited them.

The captain inquired if she had any Rebel cotton. He seemed faintly bored by the whole affair, as the sobs and wails of the Lockwood children made it difficult for him to converse with their mother. Mrs. Lockwood, of course, did not reveal the existence of her cotton, but the suave captain obtained it, anyway. Mr. Fred Grace, under duress, told him where it was. The Yankees knocked Mr. Grace about and threatened to hang him for a guerrilla. With a heavily armed escort the captain rode off into White Oak swamp, soon returning with the widow's modest bales.

They were loaded into a wagon brought for that purpose, and the captain appeared disappointed at the paltriness of the prize. However, this did not deter him from taking them.

The Yankees also took Mr. Fred Grace back to town with them. In answer to the widow's protestations, they informed her that a shotgun had been found in his possession.

Now the widow was almost crazy with apprehension that Mr. Grace would be hung. After he had gone, she'd been afraid to venture into the frigid night with the children. None of them had coats on, and all her quilts had been inside. For a while Mrs. Lockwood and the children huddled as close as they dared to the warmth from the burning house. Then as the night wore on and the temperature dropped, she took them into the smokehouse. It was there that Grandpa and Austin found them when they drove up in the wagon, ready to help kill the hogs.

Benny told Callie later that the Yankees shot his dog.

That afternoon Grandpa saddled up the mare and rode into Holly Springs. He came back with the pastor of the Methodist church, the Reverend Thackerford, following in a buckboard, accompanied by Mrs. Thackerford and several ladies from the congregation.

While the Tylers were packing up the clothes for the Lockwoods that they'd gathered out of chifforobes and dressers, it was decided that the family would move into the Riley cottage in town. Mrs. Riley had left the care of her property to the Reverend Thackerford when she refugeed to Jackson, and the house had been sitting vacant.

It would be better to have someone in it, Mrs. Thackerford said. The Riley cottage, although modest, was in a good section of town. Close by the Salem Avenue mansions, it was tucked on a little lot within sight of the Kendalls'.

The next day Blair went back to Louley's to practice the Christmas program. Grandpa took her into Holly Springs in the buggy, with his shotgun resting under the seat. Before this, he'd kept it propped out in plain sight whenever he drove them anywhere.

He had gone by the courthouse yesterday afternoon. The Yankees had Mr. Fred Grace locked up in the basement. Grandpa said the inside of the courthouse had been stacked full of cotton bales.

The Burton house was just east of the square, close by the Methodist church, and at the sight of blue uniforms strolling insolently through the streets Blair's stomach churned. Grandpa had said almost nothing on the drive into town, but when they neared the Burtons', he told her that a Federal colonel named Murphy was now in charge of the garrison. He had established himself in the Craft house.

When Mr. Hugh Craft built the white-columned mansion a few years ago, he'd had a four-inch space left between the inner and outer walls. The space had been filled with charcoal, and the house was a marvel of modern insulation and one of the most comfortable dwellings in town.

Of course, it wasn't as grand as the Coxe house on Salem Avenue, where General Grant had established his headquarters. Mr. William Henry Coxe already had a residence at his Galena plantation, but his town house had been planned with an eye to entertaining. Blair had attended numerous balls in the large double parlors, and the Coxes had a Steinway piano, which had been brought in by oxcart before the war. The house had imported marble mantels, etched glass windows, and silver doorknobs, as well as the famous bathroom.

Blair thought bitterly that the Union officers preempted only the best.

When Grandpa let her out in front of Louley's, two strange women were coming down the Burtons' front steps. They did not speak to Blair as she climbed down from the buggy, but continued down the steps, swept through the wrought iron gate, and headed in the direction of town. Both were elegantly dressed, and their

fur-trimmed walking suits and smart little bonnets
looked brand-new. She noticed that their skirts had
box pleats rather than the familiar gathers and were
shorter than any she'd seen since the blockade became
effective. They were wearing high-heeled kid boots instead of slippers. She was unable to keep from staring,
although she had an immediate premonition that
something was dreadfully out of kilter. Who were
they?

Grandpa said he would pick her up in a couple of
hours, and she tore her eyes away from the boots and
went into the house.

Louley met her at the door and said the two women
were Yankees!

Officers' wives, they were staying with the Burtons.
Louley said that several of the officers in the Holly
Springs garrison had sent for their ladies. "Yes," she
hissed, almost purple with indignation. "It seems they
like it here so much, they're bringing down their families! Now we've got to take those *women* into our
houses, too!"

The railroad down from Grand Junction had been
fully repaired and was being guarded, Louley said, and
the advance supply base was considered so tranquil
the Yankees had decided they might as well have a nice
Christmas. Undoubtedly they would have a holiday co-
tillion in the Magnolia Hotel.

Julie Ann said excitedly that one Northern lady had
moved into the Larkin house. She had perfect privacy,
because the Larkins had refugeed when Pemberton's
army pulled out.

"And Miss Lucy Blaylock was goin' by there yesterday, and she said the Yankee lady had gotten some
darkies to come in and help her, and she was packin'
all the Larkins' china in *barrels!* Miss Lucy walked up
and asked her what she was doin', and she said it was
none of her business! Miss Lucy thinks she's flat-out
stealin' it!"

Blair felt a wave of fury so intense that it made her hair rise against her scalp.

For some reason, this seemed the most blatant outrage yet perpetrated upon them.

Why? she wondered, taking off her pelisse and gloves and sitting abruptly down at the piano. Was it because a woman had done it? She looked through the book of Christmas carols with trembling hands.

Why couldn't they have let me be happy a little longer? Would it have hurt anything so much?

The girls were gathering around the piano. Blair stared blindly at the piano rack and stumbled into the opening bars of "Silent Night."

And yet she had nobody but herself to blame. She'd put on the blinders deliberately. She had refused to think of Matthew as the enemy. Then she had begun to like him too much.

I should never have let him kiss me, she thought. Now she would have to face the fact that they were on opposite sides in this war, and put an end to their relationship. Blair felt a sense of loss so acute that it was almost painful. She thought suddenly: *I can't go home!*

Finally the practice session was over, and Grandpa was waiting to take her home.

He said that he had been at the Riley cottage, checking on the Lockwoods. It looked as if the widow would have to go to her people in Georgia. Benny Lockwood might stay with the Thackerfords. The Reverend and Mrs. Thackerford wanted him to.

"You mean Mrs. Lockwood's going off and leave Benny here?" Blair said.

"Her family ain't got much. She don't think they can feed five extra mouths."

She looked with unseeing eyes at the mare in front of the buggy.

"Well, she ain't gone yet," Grandpa said. "She give me a key to the Riley place. As long as they're here, we'll help keep an eye on 'em."

When they got back to Waverley, a red-eyed Aunt

Sophie met them at the door. While they were gone, a squad of soldiers had searched the house for firearms. Mr. Weems had told them the Tylers were Unionists, but they'd gone through the house from top to bottom anyway.

Aunt Sophie's chins quivered as she related the rest of it. They had *ordered* Anna Mary to unlock all the trunks. The silver julep cups Eugenia'd sent from Memphis fifteen years ago were missing. Aunt Sophie knew without doubt the Yankees had taken them. The Tyler ladies had tried to stay with the soldiers while they were searching, but there were so many of them, it'd been impossible to follow right on their tracks. Aunt Sophie had been almost prostrate with nerves and had come near swooning several times. What had things come to when whole crowds of strange men could come thronging into one's bedroom, opening chifforobes and pawing through ladies' intimate apparel?

Blair's stomach knotted.

"You mean they went through my—my clothes, Aunt Sophie?"

Aunt Sophie nodded vehemently. "They were particularly careful to look through dresser drawers."

So their filthy hands had been all over her chemises and her lovely lawn petticoats and—Blair knew that before she could wear anything again, she would have to wash it. Wash it and boil it . . . She went running up to her room, opened the door and stared inside. Callie was sitting on the floor by the chifforobe, folding up underwear and putting it back into drawers.

She looked up at Blair. "They *tried* to get my thrillers! But they put them down for a minute and I grabbed them back! I ran and got my journal as soon as they started upstairs!"

Blair sat down on the bed.

"Grandpa had the shotgun with him."

"Uh-huh," Callie said. "I knew he did. That dumb

sergeant didn't find anything. I told him they were just wastin' their time."

"Oh, I don't know," Blair said bitterly. "They got the julep cups."

Callie folded a few more things and said in a hesitant voice, "I think they got your amethyst earrings, too."

Blair got up, went to the dresser, and rummaged through her jewelry box. "My graduation pearls are gone. And the cameo brooch. I don't see the garnet necklace and earrings, either."

"Well," Callie said, still folding, "we've got more left than the Lockwoods did."

This didn't make Blair feel any better. In fact, it made her feel worse.

"Callie," she said tightly, "don't take any more thrillers from Captain Harwell."

Callie stopped folding and looked at her in amazement. "Why?"

Blair slammed her jewelry box shut. "Just don't."

"But he's already *read* them! And—"

"They're not his old ones. He doesn't read them. He's been buying them for you."

Callie's eyes were round. "Then I'll *pay* him for them!" Her voice was beginning to quiver and Blair felt like a monster, but she had to go on with it. Callie still had her blinders on, and if she didn't warn her, it would hurt worse.

"Callie," she said. "You can't—you can't accept things from people like that! I found out today the Yankees have their wives down here! One of them stole the Larkins' china! Callie, they hate us and *you can't be nice to them!* Don't you understand?"

"Captain Harwell didn't steal the Larkins' china!" Callie cried. She suddenly jumped up, dropped the clothes she was holding, and stared at Blair. "He likes us!" she wailed. "And I think you're *awful* to say that!" Callie's small freckled face was working now, and Blair knew she was getting ready to run from the room. "You're just jealous, Blair! You never want anybody to pay any attention to anybody but *you!*"

Callie fled from the room.

Blair stood dully by the dresser and listened to her little sister clatter downstairs. She hadn't thought she could feel any worse. But she did now. And yet, what she'd said to Callie was true!

She went to the bed and lay down on it, staring at the ceiling.

That night the camp of the 28th Iowa was dark. Around the edges of the pasture only a few fires from their picket stands twinkled softly in the night. Mr. Weems said they would be pulling out soon. Then only the garrison would be left in Holly Springs. The rest of Grant's army would be pushing south, Blair supposed.

In the parlor her mother and Olivia were knitting. A fire crackled brightly in the fireplace, and to look at Olivia's and Anna Mary's serene faces, one would think the day had been like any other. Yet she had heard them talking about it at the supper table. Mostly expressing thankfulness for Mr. Weems.

Didn't they know that, sooner or later, Mr. Weems would leave them? His regiment would pull out, too. And then Mr. Weems would go to Vicksburg and try to kill Preston.

Someone pounded on the front door, shouting for them to come and open it.

The noise had broken into the tranquillity of the parlor without warning. All three of them jumped, and Olivia dropped her knitting. *Dear God!* Blair thought as she watched her mother get up quickly from the chair, put her knitting in it, and go hurrying toward the door.

Don't, Mama! Don't go!

Olivia jumped up and stared toward the ceiling, as if trying to see upstairs, where Robbie slept in the trundle bed in her room.

Blair felt as though she had put out roots into the

sofa. She did not think she could ever get off. Her
mother was in the hallway now, and she could hear
her opening the front door.

Oh, Mama, Mama! You never will learn, will you?

"Thank God!" a voice cried.

Olivia ran into the hall. Blair sat and looked at the
ball of yarn. Now they were going to get Olivia. In a
minute they would come in and get her. She sat there
and waited for them to come.

Her mother's soft voice was questioning someone
and then the other voice said, "He's been shot! Jesus,
lady! I don't know! Can you—"

Anna Mary said, "In here. Quickly. That door there."

More footsteps were running up the veranda steps.
Blair got up from the sofa, her heart pounding so noisily it was difficult to breathe. Catching the arm of the
sofa to steady herself, she took a deep breath and went
into the hall.

Anna Mary had disappeared into the office, where
Yankee soldiers were crowding around the door.
"Where were they?" one of them said.

"Bailey'd just come out to relieve me on picket, and
we heard the firin'—Jesus Christ! They must've been
out there *watchin'* me all that time!"

Blair remembered the campfires of the Iowa pickets
across the pasture. Now the pickets were in the
Waverley hall. *Oh, God! Don't let it happen all over
again!*

"Please," she said, trying to work her way through
them and follow her mother into the office. "Please let
me get by."

The Iowans looked down at her with startled cold-
chapped faces. "Please," she repeated, finally making
her way through the door.

In the office Matthew sat slumped on the sagging
couch. Anna Mary, sitting beside him, took a folded
pillowcase away from his shoulder, which was streaming with blood. Quickly she reached down for a towel,
which she pressed in its place. She had unbuttoned his

uniform coat and cut away part of his shirt. His face was clammy with perspiration and whiter than the shirt. The shirt was clotted with blood.

"No," Blair whispered. "No. Please." She could feel her lips moving, but no sound had come out. She pressed her hands over her mouth.

Anna Mary looked up and saw her. "Get the bandages. Hurry. They're in my bureau drawer."

Blair turned and went stumbling blindly up the stairs. The soldiers in the hall stepped aside for her, but she couldn't see the stairs, or the door to her mother's room, or the drawer in the bureau. But she found the bandages at the bottom of a mangled pile of her mother's nightgowns. The nightgowns had been crammed hurriedly back into the drawer. *Callie*, Blair thought. She had time to think it. A million years passed while she was getting the bandages. She had time to think of everything. With her hands full of muslin and lint she ran back down the stairs. In the office she stopped beside the couch and looked down at Matthew. His eyes were closed.

"Mama?" she said. "Is it—is it bad?"

Anna Mary reached up for the lint.

"He's lost a lot of blood. I don't think there's a fracture. I don't believe it hit the bone."

Matthew opened his eyes and looked at Anna Mary, who smiled at him and removed the towel, replacing it with a heavy wad of lint. "You're going to be all right, dear," she said. "We're trying to stop the bleeding. One of the soldiers has gone for a surgeon. He'll be here soon."

He closed his eyes.

"The muslin," she said to Blair.

Blair's hand was shaking so badly that her mother had to turn and take the muslin from her.

"Hold this on for me," she said. "Tightly. Don't let it slip."

She moved around her mother, leaning over to hold the bandage against Matthew's shoulder. She could scarcely see. In the office door the Iowa pickets were watching them in silence. *Don't let him die. I don't care what any of them did. Just—don't let him die.* She kept holding the lint while her mother worked with the muslin, securing it in place.

Matthew, she thought. *Please look at me. I'm here.*

Had he lost consciousness? She didn't know. She didn't know anything, and she was afraid he was going to die. She looked down at his hand, lying limply on the couch.

"Mama?" she said softly. "Shouldn't—shouldn't he be lying down? Are you *sure*? Has he lost too much blood?"

"Wait," Anna Mary said. "I've almost finished. Now. Captain Harwell?"

She was looking at him intently. Matthew moved his head a little and Anna Mary turned toward the soldiers in the doorway. "Would one of you come and help us? He should lie down, now. And I don't think he's hearing me. I believe he's in shock."

Two of them came forward quickly and with Anna Mary's help slid him carefully down until he was lying on his back. One of them said, "I don't see how he got as far as he did."

Anna Mary got two quilts from the bed beside the rolltop desk and began tucking them around Matthew's shoulders. "Where did it happen?"

"Pretty far back up the road, ma'am, from the sound of the firing. He was pretty near out of the saddle when he rode up to the picket stand. I guess his horse just came on by itself. The captain's been staying here, hasn't he?"

"Yes," Anna Mary said, looking down at Matthew. "But we didn't know he was coming back tonight."

The front door opened and there was a new voice in the hall. In a moment a gray-haired man with the black facings on uniform collar and cuffs that distinguished members of the medical corps came into the office. He nodded briefly to Anna Mary and without introducing himself went over to the couch and pulled back the quilts.

As Blair stood and watched, he leaned over and examined the bandage. "You apply a creditable dressing, madam," he said. "The bleeding appears to have lessened." Turning around, Blair went to stand beside the rolltop desk. Her back was to the couch. Whatever he was going to do, she knew she couldn't watch it. She reached down and touched the surface of the desk.

Eventually the surgeon said to Anna Mary that there was no fracture of the bone. The ball had passed through the shoulder and no probing would be necessary. He would leave a sufficient amount of morphine to relieve the pain, which would probably be most acute in a day or so. He said to give the patient stimulating food to compensate for loss of blood. Which had been rather copious, it appeared. He would check back tomorrow. They were in the process of converting the Rebel armory into a hospital, and he was usually out this way at least part of each day. He did not think it advisable to move the captain to the hospital in town. It was overcrowded and understaffed.

"Unless, of course," he said, "you do not wish to assume the responsibility of caring for him."

Blair heard her mother saying, "Captain Harwell is a friend of the family. We shall be happy to care for him."

After a brief pause the surgeon said, "I see," and left the room.

In a few minutes the soldiers left, too, and Blair went back to the couch and looked down at Matthew. He was so pale it frightened her, and his breathing was rapid and uneven. Although his face was still wet with perspiration, she could see him shaking beneath the quilts.

She felt a sensation of such helplessness that her knees almost gave way. She wanted to sit down on the couch where her mother had been and take him into her arms and hold him until he stopped shaking.

I love you, she thought. *I love you so much.*

Anna Mary said, "You can go now, dear. Olivia will help me. We'll take turns sitting up."

"He's cold," Blair said.

"No," her mother said. "He's in shock. I'll make sure he stays covered. The surgeon gave him some morphine, and he won't wake up until morning. There's nothing else we can do now. He must rest."

Blair started to reach down and touch Matthew, but she was afraid it would hurt him. And what good would it do for her to touch him? Anna Mary had done everything for him already.

"If anything happens, call me," she said.

Her mother was getting settled in a chair.

"Olivia will be here. And your grandpa's right there in his—"

"Mama—please."

Anna Mary didn't say anything for a moment.

"All right, dear. Now you must go upstairs. Make sure Callie's in bed. And if Robbie wakes up, someone should be there. Don't worry. Everything's going to be all right."

Blair had no feeling in her legs, but she turned and started upstairs. "Be sure and call me," she said as she passed her mother's chair.

Anna Mary nodded, taking her knitting out of her sewing basket. Blair didn't remember her putting it in. The last time she'd seen it, Anna Mary'd left it in the chair in the parlor.

And she hadn't wanted her mother to go to the door.

14

Matthew, propped against the pillows on his bed in the office, looked over a sheaf of commissary requisitions. The papers had been brought out by his orderly sergeant, Frank Evans, who sat in a chair drawn up by the hearth.

Matthew was able to get dressed by himself now, and this morning Dr. Wirtz had said briefly that the shoulder was progressing satisfactorily. There'd been no inflammation and the healing was coming along faster than he'd expected. The two Mrs. Tylers had been scrupulous about changing the dressings, and Matthew had been vaguely aware, through the haze of morphine, of someone or other always fussing over him when all he wanted was to be left alone.

After the bandages and the continual spongings, Aunt Sophie moved in on him with the beef broth. He had consumed gallons, but she was never satisfied, and kept saying the surgeon had recommended stimulating food.

Grandpa said what he needed was a good shot of brandy. But unfortunately, he added, fixing Matthew with a gimlet eye from the office doorway, his brandy was all gone. He'd had a good supply, but a pack of vandals had come through his house and relieved him of it. Grandpa seemed to be waiting for him to comment on this.

This was the first hint he had gotten that every member of the Waverley household might not be consumed by charitable instincts toward him. Grandpa's craggy face had been guarded and, Matthew trusted, so had his.

As he watched Grandpa, he thought that the rifle blast had caught him a little past the Cooper plantation. He also remembered the slatternly Sharp woman at the back door of Waverley and thought it damned strange that guerrillas could be lying in wait on a man's property without his knowing about it.

Eventually Grandpa left the doorway without further remarks.

Matthew's troopers came out to Waverley the morning after his ambush but were forced to leave until he recovered from the effects of the morphine. Then most of them came crowding into the office, in spite of protests from Mrs. Tyler, who feared so many visitors might prove a strain on her patient. Company D said they were going to clean out the nest of guerrillas if they had to burn down White Oak swamp to do it.

The cavalrymen caught Jake Sharp the next night. Identified by a black patch he wore over one eye, he was emerging from his cabin. The troopers were lying in wait in the woods surrounding it and had ridden the man down without having to shoot him. They preferred to hang him, and this, Sergeant Evans informed Matthew, was done.

The military authorities performed the execution in public, outside of town. The body of Jake Sharp was left on the rope for the rest of the day, as an example to the Rebels, and his wife forcibly put on a train going south. She had been providing food to the bushwhackers, and it was necessary to get her out of the Federal lines entirely.

Today, as Matthew looked over the commissary requisitions, Sergeant Evans told him that the main

body of the army had been halted at Oxford, waiting
for rations, forage, and ammunition to be brought
down before pushing on south.

There were still plenty of sick in the hospitals in
Holly Springs, and some infantry encamped northeast
of the square. Additional troops were along the railroad farther north. But the cavalry had been depleted.
Grant had ordered a raid on the Mobile & Ohio Railroad, to cut Pemberton's communications to the east,
and yesterday Colonel Dickey had taken most of the
Union cavalry off on that. Evans regretted missing the
raid, because to tell the truth, it was getting a little
monotonous here with nothing to do except root out
guerrillas. Matthew knew Evans was hoping for a furlough. His wife had just had a baby, and Frank wanted
to go home to his farm in Illinois for Christmas and see
his son. But of course there was slim chance of that.

Christmas in Springfield had always been a festive
occasion and Matthew had a feeling that any day now,
he was going to receive a package. He had, of course,
written before this about where he was staying, but
had not gone into detail. As soon as his mother found
out how well they'd been nursing him, she would want
to know all about the Tylers, and he thought the less
said about it, the better.

He had no idea where he stood. . . .

Matthew realized that Sergeant Evans was gathering
up his papers and preparing to leave.

"That'll be fine, Frank," he said. He started to stand
up and then thought better of it. He still felt a little
dizzy when he first got to his feet. He'd been forcing
himself to walk around pretty regularly, though. They
said he'd lost a lot of blood, and he supposed that
caused the dizziness.

"Don't overdo it, now," Evans said as he was leaving.

Matthew had set a goal for himself of being up in
time for the Christmas party.

Eaton had been out to see him on a tardy condolence

call and had arrived bearing an invitation. His civilian friend Kendall was hosting the largest soiree Holly Springs had ever witnessed, and every officer in the garrison had been invited. The officers' wives, many of whom had come down to join their husbands, would also be present. When he'd heard this, Matthew thought perhaps he ought to attend. The sight of a Northern female face might pound some sense back into his head. . . .

A discreet knock sounded on the office door, and Austin entered carrying an armload of wood. Austin had been in several times a day during Matthew's convalescence to perform certain chores for him, and although he never said much, his hands had been gentle and surprisingly strong for a man of his slender build. As he crossed the room he nodded at Matthew. "You gettin' yo color back, Cap'n. You be out an' about pretty soon."

"What was all that commotion I heard before Evans came in?" Matthew asked him. "Was it Telithia?"

Austin knelt by the hearth and began stacking the wood.

"Yessuh," he said. "Our boy, he come home."

"Little Austin?"

"Yessuh."

"How's he doing?"

Austin got up and wiped his hands on his trousers. "He cryin' an' carryin' on right now. But he be all right."

Carefully swinging his legs over the edge of the bed, Matthew put his feet on the floor. "Where did he go?"

Austin turned from the fireplace and looked at him soberly. "To the army. Reckon he thought they'd make him a soldier. Said they treated him mo' like a mule."

"Is that right?" Matthew said. Loaded him down with haversacks and equipment, probably. Let him trot along the line of march for a while. Or put him to digging drainage ditches around the tents, or emptying slops.

Yet wasn't that better than slavery? Matthew remembered the mutilated runaway he had seen in Memphis. Even beneath the benign facade at Waverley he saw the same dark cancer that infected the South.

"Austin," he said, "I understand colored regiments are being recruited in South Carolina. And General Butler in New Orleans has been taking enlistments. There's no official policy on it as yet, but maybe your son could get in touch with one of them."

"How he gone get to New Orleans?" Austin said.

"Have you got any money?"

"Nosuh. Had a gold watch, but Little Austin took it with him. And they said they shoot him, didn't he give it to 'em. That one thing he was cryin' about." Austin paused for a moment. "His mama saved up her egg money an gave me that watch for Christmas. Reckon it shamed him pretty bad."

"There's a contraband camp at La Grange. But I wouldn't recommend it."

Matthew had seen it, and like all the others it had quickly turned into a pesthole. Sanitary precautions were nonexistent, epidemics rampant, and the problem of providing food for the Negroes was fast developing into an albatross around Grant's neck.

"My wife has a little money," Austin said. "She been sellin' corn dodgers to the soldiers."

"Look, Austin. I'll probably be pulling out pretty soon and if your boy's willing to be a body servant for a while, I could use one. At least, that'd get him out of here. Then who knows? Maybe this army will start organizing colored regiments, and he can enlist in one of them." He paused. "I've sometimes wondered why any of you stay around."

"Yessuh," Austin said. "I appreciate it. An'—Cap'n, I wouldn't say nothing 'bout this to the white folks, if I was you."

He started going back out. Halfway to the office door he hesitated, turned to Matthew, and said, "You best not come ridin' out this way by yo'self after dark no more."

And of course, Matthew thought, if he'd had any sense he'd have camped at the fairgrounds that night, too. But he'd had to see her right away. He hadn't been able to wait until morning. If he'd had any sense, he'd have stayed at the fairgrounds from the very beginning. It was where he belonged.

"Think they'll be trying for me again?"

"Yessuh. Ole Bob Sharp, he wants you mighty bad, now. He ain't the only one, neither."

Matthew waited for him to go on, but Austin remained silent.

Then he said, "You be fairly safe in the daylight, though."

"All right. That's good advice and I'll take it. And—thank you."

"Thank you, Cap'n," Austin said seriously and continued across the room.

Callie knew she had to tell someone about Colonel Dickey taking the Yankee cavalry on the raid to cut the Mobile & Ohio Railroad.

The knothole had finally been productive, and the information was important. She had known with a terrible finality that she wasn't going to sew any secret messages into her bloomers and cross the lines.

So she went to Grandpa and told him.

Grandpa listened to her in craggy-faced silence, not laughing at her or anything. Then he said, "How come you heard 'em talkin'? Have you been hangin' around that office door?"

"Yessir," Callie said softly, because she wasn't ready to reveal the existence of the secret knothole.

"I don't want you spyin' on 'em anymore." Grandpa fixed Callie with his gimlet eye. "You understand that, missy? Don't want to end up in the courthouse basement with old Fred Grace, do you?"

"Do you think they *would?*" she asked, a touch of

delicious horror traveling up her spine. Mrs. Rose
Greenhow, the famous Confederate spy, had been in-
carcerated in Old Capitol Prison in Washington; and
Lord knows where they'd put Belle Boyd, if they ever
caught her!

"Well, if they do, Santy Claus won't be able to find
you. Don't want to spend your Christmas in the courthouse basement, do you?"

"Oh, Grandpa!" Callie said, embarrassed, because
she knew he was teasing; and yet, she did still hang up
her stocking. She guessed she'd hang it up as long as
they'd put oranges and licorice in it. Though where
they'd get any this year, she didn't know. Maybe off the
sutlers' wagons.

Grandpa left right after that, because Blair was waiting to be taken into town for the Musical Society re-
hearsal. When they came back, Blair said that the
Lockwoods had moved out of the Riley cottage and
gone to Georgia to live with the widow's people. Mrs.
Lockwood had left Benny with the Thackerfords!

And, she said, Mrs. *Grant* had moved into the Walter
place!

Julia Grant had her little boy and her Negro maid
with her. The maid was a slave. "And how do you like
that," Blair said. "The Yankees have stolen our darkies
away from us, but they still keep theirs!"

Blair said there were still Yankees in the Coxe house,
too, although Grant had moved his headquarters to
Oxford. The Grants were planning an officers' ball and
Christmas dinner for the commanding general's staff
at the Coxe house, and Mrs. Grant had invited Lida
Coxe to attend!

Imagine being invited to a party in your own house!
Callie thought. *That somebody else is giving!*

"The Kendalls are having a party, too," Blair said, in
a tone of furious disgust. "Isabella is going to play
hostess. She has a new gown. Ivory satin. With black
lace."

"Uh-huh," Callie said. "I know it."

Blair looked at her sharply. "How did you know it? Louley just told *me* today."

"Uh—" Callie said, twisting about a little and thinking fast. "Uh—Captain Harwell's goin' to it."

A frown flickered over her sister's face. Blair's eyes narrowed and she didn't say anything for a moment.

"Are you *sure?*"

Callie nodded. "He wants to."

Blair frowned again. "He's not well enough for that."

"Well, it's not until next Friday."

"How *can* he?" Blair said, scowling at the rug.

Callie knew what was the matter. Isabella would be there in her new dress and Blair was jealous. There was nothing she liked better than parties, and she wanted to go, too.

"Why don't you ask him to take you?" she said.

For a minute she thought Blair was going to box her ears.

"Are you crazy?" she cried.

"Well—I just thought—if Lida Coxe goes to Mrs. Grant's party, what's wrong with you goin' to—"

"You *are* crazy," Blair said shortly. "Lida's not going to that dreadful woman's party. Callie, you have no sense at all!"

By Friday, Captain Harwell was feeling so much better that he did go to Isabella's party. He got Telithia to press his dress uniform, so they knew he was going, although he hadn't mentioned it to Blair, which Callie privately thought was a good thing.

The Musical Society planned to present their program in Christ Church this year, because the Masonic Hall was full of ammunition crates. But that wouldn't be until the twenty-third, so when Friday rolled around, Blair hadn't been to a single Christmas festivity. When Captain Harwell left at about five o'clock, Callie could feel the waves of resentment vibrating through the air.

Then around six o'clock, Mr. Cooper came by and he

and Grandpa got to talking out in the hall. Mr. Weems had already gone back to camp. Callie hadn't meant to eavesdrop, but she was sitting in the dining room trying to wire some pine boughs into a wreath. She couldn't help overhearing what they were saying.

"The scout get back all right?" Grandpa asked.

"Yeah," Mr. Cooper said. "He wears civilian clothes. Goes and comes pretty much as he pleases. Keeps to the woods."

"Where're our boys now?"

"Well, if everything went like it was planned, they're about halfway between here and Ripley. They was due to pull out from Grenada on the seventeenth, and come by New Albany. Should be getting close to Holly Springs sometime tonight."

"The First Mississippi and who else?" Grandpa said.

"Bob Sharp said just about every damned cavalry unit Van Dorn's got. Second Missouri from Price's command, and the Tennessee and Texas brigades."

"Are they goin' to hit the Yanks tonight?"

"No," Mr. Cooper said. "The plan is to come into Holly Springs in the morning. Around daylight. Hell, Sam! They ain't expectin' *nothin'!* It'll be like clapping a stopper in a jug!"

"So our cavalry'll be encamped out on the roads around town tonight?"

"Ready to move into town in the morning! By God!"

They walked down the hall after this and must have gone out on the front veranda, for Callie, sitting in stunned silence at the dining-room table, had heard nothing more.

She could hardly believe what she had already heard.

There was going to be a great cavalry raid! The Confederates were coming into Holly Springs *tomorrow morning!*

They were going to be defended. They were going to be *saved! And here's three cheers for Southern rights! And for the Southern boys!*

Callie could feel goose bumps popping out all over. Even on her scalp. Trembling with excitement, she got up from the table, spilling pine boughs in all directions.

Most of the Union cavalry had taken off on *another* raid! It would be like clapping a stopper in a jug—

Callie stopped.

Captain Harwell would be coming back from Isabella's party late tonight. He would run right into the 1st Mississippi's pickets. They would shoot him for sure. They would *kill* him, this time!

Callie ran out of the dining room, into the hall, saw that Grandpa and Mr. Cooper were gone, and went leaping up the stairs. "Blaaair!" she wailed.

15

Blair drove into Holly Springs in the buggy. She slipped away without anyone except Callie knowing that she'd gone.

When she drew up near the Kendall mansion, lights were blazing from the windows and she could hear the sound of music. The party was in full swing. But she guided the mare down Salem Avenue past the mansion. She wasn't going to go in and ask for Matthew. She was going into the empty Riley cottage to wait until he came out. She knew that she couldn't set foot inside that party. Never in this world! Even if she could, the Yankees would know as soon as they saw her that something was wrong.

Callie was the one who'd remembered the Riley cottage, that it was on Salem Avenue within sight of the Kendalls', and that the Widow Lockwood had given Grandpa the key. He still had it, and luckily, Callie had seen him put it in a drawer in the dining-room sideboard.

It had taken Blair and Callie until nine o'clock to think of that. By that time the rest of the family had gone to bed. What Callie would tell them if they woke up and found Blair gone, they hadn't decided. They could only think ahead so far. But nothing mattered now except keeping Matthew away from the 1st Mississippi's pickets.

If anyone shoots him again, I'm going to die, Blair thought.

Shivering in her heavy shawl, she climbed down from the buggy, unhitched the mare, and led her into the stable behind the Riley cottage. Then she took the key out of her reticule and unlocked the front door. She had thought to bring matches, and after striking one, she managed to find an oil lamp by the fireplace and make a light. She realized she'd have to go back outside and search for the woodpile. The fireplace was bare.

Kindling and wood were stacked close by the back door, and she brought in a load and spent the next fifteen minutes starting a fire. When the flames began leaping toward the chimney, she glanced at her small enameled chatelaine watch. Ten o'clock.

She sat down on the parlor sofa. Somehow she couldn't make any plans about what she was going to say to Matthew. Her brain had turned numb.

She got up and took a peek out the door, to make sure the party was still going on. As she stood looking up the street toward the Kendalls', she remembered what their balls and cotillions were like. In the third-floor ballroom eight matched chandeliers reflected in gold-corniced pier mirrors lining the walls. One could see oneself dancing by in reels and schottisches, while in the blazing light from the chandeliers the ladies' dresses made whirling kaleidoscopes of color.

Blair wondered if they were dancing a reel in there now.

Those two women she'd seen coming out of Louley's were probably there. What kind of ball gowns did they have?

They were probably dancing with Matthew.

A fist closed slowly around her heart. Her ball gowns were all stored away in boxes on the top of her chifforobe. Would she ever wear them again? The white silk moiré was her favorite. A cloud of pale rose chiffon crossed the décolletage neckline, and the skirt boasted ten yards of material. She had to turn sideways to maneuver it gracefully through a door.

She felt almost sick with frustration.

If she were at that party, dancing that reel . . .

But Matthew would never know how she looked in the white moiré, because all she could ever wear around him was sensible blue delaine.

Blair looked down at her dress. Those dreadful women were going to take Matthew away from her. And that had been the worst part. Knowing that he would be at a party where they would flirt with him and dance with him—and she couldn't be there! If she were there, there'd be no problem. He wouldn't think of anything but her.

But she couldn't *go!*

The Yankee officers had surely brought their marriageable daughters down, too. All of them would be chasing Matthew! Blair feared she was going to cry.

Closing the door, she went back to the sofa and sat down. She'd stood in the cold night air for so long she was shaking. She hugged herself and tried to get warm. *If I can just get him in here,* she thought, *he'll be safe. I'll make him stay here until the cavalry raid's all over. The fairgrounds are too far away for him to get to his company in time.*

But—how?

Blair added a few more sticks of wood to the fire.

By the time her chatelaine watch said eleven, she had checked on the party six times.

It would never be over! She got up from the sofa and began to pace the room.

By midnight, she was almost frantic. The music was still blaring on. She could hear it when she stepped outside the front door. Jonas Kendall must have hired an orchestra from somewhere. Or maybe it was a Union Army band.

Later she had fallen into a sort of stupor. She had

been sitting on the sofa for a long time, and suddenly realized that she must've dozed. She looked at her watch.

God in heaven! It was 3:00 A.M.! She went flying to the door. What if she'd slept through the end of the party, and Matthew had already gone!

The Kendall mansion was still ablaze with lights and gaiety, but now a group of officers were coming down the front steps. Blair drew back against her doorway and watched.

As they reached the wrought iron gate in front of the mansion, the men separated, and three of them started walking toward the square. The other one turned and headed in the direction of the Riley cottage. Blair drew back a little farther against the door. Was it—? Could she possibly be so lucky?

It was!

"Matthew!" she called softly.

He came to an abrupt stop, hesitated, and walked over to peer into the shelter of the doorway.

"I thought you were *never* coming out of there!" she said. "Could you—could you come inside for a minute? I'm about to freeze!"

He leaned forward a little unsteadily to take a closer look at her. The doorway was rather dark, and although she thought that, surely, he had recognized her voice by now, he still did not seem entirely certain of her identity.

"It's me!" she whispered.

The moonlight revealed Matthew clearly, and she became aware of a slight flush on his features that she couldn't recall having seen there before. His eyes appeared to be having more than the normal amount of difficulty adjusting to her gloomy doorway—*Why*, she thought in a flash, *those—those Yankee vixens have gotten him intoxicated!*

"Blair?" he said, narrowing his eyes in concentration. He straightened up and frowned.

"I want to talk to you for a minute," she said.

"Why—it *is* you," he said in wonder and smiled. He weaved slightly forward, reached out and touched her face and added, "You pretty thing!"

Lord! she thought, removing his hand, which she kept tightly in her own. How much has he *had?* She opened the door without turning around. When Preston came home in this condition—which was seldom; usually, she suspected, when in this condition Preston did not come home—he generally wound up in the office on the couch, snoring boisterously. Maybe she should simply lead Matthew inside and show him the sofa? In that case, this would be the easiest thing she'd ever done!

Matthew wasn't exactly resisting her, but he wasn't following her through the doorway, either. He was just standing there. She tugged at his hand impatiently. "Come on," she said, trying to pull him through the door. "Aren't you cold?"

He smiled again. "Where are you taking me?"

He had such a nice smile. Little butterflies went fluttering through her stomach and she was conscious of a quick disappointment. *I hope he doesn't flop down on the sofa and go* right *to sleep*, she thought.

She smiled back at him. "You'll never find out if you don't come in and see now, will you?"

"All right," he said obligingly, allowing her to lead him into the house.

As she reached around him to close the door, he suddenly hugged her until she thought her ribs would crack. Leaning down, he whispered in her ear, "I don't trust you for a minute!"

Blair had the unsettling experience of undergoing two conflicting emotions simultaneously. Her knees were melting at her unexpected proximity to Matthew's chest. At the same time she felt a jolt of dismay to hear that, in spite of his obvious inebriation, he already suspected she was up to something.

"Matthew," she said firmly, attempting to untangle his arms from around her. "You must let go of me."

"Ahhh!" he said, leaning heavily against her and not being of any assistance. "Why do you have to be this way? I never know how you're going to be next!"

Withdrawing her hand from his, she edged out of the circle of his arm. For a moment it appeared that he would lean all the way over until he fell flat on the floor, but she quickly adjusted him to an upright position.

"I think you'd better sit down," she said. "See that sofa over there? You'd better sit on it."

He looked around the room for the sofa.

"Here," she said, guiding him toward it. "There." She gave him a little downward pull. Matthew sat down.

Should I try to sober him up? she wondered, looking down at him. He seemed pretty tipsy, but then wasn't that the best way for him to be at the moment? If he really got sober, he would certainly begin to wonder just what she was doing here. Probably if he hadn't been in this shape, she'd have never gotten him through that door in the first place.

Blair put the tip of her finger between her teeth and bit down on it speculatively. On the other hand, she didn't think she could bear it if he started snoring. She would go mad sitting here for the rest of the night with nothing to do except think about what was going to happen tomorrow. At least, if he were reasonably in command of his senses, he might talk to her. Or something. *Thunderation!* she thought, wondering if Isabella had dared to flirt with Matthew.

"I'm getting you a cup of coffee," she said.

He looked up from the sofa and held his arms out invitingly. "I don't want any."

"You have to drink it."

He shook his head, smiling again. "That is not what I would prefer," he said in a loving manner.

Turning quickly, she went to the kitchen to find the coffee. As she searched for it, she said loudly enough for Matthew to hear her in the parlor. "And what do you mean, you never know how I'm going to be next?"

She couldn't find any coffee. "I've been pretty much the same lately, haven't I?"

He hadn't responded to any of her remarks, and she feared that he'd toppled over on the sofa and already gone to sleep.

Hurrying back into the parlor without the coffee, she saw that he was still sitting up, but now he had his elbows on his knees and was holding his head between his hands.

"Well?" she said. "Are you feeling better?"

He dropped his hands, slowly raised his head, and looked at her as if she were a perfect stranger. "How in the—" he began. Then he stopped and said, "Where am I?"

"At the Riley cottage. Right down from the Kendalls'. You went to a party there tonight. Remember?" She was unable to keep a sarcastic underlining from creeping into "party."

"But how in the—how did I get in *here*?"

She smiled. "Oh, you just sort of—wandered in."

"Good God in the—" He suddenly stood up, swaying in front of the sofa. "Where's some water? I want to wash my face."

"There's some back there," Blair said, indicating the kitchen. "And," she added as he stumbled toward it, "there's a dipper and bucket on the washstand." He disappeared into the kitchen. "To your left as you go in," she called, sitting down on the sofa.

Several minutes passed while she listened to him moving about in the kitchen. When he came back into the parlor, his hair was damp about the edges and his gait was much steadier, although there was still an aura of dazed disbelief about him.

"Where is everybody?" he said. "Are they asleep? Did I—God! Did I scare 'em off?"

Blair thought the dampness of his curly hair added to its charm and her fingers fairly itched to smooth it back from his forehead. She felt her knees going mushy and wished he would come and sit beside her on the sofa.

"Who did you say lives here?"

"The Rileys. I don't think you know them." She looked down at her lap. She said as offhandedly as possible, "Anyway, they're not at home."

After having said it, she was afraid to look up at Matthew. It was a few moments before he spoke again.

"Then would you mind telling me what *you're* doing here?"

"Well, I was—that is, their daughter is one of the girls in the Musical Society. She'd been begging and begging me to come for a visit, and tonight I was feeling awfully blue, so I decided this would be a good time to come. And Mama said it would be all right, so —I did."

"So—you did. And then when you got here, and saw they weren't at home, you just decided to stay, anyway?"

Blair saw now the decision to try and sober him up had been a mistake. An unpleasant little warmth rose in her cheeks.

"Well, Grandpa dropped me off, and by the time I found out they weren't here, he had already taken the buggy and gone home."

"How did you get inside?"

"We have a key," she said with perfect truthfulness, although she had the uncomfortable feeling it sounded like a lie.

Matthew's face was blank, and yet somehow, he reminded her of an unfriendly prosecuting attorney. "Why didn't you go to another friend's house? They can't all be out of town."

She couldn't think of an answer to that and felt her stomach tighten nervously. He suspected her again, just as he had that day in the woods. Well, she would just have to brazen it out.

Pouting prettily, she said, "I don't know why you're

asking me all these tiresome questions. Do I have to give you a complete account of everything I've done today? And the reasons for it?'' She turned gracefully about, draped her arm across the back of the sofa, and tried to look as tempting as possible.

"Put your coat on,'' he said shortly. "I'll get a buggy from somewhere and take you home.''

Panic swept over her, and she almost cried, "But you'd be killed!'' However she caught herself in time and tried desperately to think of some reason why they could not do this.

"No!'' she said. "I—I can't go home *now.*'' A reason was beginning to come to her. "Don't you know what time it is?'' She showed him her watch. "It's after three o'clock in the morning!''

Matthew looked at the watch and she saw to her relief that he had not been aware of the lateness of the hour. He looked from the watch back to Blair, as if finding both of them surprising. Only—he seemed to be finding her something in addition to surprising. Oh Lord, why couldn't he smile at her again? Didn't he think she looked at all attractive? He had a little while ago—

"Do you mean to tell me,'' he said slowly, "that you've been sitting here all this time—alone? And why in the devil am I in here? Would you mind telling me that?''

"Well . . .'' She moved her hands about vaguely. "You were—you were rather inebriated. And I was afraid—afraid you might fall down on the street and freeze to death. That *has* happened, you know. You read about it all the time in the papers!''

His jaw tightened. "You can't stay here by yourself. If you won't tell me where you have some friends who'll take you in, I'll have to turn you over to the provost guard.''

Was he joking? Blair heard a small gasp and realized it had come from her. "Matthew!''

He whirled around and all but snarled at her. "What in the hell are you up to?"

Her hand flew to her mouth. "How dare you use such language in front of me!"

"Are you going to tell me?" he said menacingly, advancing toward her.

She felt a flicker of fear, and then decided that she'd better cry.

"How can you be so suspicious?" she sobbed, burying her face in her hands. She wondered if he were getting ready to choke the information he wanted out of her. *I'll die before I tell him*, she thought, squeezing her eyes shut behind her fingers.

The springs of the sofa squeaked and she knew Matthew had sat down beside her. She huddled against her side of it and didn't open her eyes.

"Please don't do that," he said in a rather helpless voice. "I know you're not really crying."

Taking her hands away from her face, she stared at him. He looked so pitiful that she almost felt sorry for him.

"Blair—" He cleared his throat. "How can you expect me to believe that you just happened to be here all by yourself at three o'clock in the morning, and you just happened to see me coming by, and you just happened to get me inside—" He paused and sighed deeply. "And for some inexplicable reason, you seem determined to stay here. I'd just like to know where I fit into the picture. That's all."

Some of her trepidation ebbed away and was replaced by a sensation of relative safety. Matthew was looking and sounding like his old self again. Perhaps she'd been a little silly to assume that he intended to work some violence upon her. He looked so nice in his dress uniform—even if it was a hateful Federal uniform—and every girl at that horrid party had probably been casting admiring glances in his direction—she could hardly stand to think about it! Without stopping to think what she was saying, she cried, "How could you *go* to that awful place? You knew I didn't want you to!"

"What awful place?"

"Do you know how long I've been waiting for you to come out of there? Five hours!"

Matthew frowned at her inquiringly. He honestly seemed to have forgotten that he and the rest of the Holly Springs garrison had just been feted by the unspeakable Jonas Kendall. "You mean the party?"

"What do you think I mean?" she said indignantly. She would have enjoyed running up the street and scratching all their eyes out!

"Have you—" He seemed to be having difficulty articulating. "Have you been waiting all this time for me to come out of that party?"

Why, she wondered with a surge of irritation, did he have to keep saying "party" in that astonished manner? As if it were some innocent little word with no particular connotation. Nothing for her to get upset about. Just a harmless little party.

"You are completely insensitive," she said. "You have no understanding whatsoever. You are—you are *dense*, Matthew."

"You mean—you didn't want me to go over there? Tonight?"

"You knew I didn't want you to," she repeated, seething.

"But why?" he said in a tone of overpowering wonder.

Blair knew she had passed the point of no return. Never in her life had she behaved so shamelessly. Now he would think she was in the habit of throwing herself at men, and flying into a fury when they ignored her, and—the unfairness of it almost drove her to sobs again. Because she was not that way at all! Oh, if only things had been the way they used to be, and parties were being given by respectable people, and she could go to them, and dance reels and waltzes and fascinate her quarry in the accepted manner! *Then* Matthew would see that she could get anyone she wanted! But now—oh, now! He would think she was absolutely desperate! Waiting for him five hours!

She had fallen so low that nothing mattered anymore.

"Because," she said with an angry little sniff, "those dreadful, awful *women* would be there!"

Matthew didn't say anything. Blair couldn't have looked him in the face now if someone had offered her all the gold in the Confederate treasury. She sat burning with humiliation, her reputation in shreds around her. To think that at one time in her life—some million years ago—she had felt contempt for girls who couldn't fill up their dance cards.

She heard the sofa squeak and presumed he was getting situated to gaze upon her abject disintegration. In fact, this was exactly what he was doing, because from beneath her lashes she could see him stretch out his blue-uniformed legs in a relaxed sort of way and lean comfortably back against the sofa.

"Now that you mention it," he said, as though savoring a pleasant recollection, "I *was* the center of a good deal of attention."

There was a short silence, as if he were waiting for her to respond.

When she did not, he added, "I don't know when I've had a better time."

Blair stared steadily at the wall, trying not to imagine what Matthew had had such a good time doing. With those wanton females he'd been associating with, it could have been almost anything. *Lord*, she thought, praying, *don't let him tell me about it!*

He laughed and said, "I don't believe it!"

She found that she was able to face him again, after all. Whirling around, she saw that he was watching her with an air of delighted amusement. His brown eyes were twinkling merrily, and although a moment ago she would have given anything to see him looking so agreeable, now it made her want to hit him.

"You poor girl," he said, grinning like a possum. "Did you wait all this time to make sure they wouldn't overpower me and spirit me away from you?"

"They can have you!" she said, quivering with humiliation. "I hope—I hope General Grant's daughter got you! I hope she looks just like *he* does! If she's squint-eyed and has a beard, you'll make a charming couple!"

"But," he said, "she wasn't present."

She was afraid to make another remark. God alone knew what it might be. She sat and glared at him in silence.

He leaned forward and took her hand between both of his. "Every lady there was fat, over forty, and married. Now. Are you still mad at me?"

Blair told herself that she shouldn't be surprised at this impudence, this reaching out without a by-your-leave and grabbing her hand. No, she had invited it. Her behavior had been without precedent in civilized society, and anything he did would only be a result of it. However, she did feel an additional quiver at this bald-faced lie that had just been presented to her.

"Is that so?" she said coldly, trying to sound as intimidating as Grandpa. "I never knew that Isabella was over forty. Although you are quite right about her being fat."

He cocked an eyebrow and cut his gaze around at the ceiling. She frowned and pulled away from him.

"Who is this Isabella you refer to?"

"You must have been extremely inattentive, Matthew. I am referring to your hostess."

"Ahhh—you mean, then, Miss Kendall? The beautiful brunette? With the magnificent eyelashes? Well, yes. I suppose I neglected to mention her."

"She's a cow," Blair said shortly.

"You think so?" he said with false astonishment. "I imagined she was a friend of yours."

Blair didn't answer.

"Well," he said soothingly, "I really didn't see too

much of Miss Kendall. It seems that Eaton keeps her pretty well occupied."

A little pain nipped idly at her heart. Looking down at his hands around her own, she unconsciously clenched hers into a fist.

"Blair? Is something wrong?"

"Oh, Matthew! I—I think she's contemptible! She was supposed to be Preston's girl!"

He watched her closely for a moment. Then he said, "I see," and released her hand.

"Don't you remember? Isabella was with Pres that time you captured him. He had to take care of *her*, and that's why he couldn't defend himself." The memory of Isabella's swollen violet eyes at church that morning rose before her and she cried, "How could she forget him like this? And then, to take up with that—that unspeakable little Yan—" Blair stopped.

The dreadful silence that followed went on and on, until she could almost feel it beating around her like a great, pulsating heart. She massaged her temple, thinking: *I wish that I could die. Just die. Right here. Right now.*

Finally Matthew broke it. "Forgive me if I'm becoming a little personal, but would you tell me something?"

"I don't know," she whispered. "What do you want to know?"

"I seem to remember you inquiring about someone. I've forgotten his name. Anyway, it was that fool with the red feather in his hat."

But I never really liked Dan Phillips, Blair thought, feeling wretched. *And I couldn't help it if he liked me better than I liked him!* And what was Matthew implying? That she was some kind of heartless monster? Like Isabella?

"I—" she said, suddenly ending her silence. "I hadn't known Lieutenant Phillips very long."

"I wondered if I were serving as his temporary replacement. If that's the case, I'd appreciate your being frank about it."

Blair took her hand down from her temple. "How can you say such a thing?"

Oh, what kind of person did he think she was? Did he have no conception of the torment she'd been through to overcome her antipathy to that—that ghastly blue uniform? Just because *he* was inside it?

"Matthew," she said pleadingly, "don't you think I like you at all?"

"I'm not sure," he replied.

He looked so uncertain when he said it that her heart ached. Why, why didn't he reach out and take her hand? Or put his arms around her, as he'd done when he first came in? She had never wanted anything so badly in her life! *Oh, Lord*, she thought. *How can I make him do it?* There were a hundred ways in which a young lady could modestly signal to her companion that she wouldn't react negatively if certain liberties were attempted. But, she thought, looking helplessly at Matthew, who continued to sit there with that hurt look on his face, probably none of them would work with him!

Why did he have to be so aboveboard and honest? In a flash a voice inside her head said: *That's the very reason why you like him, you foolish girl!*

Blair took a deep breath, cast aside her last remnant of respectability, and threw herself into Matthew's arms.

"How can you say such a thing?" she repeated, clasping him around the neck and looking over his shoulder, wondering if the Lord would punish her for this sinful behavior, but not caring much if He did. Matthew felt so good—so nice and solid—and her heart was going like a steam engine, and—finally!—he would have to kiss her again! There was just no way he could avoid it, now!

16

Well, Matthew thought, descending into an oblivion of soft yielding curves, blue delaine, and crushed rose sachet, *if this is another ambush, at least I'll die happy.* And who in his right mind could argue with that?

He turned Blair's face up to his, slid her into a more accessible position, lowered his head, and began to kiss her.

After some time had passed, he became cognizant enough of his surroundings to realize that—perhaps—he should stop and let the object of his fervent attention come up for air. Blair seemed to be having a little difficulty with her breathing, although her arms were around his neck as tightly as ever, and she had made no indication that she wished him to pause. Matthew moved his mouth over to the delectable neck. A few strands of wheat-blond hair curled against it, and they brushed across his forehead.

"Oh—Matthew!" she sighed.

He felt a strong impulse to reach out and pull her hairpins out so her hair would tumble down her back. As he rested against this garden of potential delights he wondered, *Just how far am I going to go?* He looked down at Blair, who fluttered her eyelashes upward and curved her lips in a slow little smile. "You're so nice," she whispered, hugging him again.

God! he thought. *What a question! I know damned well I'm going as far as she'll let me. Maybe*—debilitating realization—*even further than that!*

What he should do was get up immediately, wrap her up in her coat, and take her home. That was what common decency demanded. She thought all he was going to do was a little harmless kissing. Obviously Blair liked to kiss.

Matthew slid her even farther down on the sofa and kissed her again.

When that one finally ended, she moved away from him, sat up straight, and adjusted the havoc he had wreaked on her hair.

As he sat and watched her fiddle with her hair, his eyes seemed to have a peculiar mist over them. She was as beautiful as ever, but there was a soft hazy quality to his perception of her; it was as if she were blurred.

"How long *is* your hair?" he said stupidly.

She reached around and touched the small of her back. "About down to here."

Her watch now said almost a quarter to four. Too late to take her home now. Grandpa would shoot him without waiting for explanations. God! There was nothing to do but stay here with her until morning. How many—how many hours until daylight?

"Matthew?"

Blair was addressing him in a small, hesitant voice. "Would you—would you like for me to take it down?"

"No," he said, hanging on to the arm of the sofa.

A delicate flush colored her cheeks. "You must think I'm awful. I—I've never done this before." Her eyelashes fluttered upward. "It's just that I thought you might like it. And what harm could it do?"

God Almighty! Did she have any idea of what she was saying? He wished suddenly that he had taken Eaton up on the invitation to Memphis. "All right," he said hoarsely, bowing down to the inevitable. "Why don't you? I won't think you're awful. I love you too much for that."

He had the odd impression that Blair had started to melt. Blue-green eyes limpid with what appeared to be starry devotion, she clasped her hands, raised them to her chin, and sat gazing at him above them. She looked softer and more appealing than ever—if that were possible—and he wondered what had happened to make her look like that.

"Oh, I wanted you to say it!" she cried, clinging to him. "I was just hoping and praying that you would!"

Say what? he wondered; and then, of course, realized that he had just surrendered his last line of defense. He had told her how he felt.

Yet her response, instead of being what he had feared, had been just the opposite. Blair was overcome with delight. Matthew knew that he would be happy for the rest of his days.

She loved him, too.

"Blair," he said into her ear. "I won't be here forever. The army's still advancing. We may get pulled out any day. I can't go off and leave you here. We've got to think about what we're going to do."

She was suddenly very still against him.

"Blair?" he said, attempting to move her gently in front of him, so he could see her face. "Are you listening? Look at me, sweetheart."

She buried her face against his shoulder and refused to be moved. "Do we have to talk about that?"

He felt a premonition of something unpleasant. "Yes, we do."

She raised her head from his shoulder and looked at him in a stricken, frightened way. "Oh, Matthew! I just die when I think about you going! And I love you so much! I didn't mean to at first, but I couldn't help it! And I—I felt awful about it! Don't you see? I felt like a traitor! And—"

"Blair, that doesn't matter."

"Yes, it does!" she said in a voice so low he could barely hear her.

"Listen to me. I want to send you to Springfield. You'll be safe there, and—"

"Up *north!*" she cried, as if he had suggested something obscene. "How can you think I would—even for a minute—You mean go off and desert my family? And —and those people up there would hate me!"

He thought that, on the contrary, they would all love her in Springfield, but he saw there was no reasoning with her along those lines now. "Do you want to stay here and wait for me?" he asked. "Until I can come back?"

She looked at him in relief. "Oh, yes!"

Maybe, he thought with a renewed flicker of optimism, *after we are married, she will see things a little differently*. A wife's place was with her husband, and she could hardly refuse him that. He would send the whole Tyler family to Springfield, if that was what she wanted. Anything to make her happy. God! He'd be glad when this rotten war was over!

Then, although he had never brooded about getting killed before, he found himself thinking: *What if I die at Vicksburg? I'd never see her again!*

"Blair," he said, taking her hand. "Let's get married right away. There's no need to wait. Will you do that, sweetheart? We could be married tomorrow."

She drew back from him a little. "Matthew—I can't."

For a moment he had the feeling that she'd hit him in the face. Some of it must have come through in his expression, because she lifted his hand and put it against her lips.

"I love you so much," she repeated, not looking at him. "But I can't marry you. Not—now."

"Why not?" he said in a voice he didn't recognize as his own.

"Because—because everybody would think I was—a

traitor! Oh, Matthew, can't you understand? We'll
have to wait until—until we've won the war."

He was vaguely surprised to hear himself saying bitterly, as though that was of any consequence now that
he realized she wasn't going to marry him at all, "Then
we'll have a long time to wait."

"Well," she said in a small, tear-choked voice, "I
didn't mean we'd have to wait until *we* won. I just
meant, we'll have to wait until it's over. Don't you—
don't you see what I mean?"

"No," he said dully. "I'm afraid I don't."

The soft arms were around him again. She was whispering against his neck. "It won't be too long, will it?
Oh, I'm so scared something's going to happen to you!
I couldn't stand it if it did! Do you have to go? Isn't
there some way you can stay in Holly Springs?"

So I can see you every day? he thought. *And keep on
wanting you? And kiss you once in a while?* There was
a strange emptiness where his stomach had been.
Numbly he began to work with the buttons marching
down the back of her blue dress. For once in his life he
would forget duty and honor and take what he wanted.

"What are you doing?" Blair murmured, nestling
against him contentedly.

"Shhh," he whispered, "I just want to see you." He
had the buttons undone about halfway down now.
"I'm not going to do anything you don't want me to,"
he added, wondering dismally if this would prove true.

She reached up and removed several hairpins. A cas-
cade of silky blond waves suddenly obscured the buttons and covered Matthew's fingers as well.

Blair sat up. "There! Do you like it, darling?" She
leaned forward and kissed him lightly on the cheek.
Her expression sobered at once. "Matthew, you're not
angry with me, are you? Please try to understand!"

She looked so sensuous in dishabille with her hair
falling about her shoulders that he thought he might
just rip the rest of the buttons off, without bothering to
undo them.

"Blair," he said, not fully decided whether he wanted to shoot her or love her to death. "Do you expect me to wait for you until this blasted war is *over*? It might be fifty years from now!"

She looked stricken again. "Why can't you understand?"

It's hopeless, he thought. *Just go on with what you started a few minutes ago.*

But this time, when he pulled her to him a little roughly and began again on the buttons, Blair showed some resistance.

"Matthew," she said, pushing against him with her palms, "I don't think you ought to be doing that."

He paused. "Listen," he said carefully. "What if I *don't* come back from Vicksburg? Have you thought about that? What if I get shot through the heart?" He watched with satisfaction as an expression of horror crept over her face. "All I'm trying to do is love you a little—sweetheart."

In an obvious quandary, she considered this dreadful possibility. "But can't you do it without—without unbuttoning my dress? And"—she went on with an ominous note in her voice—"don't think I don't know you've been doing it, Matthew!"

"You're the prettiest thing I ever saw!" he said with perfect sincerity, kissing her again. That was one thing he *knew* that she liked.

This had the desired effect, and it wasn't too long before his vision of loveliness became insensitive to what was going on behind her back.

Only, he thought, managing by a herculean effort of will to keep a clear head, he had never encountered so many ruffles and other vaguely defined obstructions in his life.

She seemed to be wearing a—what did you call it—a chemise?—and something over that, and beneath the waist was an unexplored territory that he hardly dared think about. There must be at least two dozen petticoats there.

Blair was breathing rather quickly, and he realized that she was lifting her body toward him and giving him more room to maneuver between her back and the cushions. In fact, she was helping him out.

Pretty soon, the buttons were all undone, her arms were out of the sleeves, and the bodice of the dress had somehow worked its way down to her waist. Blair herself, by various manipulations on Matthew's part, was even farther down on the sofa than she had been before.

"Oh," she said weakly, "what's happening, Matthew? I wish—I think you ought to let me get up."

"In a minute," he whispered reassuringly. "We've got plenty of time." He was about to get the damned chemise out of the way. He took a second to deposit a light scattering of kisses down the side of her neck. They proved beneficial, because she didn't say anything more about getting up.

The chemise gave way with a tiny ripping sound and there was nothing left but some tightly laced stays and a couple of straps threaded through with pink ribbons. The straps, however, were on Blair's shoulders and well out of his path.

Although his head was fairly spinning at the sight of what lay before him, he managed a moment of cold calculation.

He glanced quickly down at Blair's face. Her hair was tangled about her flushed cheeks, her lips slightly parted, and as good luck would have it, her eyes were closed.

Matthew felt reasonably certain that he had gone further than mortal man had ever ventured before.

She had liked having him kiss her. In fact, her reaction had been most passionate. Now. What else would she like?

Matthew made a reckless gamble. He decided he knew damned well what she would like.

"Oh!" Blair cried, clutching at his shoulder and making a feeble effort to rise. The tone of her "Oh!"

indicated that there were more things in heaven and earth than she had dreamed of, before now. In any case, it didn't require an ungentlemanly amount of firmness for him to keep her supine.

When he finally put his head down on the arm of the sofa, Blair rolled away from him, gathered up her ruffles and tattered chemise, tossed her hair back from her eyes, and leaned panting against the back of the sofa. Matthew knew her heart was pounding like a sledgehammer, because he'd heard it himself. His own condition was so senseless that he didn't know whether he'd have the gumption to reach out and grab her if she tried to get away. *God!* he thought. *I've got to have her! And soon!*

He managed to stand up, lean down and gather Blair into his arms, and stand up again. He was damned if he was going to consummate this moment of long-anticipated ecstasy on that goddamned narrow sofa. There had to be a bed somewhere. People lived here, didn't they?

Like a limp, warm little bundle of boneless surrender in his arms Blair made no protest as he located the bedroom. In spite of his agony of desire for her, when he lowered her onto the bed, Matthew experienced a sharp stab of guilt. He shouldn't be doing this. And he knew he would hate himself after it was over. He almost wished she would tell him to stop.

"Matthew?" she whispered, clinging to his neck. "Your shoulder?"

He had no idea what she was talking about.

He removed her arms from his neck and sank down beside her. "Do you know how much I love you? God! I can't tell you how much!"

"Is it all right?" she insisted. "I don't know that all this exertion is good for it. You might reopen your wound."

"It's all right," he murmured, taking her into his embrace again. He didn't recall having a wound.

"Oh, Matthew," she said softly from the vicinity of

his chest. "You must think I'm absolutely shameless! I've *never* behaved like this!"

"I know you haven't," he murmured, rocking her gently in his arms. "It's all right. We're getting married after the war. Married people behave like this all the time."

"What"—Blair asked uncertainly—"are you going to do now?"

Jesus! he thought. *How can I?*

He untied his sash and unbuttoned his uniform coat. "I'm just getting ready to love you some more."

She flopped back voluptuously against the pillows, sighed in what appeared to be anticipation, and stretched her arms above her head. "I'll be so glad when this stupid war is ended. I don't see why people can't be decent and get along with one another."

She had neglected to hold her chemise together, and Matthew suspected, as he took in the view, that his vision was well aware of what riches she presented. But, he thought, unbuttoning his shirt, who had torn the chemise in the first place? He could hardly blame her for that.

Blair suddenly sat up straight on the bed and cried in a tone of disbelief, "What are you *doing?*" She stiffened with shock. "Are you taking off your *clothes?*"

"Yes," he said.

She began edging away. "Don't you dare, Matthew! I'm not going to stay here another minute if you try such a thing as that!"

Matthew performed another admirable exercise in mental control.

"All right," he said, spreading his hands in a gesture of capitulation. "I was just trying to get a little more comfortable. You were right about my shoulder. It's not feeling too well. Would you mind darling, if I— well, if I lay down for a minute?"

She paused on her knees close by the edge of the bed, pushed her hair back from her face, pulled the chemise together in front, and looked at him suspiciously.

He sighed as though suffering nobly, and waited for her to grant him permission.

"I knew you shouldn't have picked me up," she said, frowning. "The strain was too much."

"If I could just lie down—"

Blair's frown evaporated and was replaced by a look of loving concern. "Of course, darling. You don't have to ask me."

Matthew, every nerve in his body shouting for immediate attention, eased himself painfully down on the pillows and tried to look as if he were getting situated for the rest of the night.

Putting his arm over his eyes, he lay there for a few minutes, listening to the sound of Blair's breathing. She had not moved off the bed, after all, and he could feel her watching him. If she did get off, he would be forced to give her an alarming surprise.

But as the seconds ticked by, he became more confident that wouldn't be necessary. In fact, he was beginning to feel a perverse pleasure in *not* doing anything. *Let her wonder about it*, he thought.

Eventually a warm little voice was breathing close to his face. "Are you all right, darling? You're not—you're not going to sleep, are you?"

Stirring slightly, he reached out and found a naked shoulder. Blair leaned over him, bracing herself on one hand, while with the other she pushed his hair back from his forehead.

He moved his arm from over his eyes.

Her face directly above him had a dreamy, mystical look. Her fingers moved tenderly, still adjusting his hair. One pink-ribboned strap had fallen completely off her shoulder and was halfway down her arm.

She leaned down and kissed him on the end of his nose. "I'm sorry. I just love you so much, I can't seem to stop touching you."

* * *

Blair knew she shouldn't be behaving like this. But for some time now, she had pushed that knowledge to the back of her mind. At last, at last, after all those weeks of wanting to touch him, she had her hand in his hair. Bending over Matthew with his springy curls entwined in her fingers felt so delicious that she wanted to stay there forever. Although she should probably move and let him rest. But then he squeezed her shoulder reassuringly, to show that he didn't mind her touching him. Encouraged, she snuggled closer. His body felt exactly as she'd imagined. Muscular and solid and capable of protecting her from any disaster. Pressed against him like this, her own body had a disturbing reaction. Delicious little shivers shot through her. She wanted to slide her leg over his and move slowly and languorously against him.

She looked down at his unbuttoned shirt. Silky dark hairs grew on his chest. The sight of a naked male chest so close to her face had a pleasantly shocking effect. She wanted to caress it. Giving in to the impulse, she slid her hand inside his shirt. "You feel so nice," she murmured, rubbing his chest. At this rate, the poor man would never get any sleep.

Matthew suddenly turned over, taking her with him.

Blair looked up at him in surprise. Now he was gazing down at her. She smiled. Maybe he wasn't going to sleep, after all. She hoped not, because she remembered what they had done on the sofa, and—she blushed, because the thought was wanton—she wanted him to do it again. She sighed, lowered her sweeping eyelashes, and slowly raised a hand to push back her hair.

She felt Matthew's hand on her torn chemise, impatiently pushing back the ribbons and straps. Then, as his hand moved over her breast, her nipple hardened. Blair closed her eyes and gave a little moan. She knew she should stop him, but she simply could not. She went limp with desire. She felt his moustache tickle the soft mound of her breast, and then, when his mouth closed on her nipple, the excruciating pleasure left her almost senseless. When, finally, his lips moved to her throat, she clung to him, burning with sensations that she had never experienced before. "I love you," she gasped, almost in tears.

"I love you, too," he said hoarsely, working her out of the blue dress, which was still partially on her. Blair helped him, impatiently tugging it down from her waist. Tossing it aside, Matthew took her into his arms again, and they collapsed on the bed in a flurry of ruffled lawn petticoats. As she feverishly planted kisses all over his face, Blair moaned that she—mustn't—she couldn't—keep on behaving like this. Matthew didn't bother to reassure her. He seemed past the point of articulation, and grew bolder by the second. But Blair, throbbing at his every excursion, no longer cared. When his hand moved under the petticoats and pulled down her lace-trimmed drawers, she didn't protest. Then she felt his touch in the most private, feminine part of her. For a moment she stiffened, because she wasn't expecting it. Did married people really do this? This seemed the ultimate intimacy. And yet, because of his previous lovemaking, she was already poised on the brink of passion, almost ready to plunge over the edge. At this first preliminary invasion, she responded with inarticulate little sounds of desire. She was incapable of resistance. She didn't know what she was feeling, but she melted, wanting him, wanting him. Desire blossomed inside her like the opening petals of a crimson rose, velvet-soft and wet with dew.

Then, beneath his hands, she exploded. Blair didn't know what was happening. She gave a sharp little gasp and went rigid. She moved her head against the pillow in a wild, agitated manner. "Ohh," she gasped. "Oh, stop! Stop it! Stop it! Stop it!"

Matthew stopped, holding her tightly in his arms. She clung to him as though clinging to a lifeline. "Ohh," she gasped for the third time, but in a weak, lingering amazement. "What's happening? I can't—I can't—"

He put her back down and leaned over her. "Be quite now," he said in a low voice. "I'm going to make love to you."

She felt a brief astonishment. Did he mean there was more? What else could be left? After being gripped by that incredible explosion, she didn't see how anything else could compare. A melting, languorous contentment crept over her and she closed her eyes. Still pleasantly pulsating, she lay back against the pillows in a tangle of blond hair and glowing curves.

Matthew was taking off the rest of his clothes. When Blair looked over, a blush stained her cheeks. She had never seen a man naked, much less in that—condition —before. Hastily she averted her gaze. No one had given her a clinical explanation of what men and women did in bed together, but after that glimpse, she had an idea. Still, it scarcely seemed credible. But then Matthew was beside her again, and at the feel of his solid warm body against her, and the touch of his hands, she trembled, responding again. Then he lowered himself over her, and in a mixture of passion and pain she gave herself to him. He made love to her with a tender fury. For a few moments, and for a lifetime, they belonged to each other.

17

After a certain amount of time had passed, Blair became aware that the bedroom was cold.

She reached down, pulled up a quilt from the foot of the bed, and drew it over them. As she got beneath it, lying close against Matthew's shoulder, she was conscious of a lingering surprise.

A faint blush seeped over her face. It still didn't seem decent. But to be perfectly honest, she didn't regret a minute of her scandalous misconduct. No, it had been worth it. Who would have dreamed that such feelings existed? And that all those marvelous, wicked things you weren't supposed to allow would produce them? Blair blushed again at the recollection of *that*.

She wished they were already married! How could she bear to wait until the end of the war? Maybe Vicksburg would be the last battle. All the papers said the batteries were impregnable, and maybe when the Yankees saw they couldn't take it, they would give up and go home. Everybody knew General Lee would beat them in Virginia. That was just a question of time. She lightly closed her fingers around Matthew's lovely muscular bare arm.

He stirred a little and said, "I love you."

"I love you, too," Blair whispered. She wished they

could stay here forever like this. It must be almost daylight, and although today was Saturday and he
shouldn't have anything urgent to do, pretty soon now
they would have to think about going home—like an
icy dash of water down her spine she remembered
what was going to happen today.

She had literally forgotten about the cavalry raid!
She bolted up in bed and almost cried out aloud.

Matthew reached over and said, "What is it?"

She forced herself to settle back beneath the quilt.
Oh, God! What time was it? When were they coming?
She began to pray as she'd never prayed in her life.
Don't let anything happen to Matthew! Let him stay
right here with me until it's all over! Let them come
quick and get it over with! Oh, God!

"It's not anything," she said through chattering
teeth. Why did men have to fight and try to kill each
other? Did they like doing it? Oh, they must, or why
would they do it? *Dear Lord! How can they put us
through this?*

"You're trembling," Matthew said, raising himself
on one elbow and catching her arm. "Blair—"

"I'm just cold," she said desperately, burrowing further down beneath the quilt. "Just—just leave me
alone, Matthew. And—and let me get warm."

To her consternation he followed her, and she could
feel him leaning over her, and then his arm was
around her, and he was saying in a low voice, "Don't
you know how much I love you? You're not sorry
about that, are you?" He was holding her so tightly it
was almost hurting her. "Dammit!" he said, sounding
inexplicably angry. "We're getting married. This
morning."

An excited voice shouting outside broke the silence
in the room.

All the blood drained from her face.

Now, she thought. *They are here. Now. Already.*

She had a sudden, wild urge to grab Matthew
around the neck, hold on to him, and refuse to let him

get out of the bed. *He can't fight a battle with me hanging on to his neck—*

"Lieu—ten—ant!" the excited voice outside shouted. It was coming closer. Blair thought its owner was probably running down the street past the Kendalls' house, now. "By God!" it added, and she could almost hear the pounding of feet. "Where the hell have you—I can't find anybody! They're spread out all over town!"

She turned over and stared up at Matthew, unable to speak. Her terror had grown so enormous it had constricted her throat. *Oh, how I love him!* she thought. *I love everything about him! His curly brown hair, and his beautiful eyes, and the way they twinkle when he laughs at something, and his moustache—if anything happened to him, they would all vanish. He simply wouldn't—be anymore.*

"—Goddamned Rebel cavalry!" the voice outside was yelling. "About—six goddamned—thousand—of 'em!"

There was a pause, as though he were being urgently questioned. Blair's heart began a slow, measured thudding.

Suddenly Matthew tensed, and then turned his head. He had heard them. And now, he was listening.

Two pairs of feet were running down the street. Before she was aware that Matthew had moved, he was off the bed, had grabbed his shirt and pants from the chair beside it, and gone halfway across the room. *No.* Her lips moved silently. *No. Don't.*

She sat up and pulled the quilt around her.

Matthew had disappeared.

A cold draft of air poured into the bedroom from the parlor. He had opened the front door, and she could hear the footsteps clearly now, and Matthew shouting. The footsteps paused, and then came pounding back. Still holding the quilt, she got down off the bed and found that the floor was surprisingly cold. Aimlessly she turned around in her bare feet, looking for her clothes. She still had on one petticoat and her stays.

And, she realized, looking down at it, the remains of her chemise. But nothing underneath.

A measure of her strange lassitude left her and she thought: *What if those strange men come in here? And—and find out what Matthew and I have been doing?*

Snatching up petticoats, she launched a frantic search for the blue dress. Her hair kept falling into her eyes and she had to hold the quilt around her, pick up ruffled lawn underthings, and push her hair back at the same time. She felt a horrid impulse to burst into tears.

And what was Matthew doing? He must be getting dressed as he talked. Oh, what would they *think*?

They wouldn't think anything, if they didn't see her! They would think he was just getting dressed, because he'd been asleep in the normal fashion! If they came in here, she would die on the spot!

The voices suddenly stopped. She didn't feel the cold air coming in anymore, although enough had come in previously to make the room like an icebox. Matthew abruptly walked in from the parlor and picked up his coat from the back of the chair. Blair held her quilt around her like a shield.

"You knew about this all the time, of course," he said, getting into his coat.

"Matthew—" she managed to say.

"Now," he said in a flat, dead kind of voice, "if I can find some side arms out at the camp"—he began to button his coat—"and somebody has gotten the horses out of the sheds, and rounded up the rest of the drunks"—he finished buttoning his coat—"maybe we can get out there and kill us a few." He picked up his sash, folded it over his arm, and looked up at Blair. "Would you like that?"

She couldn't breathe. She could only stand there, clutching her quilt.

"I didn't . . ." she began.

Matthew looked as if he hated her. As if he actually would like to kill her! But she had only been trying to protect him! *Oh,* she thought, *how can I explain to him? I did know it all the time, like he said, but it isn't what he's thinking!*

"Matthew," she said, her heart shriveling away to nothingness—for she couldn't let him go away thinking that—"yes! I knew they were coming! But I didn't want you to—"

"Stop lying!" he shouted. "By God, is there *anything* you won't do for your glorious Cause?"

The breath left her lungs in a painful gasp. She bent over, her stomach hurting as if he had struck her there with his fist. Did he really believe that the raid was the only reason she'd done—what she'd just done? He meant that she was a—a—Blair's mind writhed away from the unthinkable word. How *could* he? *Oh,* she thought in an agony of revelation, *as soon as they've done that to you—then that's what they think!* She should have *never—never—*

She said, "I hope they kill you."

When she looked up, Matthew had gone. Then she was in more torment than ever, because Matthew's being killed was the thing she feared most! No matter what he said, she still loved him. And now he hated her. And she might never see him again!

Blair threw off the quilt and stepped into her petticoats, hands shaking so violently she almost dropped the garments before she could get her foot off the floor.

Putting her dress on proved easier, because the long sleeves warmed her a little. But as her fingers fumbled with the buttons in back, she began to sob in frustration as she realized that fastening them without assistance was going to be impossible. Finally she did the bottom ones as far up as she could reach, and the top ones as far down, and then gave up on them, leaving a large gap in the middle of her back.

I'll have my shawl on over them, she thought as she sat down on the edge of the bed and hastily drew on her stockings. When had she taken the stockings off? She didn't remember. Slipping into her shoes, she hurried to the mirrored dresser and almost cried again when she saw her hair.

It hung in a snarled mass of blond waves and curls halfway to her waist. She would never be able to get the tangles out in less than half a day! Blair went flying into the parlor to get her reticule. She found it, rummaged inside it for her comb, and went flying back to the mirror again. A few minutes of frenzied tugging proved the futility of her efforts.

It was all Matthew's fault. He had absolutely—

Oh, what was she doing! Standing here like a complete idiot, trying to comb her hair, when every second was so precious! She would just have to go down Salem Avenue with it looking like this! Blair dropped the comb, picked it up, ran back into the parlor, and put it into her reticule. She looked around for her shawl.

An eternity passed while she searched for it and couldn't find it. A breathless, heart-stopping panic began to clutch at her. What was happening out there? While she ran about in here like a lunatic? Blair found the shawl, wrapped it around her with trembling hands, and hurried through the door.

The bitter cold of the early-morning air slashed at her like a knife, cutting through the heavy woolen shawl as if it were filmy, ball-gown mousseline. Hugging the shawl around her, she hurried down the sidewalk, her feet in the thin slippers turning numb.

It was still dark, but with that faint shadowing of grayness that foretells the coming of daylight. The horses and carriages were gone from around the Kendall mansion and all the houses that she passed were dark. Everybody was still asleep. Or if they were awake, they were behind drawn draperies and tightly closed shutters.

She had not consciously thought about where she was going. Something propelled her running feet without her having to think. *Don't let anything happen to him before I get there!* she prayed. It was such a long way to the fairgrounds, and she had to reach them in time!

Blair heard firing from the infantry camp northeast of the square.

She stopped to listen. The sharp, cracking reports were coming sporadically and sounded like uneven strings of firecrackers going off. Throwing her hair back from her face, she began to run again. Cotton warehouses were on the east side of the fairgrounds and she could see them now. Generous splashes of soft pink and gold lined the sky behind them. The gray was lightening, and it was almost dawn.

Blair swung around the corner of the nearest warehouse, caught the edge of its icy brick wall, and stopped.

In front of her, on the bare dirt of the fairgrounds, a kind of frenzied pandemonium was taking place.

Men were running about, some of them pulling on shirts and dragging sabers and buckling on pistol belts as they ran. Others were throwing saddles on horses, and still others were leading more horses from sheds behind rows of white tents. A small, tousle-headed, young-looking boy ran out of one of the tents in his underwear and began to blow on a bugle. The notes had a tremulous, earsplitting urgency, and Blair jumped a little against the wall of the warehouse. Where was Matthew? With a sinking foretaste of disaster she thought that she would never be able to find him again. There were so many men and horses milling about on the fairgrounds, and even if she did find him, he wouldn't stop and listen to her, and—

To add to her terror, she became dreadfully aware that there couldn't be that many Yankees out there, after all. For most of the Union cavalry had gone with Colonel Dickey on that raid to cut the Mobile & Ohio, and only a handful had been left in Holly Springs.

Surrender! she thought savagely. *Surrender, you fools!*

Were there really six thousand Confederates coming? She had no way of knowing, but if it were only five hundred, it would still be too many. Matthew would be ridden over by sheer force of numbers! They would cut him to pieces; they would smash him beneath their horses' hooves without even pausing to look at him—oh, God! She couldn't stand it! Why had she come? It would have been better if she hadn't been here to see it—

From the north came the sinister, rhythmical drumming of hoofbeats, and she looked over her shoulder to see the first of a long column of cavalry. Emerging ghostlike from the mists of the morning, the Confederates approached at a slow, sweeping gallop, looking out to right and left as they rode. Her heart began to keep time with the rhythm of the hooves.

She suddenly recognized some of the faces and realized that they were the 1st Mississippi Cavalry.

A high, yipping, drawn-out cry from the advancing Southerners curdled the blood in her veins. Putting spurs to their horses, the lead riders in the gray column leaned forward in their saddles, still emitting the same earsplitting yells. The small hairs on the back of Blair's neck rose as she watched them veer off the road and go thundering toward the fairgrounds.

The 2nd Illinois Cavalry companies were closing ranks. Most of them were mounted, and the ones who were not were swinging into their saddles in a hurry. She heard hoarse shouts of command and realized that the small Yankee had stopped blowing his bugle. She jumped at the first sharp report of a pistol. The Confederates had drawn their side arms and were starting to fire.

The Yankees' horses, drawn up in formation, moved restlessly, tossing their heads and rolling their eyes. Hoarse, shouted orders from a dozen of the officers went down the line.

"DRAW SABERS!"

Blair's throat was so dry she couldn't swallow. They weren't going to surrender! They were going to—

Blue-uniformed men tensed forward, sabers glinting, hands lifting reins loosely—there was a strange, mingled, furious bellow of command.

"CHARGE!"

Still yelling, the advance units of the 1st Mississippi came thundering in to meet the Yankees' charge.

When they collided, Blair covered her ears. She didn't want to keep looking, but her eyes refused to close. She saw and heard an ear-shattering imbroglio of neighing, frantic horses, clashing sabers, smoking, barking pistols, flying clods of dirt, and mingled shouts and curses.

They are all crazy, she thought, without being conscious that she was thinking at all. This was the most incredible thing she had ever witnessed. Why would grown men want to behave like this? Something suddenly flew out from the wall of the warehouse and lodged in her hair. Slowly she reached up and pulled it out. She tore her eyes away from the scene before her and looked at what she held in her hand.

It was a small piece of mortar. Looking back at the wall, she saw a bullet hole in it just a few inches above the top of her head.

Why, she thought, *I almost got killed!*

She stood there, holding the piece of mortar. Was Matthew dead or alive? A small twinge of frustration reminded her that she had failed to see him at all. Turning slowly, she edged toward the nearest doorway of the warehouse, staying close by the wall. She tried to open the door and go into the warehouse, but it was locked. In the street a man screamed as though being tortured, and she closed her eyes. Staccato hoofbeats drummed so close behind her that they seemed to be headed right through her door. Listlessly she turned around and leaned back against the door.

In front of her, a large, broad-shouldered Confederate was having his horse shot out from under him. As his mount was falling, the trooper managed to disentangle himself from his stirrups and rolled free before the wretched animal caught him under its side.

The cavalryman swiftly recovered his balance, rose on his hands and knees, and ran back in a half-crouching position. Using the quivering carcass for a breastwork, he hunched down behind it, firing his revolver into the melee.

Blair leaned against the door and watched him. After a while he paused, reached into his cartridge box, and began to reload. *For heaven's sake, Preston,* she thought with faint irritation. *Don't you ever get tired of shooting? And you don't act like you even care about your poor horse.*

A tremor of awareness went scooting over her spine. Good Lord! It *was* Preston!

"Preston!" she screamed. She took a quick step to the edge of the doorway, gripped her shawl in both hands, and waved it at his dusty back.

Preston whirled around, still holding his revolver, and she drew back. "Pres!" she screamed again. "It's me!"

Lowering his revolver, he shouted, "What in the hell are you doing? Are you out of your idiot mind?"

Blair went running out and tumbled down in the dust beside him, right behind the pitiful horse. "Oh, Pres, don't let them hurt Matthew! Oh, please, *please*—"

Preston gaped at her in what appeared to be a mixture of incredulity and rage. *Oh,* she thought, *now he's mad because I've interrupted him in the middle of his glorious battle!*

"Are you crazy?" he demanded. "What are you *doing* out here?"

"I spent the night with Louley Burton," she said. "Pres, you've got to—"

He suddenly jumped up, grabbed her by the arm, and jerked her on her knees back toward the warehouse. Pebbles and dirt cut into her flesh and she heard her dress ripping as it dragged across the ground.

"Turn me loose!" she shouted, trying to get to her feet while her brother was wrenching her arm out of its socket. "Let me walk!"

"Keep your damn head down!" Preston shouted, dragging her all the way into the doorway and shoving her against the door.

He looked as if he might be heading right back for his temporary breastwork, so she clamped on to his arm and hung there with all her strength.

"*Listen* to me, Pres!" she begged, almost sobbing. "They're going to kill him! I know they are! Can't you make him surrender? Pres, you've *got* to help me! I'm about to die, I'm so scared!"

"Sis," he said, trying to pry her fingers away from his sleeve, "get ahold of yourself. I don't know what you're talking about. I can't stop and talk now—"

Blair made a serious effort to calm her racing emotions enough to get through to him. Because if she didn't, there would be no hope again. The battle on the fairgrounds was still raging, but the firing seemed to have lessened in intensity. Did that mean it was almost over? She was afraid to look out there and see.

"Matthew, Pres!" she repeated. "Please—please—find him for me!"

Her brother looked at her blankly and said, "Who?"

"Matth—" she began again, and then stopped. As incredible as it might seem, Preston did not have the slightest idea who she was talking about! How was that possible, when Matthew was the most important thing in the world?

Frantically, she tried to think of how to identify him.

"He's out there right now! With Company D! Don't you *remember*, Pres? You told us we should ask Matthew for a guard for the house. You told Grandpa and everybody! And we—"

"You mean—Captain Harwell?" Preston said, as though recalling that there was such a person. As though, she thought, he'd had trouble remembering Matthew's *name!*

"Yes!" she cried. "Pres, he's got a hurt shoulder! And I'm so scared! He can't go on fighting much longer! Oh . . ." She began to cry in earnest. "They're going to kill him! I know it! I know—"

"Sis," Preston interrupted, putting his hands on her shoulders and standing away from her. "Slow down for a minute."

Blair took a deep breath, tried to control her sobbing, and briefly closed her eyes. Pres was sounding better, now. Almost cooperative. She had to make him understand how important this was to her. And if she didn't do it quickly, it was going to be too late.

She swallowed and said, "Just find out for me whether he's dead or alive."

"All right," Preston said.

Blair opened her eyes.

"You may have to wait for a few minutes, though. But this little skirmish is about over. When it is, I'll go out and check the casualties for you. All right?"

Little skirmish? He had sounded almost offhanded. Was that all they considered it?

"Oh, Pres," she whispered, looking down at her shawl. "If anything's happened to him, I'll just die."

Preston let go of her shoulders and laughed.

Blair stared up at him, too stunned for anger or anything else. He was shaking his head and grinning beneath his sweeping blond moustache.

"Saints above us!" he said. "I'm finding this hard to believe!"

The color returned to her face. How *dare* he laugh at her at a time like this! What would ever possess even Preston—who was a total, utter varmint—to do such a thing!

"You think it's funny?" she said, in cold fury.

"Oh, not you, sis," he said quickly. "It's just that— well, skip it. Never mind. Look, I told you I'd go find your Yankee for you didn't I? Now, you must excuse

me, because I've got to get back to my derring-do." He
started leaving the doorway, then turned back and finished loading his revolver. "Now, for God's sake, stay
here until the shooting stops. Don't go flying up the
street to look for Harwell yourself. He's probably halfway to Oxford by now, anyway. And wait for me.
Maybe you can deliver some messages to the folks."
Cocking his revolver, he went cautiously back outside,
muttering, "We'll likely be here all day."

Blair leaned back against the door, conscious of a
slight relaxing of tension. Another covey of noisy gray
horsemen went thundering past, but their yells
sounded less intimidating and more like whoops of delight. She could hear only scattered firing, and it
seemed to be getting farther away. In spite of Preston's
warning for her to stay back in the doorway, she edged
forward. She saw a familiar face. It was Jim Watkins,
who had been a friend of Preston's since childhood.
Jim was walking with a peculiar, tottering gait, holding his left hand stiffly in front of him, clasped in his
right. He had wrapped his handkerchief around it, and
the handkerchief was crimson with blood.

"Jim!" she called, dashing out to intercept him.
"What is it?" She stared down at the soaked handkerchief, which was dripping blood in the street.

Jim stopped, smiled, and said, "Why, Blair! This is
an unexpected pleasure. I didn't think we'd be running
into any ladies so soon."

"Jim, what's wrong with your hand?"

Drawing the hand back protectively, he held it
against his chest. "Of all the rotten bad luck," he said,
looking at it in a kind of bemused indignation. "Some
Yank has managed to slice off my thumb."

Blair's stomach turned over.

"You've got to do something about it! You're bleeding to death!"

Jim wobbled over to the warehouse and leaned
against the wall. She tried to support him, so he
wouldn't collapse from loss of blood while she tried to

think of what to do with him. "Does it hurt much? Can I help you walk up to the hospital on the square?"

"No," he said. "You'd better stay here where it's safe. They're still fighting up around the square, but I think we've pretty well cleaned them out from down here. And anyway, it doesn't hurt much. It feels kind of numb."

Blair's heart beat faster.

"Jim, did you-all—did you beat the Yankee cavalry?"

He looked down at her and smiled. "Why, of course we did, hon. Don't you know we always do that?"

"Did you—did you kill many?"

"I reckon so. They gave us a pretty good fight. But we're driving 'em back toward the infantry camp." He frowned at his bloody handkerchief. "Da—blast! Why did this have to happen?"

"What will they do now, Jim? Will they surrender?"

"Surrender? He grinned slightly. "They didn't look like they had that in mind."

"Sis!" a familiar voice was shouting.

She looked over to see Preston approaching. As he reached them, he remarked to Jim Watkins, "I see you're skulking again."

"They cut his thumb off!" Blair cried.

Jim looked up, smiled sourly, and shifted his hand.

"Pres?" she said urgently. Then she realized that Preston couldn't tell her about Matthew with Jim standing there listening. He would never understand. He would think—

Preston looked at Jim. "Would you excuse us for a minute? Sis is dying to find out something, and we'll have to step aside for a second while I put her mind at ease. Then she'll be able to come back and admire your sacrifice some more."

"Of course," Jim said, leaning back against the wall and looking gallant, although pale. Hurriedly Blair followed Preston into the doorway. He stepped between her and the fairgrounds, looked serious and said, "I didn't find Harwell. He's not dead, he's not captured,

and as far as I know, he's hightailing it out of town
with the rest of Company D. Now. Are you happy? I've
done all I can do."

Her legs buckled with relief. "Thank you," she whispered.

"Blair," Preston said in a low voice. "What does the
rest of the family think about this?"

"They—don't know about it," she said, looking
down at the ground.

"You haven't told them?"

She shook her head.

"You'll get over it," he said shortly.

She looked up in surprise. "Oh, no!" she whispered.
"Pres, I love him!"

Preston's face was expressionless. "What about Harwell? Have you mentioned this grand passion to him?"

The color flooded her face. "Pres, you don't know
how it's been! After y'all left, they came in and—and
took everything! It was awful! They stripped the
smokehouse and took all the corn from the cribs and I
thought we were going to starve! I thought they'd
come in the house and take everything there! And they
would have, Pres! They burned the Widow Lockwood's
house! And they stole people's cotton—they just went
out and took it! And"—Blair twisted her shawl—"Pres,
don't be angry with me! Matthew's been so—so good
to us. He gave us the guard and the commissary rations and he's been staying with us—and I couldn't
help it, Pres!"

"All right," he said, and his face had a tight dark
look. "I guess you couldn't. And don't start bawling,
for God's sake." Preston stroked his moustache. "So,"
he murmured. "They burned the Widow Lockwood's
house, did they?"

"Yes!" she answered with a surge of outrage at the
recollection of it. "She didn't even get to take her
clothes out! Nothing but the—"

"Hey!" Preston said, suddenly looking pleased—in
an evil kind of way. "What would *you* like to burn,

sis?'' He grinned and gave her a nudge with his elbow.
"Think hard, now! There must be something you'd like
to set on fire!"

Blair pressed her hand over her mouth in delight
and gave an excited little jump. "Did you know that
Mrs. Grant is in Holly Springs right now? Oh, Pres!
Let's burn her trunks, and her clothes, and her saratoga, and her carriage, and—and everything she has!"

"Why not? That should give Ulysses a shock."

"She's staying at the Walter place! Oh, hurry, Pres!"

Following her brother out to the street, she saw Jim
Watkins, supported by two privates, go lurching away.
Someone will do something for him, she thought. Up
toward the town she could hear excited shouting. The
sun had come up completely and it was a bright glaring cold now, instead of a depressing gray one. Blair
picked up her skirts to run behind Preston.

Then she remembered her ungodly appearance and
stopped. It dawned on her that she had been talking to
Jim Watkins looking like this! Automatically she raised
her hands and tried to smooth her wildly cascading
hair. She looked down at her dirt-stained blue skirt,
which was ripped in two places over the knees, where
Preston had dragged her across the road on it. Hastily
she shook it and dusted the dirt off with her hands.
Then she wiped her hands on her shawl. Was her face
dirty, too? She took the other end of the shawl and
scoured it hurriedly over her cheeks.

When she looked up, Preston had vanished, and she
picked up her skirts and headed for the center of town.
She couldn't help it if people thought she looked like a
tatterdemalion. She wasn't going to miss this for the
world!

18

Cavalrymen were galloping along the road from the fairgrounds, and one of them stopped and gave Blair a lift back to town. When she slid down from the horse in a flurry of petticoats, she had to dodge her way through more soldiers who were hurrying along the sidewalks. But what a blessing it was to be able to move among men in uniform without having that awful, frustrated antipathy boiling inside her. *Our soldiers!* she thought. *Oh, thank God they're back!*

As she reached the corner by the Methodist church, she began to meet people who were pouring out of houses and mingling with the soldiers. Some of the troopers were hugging relatives, others pushing and pleading with the townspeople to go back inside. Shrieking with excitement, Louley Burton came flying across the street. Backless bedroom slippers flapped on her stockingless feet, her faded pink wrapper billowed behind her, and her long brown hair streamed straight down her back. Tight little curl papers encircled her face.

My God! Blair thought. *At least* I've *got my clothes on!* Just as Louley made it to the sidewalk, a spattering of gunfire rang out. The civilians in the street scattered like quails, and Louley whirled to clutch at Blair. She didn't seem to notice the condition of Blair's coiffure or her raggedy dress.

"They're firing at our men from the houses again!" she screamed. "The filthy little cowards!"

Blair looked around in consternation. "You mean there're Yankees still in the houses? Where, Lou?"

Louley pointed behind her, her pink wrapper falling open to reveal her white flannel nightgown. "There!" she screamed. "Where they've been staying! At our house, for one! Oh, God! I hope they get that impudent wretch of a major!"

More shooting peppered the air, but now it was coming from the Confederates, a group of whom were advancing toward the Burton house and returning the fire. It seemed to be coming from the sidelights on either side of the front door. A square of white material fastened to the end of a poker suddenly emerged from the jagged pieces of glass and waved back and forth. The Confederates paused in their firing. "All right!" they shouted. "Come on out!"

In a few moments the door opened slowly and two Union officers in night attire came through it, holding their white flag of surrender aloft.

At the sight of them Louley began to clap her hands and jump up and down. "They got him!" she screamed. "I hope they shoot him right now!"

"No, no," a flustered voice said, and Blair turned to see the Reverend Thackerford, who stood just behind them on the sidewalk in front of the church. A swallow-tailed dress coat covered his long cotton nightshirt and he was wearing shoes without socks. "Now, girls!" he said. "You know we don't shoot people after they've surrendered. It would be unchristian and against the rules of war."

Turning back toward the Burton house, Blair recognized the two Yankee females she'd seen that day coming down Louley's front steps. Huddled in agonized apprehension just inside the doorway, they clutched their cambric wrappers as they watched the Confederates lead their husbands away under guard.

With a surge of savage satisfaction she thought, *Now let's see how you like it!*

"Did you know the infantry has already been captured?" Louley screamed at the Reverend Thackerford. "Anson Harding told me they caught Colonel Murphy in bed and he's getting ready to surrender the whole garrison!"

"Well, well." The Reverend Thackerford nodded. "That would probably be wisest. Let us pray there will be no unnecessary bloodshed. Have either of you girls seen little Benny Lockwood? He seems to have disappeared—"

"I'll go look for him," Blair said quickly. She couldn't wait another minute to find out what was happening in the square. *Oh,* she thought, *I hope they go back and search those Yankee women's baggage for weapons!* And had Pres gotten to the Walter place yet? Later, she would have to go around there!

When she stopped in front of Levy's Dry Goods store, the square looked like a madhouse. Confederate cavalrymen were swarming among the bales of cotton stacked in the square, pulling more cotton bales out of the courthouse, and carrying crates and barrels from the converted warehouses on the north and east sides. Surging mobs of civilians were running and whooping through the tangle of sutlers' wagons, army vehicles, and buggies and carriages hitched in front of the Magnolia Hotel.

Blair recognized Mr. Fred Grace, helping the soldiers carry boxes from one of the livery stables. *Oh, thank God!* she thought. *They've let him out of the basement!* She went running toward him, crying, "Mr. Grace! Mr. Grace!"

Mr. Grace eased a box down and turned to greet her.

"By George! Where's your grandpa? Tell him to get down to the depot! They've thrown open the commissary stores!"

"Oh, I'm so glad you're out! Are you all right, Mr. Grace? What are you doing? What are those?"

"Federal ammunition!" Mr. Grace cried. "By George, this is one round they'll never fire!"

A grinning Confederate cavalryman appeared and added another ammunition box to Mr. Grace's pile.

"That's right, ma'am," he said to Blair. "Have to bring 'em out in the street and set 'em off a few at a time. Can't explode it all at once, or it'd take half the town with it."

"Better hurry to the depot," Mr. Grace said. "It's goin' fast."

"You mean—I can go get whatever I want from the commissary stores?"

"Help yourself," the cavalryman said, grinning again. "Courtesy of Ulysses S. Grant!"

She couldn't believe it! It was too good to be true!

Lifting her skirts, Blair went flying up the sidewalk again. But there were so many people on them now that she had to slow down. Everybody in Holly Springs was dashing around the courthouse square! People were laughing and shouting like the Fourth of July!

An excited mob crowded around the door of a sutler's store. Miss Lucy Blaylock, her gray hair covered by a white ruffled nightcap, pushed her way out carrying a sack of white flour and several large boxes of raisins. Lemons peeped from the pockets of her silk peignoir. Blair had a brief sensation of amazement that Miss Lucy owned a peignoir.

"Miss Lucy!" she cried.

Miss Lucy stopped, juggled her raisins, and said, "The darkies are in the post office looking for money! They're opening all the letters! Someone should put a stop to it!"

Blair looked at the mob around the sutler's store. If she didn't get something pretty soon, everything would be gone! She started to push her way through but was distracted by another commotion from the direction of Butler's drugstore.

Down that way, three or four Yankees were fleeing up the street on foot. Citizens standing on the sidewalks and in the doorways of stores began to shout encouragement.

"Run, Yanks!" they yelled derisively, and some of them began to cheer and catcall. A hoarse masculine voice rose above the others. "Run, you blue-bellied varmints! Run! Damn you! Run!"

A single Confederate horseman dashed out in their path, drew his saber, and blocked their progress. The panting Yankees came to a skidding halt. One of them raised his hands.

"Kill them!" Miss Lucy Blaylock screeched. "Kill them! Kill them! Kill them!"

Lord! Blair thought. *I'm glad Matthew's not here!*

Miss Lucy dropped a box of raisins and Blair picked it up, put it hurriedly back on top of the stack in Miss Lucy's arms, and pushed her way through the crowd on the sidewalk again. Someone shouted that there was a train at the depot loaded with supplies and waiting to pull out for the front.

"The Texas brigade came in that way!" another voice shouted. "The Yankees can rake hell and skin the Devil before that train gets to Oxford!"

Blair discovered that she couldn't fight her way through the mob around the sutler's store, so she went into Levy's Dry Goods. Mr. Levy was nowhere to be seen, but the store was wide open and several large wicker baskets were sitting on the counter in front. Blair snatched up one of the baskets, considered leaving a note for Mr. Levy, thought better of it, and went running out onto the sidewalk again.

She almost bumped into little Benny Lockwood, who was running in the opposite direction.

"Benny!" she cried, grabbing him by the arm. "The Reverend Thackerford is looking for you!"

Benny's pale little face was agog with openmouthed excitement and his straw-colored hair stood up in all directions. He had a coat and pants on, so he had got dressed before he escaped from the parsonage.

"M-m-money!" he stammered. "There's money all over the place!"

What was he talking about? She held on to his arm tightly for fear he'd go scampering away.

"You go back to the parsonage right this minute!"

"It's all over the sidewalk! Stacks and stacks of it! A million dollars, I bet!"

Blair heard a crash and the splintering of wood to her right. In the street an officer was knocking in the tops of whiskey barrels and turning them over so that their contents would pour into the gutter.

White men and Negroes alike saw what was happening and went running toward him. Some of them got down on their knees and cupped their hands to funnel the draining whiskey into their mouths. Cursing, the officer shouted for somebody to come help him pour out the rest of the whiskey before the damned rabble got to it.

Benny Lockwood pulled at her hand in a kind of frenzy, and Blair got a firmer grip on her basket and allowed him to lead her away from the vicinity of the whiskey. They really should go out to the depot, she thought.

"Here!" Benny screeched. "Here, Miss Blair!"

Blair stopped and stared down at the sidewalk.

It was covered with money.

Crisp Federal greenbacks in all denominations lay under their feet. Five-dollar bills, ten-dollar bills, twenty-dollar bills . . .

She looked up at the building they were standing in front of. It was the Federal paymaster's office.

"Benny—" she whispered.

Leaning down, she gathered up greenbacks and crammed them into her basket. "Oh, Benny, help me! Oh, quick—"

She and little Benny Lockwood had the sidewalk to themselves. Nobody else was interested, and they had

almost filled the wicker basket! Blair reminded herself
to go back by Levy's Dry Goods and leave a greenback
in payment for the basket.

As she and Benny scrambled madly about picking up
the money, cheers and applause rang out from around
the courthouse. Blair stopped, straightened up, and
pushed her hair back from her eyes.

The cheers followed in the wake of a group of officers, riding past the Magnolia Hotel. When the cavalcade turned the corner and drew nearer, she recognized the slim, dapper little figure riding slightly ahead
of the others. The screams and applause from the citizens on the sidewalk became almost hysterical. "Look,
Benny!" she screamed. "It's Earl Van Dorn!"

As the horses and riders passed in front of them,
Blair and Benny shrieked with excitement. The handsome Van Dorn went by at a trot, acknowledging by an
occasional nod the frenzy of his admirers. His vindica-
tion from the defeat at Corinth was complete. He had
led his cavalry around the flanks of the mighty Union
Army. The Confederates had struck deep in Grant's
rear, and the gargantuan Federal stores at the supply
base in Holly Springs were now in his hands.

The elegant general had always had an eye for the
ladies, and for one heart-stopping moment he smiled
at Blair as he passed. She thought she would explode!

"Look, Benny!" she screamed. "Look! Look!"

Van Dorn and his staff passed on, and their progress
could be marked by the pandemonium of delight that
followed them.

Blair leaned down and began snatching up Federal
greenbacks again.

A group of Texans went by with another covey of
captured Yankees, and a bored-looking Confederate
stuck his head out the door of the paymaster's office
and yelled, "When the *hell* you gonna come and get the
ones we got in here?"

The cavalrymen in the street shouted that the prisoners were coming in faster than they could detail guards

for them. They were taking these down to the depot to
the prison corral.

"Well, step lively!" the soldier in the doorway replied. "You think we wanta set on our asses playin'
nursemaid all day?"

He looked like one of General Price's Missourians,
and Blair lowered her head over her basket. The Missourians had no sense of delicacy at all!

One of the cavalrymen in the street had suddenly
stopped and turned back, and now she heard a vaguely
familiar voice calling her name.

She looked up to see—of all people!—her erstwhile
beau, Lieutenant Phillips. She had a brief feeling of
discomfiture. *Oh dear,* she thought, quickly smoothing
her hair. *Why did* he *have to show up right now?*

As Dan Phillips swung down from his saddle, his
face was agleam with delight. "Hey, boys!" he yelled,
turning his head and motioning for his companions to
follow. "Here she is!" He ran up on the sidewalk,
grabbed Blair by the hand, and looked down into her
basket.

"Honey child," he said, "what are you doing with
those?"

"It's *money!*" she cried. "It was all over the sidewalk! We've been picking—"

"You want money?" he said gaily and pulled her up
the steps of the paymaster's office. "There's more inside. How about a thousand dollars?"

With little Benny Lockwood trotting behind them,
they entered the paymaster's office. Blair gasped.
There were huge piles of greenbacks tossed all over the
floor! She was dimly aware of Yankees leaning against
the walls of the room, and of more Missourians slouching over their rifles in long-suffering silence.

"How much do you want, honey?" Lieutenant Phillips asked Blair, sending a flurry of greenbacks into the
air with a kick of his cavalry boot.

She thought that if you didn't know better, you
would think just from looking at him that he was a

Yankee, too. Warmly encased in a caped overcoat of
Federal blue, he had four breechloading carbines
slung about his shoulders, two shiny Colt army revolvers bulging in holsters on his hips, and innumerable
cartridge boxes dangling from his belt. Each one of the
cartridge boxes was plainly marked U.S.

Suddenly whipping a twenty-dollar greenback out of
his pocket, he extracted a match and a fat black cigar.
With a debonair flip of his thumbnail he set fire to the
twenty and lit the cigar.

"Ahhh!" he said, rocking back on his heels. "The
Union Army thinks of everything! Now that's what I
call going first class!"

"That's money, you idiot!" Blair cried.

He grinned at her and blew out the match.

"Miss Blair, that's United States currency! Now,
don't you mess up your pretty little hands with any
more of that trash!"

"You mean"—she could hear the hesitation in her
voice—"you mean—it's not any *good?*"

Dan Phillips reached back inside his new Federal
overcoat and pulled out a huge swath of greenbacks in
uncut sheets.

"Honey, that train sitting down at the depot had a
paymaster's car! I just picked this up for a souvenir.
You think for a minute now. Where're you going to go
to spend that stuff?"

Oh, no! she thought. No wonder she and little Benny
Lockwood had been the only ones picking it up! They
were the only two people in Holly Springs dumb
enough to! And now they'd wasted so much time the
commissary stores were probably all cleaned out!

Lieutenant Phillips looked over her shoulder with a
delighted gleam in his eye. "Boys," he cried, "take a
look at her!"

Taking Blair's elbow, he turned her lovingly around,
as if he were presenting her for the approval of the
court.

"What did I tell you? Wasn't I right? Boys, I want

you to meet the prettiest girl in the state of Mississippi! Miss Blair Tyler!"

"Oh," she said, smiling in spite of herself. "Hush! You're embarrassing me!"

The "boys," evidently members of the Texas brigade whom she hadn't met before, were streaming into the paymaster's office. Some of them stopped to kick a few greenbacks over the floor, exchange jeers with the Missouri guards, and comment upon the number of Yankee prisoners lining the walls. Little Benny Lockwood watched in bug-eyed admiration but, she noticed, he didn't stop gathering up greenbacks, either. He stuffed them into the pockets of his coat.

"Dan," one of the Texans said to Lieutenant Phillips, "for once in your life, you didn't lie. Ma'am," he added, bowing to Blair, "allow me to say that you are what we are fighting for. To defend the beauty and purity of the flower of Southern womanhood. For the—"

"You're all absolutely marvelous," she said to him and smiled. "And we love every one of you! Do you know how much we've been wishing you'd come back?"

The Texan bowed again. "With such charm and sweetness waiting at home, we would gladly saber every Yankee in sight just to get within range of your radiant smiles. We would—"

"Be quiet for a minute!" another of the Texans shouted. "And let me say a word!"

Blair put her hand over her mouth and giggled, beginning to wonder if they weren't all tipsy! Some Federal commissary whiskey must've been at the depot along with the paymaster's car! But she was enjoying the flowery compliments just as much as they were! They were obviously full of themselves, and why not? They'd just successfully executed the greatest cavalry raid in the history of the world! *Oh*, she thought, *they're magnificent! Just think what they've done!*

"Tell me about it!" she cried. "Did you come all the way from Grenada? When did you leave?"

"Three days ago," the latest Texan said. "Ma'am, you cannot conceive of how long I've been glued to that saddle. Why, we rode all night on the seventeenth, and then just stopped long enough to feed the horses! And then—"

Lieutenant Phillips interrupted.

"Thirty hours before we made camp at New Albany."

"Yes," the first one agreed. "And then what happened but a storm came up. But when we passed through Pontotoc, the charming ladies there ran out in the streets and handed us up the nicest little picnic baskets."

A third member of the Texas brigade joined in the conversation. "Yes, ma'am," he said. "We ate as we was ridin' along. When we was about through Pontotoc, what come trottin' across our rear but the whole goddamned—excuse me, ma'am—but the whole Union cavalry!"

"Oh!" she cried. "But why didn't they attack you?"

Delighted hoots of merriment rose from the Texas brigade.

"That's what *we'd* like to know, ma'am!" several of them said.

Lieutenant Phillips began to tiptoe across the paymaster's office with tiny, mincing steps.

"Hey!" he cried. "Here they come! Goddammit! I mean it! That's just the way they went! Ridin' all closed up an' starin' at us! Like they thought if they stayed real quiet, they'd be invisible!"

Little Benny Lockwood stopped stuffing greenbacks in his pockets and laughed.

The Texans and most of the Missouri guards joined in, but the Yankees lining the walls were pointedly silent.

"You must have scared them to death!" Blair cried in delight. "Oh, you're all just wonderful! Oh"—her heart swelled at the memory of General Van Dorn and his staff trotting around the courthouse square—"I could—I could kiss every one of you!"

Impulsively she stood on tiptoe and gave the nearest Texan a peck on the cheek.

"Ma'am!" he cried. "Would you do that again?"

But now they were all crowding over, so Blair made the rounds. She gave them all a kiss on the cheek, and Dan Phillips was once again beaming with pride. "What did I tell you?" he kept repeating. "I've got the best-looking girl in the state of Mississippi!"

She decided that if he wanted to fib about it, this wasn't the time to argue with him. And anyway, she did love them all!

"Hey!" one of the Missourians shouted. "You dudes git back to yur Yankee herdin'! You think we gone set in here all day guardin' these prisoners? We want a crack at them Colt's six-shooters!"

The Texans responded with what Blair suspected was unusual mildness of phrase—due to her presence —and leisurely made their way out of the paymaster's office.

Lieutenant Phillips bowed over her hand and said he hoped they would meet again before the day ended.

Well! she thought, watching the last of them leave and patting her hair. *That was rather pleasant!* Blair suddenly became aware that one of the Yankee prisoners was watching her. Looking over, she met the gaze of Captain Stephen Eaton.

Resplendent in his dress uniform, he lounged against the wall of the paymaster's office, almost beneath the elbow of a hulking Missouri guard. Obviously he had lingered at the Kendalls' festivities even longer than Matthew. He'd not had time to change from his ballroom accoutrements. Eaton's expression indicated no discomfiture at his prisoner-of-war status. Blair felt a surge of dislike so active that it left a bad taste in her mouth.

The conceited little worm didn't seem to be aware of

the fact that he had finally met his masters. She thought of those endless hours spent waiting for that horrid party to be over. And—of Isabella.

From his position against the wall Captain Eaton inclined his head slightly in a form of salutation and murmured, "Miss Tyler." Then he smiled in a particularly suggestive manner.

It occurred to her that now—at last—she could tell him what she really thought of him! And every thieving Yankee like him! For today the Confederacy was in the ascendancy. Nobody was going to drag her off to the courthouse basement for insulting the Federal uniform.

She straightened her shoulders, gave Captain Eaton a glare of withering contempt, and said, "Shut up. You little—animal."

Eaton's eyebrows shot up and he colored slightly.

"Certainly," he said softly. "Anything to oblige a lady."

There was a faint emphasis on "lady."

Blair tried to think up another epithet to hurl at him. What she'd really like to do would be go over and give him a good slap across his nasty, leering face. But perhaps that would be beyond the bounds of acceptability. Little Benny Lockwood was watching her and would undoubtedly go and tattle to the Reverend Thackerford, who would be shocked and hurt to learn that one of his parishioners was capable of such violent behavior. She would have still enjoyed doing it, however.

Benny tugged at her arm. When she looked down to see what he wanted, he tiptoed and whispered in her ear, "That's the one that took Ma's cotton!"

Why, she wondered, couldn't someone have shot him?

Yet—here he was. As healthy and obnoxious as ever! Not a scratch on him! While Matthew, who was worth twenty of him, had had to face the worst the 1st Mississippi could throw out against him!

"Ma'am," the Missouri guard at Captain Eaton's shoulder said, "did I hear this Yankee addressin' you?"

"Yes," Blair said.

"Where you hail from, Yank?" the guard said, looking down at Eaton, who was a good five inches below him.

Eaton continued to lean against the wall and radiate superciliousness. He didn't bother to turn toward the Missourian.

"God's country, Reb. That's Springfield, Illinois."

The Missourian chewed on a large plug of tobacco.

"You better be glad you ain't from Kansas, Yank." He turned, spat on the floor close by Eaton's feet and added, "You ever heard of jayhawkers? You better be glad you ain't one."

"Captain Eaton specializes in confiscating cotton," Blair said. By God! She wasn't going to let *that* get past the wild Missourian! "He takes it away from women whose husbands have been killed in the Confederate Army. And then he burns their houses."

"Is that a fact?" the Missourian said slowly. "Well, Yank, I tell you what. I *did* hear you addressin' this here lady. And to tell you the truth, we don't like no Yankee scum addressin' our womenfolk around here." He fingered his rifle lovingly. "Why don't you tell the lady you're just a sniveling, burr-tailed puppy, and you're mighty sorry you so forgot yourself as to speak out in her presence?"

Captain Eaton smiled again. But he did not respond to this suggestion.

Blair thought, *Make him do it!*

Obligingly the Missourian gave him a sharp nudge in the ribs with the butt of his rifle. "Speak up, possumguts. We ain't gonna wait all day for you to do it, neither."

"Go ram that up your—" Eaton began.

The rangy Missourian suddenly raised the rifle butt, and in a seemingly effortless maneuver brought it crashing against the side of Eaton's jaw. The impact must have been terrific, and Blair gasped and winced in sympathy. Eaton's head bounced back against the wall, he grasped his bleeding jaw in both hands, and his knees buckled.

"Watch your language!" the Missourian said warningly. "There's a lady here, you goddamned Yankee horse turd!"

Little Benny Lockwood jumped up and down at Blair's side in delighted excitement. "Hit him again!" he trebled.

The other Yankee prisoners had been watching the exchange in silence, but now they shouted words of disparagement at the Missourian. The big Confederate looked down at his victim in an almost affectionate manner.

"We still waitin'," he said pleasantly and spat again. "Now you gone say you sorry? Or you rather I took my knife to you?"

Little Benny Lockwood was now almost beside himself with anticipation. He was piping to the Missourian to kill the Yankee pissant.

Mercifully an officer came to the rescue. He had been outside, heard the commotion, and come in from the street. Eaton's tormentor began to argue with him. "By God!" he shouted. "I'll carve his damned guts out for him!"

With a little moan of terror Blair grabbed Benny by the arm and dragged him down the steps of the paymaster's office. If the officer wasn't able to stop it, she didn't think Benny should be there to see . . .

Fewer people were on the sidewalks, and thick clouds of smoke rose around the courthouse. The soldiers were setting fire to the bales of cotton piled in the square. A loud series of explosions suddenly boomed out from the direction of the depot, and someone shouted that they were blowing up the roundhouse and the supply train.

Oh, she thought, still holding on to Benny and running aimlessly up the sidewalk, there were tons of commissary rations stored at the depot, and by the time she got there, it would all be destroyed!

As they ran by Butler's drugstore, they passed Mr. Fred Grace again.

"Get back! Get back!" he shouted. "You can't stay here! They're getting ready to set off the ammunition in the Masonic Hall!"

Smoke and flames were now pouring from the buildings on the east side of the square, and Benny started coughing. Blair's eyes watered as they turned the corner and ran toward the parsonage. Grandpa was sitting in the buggy in front of the church. She came to a halt.

Lord! she thought. *How did he get here? What—what am I going to tell him?*

Craggy face set in lines of thundering disapprobation, Grandpa stared down at her from the jump seat of the buggy and without moving said, "Get in."

Blair let go of Benny, ran over and clambered onto the seat beside him and set her basket in her lap. "Grandpa," she said hurriedly. "I saw Pres! He's in town! He wants to leave some messages for the rest of the family. He—"

"I seen him," Grandpa said, giving the reins a flick. The mare, laying her ears back, pranced in the traces every time the boom of another explosion sounded from the square. Grandpa turned the buggy around in the middle of the street and headed it in the direction of Waverley. "Pres was out at the depot. Says they'll be pullin' out of town this afternoon."

"Did you get any commissary rations?" she asked, praying that Preston hadn't told him about Matthew.

Grandpa nodded briefly toward the back seat of the buggy. Blair turned to look behind her. The seat was piled with commissary crates.

"Oh, Grandpa! What's in them? What did you get?"

"How would I know? I ain't opened 'em yet. They was throwin' out stuff as fast as they could. It was catch as catch can."

"Grandpa, I got some money!" She tried to show him her basket of greenbacks, and to her relief he glanced at it for a moment. "But," she added in a small voice, "they say they're not any good."

Grandpa turned his eyes back to the road ahead. "Hold on to 'em."

As they passed the intersection of Salem Avenue, a group of Confederate cavalrymen came toward them. They were all on horseback and seemed to be escorting a civilian, who was on foot.

Blair recognized Jonas Kendall. He trotted ahead of the cavalrymen, who were encouraging him to run faster by periodic whacks with the flats of their sabers across his rump.

As the strange little procession drew nearer, Grandpa reined the mare to a halt.

Mr. Kendall was sweating, his protruding eyes almost popping out of his skull. His heavy jowls had turned a fiery red and bounced a little as he ran. Blair heard him panting in short little breaths, "For—God's —sake—boys! For—God's—sake—"

Mr. Kendall crossed in front of the buggy and looked up at Grandpa. Grandpa smiled.

"You damned traitor," he said. "Try buyin' your way out of this."

After the cavalrymen had passed the buggy, Grandpa flicked the reins again. Blair wondered if Preston had gone around to the Kendalls' to see Isabella. Grandpa didn't say anything else and they rode in silence until the buggy was outside of town.

"Now, Mary Blair, suppose you tell me where you've been."

Her hands tightened around the basket's handle. "At —at the Riley cottage."

"All right, Callie's already told me you come in last night to tell that Yankee our cavalry was a-waitin' for him."

"Oh, no!" she said, turning to stare at Grandpa's

stony profile. "I—I wouldn't have told him that! Grandpa, I—"

"Now you listen to me. Anna Mary's been half out of her mind. I know you ain't got any sense, but you'd better never pull a fool stunt like this again. I ain't goin' to ask you any more questions, Mary Blair, and the less you say about this the better. As for that damned Yankee you're so all-fired concerned about, you can forget him in a hurry. He ain't ever settin' foot inside my house again."

The handle of the wicker basket cut into her flesh.

The loudest noise she had ever heard rent the air around the buggy. The mare snorted and leaped forward, careening wildly down the road. Grandpa braced his boot against the dashboard while his arms strained to control the mare. The sudden forward motion almost threw Blair from the buggy, and she grabbed the brass-plated seat rail.

"Whoa, girl!" Grandpa shouted. "Whoa there, I say!"

As they went bumping and swaying over the rutted road to Waverley, Blair looked back over her shoulder. Above the trees around the courthouse square, all three floors of the Masonic Hall, packed with crates of Federal ammunition, were rising in a crescendo of smoke and exploding shells over Holly Springs.

19

After the fight at the fairgrounds, Company D had battled its way through Holly Springs to the infantry camp northeast of the square. They found it already captured. In a melee of trampled tents, startled Confederate guards, and shouting Union prisoners, the camp had been briefly retaken. Almost as soon as it was regained, they had been forced to abandon it.

Matthew drew rein beside a disheveled trooper who sat on the ground watching dazedly as the Federal cavalry thundered around him. The man had made no move to reclaim his rifle, which the Rebel guards had stacked not ten yards away. With bullets from the retreating Confederates whizzing around them, Matthew leaned over from his saddle and took a swing at the trooper with the butt of his pistol.

"You blasted coward! Get up and fight!"

The trooper made a quick duck and crabbed sideways, scuttling away from Matthew's prancing horse. "You crazy?" he cried, gaping back at him over his shoulder. Jumping to his feet, he scampered behind a handy tree trunk. "You better get your damned tail out'a here! You damned cavalry! While you got your damned horse!"

And where had Matthew been as the onslaught drew

nearer? Not at the fairgrounds with his men. That was for sure.

"By God!" he bellowed. "I ought to shoot you!"

"Cap'n!" Sergeant Evans yelled, wheeling his sweating horse and grasping his bloody thigh. "There's more comin' in from the east!"

Matthew took one final look at the chaos around him. Where were the officers? Where were the pickets? Where were the patrols that should have been out on the roads around Holly Springs last night? There had been enough soldiers in the garrison to hold the damned place! For at least as long as it would have taken for reinforcements to be rushed up from Oxford! Jesus Christ Almighty! Grant's entire army was less than thirty miles to the south!

"Head out north for the railroad!" he shouted to Sergeant Evans. "There's some infantry at the river bridge!"

Company D left the infantry camp and galloped north for the Coldwater, their escape only mildly contested by the Confederates, who had bigger fish to fry.

Upon reaching the Coldwater, they were greeted by a small detachment of Indiana infantry, which was guarding the railroad bridge. It was then that Matthew discovered Sergeant Evans had taken two bullets in the thigh.

It had happened during the fight at the fairgrounds, but Evans had refused to be dislodged from his saddle and had made the ride to the Coldwater clutching his leg in one hand and his reins and revolver in the other. The troopers eased him down off his horse and carried him over to one of the Indianans' tents, where Matthew examined his wounds. There was no surgeon present, and all they could do for Evans was apply clumsy bandages in an attempt to stop the bleeding.

Six other members of Matthew's company were missing. Two of the privates had been seen to go down on the fairgrounds. The other four could have been either killed, captured, or wounded and left behind. Nobody knew.

Later the faint boom of explosions came from the direction of Holly Springs. Artillery? they questioned each other, listening toward the south. Brought up from Oxford with some infantry regiments? Half the army had had time to come up on the Mississippi Central by now. But did Grant know about it? Telegraph wires could have been cut, somebody said. The guerrillas could have torn up the track.

Later there was an explosion of such magnitude that the force on the Coldwater ceased their speculations about any kind of battle around Holly Springs. One of the Indianans said, "That's our ammunition stores going up."

Matthew leaned dully against a pine tree and listened. The whole supply depot was going up. The charge at the fairgrounds had been doomed from the start. A senseless token of resistance that had accomplished nothing but the loss of six of his men.

Seven, if you counted Evans, who was one of the best.

Matthew knew that if he had been the sole Union cavalryman on the fairgrounds, he would have charged the Confederates by himself.

"I hope they kill you!" she had said.

His shoulder had set up a dull ache. A dozen little imps sawed away inside it with a dozen rusty little saws. But they were as nothing compared to their cohorts, who sawed away behind his eyes.

He went back into the tent to check on Sergeant Evans.

Evans wanted him to write a letter to his wife. Right now. Find a stamp and some paper and sit down and do it. Ella was a fine woman, he said, but she didn't have much of a head for business. There were certain instructions he wanted to give her about running the farm.

"Frank," Matthew said hoarsely, "we've got a new

hospital out at the Rebel armory. It's not far from here. In a little while, I'll take you to it."

Around midnight he borrowed a blanket from one of the Indiana troopers, rolled up in it, and lay down on the bare ground of the tent. His shoulder was throbbing all the way down into his arm, a whole panel of judges sat in accusation inside his skull, and his legs were so rigid with exhaustion that his knees kept jerking and waking him up.

Matthew's slumber was fitful for the rest of the night. Once he sat up straight, threw off the blanket, and grabbed for his revolver, lying in its holster close by his side.

"Take it easy, Captain," one of the Indiana privates said. The man had been standing picket, and had just been relieved. Stumbling around Matthew in the darkness, he searched for another blanket. "Who's Blair?" he said.

Matthew looked at him blankly.

The private found the blanket, wrapped up in it, and eased down beside him. "That's what you just said, sir. You said—"

"Nobody," Matthew said, lying down and turning over.

"Well, sir, I just—"

"Shut up," Matthew said.

He lay there for a long time before he slept again. What was eating at him? Hurt pride? The knowledge that he had made a complete fool of himself?

Opening his eyes, he stared at the top of the tent. His mouth was so dry it had a foul, acrid taste. He tried to swallow. Crazy. That was what he had been. Stark, raving mad. Lovingly he had lifted out his heart and handed it over; and now there were sharp little teeth marks all over the thing. She was a damned little cannibal, that's what she was. Probably had a whole cache of hidden necklaces, made out of Union soldiers' knuckle bones. Blasted savages, Matthew thought.

Goddamned guerrillas. Mutilating away. What was

he doing here? Let them all go to perdition and take their damned Confederacy along with them!

Slave-owning sons of bitches, with their whips and their branding irons.

He ground his teeth, turned over, and felt his shoulder give a violent twinge of protest. Dammit to hell! He couldn't keep on like this!

Early the next morning, the cavalry scouts reported that the road to the south was clear.

Now Matthew could get Sergeant Evans to a surgeon. Frank's leg, swollen and inflamed beneath the bandages, looked god-awful. He turned green when they lifted him onto a makeshift litter. There was no way he could ride his horse, and he had to be put in a wagon for the trip to the armory.

The journey was torture every inch of the way. Soon Evans was babbling, completely out of his head. Every time the wagon hit a bump in the road—and there were plenty of them, and plenty of ruts—he screamed. The sounds went through Matthew's skull like ten-inch spikes. Evans thought he was back home in Illinois, with Ella. As nearly as Matthew could ascertain, the whole family was in the wagon, coming home from church. The sergeant seemed to have forgotten about the new baby.

When Company D got to the Rebel armory, they found a smoking pile of bricks.

A tight-lipped Dr. Wirtz picked his way through the rubble to meet them.

"Yesterday," he said to Matthew, "this was a two-thousand-bed hospital. Just made ready to receive the sick." Across the surgeon's thin, aristocratic face a sneer trembled and jumped. "Van Dorn's adjutant promised that the hospital would be spared. He gave me his word as an officer and a gentleman. Then they came back and burned it."

Wirtz examined Evans and did what he could. Which wasn't much. All his chloroform, morphine, opium, bandages, bedding, and splints had also gone up in smoke. "I protested," he said coldly. "But to no avail. You'll have to take this man on to the general hospital in town."

"You think it's still standing?" Matthew asked bitterly.

"An attempt was made to destroy it. Although it contained five hundred patients. However, I understand it survived."

After another endless, jolting mile, they were in Holly Springs. The entire east side of the courthouse square was a smoldering ruin, the buildings completely blown up. On the north side of the square only the three-story Magnolia Hotel, a monument to private enterprise, remained. The cupolated courthouse still stood, but the square was littered with debris. Blackened remains of cotton bales smoked pungently about the grounds. Down the side streets off from the square, bits and pieces of exploded ammunition shells, splintered commissary crates, and unidentifiable junk lay as if scattered by Satan and all the demons of hell.

The streets were thronged with paroled Union prisoners from the garrison force, officers' wives loaded down with baggage and hurrying to the depot for the first train north, popeyed Negroes, and drunken bums.

It was difficult for Matthew to escort the wagon bearing Sergeant Evans through the mob. Soldiers tooting on large bronze pipes were prancing through the square. On the residential streets more soldiers were busily foraging in Rebel backyards and kitchens.

Taking a detour to avoid the conglomeration in front of the Magnolia Hotel, Company D passed under the windows of a two-story white clapboard house. On the flour-powdered sidewalk in front a large barrel of molasses had been turned over and left on its side. The sticky residue from the bottom of the barrel, draining slowly out and mixing with the flour, had created a sweet, brownish glue. Some of the soldiers had stepped in it, and Matthew could see footprints going up the steps of the house.

A woman leaned out of one of the second-story windows and started screaming at him. "Are you an officer? For the love of God, f-f-find an officer! They're all over my house!"

Evans stopped babbling for a minute on the bed of the wagon. "Ella?" he said.

The woman leaned farther out the window, gripping the sill. "I've got the children up here! We've locked ourselves in! They keep—they keep trying the door! For the love of God! Find an—"

"I'm taking this man to a surgeon," Matthew said.

Company D rode on for the hospital, still guiding the wagon. Some of the troopers looked back over their shoulders toward the white clapboard house.

After the orderlies got Evans on a stretcher, Matthew told one of the corporals to do something with the horses and camp where he could. Then he followed the stretcher inside.

They didn't know where they were going to find a place to put him, the orderlies said.

"You'll find a place," Matthew said. "If I have to throw somebody out of a bed."

The orderlies located a bed and put Evans on it, and Matthew went through the wards searching for a surgeon. After a while he found one of them. The surgeon's diagnosis of Evans's condition was not optimistic. He spoke of shattered bones, infection, probing, and the possible necessity for radical surgery.

"Doctor," Matthew said, "you make damned sure you can't save that leg before you start carving on it."

"Sir," the surgeon said, "you are obviously under a strain. How long since you slept?"

"Did you give him any morphine?"

The surgeon smiled in resignation. "Opium."

Later Matthew went back and sat beside Evans's bed. Eyes sunken, the sergeant was breathing through his open mouth. The so-called surgeon had cleaned his wounds and dug the ball fragments out. The bandaged leg lay on a bare mattress stained with the dried secretions of former patients. The whole hospital stank.

Matthew thought of the two Mrs. Tylers, scrupulously changing his dressings and bathing his wound.

He stared down at Evans's leg. It swam before him in a blur.

All of Matthew's muscles were jumping now, the inside of his head one huge, congealed ache. The imps sawed away with their shrieking little saws.

Outside, he could hear drunken yells and the shattering of glass.

Blair couldn't have meant that. There had to be some mistake. He had to straighten it out. . . .

The troopers were running through the streets out there like maniacs, and not a voice was being raised to stop them. The officers didn't care; Matthew himself didn't care. Let them take all the flour, all the barrels of molasses, let them burn the rest of the Secesh hole down to the ground—but God Almighty! He couldn't let anything happen to her!

Matthew stood up.

On the bed Evans groaned and tossed feebly about under the effects of the opium.

That's right, he thought. *Go off and leave him again. Let him die in his sleep. That damned sawbones will hack him to pieces as soon as you step out the door. . . .*

You're a glutton for punishment, aren't you, Harwell? You never get enough.

God, but he'd tried! He'd wanted to send Blair to Springfield—but she wouldn't go!

She'd go this time if he had to handcuff her and drag her to the depot and throw her on the train. But what if he was already too late? Matthew imagined floury footprints going up the Waverley front steps.

He headed for the street.

As he neared the hospital door, a muffled croak caused him to halt.

"Well," it said. "I see—you survived."

He looked down at the man sitting on the edge of the bed nearest the door. For a minute, he didn't recognize him.

"Good Lord, Steve!" he said in a low voice. "What happened to you?"

The right side of Stephen Eaton's face had swelled up like a rotten tomato. A jagged line of stitches swerved across his jaw. "The Twentieth Illinois—came in this morning," he said slowly. "Up from Waterford. On the train. Their damned—" He paused and raised his hand tentatively to his jaw. "Their damned colonel stopped—the train. About seven miles down the track."

"Stopped the train? Why?" Matthew couldn't keep from staring at Eaton's jaw. It didn't look like a gunshot wound.

"Who the hell—who the hell knows? Stopped the train. Took all the troops off. Marched—marched 'em the rest of the way. Slowest advance in the annals of warfare."

"Steve, what happened to your face?"

"Oh. This?" Eaton shifted his feet gingerly about on the hospital floor. "Got it—at the paymaster's office."

He realized Steve was still wearing his dress uniform. The same one he'd worn to the party Friday night.

"See those stitches? Damn near ruined my—face."

Jesus! Matthew thought. It damned near did! Eaton's suave countenance might be permanently marred. "You were in a fight? At the paymaster's office?"

"Hell!" Eaton said. "I'd already—surrendered!"

"Well, then, what in the deuce—"

"I've got your little lady friend. To thank. For this."

"Who?" Matthew said.

"Your little Miss Tyler! That's the—hell who!"

"What are you talking about?"

"Turned—that damned buffalo loose! On me!"

"Steve, you—"

"She was in the paymaster's office. Robbing us—blind. I'll bet she picked up—ten thousand dollars! In there!"

"Steve—"

"Seems she didn't like something—I said."

"What the hell did you say?"

"I said—'Hello. Miss Tyler.' "

"You goddamned liar—"

"What's the matter with you? Ask anybody. That's—what I said!"

Eaton fingered his stitches and looked at Matthew in aggrieved surprise. The patients on the surrounding beds were beginning to look at him, too.

"Make sense, dammit!" Matthew said through gritted teeth. "She didn't do that to your blasted face!"

"The guard! The damned—Johnny guarding me! You damned crazy fool! Matt, what's the matter—with you?"

"What'd he do? Shoot you in the jaw?"

"No! Hit me! Hit me, dammit! With his—rifle butt! I said 'Hello—Miss Tyler.' And they don't like no Yankee scum addressin' their womenfolk—around here!"

"Did she tell him to? Is that what you're—"

"She told me to—shut up. Called me an—animal. Matt, what in the hell are you—so excited about? Are you—"

Eaton paused and stared up at him in dawning amazement.

"God—Almighty! Are you serious about that—little—"

"Shut up!" Matthew said.

"Well, I wish," a nasal voice remarked querulously from the adjoining bed, "that you would stop abusing that man. Can't you see he's wounded?"

"You," Eaton said, "are ten times—a fool! Jesus Christ! She had her—lover—in there!"

Matthew feared he was going to be sick to his stomach. He knew he should leave. Immediately. Not wait another minute. But a kind of horrified fascination was gluing him to the floor. It was like deliberately standing under the guillotine, waiting for the ax to fall. And he knew Eaton was going to let him have it. Probably in the very next breath.

"Damned Texan!" Eaton said, letting him have it. "Lighting his cigar with—greenbacks from the paymaster's office! Showed her off to the whole—damned troop! Said, 'This is my girl! Ain't she—pretty!' Laughing about how they—scared off our cavalry!"

"Is that right?" Matthew said, mildly surprised to discover that he was still breathing. To realize that his head was still attached to his neck. The way his head was pounding, it would have been a relief to get rid of it. Let it roll across the hospital floor under the bed of that old carper on Eaton's left. Give the surgeons a thrill.

Eaton wasn't through yet.

"So then she—gave them all a—congratulatory kiss!"

Still warm from my arms, Matthew thought.

Soft and blond and pink and white. Delectably curved and delicately scented and all atremble. Think about it hard. Remember every tingle. Because after this, you're not ever going to think about it again—

"Ye gods!" Eaton said. "And you *lived* in that—nest of rattlesnakes out there! You better be glad—you didn't get stabbed in—your sleep!"

"I got shot," Matthew said.

He suddenly remembered that his baggage was still out there.

Forget it. Forget that, too. Forget everything. Die, if he could.

"Well," Eaton said. "I'm getting out of—this damned hole. Thank God the Magnolia Hotel didn't get—blown up."

Later that afternoon, acting on some ingrained devotion to duty—perhaps he ought to report in at headquarters—Matthew found himself in the smoke-blackened building that had served as command post for the garrison.

The rooms were thick with cigar smoke and officers, and rumors were shooting through the air like corn on a popper. Matthew sat down and stared dully in front of him. An excited voice close by his chair said that warning of Van Dorn's attack had come over the wire from Oxford on the afternoon of the nineteenth.

"From who?"

"From Colonel Dickey!"

Dickey's cavalry force had passed across Van Dorn's rear at Pontotoc a little before sunset on the eighteenth. Every darky in the neighborhood had reported to the colonel that thousands of Rebels had been passing through the town all day, going northwest. When Dickey reached Oxford and reported to the commanding general, Grant had immediately ascertained Van Dorn's objective and gone down to the telegraph office in person. He had fired off wire after wire to Colonel Murphy in Holly Springs.

Here the stories became confused.

Murphy had not received the dispatches in time. Murphy had received the dispatches and wired back that he was ordering out his handful of cavalry. Major Mudd, in command of the cavalry, had said he knew nothing of the coming attack until after the infantry camp was overrun. Major Mudd said he had had patrols out on every road around Holly Springs until well past midnight. No, the truth of the matter was that Major Mudd and Colonel Murphy had both been at some party all night. They were both drunk.

That sounds about right, Matthew thought.

An acquaintance in the 6th Illinois Cavalry passed his chair. He stopped to say that Colonel Grierson was pacing up and down the telegraph office in a lather of impatience, trying to get the go-ahead to move out in pursuit of Van Dorn. The 6th was mounted and ready to go. Adjutants were firing off wires to Oxford. More

Union cavalry was moving in from the Tallahatchie to join in the chase. Infantry and artillery were being rushed up on the Mississippi Central.

Matthew nodded and listened. As he recalled, Colonel Murphy had been the one to pull out of Iuka last September and abandon his supplies to the Rebel general Price. There had been some talk of a court-martial at the time. He wondered how Murphy had managed to get the assignment in Holly Springs.

The cigar smoke was making his eyes burn, so he went back to the hospital to sit with Evans. When he reached the sergeant's bedside, one of the company privates—Joe Phipps—was there. Phipps, a buoyant, downy-cheeked youngster of eighteen, said that Old Sarge had been resting fairly well. They kept watch together until it was almost dark. Then one of the surgeons came through the wards and said all visitors had to clear out for the night.

As Matthew and Private Phipps emerged from the hospital, a young Negro accosted them. He had been crouching on the sidewalk close by the side of the building.

"Cap'n Harwell?" he said, jumping up almost in Matthew's face. "Cap'n Harwell? Here I is!"

What in the devil—?

Through the buzzing in his head he attempted to identify this strange apparition. He saw a large, rawboned, mahogany-colored figure, clad in linsey pantaloons, gunboat brogans, and a frayed jacket. The boy's features were working with excitement and he caught the faint odor of whiskey.

"I'se ready to go with you!" he cried. "Like you told Pa!" Then, at the blank look on Matthew's face, a faint shadow of doubt crept into his voice. "You ain't changed yo' mind, is you?"

"Ahhh—" Matthew breathed in belated recognition. "Little Austin!"

Smiling, the boy nodded in agreement. "Yessuh.

Thass me! I been lookin' for you most all day, Cap'n!
When you reckon we gone leave?''

"Wait for me a minute, Joe," Matthew said to Private Phipps. He drew Little Austin aside and stepped back a few paces. "Look. You're going to have to stick around for a while, because I'm not sure when—well, just stick around. Then—"

"Pa say you say they might take me for a soldier! I say, freedom, I sees you comin'! You on yo' way!"

In spite of himself, Matthew smiled. "Glad to see it, are you?"

"Jesus, Cap'n! Wouldn't *you* be?"

In Tennessee, there had been a song—a chant—the contrabands sang as they worked on the fortifications.

No more driver's lash for me . . . no more . . . no
* more.*
No more pint of salt for me . . . many thousand
* gone.*
No more hundred lash for me . . . no more . . . no
* more.*

NO MORE, BY GOD! Matthew thought.

"You meet me back here at the hospital tomorrow," he said to Little Austin. "Can you find a place to sleep? Stay in town. Don't go back out there. Have you had anything to eat?"

"Yessuh, I find a place all right! I knows how to forage, too! Cap'n, when you gonna catch ole Van Dorn? You catch 'im, you make 'im holler! You—"

"I'll be coming back to the hospital tomorrow. One of my men's in there. You stick around."

And then he heard himself saying, "How's—how's everybody out at Waverley? Is Mrs. Tyler all right?"

"Yessuh, sho' is." Little Austin nodded. Then he smiled contemptuously. "Pa ain't gonna let nothin' happen to his white folks."

"You're—sure?" Matthew said, and despised himself

for protesting that it was Anna Mary's safety and not Blair's he was concerned about.

"Yessuh, yessuh," Little Austin said impatiently. "They just like they always been."

"Tomorrow morning," he said. "Right here. I'm not going to forget about you."

"I be waitin'," Little Austin called out happily as Matthew and Private Phipps continued down the street.

Phipps said that Company D had found accommodations for the night not far from the square.

As they approached the building, Matthew realized it was a church. As the captain could see, Phipps said as they climbed the curving stairway leading to the entrance, the auditorium in this building was on the second floor. The stairs had presented difficulties when they'd attempted to lead the horses up them. So— they'd been forced to quarter the poor creatures in the basement.

"Don't worry about it, Joe," Matthew said.

When they entered the dark-paneled sanctuary, he noted that of the ten stained-glass windows lining the sides of the room, four had already been shattered. But still, it would be warmer here than outside. He realized he was hungry. That might be one reason for the buzzing in his head.

"Did you draw any rations?" he asked.

"Well now, Captain," Phipps said with a jocular yet slightly uneasy glance in his direction, "we did find a few potatoes. And some milk. And a chicken or two."

Obviously Phipps expected his stern commander to dock him fifty cents for the chickens when the next payday rolled around.

"The chickens attacked us," he added. "And we were forced to defend ourselves."

"I hope you showed them no quarter," Matthew grunted.

The troopers sat around in the pews eating and the tantalizing aroma of roast fowl drifted about the church. Matthew sat down and ate too, because he was hungry. He knew that in a little while he was going to sleep, because he was so sodden with exhaustion he could do nothing else.

While they were eating, an excited, rosy-cheeked old Rebel came into the sanctuary, advanced upon him, and expressed a desire for them to leave.

Chewing on a chicken leg, Matthew heard him out in silence.

From the general tenor of his remarks, this was not the first time the minister had presented the request. But now—he had spied a captain's shoulder straps among the ranks. They all wanted an officer, Matthew thought wearily. They just never learned to leave him alone.

"This is the Lord's house," old rosy-cheeks said sanctimoniously.

Matthew pointed with his chicken leg toward the slave gallery at the back of the church. "What do you call that, Parson?"

The plump face stared back at him with innocent incomprehension.

"Is that what you see when you stand behind that pulpit and preach?"

The Reverend Thackerford—for he had so introduced himself—looked at the slave gallery and turned back to look at Matthew. "Our people sit there."

Our people—our people. They even lied to themselves. Always glossing it over, covering it up.

"You mean your slaves, don't you?" Matthew said.

The whole damned South was rotten. They were tottering on the crust of a volcano, perched over a hole in a privy. *Knock the props out,* he thought. *Bring it down with a crash. Rub their noses in it.*

"This isn't the Lord's house," he said, focusing his bloodshot eyes with difficulty on the cherubic face in front of him. "It's a signed, sealed, and certified outpost of Beelzebub. Where do you keep your whips and your branding irons?"

The minister sighed.

"My son, I bear you no personal ill will. You are all welcome—*welcome* in this church. But you must enter in the proper spirit! A spirit of reverence—"

"Reverence for what?" Matthew said.

"Your holy Father, my dear boy! Who is Lord of us all! Why, your wounded were brought here yesterday! We didn't refuse them! We are all God's children! We cared for them all—"

"Now, Reverend," he said slowly. "You get out of here. And don't bother my men again. We're tired and we're going to get some sleep."

Company D spent the night stretched out on the pews. Before he drifted into oblivion, Matthew's gaze rested on the soaring bronze pipes of the organ behind the pulpit. They reminded him of something, and in the few minutes before he went to sleep, he figured out what it was.

They were the same kind of pipes the soldiers had been tooting on as they pranced through the square.

Before daylight the next morning—December 22—Colonel Grierson moved out of Holly Springs at the head of eighteen hundred Union cavalrymen. However, a precious twenty-four hours had been lost.

Van Dorn had already gone past La Grange, cut the Memphis & Charleston a few miles to the west, and was heading east toward the Jackson & Mississippi at Bolivar, Tennessee.

On December 23, Evans's leg was amputated, and on December 24, the sergeant died.

Matthew spent Christmas day at Ripley, where in the early winter twilight there was another cavalry clash as Van Dorn passed through the town heading south for Grenada.

20

Early in the afternoon of December twenty-third, the third day after Van Dorn's raid, the first group of Yankees came into Waverley.

Blair was in the dining room putting the dinner dishes back into the sideboard when she heard their voices in the yard. They didn't knock or demand to be admitted. They just opened the front door and came pouring into the hall.

Still holding the plates in her hand, she straightened up and saw the double doors from the parlor swing open and five Yankees come through them into the dining room. They brushed past her to grab the Sheffield candlesticks Olivia had decorated with holly sprigs for Christmas. As she stood and watched, they started scooping silverware from the sideboard drawers.

From the hallway, she could hear feet pounding up the stairs, and from the second floor, startled screams from Olivia and Aunt Sophie. "Here we come!" a man's voice shouted. "Come and see the Yankees and tell us how you like us!"

As Blair ran from the dining room into the hall, the door from the back veranda opened and Grandpa strode in. He went to the foot of the stairs, grabbed one Yankee by his uniform collar, and with a mighty heave sent him crashing against the wall. Grandpa dragged him to his feet and began to choke him.

Blair pressed her hands to her face. Other Yankees ran out of the office, yelling, "By God! He's trying to kill him!"

As the blue uniforms surged around Grandpa, she could see the back of his neck, his shoulders, and the top of his head. There was a brief, urgent struggling back and forth of bodies, and then the dull, sickening thud of a revolver butt against Grandpa's skull. He disappeared.

Somehow she pushed through the soldiers crowding over him. "Hang the damned Secesh," one of them said. She got down on her hands and knees and bent over him. A thin trickle of blood crept down from the white hair above his temple. His eyes were closed and his face had a strange ashen cast.

Blair couldn't speak. She could only crouch there, shivering, trying to push Grandpa's hair back and see where the blood was coming from. The Yankees standing over them were talking. "We ain't found any money yet," one of them said.

"Yeah, and now you've flattened the old boy out, he ain't going to tell you nothing. That was pretty damned smart."

"There's a nigger outside. He'll know."

"Well, if we leave now, somebody else'll come through and get it. Let him lie for a while. He'll keep."

As they walked away, Blair continued to huddle on the floor beside Grandpa. Occasionally Yankees going back and forth through the hall would give him a kick as they passed. She was afraid to leave him and go look for the rest of the family. Finally she stood up, caught him under the armpits, and tried to drag him into the parlor. For a few minutes she thought she wouldn't be able to move him. He was so heavy and his head sagged alarmingly when she tried to raise him by his arms.

Easing him down, she managed to slide him along

the floor without lifting him. None of the Yankees offered to help her, and as she pulled and tugged Grandpa into the parlor, she thought this must be what hell was like. She maneuvered him onto the rug in front of the sofa, sat down on the floor beside him, and cradled his head in her lap.

A smothering panic closed around her. Where was Matthew? Why didn't he come?

A Yankee entered the parlor, carrying one of the Tylers' pillowcases, bulging with loot. When he saw Blair sitting on the floor he stopped, stared at her, and came over and sat down on the horsehair sofa. Opening the pillowcase, he pulled out one of her stockings.

"What's this?" he said, dangling it in front of her face.

Blair said nothing, but her fingers found the edge of Grandpa's coat sleeve and tightened around it. She could smell the Yankee without turning around. A rank, heavy odor of stale sweat and whiskey steamed behind her from the sofa.

"Show me how you put these on, sweetie."

Where was her mother? Blair had a sudden, terrible desire to push Grandpa's head out of her lap, jump up, and run screaming for the trees of White Oak swamp.

Smiling, the Yankee leaned over and looked into her face. She drew back. His breath was fetid and some of his teeth had turned black with decay.

"You're a pretty one, ain't you?" Putting her stocking back into the pillowcase, he pulled out a pair of lace-edged white dimity pantalets. "Where do you wear these?" he said, bending forward so that he could watch her expression. "A fellow could get a hard-on just thinking about it." He laughed. "I'll bet the sight of your little rump in them drawers could put a whole regiment at fixed bayonets."

Blair looked down at Grandpa. He was still breathing, but maybe they had done something to his brain when they hit him. Grandpa had been unconscious for too long. Maybe they had broken his skull.

Wake up, she thought desperately.

"Leave me alone," she said softly to the creature behind her on the sofa, wondering as she said it if he was going to drag her into the middle of the parlor floor and rape her. Right in front of all the others. While that stinking breath blew into her face.

"You damned Rebs getting a little sorry now you started this war? Think now you ain't going to be quite so proud?"

She wanted to say, "Get out of my house." If he grabbed her she didn't think she could stand it. Already she was feeling dizzy. She held her breath for a moment to get relief from the smell.

The Yankee suddenly swore and got up from the sofa. Blair didn't watch him because she didn't want to know what he was doing. But when she heard him saying, "Well, now, that's a right fine piano," she had to look up.

As soon as he saw that it was important to her—that she wanted it—he put down his pillowcase and grinned.

"Too damned fine for a Rebel," he said.

He picked up his rifle, turned the butt down, and smashed it against the piano keys. There was an insane, crippled arpeggio of chords and shattering ivory, and he stabbed up and down the keyboard, bringing the rifle butt down with all his strength. When he had finished, the piano was a ruin, a wreck, a broken snarl of ivory and rosewood. Blair's music had been taken away from her, too.

She continued to sit on the floor. In the inner recesses of her memory Miss Lucy Blaylock was screeching "Kill them! Kill them!"

Her mother came through the parlor door. Anna Mary stopped and looked at the piano, and the Yankee picked up his pillowcase and brushed past her. Then Anna Mary saw Blair and Grandpa in front of the sofa and came forward swiftly. She knelt down and put her hand on Grandpa's forehead.

"He tried to kill one," Blair said. "And they hit him with a pistol."

"We must get Papa Tyler to a doctor—"

"Mama," Blair whispered. "Your ring . . ." Her mother's heavy gold wedding band was gone.

Anna Mary's face twisted and tears rose in her eyes. "I didn't want to give it to them. They forced it off—"

From the backyard Telithia's shrill screams pierced the parlor. Anna Mary got to her feet, said, "We have to find someone to help us!" and went hurrying toward the back. After she had gone, Blair saw more Yankees coming down the stairs. One had a drift of rose chiffon against his uniform. Her white moiré ball gown, hanging over his arm—

Anna Mary came back into the parlor with her arm around Telithia. A soldier was following behind them, and Anna Mary gave Telithia a shake and said, "You must be quiet!"

Telithia broke away, sinking down onto the parlor floor close by the wall. Putting her face in her hands, she leaned over until her red bandanna almost touched the rug. Then she straightened up, leaned down again, and began to wail.

Anna Mary and the Yankee soldier came over to the sofa and the Yankee looked at Grandpa. "I guess we can take him into town in one of the forage wagons," he said.

"There's a mattress in the office," Anna Mary said, speaking in a loud voice in order to be heard above the sound of Telithia's wails. "Please help us carry it to the wagon. My father-in-law may have a concussion. If he's jolted about too much, it may be fatal."

"All right," the soldier said. He was young and clean-shaven and Blair hadn't noticed him running through the house before. "He's under arrest, you understand," he added. "But I'll try to have a surgeon see him after we get into town."

Eventually two privates went through the hall carrying the mattress from Matthew's bed. In a little while they came into the parlor and, with Blair and Anna Mary helping, lifted Grandpa and carried him out to an army wagon. In the barn lot, Union soldiers were untethering the milk cows.

Anna Mary said, "They've taken one of my servants into the swamp. His wife is hysterical. Can't you do something? There was something about money—"

"Ma'am," the Yankee said, "I'm just in charge of the foraging detail. You've got a rough bunch there in your house. I'm just a corporal."

"Please. Please make them—"

"Ma'am, I got no *control* over 'em. You people just all stay together. They aren't going to hurt you."

He climbed into the wagon, and the foraging detail drove away, with Grandpa in the back on the mattress, surrounded by sacks of meal, hams, pots and pans, and chicken carcasses.

"Mama?" Blair said to Anna Mary. "What are they going to do to Austin?"

Anna Mary's face was white. "They think we have money hidden somewhere. They're trying to—to make Austin tell them where it is."

As soon as they'd returned from Holly Springs on the day of the raid, Grandpa had hidden the greenbacks, as well as the commissary crates. He hadn't told anyone where he'd put them.

"Austin doesn't *know* where the money is," Blair whispered.

"Little Austin has run away again," Anna Mary said. "Telithia said he left Sunday morning. He told her he was going to look for Captain Harwell."

Blair felt a sinking sensation in the pit of her stomach. Her mother was watching the forage wagon creak away between the line of crape myrtles. "But why? Why would Little Austin want to find Matthew?"

"Telithia said he offered to take him with him when his company pulled out. We've got to get back inside, Blair. Olivia and Callie are still upstairs."

Unable to decipher anything anymore, Blair followed her mother into the house. Why would Matthew want to take Little Austin away from them? It was all she could do to force herself to go back into the house. It was like walking into purgatory, where a thousand demons were waiting for her—and Grandpa had gone.

To her surprise, the Yankees were leaving. They had stolen all they could carry. Descending without warning, they had passed through Waverley like a tornado and now were leaving in the same way.

When the last of them had gone, Blair closed the front door. For a moment she turned and leaned against it.

Austin was still in the swamp.

Callie appeared at the head of the stairs and stood looking down at her. "I saved a lot of your dresses."

Mindlessly Blair climbed the stairs. She went into her own bedroom first. For a confused second she thought it had been snowing. Drifts of a white, fluffy substance lay all over the room.

"They slit the mattresses open," Callie explained.

Feathers. Feathers all over the place—

"They took your dresses out of the chifforobe," Callie said. "But I ran and got most of them. I wadded them up and sat on them. I think—I think they tore some."

Blair walked over to a pile of her dresses on the floor by the table where Callie had been sitting on them. She had managed to save quite a few. "Why did they slit the mattresses open?"

"Lookin' for money, they said."

Large, jagged pieces of paper covered with writing were scattered on the floor in front of the table. Blair suddenly bent down. "Callie," she whispered. "Your—"

"Nooo!" Callie wailed, rushing over, falling on her knees, and picking them up. "Don't read it! It's my j-j-journal! I don't want you to read it!"

Blair let the pieces of paper in her hand flutter to the floor. "They tore it up, didn't they?"

Callie nodded, her bright red pigtails lowered over the scraps of her journal as she worked to get them all before somebody could read them.

"You couldn't get it away from them, could you?" Blair said in a tight, cracked voice. "You were busy saving my dresses."

As soon as they'd seen Callie was proud of her journal—that she wanted it—they'd ripped it to shreds. Had they stopped to read it first? And laugh at it?

"Thank you for saving my dresses," Blair whispered. "I can't think—I can't think of anything I'd rather save."

The Tylers spent the rest of the afternoon going through the house gathering up anything that was left. They brought most of it into the parlor.

Of all the mattresses in the house, only Olivia's had escaped the knives. That was because Aunt Sophie was prostrate on it, Olivia said. At first, the Yankees refused to believe Aunt Sophie had really swooned. They threatened to roll her off. The old woman was faking, they said. It was a favorite Secesh trick. When the Southerners had their money sewn into a mattress, they always put an old woman or a bunch of brats on it and said they were sick.

Blair and Olivia struggled with the mattress and brought it down to the parlor. Everyone was going to spend the night in there. Robbie trotted at their heels hiccuping softly, too breathless to cry. The last soldiers had terrified him. He kept asking when Mr. Weems was coming back.

His mother told him Mr. Weems had gone home to see his own little boys. Olivia was sure he had been captured in Van Dorn's raid with the rest of the infantry. What the Confederates had done with their prisoners, she didn't know.

Blair brought her dresses down to the parlor. She found her shawl beneath the bed, buried in feathers. All her bonnets were gone. A blue ribbon had fallen off one of them and been left on the stairs. She picked it up and brought it into the parlor, too.

When she went into the office she found books scattered over the floor. They had thrown them down from the shelves, still searching for money, she supposed. No one had tried to clean anything up. It would take a week to do the office alone.

Matthew's cap, with its crossed sabers of tarnished brass, sat on the rolltop desk; his uniform coat hung on a hook on the back of the door.

She leaned her forehead against the sleeve. The heavy blue material was the same kind that had been on the soldier carrying her ball-gown down the stairs. She thought of that, but somehow, it didn't matter. This coat was Matthew, and as she pressed her face against it, tears stung her eyes.

Last Monday morning, in the predawn hours, they had been awakened by the muffled pounding of horses galloping past the house. Although it had been too dark to see much when she and Callie jumped out of bed and stood shivering at the bedroom window, they had known the soldiers riding past must be Federal cavalry, in pursuit of Van Dorn.

If the Yankees caught Van Dorn, there would be another battle. Even now, they might be fighting one. If Matthew were killed, who would think to let her know about it? They might never tell her. She might go on forever, waiting for him, praying that he'd come back. And all the time, he would be dead.

I can't stand this, she thought. *They'll never stop fighting. There'll be another battle and another and another . . .*

When she went back into the parlor it was almost dark. Aunt Sophie lay on the sofa with her stockinged feet in Anna Mary's lap. She was no longer in a swoon but had been unable to find her Bible in the wreckage of her room.

This isn't real, Blair thought. *None of it is happening.* As the night wore on, she realized they had forgotten to bring in extra wood for the fire. The parlor was getting colder and colder, and although all of them were completely dressed, nobody said anything about going outside to the woodshed. Blair knew that she would rather be shot than do it, and wondered why they all seemed to think they were any safer inside the house.

A muffled bumping suddenly intruded from the hallway. To the women huddled in the parlor, it sounded as if something was being dragged across the floor.

Everyone sat perfectly still and listened. Closing her eyes, Aunt Sophie pulled the edge of her quilt over her face. In the hall someone was breathing; the sounds were heavy and labored and, every so often, interspaced with a gargling, straining noise.

Telithia jumped up from her chair and opened the door.

Now, Blair thought, *Telithia will run screaming for the swamp. Why are we all sitting here and not moving? Whatever's out there isn't human. Nothing human would be making sounds like that—*

"Sweet Jesus," Telithia whispered. "Oh, my Lawd!"

Anna Mary moved Aunt Sophie's feet from her lap, hurried to the door, and knelt beside Telithia.

Austin was in the hall, on the floor. He had crawled all the way down the hall from the back veranda door. Blood ran from his nose in thick, ropy rivulets, and his mouth was hanging open. Blair could see his tongue. As Austin looked up at Telithia, more blood swam in his eyes.

Somehow they half lifted and half dragged him into the parlor and laid him on the mattress. He wasn't as heavy as Grandpa had been, and there were more of them to drag him.

"They haven't killed him," Anna Mary said to Telithia. "You see that, don't you? You see that he's alive?"

"Why they wants to treat him this way?" Telithia said.

Finally a thin, cold daylight crept through the parlor windows and the terrible night was over.

Blair, Olivia, and Anna Mary went together to the woodshed, gathering several loads of wood for the parlor fire. When they got back in the house, Austin was able to whisper.

The Yankees had taken him into the swamp and hung him several times. They would raise him just high enough beneath the tree limb so that his toes were unable to touch the ground. Then they would let him down and demand that he tell them where the money was hidden. But Austin couldn't tell them, so they would lift him up again. After a while he blacked out. When he came to, the Yankees had gone.

Now Anna Mary insisted on setting out on foot for the Cooper plantation. Although the foraging party had taken the mare, she was determined to get into Holly Springs somehow. Austin needed a doctor, and she feared that the young Yankee had not taken the surgeon to Grandpa. Without proper care both men might die. If she went to the Coopers', perhaps they would have a way of getting into town.

Blair and Callie refused to let her go alone. As they set out down the driveway with their mother, teeth chattering in the morning air, Blair realized that it was Christmas Eve. When they reached the road, clouds of smoke were rising in the distance above the pecan grove. The Cooper house sat on a hill, and on clear days the Tylers could see the smoke from its chimneys. But this smoke was not coming from the chimneys. There was too much of it; it was too black and thick.

"What's that?" Callie said.

For a moment they stood and watched it.

"Get back inside!" Anna Mary said in an urgent, broken whisper. "Hurry!"

As Blair ran beside her mother, the driveway seemed to stretch forever between the line of crape myrtles, and she thought that she had never seen her mother run before. Callie was looking back toward the smoke as she ran. "They're comin' back!" she wailed. "Mama! Ma—ma! They're comin'—"

"Run!" Anna Mary said, gasping.

After the Yankees had finished burning the Cooper house, they would burn Waverley. *And then*, Blair thought, *we will have to go into the swamp. Julie Ann must be in the swamp right now.* She wondered what they had done to Julie Ann.

At the front steps Anna Mary stopped. "The well!" she said. "We must draw some more water. Find a— find a pan or some buckets. Anything! Hurry, girls!"

By the time they found two buckets in the kitchen, filled them with water from the well, and carried them into the parlor, the second group of Yankees came up the driveway.

Anna Mary closed the parlor door and pushed a chair against it. The Tylers sat and waited.

Like the repetition of a nightmare they could hear feet running through the hallway and pounding up the stairs. There were shouts and curses and then the crash of breaking glass from the dining room. The doorknob turned and a Yankee pushed aside the chair and looked in at them.

"Please don't come in here," Anna Mary said.

The Yankee glanced at Austin lying on the mattress and closed the door. Olivia said, "Mama Tyler? Do you smell smoke?"

Then, of course, it was no longer possible to stay in the parlor. Callie remembered to grab one of the buckets of water, and upon reaching the second floor they discovered it was Aunt Sophie's room that had been set on fire. The soldiers had piled the contents of her chifforobe into the middle of the bed and thrown lighted matches on it. Aunt Sophie had neglected to bring her clothes into the parlor, and no one else had done it for her.

Anna Mary ran to the bed, snatched up a quilt folded at the foot of it, and began beating at the flames.

"What are you trying to do?" she said to the Yankees. "Are you trying to kill us?"

"No, you old bitch," one of them said. "We were just cold and we wanted a fire."

Callie trotted through the upstairs bedrooms armed with the bucket of water. She saw smoke curling from one of Anna Mary's bureau drawers, went running over, pulled open the drawer and poured part of the water into the flames. She soon discovered that the Yankees were being sneaky. They were dropping lighted matches in dresser drawers and then closing them. Several times she was almost too late.

Callie thought as she darted through the rooms that the Yankees were enjoying this. Some of them would nudge each other when they saw her coming. She beat at a thin tongue of flame curling up from Olivia's chifforobe. *Santa Claus!* she thought suddenly. *Santa Claus is coming tonight!*

Robbie thought he really *was!* Olivia and all of them had told him about hanging up his stocking.

Callie heard Grandpa saying clearly: "Well, if they do, Santy Claus won't be able to find you. Don't want to spend your Christmas in the courthouse basement, do you?"

She tried not to start bawling right in front of the Yankees. They would think she was crying because she was afraid of them.

She went running downstairs to refill her bucket. When she passed the dining room she came to an abrupt halt, turned back, and stepped inside. Bits and pieces of broken china crunched beneath her feet. She guessed it had made the second group of Yankees mad when they didn't find any silver. They had smashed her mother's china all over the floor. Some of the dining room windowpanes were broken, so they must've thrown some of the china through the window. Cold air was pouring in.

Backing carefully out of the dining room, Callie ran outside to the well. As she refilled her bucket, she looked toward the house and saw that the Yankees were leaving. There had been less to steal this time.

After they had gone, the Tylers checked through the house one final time for any undiscovered fires and all came into the parlor again.

"How long is this going to go on?" Blair said.

Callie had decided that she would start walking into Holly Springs. When she got there, she would find Grandpa and then ask for a guard for the house. She would go all the way to the top if necessary, and ask General Grant.

Only—she suddenly remembered—Blair had said Mrs. Grant was in town during the raid, and Preston had gone around to the Walter place to burn her saratoga.

Maybe she'd better ask somebody else for the guard. General Grant was probably still mad about that.

She wondered if Mr. Weems had been sent to a prisoner of war camp. She didn't think they'd ever get another guard as good as him. And Captain Harwell was out chasing Van Dorn. He would be pretty upset when he came back and saw what they'd done to Waverley. Callie hoped that Blair would keep on liking him. In her opinion, he was the best beau Blair had ever had. *Well*, she thought, *when this is all over, maybe Blair and Captain Harwell will get married. Then if I can find a piece of paper, I'll write a letter to his sister.*

The smokehouse and the dairy had both been stripped, so for dinner the Tylers ate cold cornbread. After she finished eating, Callie went upstairs to look for Aunt Sophie's Bible. Her bed was such a mess that she didn't think Aunt Sophie would be able to sleep there. Some of the fire had burned down into the mattress and left a charred hole in it—Callie heard another commotion downstairs and stopped searching.

Desperately she looked around the bedroom. There just wasn't anything left for them to break or steal, this time.

But when she went softly back downstairs, she saw someone who made her feel groggy with relief.

It was Mr. Weems.

He hadn't been sent to a prisoner of war camp, after all. As the Tylers crowded around him, Mr. Weems said that Van Dorn had paroled all the prisoners. Even Aunt Sophie had gotten off the sofa and was trying to tell him about her Bible.

Mr. Weems looked as sorrowful as ever and patted Aunt Sophie on the shoulder. Aunt Sophie burst into tears and buried her face against his jacket.

He promised that he would go back into town and see what had happened to Grandpa. Callie felt as if Mr. Weems had been sent from heaven in a golden chariot.

Anna Mary asked him to let her go with him, but he said she shouldn't try it. Holly Springs was full of soldiers and no place for a woman. Mr. Weems thought the whole army was falling back. He had recognized some of the regiments that advanced as far as Oxford marching into town. Things were out of control and unsafe there, he said sadly. There had been a general breakdown of morality, even among the officers.

After Mr. Weems left, no additional Yankees came through the house and the Tylers slept the sleep of exhaustion their second night in the parlor. Austin's throat didn't seem to be hurting as much, and he was able to swallow some cornmeal gruel. He could also sit up on the mattress, but every so often a watery discharge of blood would run out of his ears.

Of course Robbie didn't get to hang up his stocking, but none of them reminded him and Callie hoped he'd forgotten about it.

Christmas morning Mr. Weems came back and said Grandpa was in jail. He brought the Tylers some field peas for their Christmas dinner. It turned out that they were his rations. He said he wasn't hungry and they could have all of them. Evidently most of the Union Army had been reduced to field peas when their commissary stores were destroyed.

When they asked about the Coopers, he didn't know what had happened to them. When he'd passed the house, only the chimneys were standing.

Christmas afternoon three more Yankees came by, but Mr. Weems wouldn't let them inside the house. For a while they hung around the backyard, and when he went out to bring in wood for the fire, they yelled and jeered at him from behind the Cherokee rose hedge.

Blair heard them calling him a traitor and a damned old Secesh. When Mr. Weems got back inside with the wood, he asked Anna Mary where they kept the ax. The woodpile was getting low, and when he'd gone to chop some more he'd been unable to find an ax.

Anna Mary told him it was usually in the woodshed, and later he went out to look again. Blair followed him to the back veranda. She didn't think he was going to find the ax. It had probably been taken by the foraging detail.

"Mr. Weems," she called, standing on the veranda and hugging herself to ward off the cold wind whistling around the corner of the house.

He stopped and patiently retraced his steps.

"Have you—have you seen Captain Harwell?"

He stood sorrowfully beside the veranda, looking up at her. He shook his head.

"No, ma'am."

The bearded face beneath its tiny forage cap was dolorous and unreadable. But Blair didn't care what he was thinking. She didn't care what anybody thought now.

"I ain't seen any cavalry in town," he said.

The last three Yankees had given up and straggled away, and the barn lot and backyard were completely empty. It was quieter there than Blair had ever seen it. No cows pulled at their tether ropes, no chickens scratched about the henhouse, and no pigs grunted in the pen. Except for the open door of the smokehouse creaking in the wind, everything was silent.

Lips blue with cold, she clenched her teeth to keep them from chattering.

"How will I know if anything happens to him?"

Mr. Weems was silent. It hadn't seemed to bother him when the other Yankees called him a traitor. Grandpa had called Jonas Kendall a traitor, too. Blair thought that Mr. Weems and Jonas Kendall were not the same.

"Well, now, ma'am," he said slowly. "Ain't nothing goin' to happen to him. Cap'n Harwell'll be back in a day or two."

"If you see him, will you let me know?"

He nodded. "But won't be no need of that. He'll be comin' out to see about you. Just like I done. You can see him yourself."

She had a cowardly desire to bury her face against his uniform jacket and burst into tears. As Aunt Sophie had done.

"You don't have to do this," she said softly. "We're not loyal Unionists. I don't know why you ever thought we were."

Mr. Weems thought about it for a few minutes. "Don't matter," he said, and continued across the back yard to look for the ax.

21

Samuel Tyler lay on a rough cot in a cell in the Marshall County jail. Tongues of flame licked briefly at his
chest, flicking along his arms and traveling down to his
fingertips. But not so intense as they had been a few
days ago. Then they had burst inside him with a fury
that turned him rigid, and finally blacked him out.
There would be some fancy medical term for it, he
reckoned, that his son would know.

"You come with us, Sam," Vince Cooper had said.

"I ain't ridin' with a Sharp," he'd replied.

Now Jake Sharp was dead. Hanged at the end of a
rope.

Samuel Tyler lay on his cot and ruminated. Which
was worse? A Yankee or a Sharp?

No difference, he decided. Jackals and buzzards,
two of a kind. He could dispose of either with no more
compunction than swatting a fly.

As he lay in the jail wrapped in his fingers of flame,
Grandpa reflected on what was happening to his family. He did not try to avoid it. There was no way. Pres
had been right. He should have sent the womenfolk to
Alabama. Pres had been right all along. Samuel Tyler
had been wrong.

The jackals wanted him but seemed to be waiting for

him to get well enough to stand trial. The buzzards were too fastidious to come into his cell and perch over his cot, carry him out, and prop him under the rope. Yet the torture of his thoughts was more exquisite than any rope. For now the carrion eaters were feeding off his living flesh; sinking their fangs in, ripping great chunks of sinewy meat from his bones.

Grandpa did not know how many days and nights had gone by. He had lost count. After he had been in the jail a long time, Austin came in. They let him stand in the doorway and talk to the prisoner under the eye of the guard. Grandpa was not sure whether Austin was real or a figment in a dream.

He sat up painfully on the cot.

"The womenfolk? All of 'em still alive?"

Austin looked at him soberly. "They's all mighty hungry. We ain't got nothin' to eat."

Grandpa had never realized that a Negro could look pale. Austin's skin had assumed the appearance of dead ashes.

"Tell Anna Mary to take the girls an' go to her folks in Alabama," he said hoarsely. "Sophie an' Olivia can go to Memphis. Eugenia'll take Sophie in."

"Mist' Sam—you know Miss Anna Mary ain't gonna leave long as you in here."

"Tell her I said—go! You got *anything* to eat?"

"A little meal. I been tryin' to trap. I can't hunt, Mist' Sam. They done took yo' shotgun."

Grandpa's eyes bored into Austin's. Hunching his shoulders, he pressed down with his hands on the edge of his cot. "Try that old creek bed down in the swamp. That stand of poplars. You know where, Austin. There's a plenty rabbits down there."

"Mist' Sam, ain't no rabbits down there—"

"Goddammit! You do what I tell you! An' you fish! There's still fish in the river! Get Little Austin out on them trot lines!"

There was a short silence. The guard said, "Hurry

up, old man. We ain't going to let Sambo stay here all day."

"Go over to Coopers'," Grandpa said. "See if they got anything. Go around to the parsonage. Go to the Burtons'. If anybody's got any food, tell 'em I'll—pay 'em when I can."

"Coopers ain't there," Austin said. "Their house burnt down. I done looked over there. Ain't nothin' to eat."

The flames licked lightly over his chest. Grandpa ran his tongue across his cracked lips. "You ain't lookin' so good, Austin. You been sick?"

Austin nodded slowly. "I'd a come befo', but I ain't —been feelin' so pert."

"You should of sent Little Austin inta town. What'd you do? Walk it? Don't let none of the womenfolk come here."

The pain was shooting all the way down into his fingertips. Samuel Tyler gritted his teeth.

"Yessuh. They done took the mare. You had a doctor in here to look at you, Mist' Sam?"

"No, but I'm all right. Don't say nothin' about it to Anna Mary. I'm all right."

"We don't let everybody and his brother come traipsing through here," the Yankee guard said.

"What day is it?" Grandpa asked.

"It's Sunday," the guard said.

Grandpa shook his head impatiently. "What day of the month?"

"It's January, Mist' Sam," Austin said.

"January fourth," the Yankee said. "Time flies, don't it?"

"The Yankees is leavin'," Austin said quickly. "They been passin' by Waverley all day. They's marchin' north—"

"That's enough jaw out of you, Sambo," the guard said, hustling Austin through the door.

Rivers of flame washed over Grandpa now. Red currents of agony crashing against the shores of his heart—

"Look under the floorboards in my bedroom!" he shouted. "Behind my dresser! Get my Bible! It's hid under there—"

"The old sinner's getting religion," the Yankee guard said in amusement, closing the door. "Want your Bible before we hang you, old man?"

Olivia had learned that as each Federal regiment passed the house, there would be supply wagons at the end of it. When these went by, she would go down to the road and beg for food. She had no fear and no pride and would stand there until all the wagons had passed. Sometimes they would give her something, but more often they would not.

Whatever they gave her, it was never enough. Olivia brought it to Robbie. He would eat anything now. The Yankees stopped to feed their horses south of the pecan grove and Olivia went there, after they had gone. She carefully picked the grains of corn out of the mud and took them home and boiled them. That got Robbie through another day.

It was hard to keep enough wood for the fire. With the ax gone, they had to search for sticks and fallen tree limbs small enough to break with their hands. The family stayed in the parlor most of the time to conserve the wood. The upstairs bedrooms were icy, and the Yankees had not left enough quilts. The mattresses had been restuffed and sewn together and Anna Mary, Olivia, and Robbie all slept together in Anna Mary's bed.

At first, they had tried to clean the house. But a lot of it remained undone. Anna Mary swept the broken china from the dining room and stuffed rags in the windows where the Yankees had thrown the china through them. In the office books were still scattered over the floor. None of them had the energy or desire to pick them up. It took all the energy they had to find wood for the parlor fire and something to eat. The worst day had been when the cornmeal gave out. That was when Austin walked into Holly Springs to see Grandpa. That day, there had been nothing to eat at all.

For Blair the days passed in a veil of unreality. A terrible voice inside her kept insisting that Matthew was mother. dead. But she refused to listen to it. In the last few days there had been cavalry as well as infantry going past the house. Every time she looked out and saw blue-uniformed men on horseback, her heart seemed to stop beating as she waited for one of them to turn into the drive.

The last, desperate link that still bound him to her was his coat hanging on the back of the office door. Blair went there often just to touch it. It wasn't as if he were dead, in spite of what the voice kept insisting. The coat had become a kind of talisman. As long as it hung there Matthew would be coming back to get it.

After Austin came back from Holly Springs, he went out to the swamp. He was gone until almost midnight, and when he came back, things were never quite as bad.

Hidden in a cave by the old creek bed, near the stand of poplars, he had found the commissary crates Grandpa had acquired on the day of the raid. It had taken him a long time to get the crates open, for the Yankees had taken every tool in the storehouse, as well as the ax. But he had finally knocked the crates apart with a rock. Austin said they all had hardtack in them.

After the family had eaten the hard little crackers, Anna Mary and Austin went into Grandpa's bedroom, moved his dresser, and pried the floorboards up. Austin felt around beneath them until his fingers touched something. When he drew it out, it was a thick leather pouch.

He handed it to Anna Mary, who opened it. It was stuffed with Blair's greenbacks from the Federal paymaster's office.

* * *

For the first time since Van Dorn's raid, the Tylers began to think of the larger events that must be taking place in the world outside. What did the Yankees' leaving mean? That Grant's army was retreating without ever having fought a battle? Were they marching back in defeat? If that were so, then Van Dorn's raid had accomplished much more than the destruction of the supply base in Holly Springs. It had saved Vicksburg.

On Wednesday night they had a downpour, with hard winds. The deluge proved a bonanza to the Tylers, for many small tree limbs blew down during the storm. The family spent most of Thursday morning picking them up.

Anna Mary decided they had enough wood to make a fire in the kitchen and do the family's long-neglected laundry. While the others were in the kitchen, Blair went into the house to gather up her and Callie's laundry. As she was going back downstairs, she heard a noise in the office and stopped. Someone was in there, walking around. A drawer opened and closed.

Blair's hand went to her throat. Matthew had come back! He wasn't dead. Oh, not ever, ever! He must have come in while they were all in the kitchen, and when he couldn't find anybody—when nobody answered—he'd gone into the office to see if his things were still there.

Heart pounding, she ran lightly down the rest of the stairs, reached out, and opened the door.

Little Austin stood in the office, searching through the drawers in a drop leaf table. He held a battered valise in one hand and Matthew's uniform coat hung over his arm. At the sound of the door's opening he looked up. Blair saw a brief confusion on his face. Then his lips poked out in their familiar sullen expression, he lowered his head over the drop leaf table, took out Matthew's shaving equipment, and crammed it into the valise.

The blood thudded in her ears with a deafening

fierceness. She couldn't believe Little Austin wasn't Matthew. She had been so sure—

"What are you doing with Captain Harwell's things?" she said.

"I'se takin' them to him," he said, not looking up at her.

The bundle of dirty laundry had slipped from her hands and lay in a heap on the floor.

"Where is he?" she said.

Closing the drawer, Little Austin hurried over to the rolltop desk, picked up Matthew's cap, and stuffed it into the valise. "We's leavin'," he said, looking desperately around the office, as if not sure whether he had everything. "His—his company pullin' out!"

Her hand gripped the edge of the door. "Is he wounded? Has he been sick? Little Austin, you—*tell me!*"

Little Austin closed the valise and started toward the door. "Cap'n Harwell in town, Miss Blair! He ain't wounded! He been back most a week!"

A dark maelstrom dipped and swirled around her as Little Austin tried to get past her and through the office door. "Liar!" she screamed. "You're lying to me!"

She snatched at Matthew's coat across his arm.

"You give that to me! You're trying to steal it! You give me—you give—" Little Austin shifted the valise and grabbed for the coat. For a hideous moment they fought over it.

Little Austin was stronger. He wrenched the coat from Blair's clawing fingers, gave her a violent shove with the valise, and bolted past her through the door.

She landed screaming against her father's rolltop desk. The edge of the desk cracked hurtfully against her hip and she lost her balance and went tumbling to the floor. She opened her mouth to scream again. Out in the hallway Little Austin was running for the back veranda. Blair reached up, caught the edge of the desk, and pulled herself to her feet. Panting, sobbing, trying to catch her breath to scream again, she went stumbling through the hall and wrenched open the back door. Little Austin was already halfway through the yard.

Telithia came out of the kitchen and started toward him, holding her arms in front of her as she ran. "Baby!" she shrieked. "Baby! Baby! Wait!"

Little Austin looked back over his shoulder, the valise bumping wildly against his legs. Gripping it in both hands, he swung it to one side, almost dropping Matthew's coat. "Ma!" he cried in great, heaving sobs. "Ma, I cain't!"

Austin emerged from the kitchen, caught Telithia, and wrapped his arms around her from behind. He held her, made her stop.

Little Austin crossed the barn lot and ran into the pasture. Blair watched him until he disappeared into the woods behind the house.

Anna Mary sat on the side of the four-poster bed with her shoulders straight and her hands clasped tightly in her lap. Her hands were red from the laundry tubs and the hot water had wrinkled her palms.

"You're so young," she said. "I blame myself. I saw what was happening, and I should have talked to you a long time ago. But I hoped—I hoped that it would be a temporary thing."

"I thought he loved me," Blair said.

Even though she was wrapped in a quilt, her teeth were chattering. They always did when she was cold, and her lips inevitably turned blue. The cold seemed to get to her more than it did other people. She hated wintertime.

"I think he did," her mother said.

"No." Blair stared at the quilt with burning eyes. "He's been back in town a week."

"There must be some reason. I don't believe Matthew would stay away for no reason. We were all fond of him, Blair. That's why we invited him to stay here."

"We invited him to stay because he gave us the guard and the commissary rations."

Anna Mary's blue eyes clouded. "Perhaps you're right. I didn't think of it that way at the time."

"I didn't want him to stay, Mama. But you and Olivia—"

"Yes, darling. I know."

"I thought you and Liv were the stupid ones. Inviting everybody in. But it was me who was really stupid, wasn't it, Mama? None of you fell in love."

Anna Mary's gentle face had a twisted, aching look. "Blair, love is never stupid—"

"It is when he doesn't love you."

Anna Mary's hand reached out and clasped her arm through the quilt. "Listen to me. The night Matthew was wounded. You felt sorry for him, didn't you? You'd never been around suffering and death before. But I have, Blair! My heart goes out to them, too! Darling, I'm not blaming you! But you must *think!*"

I loved Matthew before that, Blair thought.

But Anna Mary didn't believe it. Her mother didn't believe she was in love with Matthew now. *I wish I wasn't,* she thought. *It makes everything matter too much. Love hurts you and tears you apart. It's not worth it. But it's too late; I can't get away. I can't just stop hurting and say: I won't care anymore.*

Anna Mary said, "What did you want? To be married?"

"Yes."

"Blair, if you and Matthew had gotten married, could you forget all this?"

"All what?"

"Everything! Everything that's happened in the last three weeks! Could you forget all the Yankees have done to us?"

But they hadn't done it then.

"That wasn't Matthew," Blair whispered.

"I'm not saying it was! But could you live with him for the rest of your life—and not think about this?

Blair, I try to believe I don't have any hate in my heart! But I can't forget it! Can you?''

''Mama, that doesn't have anything to do with Matthew and me!''

''Oh, my darling, how I wish that were true! But—don't you see? It would be like a poison! Always coming between you! Blair, you'll fall in love again! You'll find someone from your own people! Someone who has the same ties, the same roots—''

Anna Mary stopped talking and raised her clenched fists to her mouth. She was silent for a moment.

''Darling, forgive me, but I think it's for the best that Matthew didn't come back.''

Her mother was glad.

They were all glad. Grandpa had said she could forget that damned Yankee in a hurry. *Stupid*, Blair thought. *How could I have been so stupid? "You'll get over it,"* Preston had said.

She'd known it the day the Yankees burned the Widow Lockwood's house. She had made up her mind not to love him as far back as then. But the next night, Matthew had been wounded, and when she thought he might die nothing else mattered. Nothing else mattered now.

Blair rolled over in the quilt, with her back to her mother. Anna Mary had given her good advice. Grandpa, Pres—all of them had. The only thing bad about it was that she couldn't take it. It was too late to stop loving him even when she knew he didn't love her. Why had he told her he did?

So he could do those things to her. That was the only reason. Her teeth started chattering again. How could she have been so wrong about a person? Why had Matthew asked her to marry him?

So he could do those things to her. That was the only reason he'd said that, too.

Anna Mary stood up. ''I'll bring some wood up here and make a fire. You're cold, dear.''

* * *

The next night they had meat for supper; Austin had caught a possum in one of his traps.

Telithia cooked it, saying through her tears for Little Austin that she was sorry they didn't have sweet potatoes and greens to go with it. When Blair sat down at the table, she looked at the meat piled on a cracked platter in front of her mother. She had seen the dead possum in the backyard before Austin skinned it. It had had the usual pointed nose, sharp little teeth, and long, hairless tail. It had reminded her of a large rat. A heavy, gamy odor drifted up from the platter and the meat was swimming in grease. Blair's stomach heaved.

She had to jump up and run from the room. Outside in the back, she held on to one of the supports of the passageway and retched until everything in her stomach came up. Her head swam and a cold sweat broke out on her face. Anna Mary and Olivia helped her back into the house and Blair lay down on the sofa in the parlor. The others went back and finished their meal.

I can't go on, she thought. *I don't have anything to go on for. Next, we'll be eating real rats. Little individual rats. Telithia will fry them and Mama will have them all stacked on a platter and serve them out one by one. This isn't real. In a minute I'm going to wake up. It'll be the middle of November, and a beautiful day, with the sun shining outside. I'll be waiting to go for a ride and a picnic. And this time, Dan Phillips and Pres and Isabella will all be here.*

Matthew—

By Saturday the road in front of Waverley was empty. The last of the Federal wagon trains had apparently passed. That afternoon the Reverend Thackerford came out in a wagon, drawn by an ancient, doddering mule.

Plump cheeks sagging like dewlaps, the minister climbed slowly down from the wagon as if every motion sprang from an infinite sadness. "I would have come before," he said, "but I did not know—I had no means of transportation." He looked at the mule. "It is only through the grace of God that I obtained this."

He said most of the Yankees had left Holly Springs. They were moving their sick out today. Most of them were being transported on the railroad, so the roads should be fairly clear. Things were bad, he said. Bad all over. There was so little to eat.

Anna Mary asked about the Coopers. Gone south, the Reverend Thackerford said. Outside the Federal lines. Then he asked to speak to Anna Mary and Aunt Sophie alone in the parlor.

Olivia, Blair, and Callie waited in the office, without a fire.

In a little while Anna Mary opened the office door. She stood there and looked in at them, a pale, thin statue carved in ice.

"Your grandpa is dead," she said.

They buried Grandpa on the cold, windswept heights of Hillcrest cemetery in Holly Springs, but he did not stay there.

He still walked about the house. He was everywhere: in his rocking chair beside the lamp on his bureau, reading the *Memphis Appeal;* walking with long strides through the barn lot, dressed in Kentucky jeans supported by a single gallus, calico shirt, and tattered straw hat. He sat in his accustomed place at the head of the table, saying, "You'd better get dressed in a hurry, Mary Blair. Henry of Navarre is a-comin' up the driveway."

The Yankee guard at the jail had come in early Saturday morning and found Samuel Tyler dead on his cot. A Federal surgeon was summoned to examine the corpse. Heart failure, he said. Then the surgeon sent for the Reverend Thackerford, who had not known Grandpa was there.

Now the minister spoke of a full life, eternal rest, and an all-loving, all-understanding God. They prayed together in the parlor. There was nothing else to do.

Callie cried constantly now. At night, in their bed, Blair held her little sister close, feeling her shoulders shaking with the never-ending sobs. Blair cried too, but the tears she shed were silent, trickling noiselessly down her face.

One night she awakened and Callie wasn't there. Blair had no wrapper to slip into, no nightgown, no peignoir. She got out of bed in the frayed dress she slept in, and on bare feet felt her way through the icy darkness of the house.

She found Callie in Grandpa's bedroom, huddled in his rocking chair. "Come back to bed, honey," she whispered, taking her by the hand. After she got Callie into bed, Blair had to go to the washbowl and throw up again. She tried to be quiet about it and muffle the wretched noises she made. She had even been sick at the funeral, but had managed to hold the nausea back until she could find shelter behind a tree.

They had potatoes to eat now, and even pork and molasses. Austin had taken the greenbacks to town and bought food. Mr. Charlie Blaylock had made a far-ranging trip outside the county to bring in supplies and was selling them in Holly Springs.

But Blair couldn't eat the pork and molasses. All she could keep on her stomach was the hardtack. Its dry, unleavened dullness was exactly what she craved. She kept a few of the crackers in her apron pocket and nibbled on them during the day. She seemed to keep them down better if she ate often, and a tiny bit at a time.

All the Yankees were gone now, yet when the Tylers went into Holly Springs for Grandpa's funeral, Blair had scarcely recognized the town. Charred rubble, half-destroyed brick walls, and blackened beams seemed to bear down on her from every side.

The beautiful stained-glass windows in the Methodist church had all been smashed, and the Sunday School rooms on the lower level were uninhabitable. The Yankee cavalry had quartered their horses there.

Piles of dried manure had been left on the floors, and nails had been driven into the walls to hang bridles and saddles. The organ in Christ Church had been dismantled, the Reverend Thackerford said, and the pews used as feed troughs.

The townspeople at the funeral looked no better than the town. Blair had not wanted to talk to anyone; everything anyone said was another blow of the hammer, reciting the bitter litanies of what the Yankees had done.

Louley Burton, sharp-faced, thinner than ever, said the Kendalls had gone. Isabella departed two days after Van Dorn's raid, on the train with some of the Yankee officers' wives. Mr. Kendall stayed a few days longer, packing up things from the house. The Confederates had taken all the speculators' gold away from them and made them watch while their cotton was burned.

Some people had been lucky, Louley said. They still had something to eat. But they were hoarding it; people weren't sharing as they used to do. After the Federal Army left, some of the citizens had gone out and picked through the litter left along the roadside and in the army camps. They were looking for food mostly, but some of them had found tin spoons, bits of harness, nails, a little girl's doll. Everything was precious now.

On the first day of February a light snow fell. A thin layer of white powdered the empty Waverley outbuildings and made patterns of lacy loveliness along the bare limbs of the crape myrtles in front of the house. Robbie was fascinated, and Callie stood with him at the kitchen window, tracing outlines of delicate snowflakes frozen against the glass.

Olivia said he could make a snowman, but Telithia didn't think there would be enough snow. "We can scrape it together," Callie said. "We'll make a fat old snowman right by the kitchen window, so you can look out and see it, Robbie. And we'll make us some snowballs, too."

After they went outside, Blair stood at the kitchen window and watched them. Callie was stumbling about in Anna Mary's cape. It was much too long for her and already wet around the bottom. But Callie's coat had been stolen when the first group of Yankees came through the house.

Turning quickly from the window, Blair hurried through the passageway and into the house. In the hallway she held her breath until the surge of nausea had passed. Then she went into the office and shivering, blue with cold, teeth chattering, began to hunt through the shelves for her father's medical books.

Except for measles and chicken pox, she had never been sick. Very rarely did she even catch cold. What was the matter with her? Her hands trembled as she searched through the books.

And what good would it do if she knew? Where would they get any medicine now? Her mother still had some of the persimmon cordial for coughs, and a tonic she dosed them with for chills and fever—but Blair didn't think she had a fever. Her forehead didn't feel hot.

When she found the book she was looking for, she took it over to the sagging couch and sat down. She hunched over it for a long time, turning pages, running her finger down the index, flipping pages again. The medical jargon was turgid, the print small, and the heavy volume had a musty, mildewed smell.

Blair paused. She read a few paragraphs intently, and then went back and read them again. Her eyes flicked up from the page and looked vacantly out the window at the snow swirling in little gusts against the pane.

The world stopped. The earth came to a halt on its axis and ceased to turn.

She put her hand tentatively on her breast. *Yes*, she thought. *Yes. It's true.*

She was not completely ignorant. She remembered

how Olivia had been two years ago, before Robbie was born.

Did I know it all the time? she thought.

No, I didn't.

There had been other symptoms, which she had ignored. She had been late like that before. In fact, she didn't even know when it should have occurred. When? About—about the first week in January. Yes. A month ago. Now, she remembered feeling relieved that she wouldn't be that way for the Musical Society's Christmas program.

But of course they hadn't had the Christmas program, because on December 23 Christ Church was full of horses. She closed the book and put it blindly on the couch.

This was inside me all the time, she thought. *Growing, spreading, digging in. Like a tumor. A fungus. A parasite. In me.*

It was there when I ran to the fairgrounds, and when I was talking to Jim Watkins and Pres. It was there when that stinking Yankee smashed my piano, and when they tore up Callie's journal and threw Mama's china through the window.

It was inside me while I was dragging Grandpa into the parlor and while they were kicking him. It was there when Little Austin pushed me and I fell down against the desk.

This final, unspeakable abomination—nothing, nothing could ever happen that would be worse than this.

Blair lay down on the couch. She put her hands over her stomach, bearing down hard.

Squeeze it to death. Kill it, kill it—oh, God! Her mother would know now. They'd all find out.

Stop eating the hardtack. You'll die.

She had wondered if God would punish her for her sinful behavior. And had thought she wouldn't much care if He did. Was that what this was?

She was so tired. *I believe*, she thought, *that if I just close my eyes and lie here for a long time, I could die.*

Matthew, of course, was the worst of the lot. She had loved and trusted him, so he had been able to do this. *They're not ever through with us*, she thought. *We keep thinking there's nothing else they can do. But there always is.*

Her hand moved out blindly and touched the faded cover of the couch. Matthew's hand had been lying about there when Anna Mary was bandaging his shoulder. She had looked down at it and that was the place.

It was odd, but she didn't feel cold. The office was very cold, and she didn't have on a coat or a shawl. She felt drifting, disconnected, as if she were floating through space.

Blair closed her eyes.

Strangely enough, it was summertime and she had on her white embroidered muslin. Her flounced skirts frothed with delicately worked flowers, and she wore the leghorn hat with the buttercup-yellow ribbons. The ribbons were as wide as her hand.

A small gold brooch with seed pearls gleamed on the bodice of the dress. It looked a lot like a brooch Olivia had had. Maybe it was Liv in the white embroidered muslin—no, Blair was sure it was herself.

Robbie's fat little hands reached for the brooch and he laughed. A gurgling, delighted little laugh.

Blair floated dreamily above the couch. She felt warm and happy and looked very pretty and Robbie's skin was like velvety satin as she held him in her arms. He had soft brown curls swirling in ringlets on the crown of his head and beautiful, innocent brown eyes. His neck, when she pressed her face against it, had a sweet, powdered-baby smell. His hands were chubby and dimpled and he was cutting a tooth. One tiny white pearl peeped up through his gum. He was the most beautiful baby in the world.

"I love you," Blair whispered. "You belong completely to me."

She smiled a little, opening her eyes and gazing out at the snow. She still wasn't cold. *I fooled all of them,* she thought. *Matthew and Mama and Grandpa and God. Every one.*

You all thought you'd kill me with this, didn't you?

Well, you didn't. Because I'm going to get the best of you yet.

She put her palms lightly over her stomach. *It's all right,* she thought. *They're not going to hurt you. You're all mine.*

22

In the early dawn of April 17, 1863, the pine-covered hills of southwestern Tennessee were shrouded in a misty blue. Little birds warbled sweetly in the trees, wild plums bloomed along the roadways, and beside the chimneys of what had once been houses, golden daffodils and fragrant hyacinths perfumed the gentle air.

Moving out of their base camp in the village of La Grange, 1,700 Union cavalrymen in columns of twos rode at a leisurely pace down the sandy road to the hazy hills. Before them lay the Wolf River and the boundary of the state of Mississippi.

The 2nd and 6th Illinois and the 4th Iowa comprised the newly formed 1st Brigade, 1st Cavalry Division, 16th Army Corps. Colonel Benjamin Grierson, former bandmaster and music teacher, headed the brigade. As a child, he had been kicked in the face by a horse. He had never liked horses since. But Sherman had called him the best cavalry officer he had ever had.

The 6th was in the lead on this first day of march, and the fine white dust thrown up by the hooves of their horses sifted back and settled on the members of the 2nd, who rode in the center of the column.

Matthew, at the head of Company D, saw that the

uniform of Corporal Joe Phipps, who rode beside him, was already collecting traces of sand.

Grierson had not informed his lower echelon officers where they were heading on this balmy April morning, but Corporal Phipps thought he knew.

"If it's not Columbus, I'll sell myself for bull beef," he said.

Matthew made no response, but he thought Phipps was probably right. A nest of Rebel cavalry operated near Columbus, sending out raiding parties to harass the Union forces stationed along the Memphis & Charleston Railroad in southern Tennessee. Matthew hoped this expedition's purpose was to clean them out. Once and for all.

"It figures," Phipps said. "We've got five days' rations with orders to make them last for ten. Columbus is a five-day march from here. We're going to hit it, do some damage to the Mobile and Ohio Railroad, and then come back to La Grange. A ten-day march."

The eagerness in Phipps's tone indicated that he looked upon it as a ten-day picnic. But Matthew was looking forward to it, too. Anything to get out of La Grange.

Early 1863 had been a period in his life he hoped he could forget. The last four months had been a nightmarish mixture of oozing black mud, heavy snowfalls that blew down the flue of his hut, half the men in his outfit down with dysentery, diarrhea, sore throats, and measles, constant picketing and patrol duty for the ones that were left, riding vedette in sleet that cut through his overcoat and stung his face, horses coming down with greased heel because the troopers didn't bother to put planks under their feet to keep them out of the snow—and the charms of La Grange.

The town was a picked-over skeleton, mired in mud. All the vacant houses had been turned into hospitals, shrubbery used as hitching posts for horses, and the streets trampled into bottomless slush. Dead-looking vines were taking over everything, curling around

crumbling chimneys and empty outbuildings like
voracious, hungry snakes. A few slivers of flesh still
clung to the bones of the town. Like all putrescent
things, it stank. Matthew, who had imbibed freely on
the long winter nights in his ill-heated quarters, could
smell it all the time. La Grange was the Confederacy.
Dead but didn't know it, rotting on its feet.

"Captain," Phipps said, "I'm pleased as punch we
got shifted to Colonel Grierson's brigade!"

"So am I," Matthew said.

Grierson was a mover; he got things done. If it had
been left up to the colonel, they'd have caught Van
Dorn. As it was, he got away clean. Back to Grenada
on the twenty-eighth of December. Mizner, who
ranked Grierson, had ordered them into camp at New
Albany, giving up the chase.

Matthew glanced over at Phipps. As always he was
fresh-faced, wiry, and ready to storm hell with a pen-
knife. Matthew had backed him for corporal in the
company elections, in spite of his youth. They'd had to
hold the elections to fill the vacancy left by Sergeant
Evans. And that was something else he hoped he'd forget.

The column passed scraggly cotton fields gone to
briar and weed. The ditches along the roadway were
full of the same white sand. He shifted his jaw, feeling
the grains gritting between his teeth. They traveled
light now. Matthew's carbine was the heaviest thing he
packed. No more saddlebags bulging with extra shirts
and handkerchiefs sent lovingly from home, no more
skillets and coffee pots, no more extra blankets, just
the one. For this march they'd been issued forty
rounds of ammunition and a double ration of salt.
Most of them had brought along their ponchos, because it always rained.

The orders began to come back along the line. "Trot,
march!" Automatically the seasoned cavalry horses responded, knowing the commands as well as their riders. Corporal Phipps had a new mount, one of Tennes-

see's finest, impressed especially for the raid. Grierson's quartermaster details had scoured the countryside for the past two weeks, replenishing their stock. Other horses had been sent down from the remount station in St. Louis. But Phipps, wise in the ways of the cavalry, had preferred the local breed. The St. Louis horses, bought from western farmers, were attuned to the plow.

"I'll say one thing for the chivalries," he remarked, deftly applying his spurs. "They sure as hell know a good horse!"

Matthew accommodated himself to the change in pace, letting unused muscles respond to the new rhythm of his saddle. As usual, it was short. Soon it was time for him to raise his hand in the signal for "Walk, march!"

Phipps took up his part of the one-sided conversation where he'd left off. Captain Harwell was a man of few words. He didn't remember him as being particularly laconic before La Grange, but maybe he was mistaken and the captain had always been that way. In any case, Phipps didn't mind. It gave him more time to talk.

"I swear, though," he said, "I do not like being on the quartermaster detail. I mean, when you've got to take some poor old jasper's horse right out from in front of his plow. And Lord—but the females! How they do take on! Crying and begging and saying, 'That one belongs to Sally! Had it since she was a baby!' And half the time—"

"It's an act," Matthew said.

Phipps rode in silence for a moment.

"You really think so?"

"Prepared especially for your benefit, Corporal."

"I'll be darned!"

But the most consummate actress had been Blair, Matthew thought. He had been right about her the first time. Now he knew with a sickening certainty that she had never loved him. He wondered how long any one conquest had managed to hold her attention. Not too damned long, he was certain of that. No doubt she had already forgotten the Texan and found someone else.

The column traveled at the prescribed cavalry rate of three miles an hour, rested for ten minutes every hour, and covered thirty miles that day. They camped for the night just north of Ripley, on the Ellis plantation, where the commissary sergeants ordered out the details to move in on the plantation's henhouses, smokehouses, and barns.

As soon as the corn and forage were rationed out, Matthew squatted by his campfire, brewed his coffee in a tin can, and drank it black.

The moonlight that night was hazy, the moon crossed by scudding clouds. It gave the woods and fields around them an eerie, haunted look.

With the April sunshine warm on her shoulders Callie sat on the back veranda steps and watched her sister making a hat.

Blair had painstakingly plaited the straw, sewn it together, and now was shaping the crown. She had already made hats for Callie, Olivia, and Aunt Sophie, and this was to be hers.

"What are you going to decorate *that* one with?" Callie asked.

Blair was using an upturned tin pan in lieu of a block. "The blue ribbon I saved. I'm going to sew it around the crown and bring it through and tie it under the chin."

"I liked the red feathers on Olivia's," Callie said, thankful that her sister was no longer throwing up.

"I don't know. The pokeberry-juice dye came out a little light."

Callie thought Blair must be getting well. This one bright spot in her existence was something she always reminded herself to be thankful for. Her sister had been sick so long.

She couldn't help hearing her vomiting into the

washbowl in their room. Finally one morning she'd sat up in bed and said, "What's the matter?"

Blair thought she was asleep; she'd jumped and clung to the washstand. When she came back from cleaning the bowl, she made Callie promise she wouldn't say anything to their mother about it. She said she just had an upset stomach, and it would pass.

It hadn't though, not for two whole months, and Callie had almost been sick herself with fear. She knew now that people she loved could be taken away from her, and she'd been afraid Blair was going to die as Grandpa had.

Across the barn lot the Cherokee rose hedge was leafed out in bright, tender green, and buds were forming. Soon the roses would be in bloom. But for the first time in her life Callie wouldn't be here to see them. The Tylers were going to Alabama, to Anna Mary's people. She and her mother and Blair would be staying with Grandmama Carter for a while.

We're refugeeing at last, Callie thought, sitting in the sunshine on the Waverley back steps. *But when the war is over, we're coming back. . . .*

Blair had gone back to shaping her hat. As she watched her working with the straw, Callie had the uncomfortable feeling that her sister was getting fat.

"I think I'll get the ribbon and see how it's going to look," Blair said.

After she had gone, Callie sprawled back on her elbows in an unladylike fashion and closed her eyes against the sun. *I don't want to go to Alabama,* she thought.

She scratched her arm. Maybe she had a chigger bite.

Back in January when Grant's army pulled out, she had thought that they were rid of the Yankees for good. But in the last two months Holly Springs had had *three* cavalry raids. And Callie thought every one of the Yankee cavalrymen ought to wear a big board slung across his back saying THIEF.

Anything you didn't want them to take, you had to hide.

Austin had dug a hole in the smokehouse floor and buried their meal and potatoes in it. Then he put planks over it, covered them with dirt, and put the empty pork barrels on top of that. So far, the raiders hadn't found it, but it surely was a lot of trouble to get the meal and potatoes out.

Of course, there were some things you couldn't hide. Telithia had tried to start a garden back in February. She'd planted early cabbage, carrots, and some onion sets. But on the second raid from Memphis, the Yankees had come by Waverley and ridden their horses through it—whooping and hollering and just ruining everything she had!

Something was tickling Callie's face. Opening her eyes, she saw a bouquet of violets close by her chin. She sat up hastily. "How did you sneak up on me like that?"

Jim Watkins laughed and eased down on the step beside her. "You were asleep," he said.

Jim had been home for almost a month, recuperating from a wound he'd suffered in early March, in Tennessee. This was in addition to his missing thumb, which had been sliced off in the battle at the fairgrounds during Van Dorn's raid.

Blair appeared on the veranda, coming back with the blue ribbon. Jim got to his feet.

"For heaven's sake," she said, "sit still."

Jim's latest wound had been in his knee. His left leg was stiff and dragged when he walked. Callie thought it was sort of a curiosity how the Yankees always seemed to attack him on the left. Pretty soon Jim's left side would be completely demolished. He would have only a right.

Blair sat down on the edge of the veranda, with her feet on the top step. Jim divided his bouquet of violets and gave half to Callie and the other half to Blair. "I brought these for my sweetheart," he said, indicating

Callie. "But I don't reckon she'll mind sharing them with you."

"You're the most durable sweetheart I ever saw," Blair said. "I can remember when you were my first beau. I was ten."

"Where did you get that *horse?*" Callie asked, looking at a dejected creature that lolled by the single post where the backyard gate had been.

"Are you referring to my noble steed? On which young Lochinvar has come out of the West?"

From under her lashes Blair peered at his profile as he lounged against the step. He'd lost a frightening amount of weight since she'd seen him at the fairgrounds. Jim had always been lean, but now he seemed to have gone completely to bone. His patched gray trousers bagged about the knees and his worn belt had been taken up several notches. Still, in spite of his gauntness, he had a well-bred, sensitive look. Jim had always been gentle, a lover of books. It was like him to stop and pick the violets, she thought.

"Speaking of young Lochinvar," he said, "what do you hear from Pres?"

"We keep up with him through the *Memphis Appeal*," Callie said. "All they ever write about is the cavalry. And General Morgan and Miss Ready."

After the Holly Springs raid, Van Dorn's cavalry had been transferred to General Bragg's command. Pres had been in Spring Hill, Tennessee, since the last of December.

"Ah, yes!" Jim said. "The beautiful Miss Ready. I hear the wedding was quite an affair."

"Bishop Polk performed the ceremony," Callie said eagerly. "And General Breckinridge was one of the groomsmen. They had a big ball afterwards and danced far into the night."

Blair drew up her knees a little, to hide her thickening waist. Clever Miss Ready. She'd had the good judgment to fall in love with her hero, John Hunt Morgan, who was on the right side. Married him, too. Blair

touched the tip of her finger to a velvety violet petal.
She didn't think about it all the time now. It was fading
a little; it didn't matter as much.

I'm getting over it, she thought. And yet—every time
another cavalry raid had come down from Tennessee,
she'd looked for him. Sick with nausea, shaking with
helpless fury and cold, thinking as they galloped back
and forth through Telithia's garden patch that they
weren't even human—they were animals who walked
on their hind legs and dressed in blue suits—still, she
had hope.

Why? she wondered. *I don't care.* The baby was all
that mattered now. She still hadn't told anyone. She
knew that sooner or later Anna Mary would have to
find out. But she couldn't bear to add to her mother's
burdens now. And if, in the back of her mind, Anna
Mary had already noticed, she turned a blind eye. Blair
could understand that. It was beyond Anna Mary's
comprehension that her daughter would do such a
thing. *But at least*, Blair thought, *I'll have the baby.
Something to love.*

Blair's finger moved tenderly across the violets. She
had even thought of a name. David. It was a name she
had always liked. She could name it whatever she
wished. This baby was hers. . . .

"Well, I'll tell you one thing," Callie said suddenly.
"I wish the cavalry was back here in Mississippi!
Maybe then we wouldn't have to keep everything bur-
ied in the ground."

Jim laughed. "Sugar, I imagine General Pemberton
wishes the same!"

Blair looked up from the violets. "Who do we have
in Mississippi, Jim? Did they leave us with any protection at *all?*"

"If you mean cavalry, not much. Chalmers is making
do with what he's got. And what he can stick together
with spit. And since the legislature authorized Gholson
to raise state troops, Chalmers is losing what little he
had."

"But I don't understand! Aren't the state troops supposed to defend the state? Isn't that what they're organizing them for?"

"Well, yes. But most of the partisan rangers in Chalmers's district were from the northeastern part of the state. Now that they're organizing into state companies under Gholson, they're pulling out of here. We're in the western district, Blair."

"So we're just left to the mercy of the Yankees! While they're over there keeping the Mobile and Ohio Railroad clear!"

"Somebody's got to watch out for Macon. Columbus has the munitions plants."

"And of course the Yankees have picked Marshall County so clean, they don't worry about us!"

Jim reached over and gave the hem of Blair's dress a lazy tug. "Stop fussing for a minute. I've got some good news."

"What?" Callie said.

"I'm going with you on your trip."

They both stared at him.

"You're going to Grandmama Carter's?" Callie said.

"Well, only as far as Meridian. But that's almost to the Alabama line. I've been assigned there."

"What will you do in Meridian?" Callie asked.

"I'll be in charge of the depot."

Blair forced herself not to look at his leg, stretched stiffly in front of him on the lower veranda step.

"Jim," she said softly. "Jim?"

"What, honey?"

"What *are* you going to do?"

He looked up at her and smiled. "I'm not fooling. I am going to be in charge of the army depot. We've got a lot of supplies stored over there. The railroads intersect at Meridian. All the ordnance from the munitions works at Selma passes through. And any troops from the East coming into Vicksburg. It's a busy spot."

"When do you have to be there?" Blair asked.

"The end of this month."

"We're leaving Tuesday, Jim. Can you really come with us?"

"Sure can."

Blair leaned over and hugged him, spilling violets into his lap. "I'm so glad!" she said. Callie pounced upon him from the other side.

"Goodness gracious!" he said, sounding pleased.

On Saturday, the second day of march, the 2nd Illinois took the lead. The long line of Union cavalrymen, with forty paces between each squadron, resumed their southeasterly course.

By eight o'clock in the morning the advance was entering Ripley, encountering no opposition, nor even any surprise, from the citizens of that town, who watched sullenly from windows and doorways at the Yankees riding past. They had been invaded before; the expressions on their faces indicated that they expected to be invaded again. Ripley held no pleasant memories for Matthew. It was here that he had spent Christmas Day. The community still bore the scars of the December twenty-fifth clash with Van Dorn, when he and his pursuers touched briefly before the Rebels broke away and hurried south for Grenada.

Now on this April morning Grierson ordered a rest in Ripley while he conferred with his staff. They were drawing near the section of the state patrolled by Confederate cavalry.

As Company D dismounted, an elderly, lantern-jawed civilian squatted on his haunches against a storefront, watching them. Corporal Phipps looked over at Matthew and grinned.

"Hey, Pappy!" he yelled to the old man. "Let's hear you give three cheers for the Union!"

The ragged figure squatting in the sunshine moved its jaws slowly, working with the inevitable cud of tobacco in its cheek. Among the lower class of Southern whites, even the women chewed. Matthew had seen young girls of ten and twelve begging for a plug. Corporal Phipps cocked his revolver. "Come on now! Loud and clear!"

Some of the troopers snickered. Looping his reins around a hitching rail in front of the store, Matthew shifted his shoulders, easing cramped muscles.

"Rah," a lethargic, incredibly hate-filled voice intoned softly behind him. "Rah. Rah."

Matthew was conscious of a feeling of surprise that the old man had understood Phipps, that they shared a common language.

"For the Union, Pappy! For the flag!"

"All right, Joe. That's enough," Matthew said, squinting up toward the white clouds beginning to swell on the horizon. He had hoped he'd never have to lay eyes on this place again.

The surgeons had removed Evans's leg the day the 2nd Illinois left Holly Springs for Ripley, and when they'd returned, Frank was dead. It'd taken a neat twenty-four hours for those amputation-crazy butchers and that pesthole of a hospital to kill him. It had been like handing Evans a death sentence to take him there. The army hospitals had killed more soldiers than all the bullets and cannon balls put together. He'd never send another of his men to one.

"All right if we mosey around a little, Captain?" Phipps inquired. "See the sights?"

"We're pulling out in an hour. Be back."

"Yes, sir!"

Matthew paced back and forth in front of the hitching rail, slapping his gauntlets against his open palm. The pale, malarial eyes of the old man squatting against the storefront followed him, going from one end of the hitching rail and back again with him, in a pendulation of rheumy hate. *Like to kill me with that look, wouldn't you, you damned sullen bastard. Grierson, hurry up.*

After Christmas, there had been the letter to Evans's widow, which Matthew had had to write.

Again Matthew squinted up at the clouds, banking

rapidly. There was a void inside him. A blank space. Something was missing. There were things other people felt that he no longer did. He could still feel self-disgust.

He blamed himself for the sergeant's death. Instead of being in camp with his troopers, he had been making love to Blair. For the first time, he had forgotten his lifelong code of honor and duty, and it had brought him nothing but pain. Blair didn't know what love was. She wouldn't remember him for five minutes after he crossed the Tallahatchie.

"You damned imbecile!" Matthew said, turning abruptly to face the rheumy-eyed old man squatting against the storefront. "Look somewhere else!"

Forty-five minutes dragged by before the troopers began to straggle back in groups of twos and threes. One of them said Colonel Hatch was already pulling out. The Iowans were heading east, toward the Mobile & Ohio Railroad. Company D got back into formation, mounted up, and prepared to ride out of Ripley. The 2nd again took the lead. Followed by the 6th, Grierson's old command, they continued south.

The narrow road was rocky and the soil along the way poor. They began to pass occasional houses, rude, dogtrot cabins for the most part. Small fields of oats and rye were greening in the sun. Each cabin had its corn patch with new stalks pushing up, evidence that a spring crop was being attempted this year. Matthew rode in his shirtsleeves, his coat in his blanket roll before his saddle, the sun beating down on his forehead and the bridge of his nose.

Late that afternoon the whole brigade, except for the Iowans, passed through New Albany and moved southwest along the Pontotoc road. The sky was now black with thunderheads and flashes of lightning scissored intermittently across the horizon to their front.

The column halted five miles south of New Albany on the Sloan plantation. Horses were unsaddled and the plantation's fence rails melted quickly away. The troopers would use them for shelters to hang their ponchos over, to keep out the coming rain. After assigning his picket details Matthew sat down at his campfire and shared a pot of coffee with Corporal Phipps and one of his sergeants, a sober man named Clark.

"We're going to knock hell out of Mississippi!" Phipps said. "Look how far we've gotten on this raid! And look what we've come up against! Not a damned thing worth mentioning!"

He took a swig of coffee and smacked his lips. "Three more days and we'll take Columbus."

Matthew slept fitfully that night, with the rain pounding against the poncho draped over his face. The pile of brush under his blanket did little to keep him out of the wet. His uniform was soon soaked through to the skin. But the weather could have been worse. It could have been sleet.

23

Before daybreak Sunday morning the Tylers sat in the kitchen eating breakfast, the unsteady light cast by the cottonseed oil in the lamp on the table sending wavering, elongated shadows into the corners of the room. Aunt Sophie suddenly put down her fork and said, "I'm not going."

Callie poured molasses on her cornbread and sighed under her breath. This was not the first time Aunt Sophie had refused to go to Memphis. But today was the day she and Robbie and Olivia were supposed to *leave*.

All three of them were dressed for the trip. Their trunks were packed and waiting in the parlor, passes had been obtained for them to cross the lines, and Mr. Charlie Blaylock would soon be arriving to escort them. All arrangements had been made.

"But, Aunt Sophie!" Blair said, putting down her coffee cup. "I've made you the lovely hat!"

Aunt Sophie raised both hands and waved them at Blair. "I refuse!" she said in a shrill voice. "I will not!"

Olivia stopped cutting Robbie's slice of fatback. "Robbie and I are going with you—"

Vehemently Aunt Sophie shook her head. "Not to live with Eugenia!" She got up from her chair, put her hand over her face, and burst into tears.

All eyes around the table turned to Anna Mary, sitting white and silent in the flickering light of the lamp. She rose, put her napkin on the table, and went to Aunt Sophie. "This is what Dr. Tyler said we must do," she said gently. "This is what Papa Tyler wanted us to do. Don't you see we can't stay here any longer?"

"You've always been so good to me!" Aunt Sophie said in a broken voice behind her hand. "You made me feel this was—this was my h-h-home!"

"It is your home."

"I l-l-loved the children! As if—as if they were my own! Anna Mary—don't make me go!"

Callie stared with determination at her cornbread and molasses. A great, white-hot poker burned inside her throat.

"Eugenia loves you, too, dear. She has written begging you to come."

"NO!" Aunt Sophie cried in such a loud voice that Callie jumped. "She doesn't like me! She never has! I've never been *grand* enough for her! Eugenia has always sneered at me, Anna Mary! I cannot bear the thought!"

"She is your sister—"

"*Why* did God have to take him? He was my mainstay! My rock! Anna Mary, I pray for him every breath I draw!"

Callie's eyes were so blinded with tears she couldn't see the cornbread and molasses. "He" was Grandpa, and Aunt Sophie was afraid he was in hell. The thought terrified her and she spent uncounted hours on her knees in her bedroom, pleading with her stern Old Testament God to have mercy on his soul. Always, she had assumed that Brother Samuel would take care of her for the rest of her life. Never had she dreamed that the cozy haven he had provided would fall about her with a crash. In her repeated warnings to her brother of hellfire eternal, never had she dreamed that he would die before she could convert him and make him come to Christ.

"Please listen," Anna Mary said. "It won't be for long. When the war is over, you can come back here. We'll all come back—"

"No," Aunt Sophie sobbed, but in a quieter voice, sounding beaten. "As soon as we leave, the Yankees will come and burn the house. You know they will, Anna Mary. They always do!"

"Austin and Telithia will be here."

"They'll burn it anyway!"

Callie wished Aunt Sophie wouldn't come right out and say it like that. She had a terrible feeling she was right. As soon as the Tylers left, another Yankee raiding party would come down from Tennessee and burn the house. They might as well leave a big sign on the front door saying, "Welcome, vandals! You can come in and burn it now!"

Anna Mary led Aunt Sophie from the kitchen, and the rest of them went back to their breakfast. Day after tomorrow, on Tuesday, Callie and Blair and their mother would be leaving, too.

Soon after sunup Mr. Charlie Blaylock arrived, driving a spring wagon. This would be Aunt Sophie's and Olivia's mode of transportation. It looked like rain, and Mr. Blaylock wanted to get an early start. Memphis was an all-day trip.

While her mother was kissing Robbie good-bye and holding him against her as though she never wanted to turn him loose, Blair kissed her sister-in-law on the cheek.

"Good-bye, Liv!" she whispered.

Olivia's brown eyes were swimming with tears beneath her new red-feathered bonnet. "Do you know what I hate about it most? Not being able to see Robert anymore!"

"You saw him just a month ago."

"They won't let *him* cross the lines," Olivia said, beginning to pick at the fringes on her shawl. "I may not see him again until the war is *over.*" She stared at

Blair. "How long do you think it's going to be? How much longer are we going to have to wait?"

Forever, Blair thought. A battle had been fought at Murfreesboro the last of December, but of course with the mail service stopped, the Tylers hadn't learned of it until long after it was over. The papers said it had been a great Southern victory, but as far as Blair could see, it had made no difference. Bragg's army had simply moved down to Tullahoma and Rosecrans had occupied Murfreesboro. What had they accomplished, besides getting the battle over with and making Robert's furlough possible? And her father's, too, of course. In March Dr. Tyler and Robert had come home together, for three weeks.

"Liv," she said. "You'll be safe in Memphis. The Yankees already have it. There won't be any raids and you won't have to keep your clothes hidden and you'll have enough to eat. I'm glad we're leaving! I'm *glad!*"

Olivia hugged her quickly, her hat brim brushing against Blair's cheek. She wondered if Liv had ever suspected. She didn't think so. Olivia had lived with them ever since she and Robert were married, and how many times had she really stopped and looked at her . . .

Austin was helping Mr. Charlie Blaylock load the trunks into the wagon. It had been rather surprising how much they'd had to pack. All of Robbie's baby clothes—miraculously spared.

Blair wondered if Olivia would have another baby now.

The sight of her brother and his wife together had been so painful she had almost been glad when Robert left.

Still, it hadn't been as terrible as the scene in the kitchen with her father. "It won't be long, Liv!" she said. "Then we'll all come back!"

"Time to go, ladies!" Mr. Blaylock said.

Robbie was passed about for one final round of kisses, and as the wagon rolled away down the drive-

way, he looked back over Olivia's shoulder, waving
good-bye. Aunt Sophie was sobbing and Blair wondered if she would ever lay eyes on any of them again.

Soon after reveille Sunday morning, Matthew and
Captain Swain of K Company were summoned by one
of Grierson's staff for special orders from the colonel.
At the Sloan house, they were informed that they
were to take their companies out to the east this morning, locate Colonel Hatch and the 4th Iowa, and, upon
finding them, convey orders for Hatch to make a feint
toward Chesterville. A Rebel general named Gholson
was organizing a regiment of state troops there.
At 6:00 A.M. the two companies rode out on their mission, shoulders hunched against the driving rain. Low-
hanging tree limbs, heavy with accumulated wetness,
brushed against the ducking men and showered them
anew. Matthew and Captain Swain had scouts riding
ahead of the two companies at long rifle range. Phipps
was among them. As they advanced cautiously through
the rain-soaked forest, the scouts would draw any unexpected rifle fire.
To Matthew's surprise it wasn't long before they
made contact with Hatch's advance guard. Grierson's
orders for the feint toward Chesterville were relayed,
and the Iowans said that after leaving on Saturday
they had gone east for only four miles and then turned
south, riding parallel to the main column. Since Saturday they had been skirmishing almost constantly with
an undetermined number of Confederates following
along their flanks and rear.
Once the orders from Colonel Grierson were delivered, Matthew and Captain Swain turned their companies back toward the Sloan plantation. The rain was
slackening and the going was quicker. They left the
cover of the woods and took to the road.
Matthew, riding at the head of his men, thought the
Iowans must be acting as decoy for the main column.
And evidently Grierson's strategy was working. The

Rebels had been concentrating on Hatch, perhaps under the impression that the 4th Iowa comprised the Union body entire.

The scouts, Phipps among them, were still riding fifty yards or so in advance. Matthew lost sight of them for a moment as they rounded a curve in the road. When they came into view again, he discovered they had halted beside a mud-splattered buggy. Putting spurs to his horse, he galloped toward them, telling the rest of the troopers to wait. When he drew rein beside the buggy, Phipps and the scouts were having a chat with its occupants. Peering inside, Matthew saw three excited young ladies.

"Joe," he said angrily. "What in the hell are you—"

"This heah's our captain," Phipps said. "An' most of our men back theah. I was just tellin' the ladies, suh, how we got ordered up yesterday from Columbus."

The young lady in the driver's seat leaned out of the buggy and looked apprehensively back toward the troopers in Matthew's rear. "Oh, do be careful!" she cried. "They attacked the bridge at New Albany yesterday!"

The young lady in the middle interrupted. "Did Willie Caskill come with y'all? Is he in your regiment?"

All three of the dainty creatures were dressed in spotless white. Ribbons and ruffles predominated. The buggy was a perfect flurry of excited flutterings and bobbing parasols.

"I'm not sure, ma'am," Matthew said, baring his teeth in a smile. "What regiment am I supposed to be in?"

"Ha, ha!" Phipps chuckled hastily. "Second Alabama, Company D. Up from Columbus, on a scout. As I was just informin' the ladies heah—"

"You must be *very* careful!" the first young lady insisted. "There were Yankees all over the Pontotoc road!"

She was a pretty little thing. As a matter of fact, all of

them were. It had been about four months since Matthew had seen ruffles and ribbons like that.

"How many troops have we got out here, ladies?" he asked, in a fair imitation of a southern drawl. He would throw in a "reckon" and a "y'all" in a minute. Phipps, he thought, was laying it on too thick.

Curls bobbed eagerly and delicate voices tripped over each other. They all wanted to tell him at once.

"Colonel Barteau's over at Okolona on the railroad! And General Gholson's got some state troops at Chesterville! And—"

"How many would you say Gholson has?"

The young ladies frowned and thought it over.

"Well—a lot."

"Yes, but so many of them had the measles, poor boys!"

"And they're not very well organized yet."

Matthew looked over at Phipps, who was drinking them in with delight. Joe's rain-slick poncho pretty well covered his uniform, but a healthy slice of his muddy blue trousers was visible above his high-topped cavalry boots. But then the young ladies undoubtedly assumed the trousers had been captured off some demon Yankee, as he lay stiffening on the battlefield.

"A couple of regiments, would you say?" Matthew inquired.

The young lady on the far side of the buggy leaned across her companions. "I *know* he's got J. F. Smith's cavalry. Willie Summers is in that! They came over not long ago from General Chalmers's western district. And he's got Weatherall's cavalry, too!"

"Are Smith and Weatherall at Chesterville now?"

The ladies held a hurried conference. They *thought* so.

Matthew thought with satisfaction that Colonel Hatch and the Iowans should be moving out on the feint toward Chesterville about now.

"Do you think we ought to go on?" one of the young ladies asked suddenly. "Is it safe?"

"Ma'am," Phipps said gallantly, "don't give it a thought! We've just cleaned out every Yankee to the rear!"

"I suppose they're all over at the railroad now, Lucy," the middle young lady said.

The first young lady smiled at Matthew and Phipps. "You Alabama troops are just splendid! We're so grateful that you've come to protect us! You don't know how much better we feel just knowin' that you're here! Why, we've been mighty near in a panic—with Yankees runnin' all over the place and nobody knowin' exactly where they were!"

"Now don't you worry!" Phipps cried delightedly. "We'll send 'em flyin' back to Tennessee! I expect we'll be layin' an ambush for 'em in just an hour or two! Why, ma'am, we'll annihilate that crew of thievin' scoundrels!"

"Oh, we *know* you will!" the bloodthirsty little darlings chorused, all but clapping their dainty hands. Matthew found them rather intriguing. They looked so soft and sweet. It was interesting to hear them putting their true feelings into words.

Captain Swain of Company K had now rounded the curve in the road and was riding cautiously forward with a puzzled expression. Matthew motioned for him to proceed and then lifted his cap to the ladies. "Time for us to be moving out," he said to Phipps and the scouts. As they were leaving, Matthew leaned toward the buggy and through his three-day growth of whiskers, showed his teeth in an evil smile. "I'll cut off a Yankee's ear and bring it to you," he whispered. "As a trophy of the chase."

The young lady closest to him drew back slightly and gave an uncertain little laugh. Matthew and Phipps rejoined the procession and Phipps, looking back over his shoulder, said that three lacy handkerchiefs were waving encouragement to the troopers as they passed.

When they reached the Sloan plantation, the 6th had

already left camp. The 2nd was saddled up and waiting for them. The column moved out on the Pontotoc road.

The earlier passage of the 6th across it had turned the road into an ankle-deep quagmire of adhesive, yellowish mud. No sun had come out to dry it, and some of the horses skidded and went down, taking their riders with them. Even the troopers who didn't fall were soon liberally flecked with yellow daubs from the hooves of the horses in front of them. Matthew kept his poncho on but could feel the little pellets drying in his eyebrows and dotting his face.

By late afternoon, as they were nearing the village of Pontotoc, firing was heard to their front. Assuming the 6th had entered and encountered resistance, the 2nd arrived at a gallop. They found the 6th already in control. A band of armed civilians, assisted by a few of Weatherall's state troops, had fired upon the advance guard but had been quickly routed.

Darkness was falling when they made camp a few miles below Pontotoc. Colonel Hatch and the Iowans had rejoined the column, having successfully made the feint toward Chesterville, with two hundred or so of the newly organized state troops nipping at their heels along the way.

As Matthew prepared to bivouac for this third night of march, his respect for Colonel Grierson grew. They were at least seventy miles into Rebel territory, and, as far as he knew, had not lost a single man.

The buglers blew reveille the next morning at two thirty. Stumbling about in the darkness, the men assembled for morning reports. Soon the company commanders were ordering, "Prepare for inspection!"

The sick and those showing signs of weakness were being sent back to La Grange. More than one hundred cavalrymen were eventually culled. The Rebel prisoners were lined up with them.

"The Quinine Brigade," Phipps said.

Grierson ordered this motley band to head back for Tennessee over the same roads the brigade had taken coming down. Their horses' hooves would further churn the yellow mud of Mississippi, giving the impression to any pursuing Confederates that the whole column had retraced its steps and was going back to base.

The ruse might be temporary, but it would add to the confusion. It would also obliterate the tracks heading south from Pontotoc.

The Quinine Brigade pulled out for La Grange in the darkness. At four o'clock in the morning the column once again headed south. Hatch's Iowans were in the lead. A chill, misty drizzle blew into Matthew's face as he hunched forward in his saddle, riding with eyes narrowed against the rain. He had a sense of portent, as though something important was going to happen. He was not convinced now that Columbus was their goal. This was the fourth day of march, and the sick men just mustered out could have made it for one more day. If the whole column would be heading back to La Grange day after tomorrow, it made no sense to send the Quinine Brigade back now.

He was beginning to believe that everything Grierson did made excellent sense. Matthew suspected the colonel had some other target in mind. What? He wasn't sure yet.

24

Monday evening Anna Mary and her daughters went into town and spent the night at the parsonage with the Thackerfords. Early the next morning Mr. Burton would take them by carriage to Abbeville, and they would go on the train from there. The railroad bridge was out across the Tallahatchie above Abbeville and had not been repaired.

At sunrise Tuesday they were off, Mr. Burton and Anna Mary on the front seat of the carriage, Blair and Callie in the back with boxes piled around them. One of the boxes contained their lunch. Creaking behind the carriage, a wagon driven by Jim Watkins carried their valises and trunks.

Their little cavalcade left town so early that nobody was on the streets. Callie sat silently watching all the familiar things she loved pass out of her life. The cupola on the Marshall County courthouse, the wrought iron fences from Jones & McElwaine, the graceful curving stairway above the columned portico on the Methodist church. Good-bye, they all seemed to be whispering. Good-bye! Good-bye!

Grandpa was staying. He would always be here. . . .

Blair, sitting beside Callie, thought, *I'm glad we're*

leaving. She was wearing her hoops today, and they spread over the boxes wedged under her feet. The greenbacks had been sewn into little bags and taped to the inside of the hoops. Anna Mary had some in hers too, and all three of them had additional greenbacks hidden in the soles of their shoes. Nowadays travelers hid their money. You didn't carry it in reticules anymore.

That morning Blair had managed to squeeze into her twilled bombazine. Before they left Monday, she'd tried on several of her dresses, standing in front of a tilt-back mirror. She had been satisfied that with the hoops, no one could tell.

The hoops were her fortress and her salvation, providing a hiding place for the money and for her. Eventually she supposed she would have to hitch them up a notch or two.

But, she remembered, once they got to Alabama, there'd be no need for a disguise. Only for lies. She'd already concocted several. Most of them revolved around a gallant Confederate husband, fallen in defense of the Cause. Blair looked out from the carriage at the rolling, wooded countryside along the Oxford road. They had already left Holly Springs and she'd scarcely noticed. She never wanted to come back.

Her father had been determined to get her out of here.

And, of course, he was right. In another month or two her condition would be so obvious that the Tylers wouldn't be able to hold up their heads in Marshall County. She would have succeeded in disgracing them all. . . .

Blair closed her eyes for a minute, feeling the lunch box jolt against her lap as the carriage passed over a bump in the road. *That's funny,* she thought. *I had so many beaux and I played the piano so nicely. I reckon Papa thought I was going to do him proud.*

Dr. Tyler had come into the kitchen unexpectedly

one morning and caught her being sick into a basin beside the stove.

He had stood in the doorway watching her. It was too late to control the nausea then and she'd had to go on. Through the whole humiliating, disgusting procedure. Knowing he was watching and not being able to stop.

Dr. Tyler waited until she was quite finished. Then he said, "You're pregnant, aren't you?"

He sounded as if he were diagnosing some loathsome disease. Blair went over to the kitchen washstand, found a damp dishrag, and pressed it over her mouth.

Her father was a tall man; once he had been redheaded, like Robert and Callie. Now his hair was gray. He was hatchet-faced and cadaverous; his sharp, deeply lined features were stiff with disgust.

"Who is the father?" he said.

Blair sank down at the kitchen table and buried her head in her arms. *Nobody!* she wanted to scream at him. *It's all mine! It's all I've got to live for! And it's not a disease, it's my baby!*

His voice cracked between them like a whip. "WHO?"

Blair couldn't answer. She couldn't say Matthew's name. *Nobody,* she thought again, her eyes squeezed shut against her arms. *There wasn't ever anybody like that! I made him up! The man I fell in love with didn't exist! The real Matthew wasn't anything like I thought he was—*

"A Yankee!" she screamed at her father, lifting her head from her arms.

Dr. Tyler took a quick breath. *There!* Blair thought. *Are you happy? Now you know!*

He turned his back to her and walked over to the kitchen window, clasped his hands behind him, and stood staring rigidly outside. "The captain who stayed here," he said, his voice drifting coldly around his back. "The one who was wounded. The one your mother cared for."

Blair's lips moved wordlessly, trying to make sounds. Mama had told him everything. Naturally, she would. Anna Mary and her father always told each other everything—

"Papa—don't say anything to Mama. Please—"

"My *God*, Mary Blair! I'd rather see you dead!"

The kitchen teetered dangerously, walls and floors seeming to swell unsteadily and then recede.

"You have strange preferences," he said. "These are the people who killed your grandfather. Who took your mother's wedding ring. Who have beggared me."

She had never really looked at her father, either. He had simply—been there all her life.

"Where is he now?"

"I don't know where he is," Blair whispered.

"I hope to God he's wounded again someday," Dr. Tyler said. "And they bring him to me."

Something cold and hateful and ugly crept across the kitchen, pulling and twisting at her.

"At Murfreesboro our wounded lay on the battlefield all night. Between the armies. We could hear them screaming. They were freezing to death."

Papa's living on hate, Blair thought. *The war has twisted his mind. He never used to talk this way.*

"I'll give you something to get rid of it. It may not be too late."

David—

"No," she said.

Dr. Tyler covered his face with his hands. "Ahh, God! God! God!"

He had told her mother, of course. Blair tried not to think about that. The pain she had caused Anna Mary she would never forget. She had begged her mother not to tell the others, and she had not. At least, she had been spared Aunt Sophie's sermons and Olivia's shocked sensibilities. As for Callie—well, she'd worry about that when the time came.

* * *

Thanks to their early start, the Tylers reached the Abbeville depot in time for lunch. The train for Oxford was due to leave at two o'clock that afternoon.

Boxes, trunks, and valises were unloaded from the wagon, they expressed their gratitude to Mr. Burton, and soon the carriage was on its way back to Holly Springs.

Callie wanted to run after it, yelling for him not to go off and leave her. Her last link with home was going up the road with him. *Now,* she thought with a terrible, lost feeling, *we are sure enough refugees.*

They ate their lunch in the depot. After that, Callie felt a little better. It was sort of adventurous, in a way. Like starting off on a vacation. She pretended they were going to New Orleans and would stay in a suite at the St. Charles. When they got there, she would visit a bookstore in the French Quarter and buy twenty ledgers and Augusta Jane Evans's new novel.

There wasn't much to do in Abbeville except sit on their trunks, and after lunch the adventurous feeling sagged a little. The passenger train to Oxford didn't leave when it was supposed to. Finally Jim learned from the stationmaster that the engine had broken down. They were trying to fix it; they were working on it right now.

It was four o'clock before they finally got it running. Callie had ridden trains before, and as she got on this one, she thought it wasn't much. There were only three cars—one passenger and two freights—and the seats had holes in the upholstery and were dusty. As the Tylers arranged their boxes around them, she thought the Mississippi Central had fallen on evil times. There wasn't even a ladies' car! Much less a sleeper. She'd felt an almost personal pride in the Mississippi Central's first-class sleeping cars. Among southern trains they were a rarity. And the Central was really Holly Springs's railroad. It had been planned and put into operation by Mr. Goodman and Colonel Walter and all the leading citizens.

Oh, well, Callie thought. *At least it's running.*

It didn't run very fast. On the ten-mile trip to Oxford, they stopped four times. Twice to clear brush from the telegraph wires along the tracks, and twice to work on the engine. The cars rattled and crashed against their couplers, clouds of pitch pine blew back from the smokestack, and they had to keep the windows closed because of the sparks.

Callie sort of enjoyed it, though. She rubbed a spot clean on the window so she could see through it.

"Next time," Jim Watkins said from the seat behind her, "we are going to stop and pick blackberries."

The trip from Abbeville to Oxford took three hours. When the train chugged into the Oxford depot, it was 7:00 P.M.

There was no conductor, but the fireman stuck his head into the passenger coach and said, "Everybody out! This is as far as we go today! Sorry, folks."

Blair and Anna Mary looked at each other in consternation.

Jim got to his feet and began picking up parcels and boxes. "Looks like we spend tonight in Oxford," he said pleasantly.

Later Callie wondered how they'd have managed without him. Besides serving as porter, Jim made a trip into town and contacted some old friends of his. This kindly couple extended an invitation for the lot of them to stay overnight at their house.

On Tuesday, the fifth day of march, the Iowans pulled off again to the east. The main column continued south, in a heavy rain. It was now obvious to even the most unobserving trooper that the brigade was not heading for Columbus. The men discussed where they might be going as they rode along. Some of them had made vain attempts to dry out their soaking uniforms by the campfires last night, but Matthew had gone to sleep as soon as he rolled up in his poncho and blanket. He had not taken his clothes off for five days, and his cotton shirt and heavy woolen trousers had a rank, sour smell. His beard was growing increasingly lush, but as far as he could tell, it harbored no lice. Lice were a bane of the marches—and even worse in the camps—and the only way to get rid of the graybacks was to strip and boil every article of clothing he had.

Mud, sowbelly, dysentery, and lice. The romance and glamor of a military life. He hated it now with a dreary, unending stoicism; a dull, day-to-day, week-to-week toughing it out. Waiting for the war to be won so he could go back to Springfield.

For what?

To get away from the mud, sowbelly, dysentery, and lice.

The Democratic peace factions in the Illinois State Legislature were yelling armistice. It seemed that they were getting tired of the war. *They* were getting tired of it. Every one of the traitorous bastards should be hung.

Day before yesterday, after leaving the three young ladies, Matthew had wanted to send a detail back to confiscate their horse. But Phipps had talked him out of it. "Captain, I'd be plumb mortified to make them tramp through the mud in those pretty white dresses! Especially after fooling them like that!"

Phipps had been charmed, hornswoggled, completely captivated. He'd asked later if Matthew had ever seen anything so nice.

Yes, he'd seen better. Not one of them could compare.

Back to Springfield when the war was won. What the hell was he going to do there?

At 4:00 P.M. the Union cavalry entered the town of Starkville, riding at a trot. Again no resistance was encountered and they stopped for a brief rest.

Starkville suffered slightly. The troopers entered all the stores along the main street, helped themselves to the merchandise, threw what they didn't want into the mud-slopped streets, stocked up on tobacco, captured the village mail boy, and robbed the mail. Executing a brilliant flanking movement, they stormed Hale & Murdock's traveling hat wagon, fortuitously in town at the moment, and took all of Hale & Murdock's hats. They gaily tossed out the hats to the colored citizens of the town, who were watching the goings-on in open-mouthed amazement. The horses and mules of Starkville, of course, quickly joined the column's reserve herd.

Matthew took no booty himself but did accept a few cigars from Corporal Phipps, who had more than he could use. He thought glumly that at the next town, maybe he would pick up a little something. He could send it home to his sister Amy as a souvenir.

Moving out of a dazed and reeling Starkville, they entered the low-lying bottomland country to the south. Swollen streams had overflowed their banks and the column struggled belly-deep in mud. Five miles below Starkville, they were forced to swim their horses across a roaring creek. Camp was made that night along another creek bank in a heavy rainstorm.

Matthew slept in an oozing puddle, with his poncho again draped over his face. He could sleep anywhere. This night, the mosquitos were swarming, ecstatic at their unexpected feast. In the swamps around them bullfrogs chur-runked, occasionally waking the men up.

Matthew was soon aroused from his slumber by a hand roughly shaking his shoulder.

"Captain! Wake up! The First Battalion's been ordered out!"

Groggy with sleep, he sat up and felt around in his pockets for matches to provide some kind of illumination. The lieutenant who had awakened him moved off among the sleeping troopers, the dull gleam of his lantern preceding him through the rain.

The 1st Battalion saddled up in the darkness without stopping to make coffee. Once again they splashed out through the swamps, ducking water-laden tree limbs, but this time they moved in starless, inky blackness. Matthew thought it must be close to midnight, and the water sucking about the horses' feet had an oily, stagnant look. A Negro had informed Colonel Grierson that a Rebel tannery was out this way.

In spite of the lateness of the hour and the unidentified slitherings and splashings around him, Matthew rode without a sense of foreboding. If a Negro had said a Rebel tannery was out in this hellhole, then a Rebel tannery would be there.

In this infernal country of yellow muck and sudden violence the blacks were the only ones he trusted. And during the exquisite torture of January and February in La Grange, he had sometimes thought Little Austin was the only thing that saved him from madness.

At this time, Matthew had fallen into the habit of putting himself to bed at night with a few drinks. It was the only way he could sleep, and with reveille sounding at four o'clock every morning, lying glassy-eyed in his bunk until all hours had been impossible. Whiskey was always available to officers, and soon the few drinks had become more than a few.

Several times he had ridden out on vedette so drunk that only the impeccable behavior of his horse had kept him in the saddle. It was a wonder he hadn't been court-martialed and shot. Perhaps at the time he had unconsciously hoped that this would happen, but he had evidently developed a facility for appearing sober when he wasn't. By not saying anything, and moving slowly, he gave the impression of being a little withdrawn but still functioning.

Only Little Austin had been aware of his true condition, and often Matthew had been awakened in his solitary hut by a voice saying solicitously, "You got to get up, Cap'n! The reveille done sounded!"

In March there had been rumors of the possible organization of a regiment of black troops in La Grange. He hoped it would come about. Little Austin was impatiently awaiting the day of his induction, and Matthew hoped to hell they wouldn't assign the blacks to fatigue duty and let it go at that.

The Tylers were at the Oxford depot early Wednesday morning, and to their surprise the train was ready to pull out. Trunks and boxes were loaded aboard, they settled into the dusty seats, and with a puffing, banging, and jolting they were once again headed south on the Mississippi Central.

Blair and Jim Watkins sat together this time. Soon a stout, ruddy stranger leaned across the aisle and said companionably, "Did you hear about the terrible accident with the nine forty-five from Grenada?"

"What?" Blair said.

"It left for Jackson on schedule!" the ruddy gentleman cried, slapping his thigh.

Jim laughed agreeably.

Blair looked back out her dirty window without replying. They rode in silence for a while. Then the stranger attempted another conversation.

"You watch," he said. "The engineer's going to stop for every bridge and trestle between here and Grenada. In my opinion, anybody brave enough to get on one of these tooters deserves a medal. Why, the M&T north of Senatobia is nothing but rust! It's falling to pieces!"

"Just as long as I don't have to get out and push," Jim said.

The stranger chuckled. "Well, I reckon that'll be next. The telegraph operator back at Oxford said the Yanks are raiding along the Mobile and Ohio. Got in a dispatch this mornin'. They're expectin' an attack on Columbus."

"Well, then," Jim said easily, "that makes it all the better for us. We'll have a clear track to Jackson."

"Jim?" Blair whispered. And when he bent his head to listen, "What did he mean about stopping at all the

bridges and trestles? Is there any danger they're going
to be *down?*"

"They're just being careful. It's just a precaution.
They always do it."

"Do you think we're going to be—to be attacked by a
raiding party?"

"Of course not! Didn't you hear our expert over
there? The Yankees are all busy at Columbus."

"What's the name of that railroad we're taking out
of Jackson? Is that the Mobile and Ohio?"

"*No,* honey! That's the Southern. The Mobile and
Ohio's fifty miles to the east of us."

Blair curled her toes, feeling the greenbacks in the
soles of her shoes. If the train were stopped—if the
Yankees swooped down on them all of a sudden—
would they search the passengers? A cold, sick feeling
rose in her stomach. What if they found the greenbacks? Would she and Anna Mary be sent to prison?
No, she thought. *Not again. Please, God, let us make it
to Alabama! Don't let anything happen now! I thought
we were getting away from it—*

"Listen," Jim said, giving her elbow a gentle
squeeze. "Stop worrying! We're almost to Grenada.
That's the northern edge of the Vicksburg defenses.
Pemberton's not going to let any Yankees slip through
there and get you! And if any of them try it before then,
I'm here to protect you. Don't you trust me?"

Blair smiled a little wanly. "Yes," she said.

Now she would pray they made it safely to Grenada.

It was about fifty miles from Oxford, she thought.
How many miles had they already covered? The delays
had started again, and the stout stranger proved pro-
phetic. The train slowed to a crawl at every bridge and
trestle. More passengers got on at Water Valley and
others departed. The train stopped again to take on
cords of wood for the engine. The coach was not
crowded, and so far Jim had been the only man in
uniform to board the train.

For Blair the turning of the wheels began to make a

singsong rhythm: *Grenada, Grenada—make it to Grenada.*

They arrived there at one o'clock that afternoon: a six-hour trip from Oxford.

The Tylers got off briefly to stretch their legs and walk up and down along the station platform. Coming in, they had seen trenchworks and Confederate pickets. Now they saw many soldiers.

When the train whistle sounded, all the passengers reembarked. A boy came through the cars selling sandwiches and fried pies. The Tylers and Jim purchased several. Blair ate hers with enthusiasm, although the bread was dry and the pies cold and soggy. She wished she had milk to go with it. Milk was good for babies, so it was probably good for her. She still ate the hardtack, too. She'd brought a supply of the crackers with her, in one of the boxes. *I've got to stop this*, she thought. *No wonder I can't get into any of my dresses. I'm going to be as big as a barrel.*

The train pulled out of the Grenada station. Anna Mary leaned around the back of the seat and said, "Are you feeling all right, dear?"

"Mmm—I'm fine," Blair said through a mouthful of sandwich. Callie had given her part of hers, saying she was too excited to eat it. Blair did feel fine. They were south of Grenada.

It had started to rain, but the train rattled on, puffing and smoking and making good time. The bridges and trestles south of Grenada were considered sacrosanct from Yankee raiding parties. By nine o'clock that night they were pulling into the state capital.

Jim couldn't believe it. He said they'd averaged almost fifteen miles an hour! That was as good as before the war.

The Jackson depot was a beehive of activity, even at that late hour. When the Tylers got off the train, the rain was pouring down in torrents. Jim went to find a hack and inquire about hotel accommodations. *Thank the Lord we've got some money*, Blair thought as they waited in the depot, surrounded by their trunks and boxes.

It would be nice to stay at the Bowman House, Anna Mary said, but she imagined it would be terribly expensive. Military supplies and soldiers were all about the station, and Callie said it looked like Holly Springs back in December, when the Federal supply base had been there. Only Jackson was bigger. General Pemberton's headquarters were somewhere around. Callie asked her mother if she thought they'd see anybody famous.

They ended up staying in a boardinghouse a long way from the station. The ride out in the hack was endless, made in darkness and pouring rain. Jim said he was embarrassed to take them to it, but it had been all he could find. Callie was just glad he was with them. What would they have done without him? Probably spent the night in the depot, on a bench.

Blair, Anna Mary, and Callie all shared one tiny room containing a narrow bed with a lumpy mattress. Callie decided she'd rather sleep on the floor. The wall beside the bed was coated with tobacco juice, the sheets looked dirty, and there were no bathing facilities, not even a bowl and pitcher. Anna Mary had been taken aback at the price demanded for the accommodations.

As Blair undressed, she put her hand to the small of her back. The fourteen-hour trip from Oxford had made it ache painfully. She was very tired now. Her neck and shoulders felt stiff from the jolting of the train.

If things were as they used to be, she thought, *we'd be staying at the Bowman House. And tomorrow morning, we'd go shopping. Mama and I would be picking out lovely dotted swiss and organdies and Irish poplins for my summer dresses. And tomorrow night we'd all go to a concert, or to see a musical.* Once they'd made a special trip to Jackson to see *Loan of a Lover,* and afterward her father had bought her the sheet music. . . .

What's happened? a little voice said. *What's happened?*

Only another hundred miles—or was it a hundred and fifty?—and they'd be in Alabama.

A new place. Untouched by war. A haven.

Blair crawled into the narrow bed and put her hand lightly to her stomach. *David. I love you . . . you're going where it's safe.*

At sunrise the column moved out again. It was now Wednesday, April 22, the sixth day of march.

The skies were clearing a little as they entered the flooded bottomlands of the Noxubee River. Creeks crisscrossed the route and the column turned to the west to avoid them. Sergeant Clark said that Company B of the 2nd had been sent out early that morning on a quick scout to Macon, to cut the telegraph wires and create more confusion along the railroad. Matthew thought that if Company B returned intact from that excursion, the only honor suitable for Colonel Grierson would be to deify him.

The citizens of the Noxubee River country, isolated by the floods, had not been alerted to the Federals' presence. Scouts dressed in civilian clothes had been sent ahead of the column, pretending to be Confederate guerrillas. Riding a mile or so in advance, they were gathering information as to roads, bridges, location of possible horse herds and forage, and the whereabouts of the enemy. If the scouts were captured out of uniform they would, of course, be liable for hanging. All of them had volunteered for the assignment.

As the column neared Louisville, a battalion of the 6th was sent ahead to set up pickets before the rest passed through. When they entered, the town appeared deserted. Every door was closed, every shutter drawn, and some of the windows had been boarded over. Louisville lay on higher ground, and evidently the citizens had received news of their approach and fled en masse.

It was almost dark now, and the silence was oppressive. All the troopers seemed to feel it, and it was as if ghostly, unseen eyes were watching from behind those locked and boarded windows. When Colonel Grierson ordered Major Graham to stay in the town for an hour after the column passed through, Matthew cursed silently. But Grierson meant to make certain nobody came out from behind those windows to spread the news of what direction the column had taken.

After the hour had passed, the 1st Battalion moved out of Louisville in the darkness on the trail of the brigade. The road to the south led through another swamp. Huge pines crowded on either side of them like towering sentinels, rising black against the sky. Still, on they marched. They had had precious little rest the night before, and some of the troopers were nodding. Others were slumped forward in their saddles, riding in their sleep. Occasionally Matthew turned to trot up and down beside his company. If the men were allowed to doze, their horses might get out of the line of march and wander into the swamp, carrying their riders with them.

"Close up, men!" he urged repeatedly, wondering if he would have to give them a whack across the shoulder blades with the flat of his saber.

At last, ten miles below Louisville, they rejoined the column in camp on the Estes plantation. Almost without halting, the troopers had covered fifty miles that day.

25

When Blair got up Thursday morning her back was still aching. The lumpy boardinghouse mattress had not been conducive to sleep, and as she began putting up her hair, she discovered that several of her precious hairpins were missing. They must have jolted out unnoticed during the long train ride yesterday. Struggling silently with her heavy coil of blond hair, she tried to secure it with the few pins that were left. She felt stiff and sore and not very clean.

Anna Mary went to ask the boardinghouse proprietress for a pitcher of water so they could wash their faces. When she returned with it, the water was cold and had a faint fishy smell. Their morning ablutions were made hurriedly. Blair took a rose-colored lawn out of her valise and wiggled into it. Callie buttoned her up, mercifully not commenting on how tight the lawn had to stretch.

The passenger train to Meridian was not due to leave until nine o'clock that morning, so the Tylers and Jim had time for a quick breakfast in the boardinghouse dining room. They were served leathery fried eggs, thick slices of fried pork, and the omnipresent cornbread. The proprietress said real Rio coffee was also available, at $2.50 a cup.

The trip back to the Jackson depot was made in the same hired hack, the driver having been engaged for that purpose the previous night. *Only one more day of this*, Blair thought. *Only one more day.*

By eleven o'clock their train had not arrived, and once again Jim went seeking information. He paid a visit to the telegraph office, staying longer than expected, talking with an officer he knew who was attached to Pemberton's staff. The officer said the Yankees were still raiding along the Mobile & Ohio and had been pinpointed at Starkville day before yesterday. A strong force was reported moving on Macon.

And strangely enough, he added, General Ruggles in Columbus kept wiring that the enemy was falling back to La Grange.

"I'm waiting for the train to Meridian now," Jim said. "Three ladies are traveling with me. Would it be advisable for them to continue on to Meridian?"

"Yes, I think so. The Southern's perfectly safe. All the trains are still running on schedule. More or less."

The Jackson-to-Meridian passenger train pulled into the Jackson depot three hours late. It was packed with refugees who had boarded in Vicksburg. When the Tylers started to get on, they were told by the conductor that there were no seats available. They could get on if they wanted to but would have to stand up all the way.

Anna Mary glanced quickly at Blair, who had been sitting in the depot since nine o'clock that morning.

"No," she said. "We can't do that. We'll wait for the next train."

"Ma'am," the conductor said, "there won't be one today."

"Mama," Blair said urgently, "*please* let's go on! I don't want to go back to that boardinghouse! I'm not tired!"

"No," Anna Mary said, her face drawn with worry and fatigue. "I won't let you stand up for a hundred miles. For another fourteen hours."

"Look," Jim said to the conductor. "I've got orders to report to Meridian. Is there any kind of train leaving Jackson today?"

The conductor looked down at Jim's leg. "There's a freight scheduled to follow us. It's going as far as Newton Station. *You* could probably hitch a ride on that."

"And the ladies?"

"Well, sir! If they don't mind sitting on their trunks!"

"Mrs. Tyler?" Jim said.

"How far is Newton Station?"

"Fifty miles, ma'am," the conductor said.

"Let's do it, Mama!" Blair said, holding pleadingly on to her mother's arm. *Fifty miles*, she thought. *Fifty miles farther along.*

The conductor looked at their bedraggled little group with a touch of sympathy. "There's a nice hotel at Newton. You could spend the night there and get the Meridian passenger train out in the morning."

A nice hotel! Callie thought. *I'll bet!*

Fifteen minutes later, they were boarding the freight. Callie thought it was about as comfortable as the passenger coach. Some of the boards along the side of the boxcar had been knocked off. Jim said it had probably been used to transport troops, and the soldiers had knocked the boards off to get a little fresh air.

It worked for the Tylers, too, and although they were surrounded by crossties and medical crates, the engineer brought back two stools, and Anna Mary and Blair sat on them. Callie and Jim sat on the floor. The engineer said a military hospital was at Newton Station and the medical supplies were being delivered to it.

The engineer also spoke encouragingly of the hotel. He knew the owners, a Mr. Moffatt and his wife, and said they ran a fine establishment. The Tylers would like it there. It was better than anything they'd have found in Jackson, that was for sure.

The trip to Newton took a little over five hours, and by the time they got there, Blair's back was breaking in half. The fireman and the engineer helped them unload their boxes and trunks before switching the cars to a siding to unload the freight. The promised hotel, across the dusty street from the depot, was a two-story building with peeling white paint. Right down the street from it was the military hospital, a hot-looking, sprawling barn of a place. There were a few unpainted stores on either side of the hotel and a nondescript building to the left of the depot. And that was Newton. *We're in the middle of nowhere,* Blair thought.

Two hours later, Callie stuck her head in the door of their hotel room and said, "Mr. Moffatt's got a telegraph machine in the depot! He showed me how it works!"

I've died and gone to heaven, Blair thought, luxuriating in a tub of hot water and frothy bubbles of soap. "I don't think I'll go to Alabama," she said to Callie. "I may stay in Newton for the rest of my life."

"It is pretty nice," Callie agreed, watching her around the door. "The Moffatts ought to be named Mr. and Mrs. Muffin, don't you think? I mean, they sort of look like that."

"They're beautiful," Blair murmured.

"We're having yeast rolls for supper! And strawberries for dessert!"

"I don't believe it." Blair sighed, squeezing warm water from her washcloth between her shoulder blades. "There aren't any strawberries left in the world! And for heaven's sake, close the door! Somebody's liable to walk through the hall and see me like this."

"We're the only ones up here," Callie said.

"Where's Jim?"

"Down at the hospital with Mama. Mr. Moffatt showed me how he sends messages in Morse code. He showed me how to make an *e*. Di—dah. And an *s* is di —di—dit—"

"Oh, Callie, I'm so glad we came on to Newton! Just think—we've got two whole rooms. One for Mama and one for you and me! And the beds! The beautiful beds! Close the door. I'm getting out of the tub."

"Supper'll be ready in thirty minutes," Callie said, banging the door shut.

Blair reached for a towel and climbed out of the tub. She'd forgotten there were such things as plenty of hot water and soap. And servants to bring it up to your room. The Moffatts had servants all over the place. You'd think there wasn't a war going on—

"Can I come in, dear?" Mrs. Moffatt's voice inquired from the other side of the door. "Have you finished your bath?"

"Yes, ma'am," Blair called, wrapping up in the towel. Mrs. Muffin—Moffatt—advanced across the room, bearing a pitcher of grape juice. Grape juice! Where in the world did she get it?

"I thought you might like something refreshin' after that dreadful boxcar! Imagine! What's the railroad comin' to? Puttin' ladies in freights! Ah—!"

Mrs. Moffatt had spied Blair's valise, sitting open on the floor with clothes tumbled about.

"Would you like to have one of your dresses pressed for tomorrow? They do get wrinkled when you're travelin', I know. But I can take it down to Ida and she'll do it in a jiffy."

Mrs. Moffatt put the pitcher of grape juice down on the bureau, clasped her hands in front of her spotless white apron, and stood smiling at Blair.

Blair felt a sensation of positive adoration for the plump, motherly little woman standing before her. Mrs. Moffatt had a neat bun of white hair and smelled of cinnamon and yeast. She reminded Blair of kittens and grandmothers and everything loving and kind and good.

"Mrs. Moffatt," she said softly. "I'm going to have a baby!"

Mrs. Moffatt threw up her hands in delight. "You precious girl!" she cried.

In the next five minutes Mrs. Moffatt made a thorough inventory of Blair's valise. She decided the blue sprigged dimity was the exact costume to press for tomorrow, and learned that Blair's back was still aching a little.

"Now you get your shimmy on, darlin'," she ordered, "and then I'll rub your back. And tonight for supper, we're goin' to give you plenty of milk. And you get to bed early! You need your rest!"

Blair put on her chemise and petticoats and sat down on the edge of the bed while Mrs. Moffatt massaged her back.

Why had she suddenly burst out and told her like that?

"But aren't you excited!" Mrs. Moffatt was saying. "And won't it be a lovely baby! With a pretty little mother like you!"

Blair was frightened now. *Why did I do it? Was I trying to pretend?*

"Mrs. Moffatt," she said. "I wish you wouldn't—say anything about it. At supper tonight."

"Not say anything about your precious baby? Why-ever not?"

"Mama—worries about me."

"Oh, well, if you say so, darlin'. Not a word! Your mama's such a sweet lady, isn't she? Those poor boys down at the hospital are goin' to love seein' her. You'll have to visit them, too! They're lonely, I'm afraid, though we do all we can—there, now! Does your back feel better?"

"Yes," Blair said.

An old-fashioned square piano sat in the hotel lobby. Blair had noticed it when they were checking in. The lobby was a comfortable, familylike room, filled with rococo chairs, settees, and Mrs. Moffatt's potted ferns. After supper Blair went to the piano and, standing over it, picked out a simple song. The piano was out of tune, but her hand moved across the familiar keyboard with a touch as natural to her as breathing. It was like touching the face of a beloved, almost forgotten friend.

The surgeon from the military hospital had joined them for supper, and soon they all began to drift into the lobby. Blair heard them taking seats behind her, and the discreet creaking of springs.

"That was our daughter's piano," Mr. Moffatt said. "It hasn't been played since she left here. Would you like to favor us with a few selections, my dear?"

"We'd love to hear someone playing the old piano again," Mrs. Moffatt said.

Blair sat down on the piano stool with a pleasure that was almost painful. She saw the mellowed ivory keys through a mist of tears.

She played tenderly, dreamily, and after a while she could hear their voices rising and falling around the music she made. "Yes," Mr. Moffatt said. "We know how terribly the northern part of the state has suffered. A correspondent from the *Appeal* stopped here two weeks ago. He'd passed through the country north of Grenada. Said that out of fifty plantations, approximately five still had people living on them."

"Did you find any boys you knew when you visited the hospital this afternoon?" Mrs. Moffatt asked.

"No," Anna Mary said. "But I imagine the medical supplies that came in on the freight with us will be very welcome. More welcome than we!"

The surgeon gave a short, unpleasant little laugh. He reminded Blair in some way of her father, although he and Dr. Tyler looked nothing alike. Three barrels of whiskey were in front of the hotel—medicinal, for the hospital, the Moffatts had said—and the surgeon had already made two trips out there before they sat down to supper. Each time he'd come back, he'd been a little ruder, a little more abrupt.

He didn't belong here. In the cozy serenity of the Moffatts' hotel lobby he was grotesque, an ugly little gnome who belonged somewhere else. *Go away*, Blair thought, playing softly.

"It's about time for the annual spring campaign in Virginia," he said. "About time for the Yankees to trot out their latest incompetent. I hear it's some idiot named Hooker this year."

"General Lee's unbeatable," Mr. Moffatt said.

The surgeon laughed. "Of course, sir! How many will they send against him this time? A hundred thousand? Keeps Marse Robert infernally busy killing them off! I anticipate another Fredericksburg!"

"I don't think this conversation is particularly interesting to the ladies," Jim said quietly.

"My apologies, then," the surgeon said. "Your visit through our wards this afternoon was appreciated, madam. Do you plan to be here long?"

"No," Anna Mary said. "We're leaving tomorrow morning."

"Alabama, I believe you said? Well, that should be tranquil enough."

"Some of the boys from the hospital come up almost every evening after supper," Mrs. Moffatt said. "One of them has a guitar. We've been having some nice little songfests. I'm sure they'll be coming up this evening. Later we can sit on the porch, if you'd like."

"I understand the Mobile and Ohio's under attack," the surgeon said. "Did you get any news in Jackson? As to what our galvanized Confederate is doing about it?"

"If you mean General Pemberton," Jim said, "the appropriate measures are being taken." He paused for a moment. "I was assured the line to Meridian is perfectly safe. As a matter of fact, our cavalry is driving the enemy back to La Grange."

"What cavalry?" the surgeon said, and laughed again. "Gholson's state troops? The sixty-day militia?"

Blair heard Jim getting up stiffly from his chair.

"Mrs. Moffatt? Why don't the ladies move out to the

front porch now? I'd like some fresh air myself. Mrs.
Tyler?''

Blair played a few more lingering bars. She had
tried not to listen. The music flowed sweetly around
her, wrapping her in moonbeams, taking her back. To
a happier place. A land of sunshine and crape myrtle,
wrought iron, and Steinway pianos, brought in by oxcart before the war . . .

Rocking chairs were on the hotel veranda and the
night air was pleasantly cool. Polaris, at the tip of the
handle of the Little Dipper, twinkled in the heavens
above the hotel. Mrs. Moffatt said the small building to
the left of the depot was a warehouse, containing small
arms and uniforms waiting to be sent to Vicksburg.

In a little while the convalescents began to drift up
from the hospital. Some of them were on crutches and
advanced slowly and laboriously. Mrs. Moffatt knew
all of them, and the Tylers were soon introduced. The
guitar owner, a Kentuckian who had not been home
since the war started, appeared carrying his guitar.

The soldiers sat on the grass in front of the hotel, in
the rocking chairs on the veranda, and on the steps.
"Are you going to play for us?" Blair asked the Kentuckian.

He was bashful in the presence of strangers, but after a little encouragement he played beautifully, a sunburned troubadour in butternut shirt and jeans.

"Sing for us, Blair," Jim said.

"What would you like to hear?"

" 'Home, Sweet Home,' " one of the convalescents
said.

"Let's all sing together."

"All right."

They sang "Home, Sweet Home," "Lorena," and
"Juanita." Blair supposed they would have sung forever in the starlight of Newton Station if Anna Mary
hadn't finally said they would be leaving early in the
morning and must be going inside. Blair was tired, but
she wasn't sleepy. The rocking chairs made a gentle

creaking on the veranda, and across the street the depot and warehouse were disguised in moonlight and soft with shadows.

As she sang, Blair had been conscious of the sad eyes of the soldiers watching her. She thought they were seeing someone else. Wives and sweethearts; all the women waiting in all the homes across the South. *I've changed*, she thought, her hands folded lightly in her lap. She hadn't bothered with the hairpins tonight, and her hair hung carelessly down her back, tied with a green ribbon Mrs. Moffatt had given her.

After they'd all said good night and were going through the hallway to the steep, narrow little staircase leading to their rooms, Jim chuckled softly.

"What are you laughing about?" Blair asked.

"You didn't hear it? That fellow sitting by me congratulated me. Said I certainly had a lovely wife."

Blair pointed to herself in amazement. "Me?"

"Yes, honey. He thought we were married."

"Didn't you tell him any different?"

"Why, no. I just sat there and contemplated my good fortune."

Blair laughed. "Jim! You should be ashamed!"

"Well, why not? We've been engaged since you were ten, haven't we?"

He smiled down at her. Callie and Anna Mary had already preceded them upstairs. For a moment Blair stood watching his face. Gentle, amused, sensitive, it told her nothing. *He's joking*, she thought. *And even if he wasn't* . . .

"I'm so glad you've been with us these last three days," she said.

"Yes. I've been a regular trump. I got you the delightful boardinghouse. And the boxcar."

"That wasn't your fault."

If she leaned toward him now, would he kiss her?

Yes, she thought. On the forehead. A brotherly kiss. And yet—maybe not. Why had he told her about the soldier on the veranda mistaking her for his wife? Was it an opening? A hint? Maybe that was the way he would like it to be.

You'll find someone from your own people. Someone who has the same ties, the same roots . . .

I can't do it, she thought. *I can't let him kiss me even if he wants to. I couldn't do that to him. He's so thin. His chest would be almost fragile. Like a bone. Oh, Jim . . .*

"Good night," she whispered. "And thank you for all you've done."

Thursday morning "Boots and Saddles" blared across the plantation fields all too early. Matthew's head was up from his saddle in what seemed five minutes after he'd put it there. This morning, however, there was time for a quick cup of scalding black coffee. They would eat as they rode. The horses, always attended to first, were fed and watered. Some of the troopers had taken out their pocket knives and were attempting to scrape the dried mud off their uniforms as they waited for the order to mount.

Matthew thought the sky was clearing.

To the south lay another swollen river, the Pearl. It was known to be too deep and swift to swim or ford. The scouts had reported increasing numbers of armed civilians, scurrying along in front of the column. But all of them had been keeping at a safe distance, well out of rifle range. Grierson feared that the Pearl River bridge had already been destroyed.

As the column neared the town of Philadelphia, a volley of gunshots erupted. A band of civilians had drawn up across the road and fired into the advance guard. As soon as the advance guard charged, the civilians scattered.

Philadelphia was soon encircled and picketed and Colonel Grierson dismounted to interview the prisoners; the elderly gentlemen appeared extremely apprehensive about what was to be done with them. One of the old men said they had been in the process of organizing a party to burn the Pearl River bridge when the advance guard galloped in. *Not even state troops this time*, Matthew thought, wondering what had happened to Barteau's Tennesseans and Smith's and Weatherall's cavalry.

Later, as they rode out of Philadelphia, Corporal Phipps cleared up the mystery to some extent. He had been talking to one of the scouts, who said Company B had reached Macon and drawn strong pursuit from that vicinity.

Good God Almighty! Matthew thought. Strong pursuit concentrated on one company, composed of thirty troopers? Where were the rest of the Rebels? Tracking Hatch's Iowans along the Mobile & Ohio? Following the Quinine Brigade back to La Grange?

At five o'clock that afternoon the column halted at another plantation to feed and rest the horses. Matthew, who had had approximately six hours sleep out of the last forty-eight, paced restlessly. He felt impatient, irritable, keyed up for a fight that refused to come. He had lost all sense of distance traveled, and thought they must have penetrated as far south as Jackson. Pemberton's headquarters were there, and the idea crossed his mind that they might be attempting an attack on the state capital. By this time, he was convinced that Grierson was capable of leading them successfully through any endeavor, no matter how preposterous it sounded.

This stop, too, was brief, and they were again on the march, moving rapidly south.

At ten o'clock that night another halt was ordered.

In a few minutes the four companies of the 1st Battalion were ordered to assemble. This time, Lieutenant Colonel Blackburn addressed them.

As his horse pranced back and forth in front of his forming columns, Blackburn told his men exactly where they were going and exactly what they would be expected to accomplish.

All last winter and into spring, he said, the Army of

the Tennessee had been struggling to get into position for the Vicksburg assault. As every member of the 1st Battalion knew, the overland campaign through central Mississippi had been unsuccessful, as had the route through the bayous and swamps. The purpose of this raid was to divert the Rebels' attention from the main thrust now being made against Vicksburg. Grant was moving his army across the river at Grand Gulf.

Blackburn said that directly to the south—now less than twenty miles away—lay Pemberton's lifeline to the east. The Vicksburg Railroad.

Over it must pass all ordnance, supplies, and troops coming in to reinforce him from the eastern states of the Confederacy. If they could cut this railroad, they would be severing his supply line at the time it was most vital to the defense of Vicksburg. If they could break his telegraphic communications, he would be cut off from his bases along the Mobile & Ohio. And hopefully they would draw off many of the Rebel troops from Grant's movement across the river.

The raid so far had been brilliantly successful, Blackburn said, and he was confident of their ability to accomplish this final mission.

The two hundred men of the 1st Battalion would leave immediately on a forced march to the railroad, with the main column to follow within the hour. The town of Decatur lay between them and the railroad, and they should be reaching it before dawn.

The temperature had fallen and the stars were out. The night air had an exhilarating briskness as it blew against Matthew's face when the battalion moved out at an easy, swinging gallop. With the scouts in the lead, the advance guard rode a quarter of a mile in front of the first company, with moving pickets strung out at one-hundred-yard intervals, searching out every by-road and crossroad for concealed observers.

"I'll be darned!" Corporal Phipps shouted behind him. "The Vicksburg Railroad!"

Around midnight two of the scouts got tangled up in

the thickets and byroads and fired on one another. Luckily they both missed. There were no other incidents, and at 3:00 A.M. Colonel Blackburn ordered a halt. The scouts, still wearing their civilian clothes, were to ride ahead into the village of Decatur and pick up any information they could get as to the disposition of Rebel defenses along the railroad.

In an hour or so the scouts returned. After arousing a sleeping citizen, they had been hospitably invited into his home. When told they were scouts from Van Dorn's command, carrying written communications to Confederate forces in the area, the citizen had informed them that a considerable force of Confederate cavalry had passed through Decatur a few days ago, going east. The scouts then inquired as to the location of troops guarding the railroad, so they might get in touch with them. The citizen said that the nearest soldiers would be at Newton Station, some ten miles to the south. He knew a hospital was there, containing about a hundred sick and wounded, but was not sure there would be any infantry.

After receiving this helpful information, the 1st Battalion continued their advance. A brief halt was made at a creek ford, where they paused to unbit and water their horses.

When the sun rose on Friday morning, the Union cavalrymen were within a mile of the railroad. They had ridden unchallenged all the way. Blackburn once again ordered the scouts to precede them, reconnoiter the railway depot at Newton Station, find out exactly what troops, if any, were stationed there, if they had any artillery, and what time the first train was due to pull in.

After the scouts had gone, Blackburn strode back and forth impatiently, talking with his officers. The prize was almost within their grasp. Lack of sleep and hard riding had made them all impatient.

26

Friday morning Blair's blue sprigged dimity hung waiting in their room. She and Callie dressed in the dewy coolness of early morning and once again, Blair struggled with her coiffure. No matter how few hairpins she possessed, a lady could not travel with her hair streaming down her back. Or without a bonnet.

The Meridian passenger train was due to arrive in Newton at eight forty-five, but the Tylers' valises had been brought down to the lobby early, just in case. Their trunks had been left in the depot overnight, as Mr. Moffatt had assured them they would be all right. The depot had a safe containing the Southern Railroad's money, as well as a storage room full of medical supplies for the hospital. Mr. Moffatt locked it securely every night.

After breakfast, Callie wanted Blair to go over and see the telegraph machine. Blair was not particularly eager to see the telegraph, but to please Callie she agreed. Mr. Moffatt went with them to unlock the depot and Jim also ambled over. As they crossed the street, several of the convalescents hobbled out to sit in the early-morning sunshine in front of the hospital. Callie waved to them, and several of the men waved back.

After climbing the little flight of steps leading to the depot, they waited for Mr. Moffatt to unlock the door and followed him inside. Another door led onto the loading platform and he opened that too. The telegraphic equipment sat on a high table, and Mr. Moffatt perched on a stool to operate it. All of them gathered round to observe, and Jim listened with interest as Mr. Moffatt explained how it worked. After a while Blair wandered over to the open door to look across the station platform to the trees beyond the railroad tracks.

It was almost eight o'clock now, and the dewy coolness of the morning was already wilting in the heat. Below the railway embankment a ditch filled with stagnant water glimmered iridescent in the sun. Clouds of mosquitoes hovered in the air above it. At home, they hadn't been bothered much with mosquitoes; the high elevation, Grandpa always said—

"Mister?" a man's voice said suddenly behind her. "You got a telegraph in here?"

Turning, Blair saw three bearded, mud-caked men in butternut trousers and linsey shirts standing against the sunlight from the street. All three had pistols buckled around their hips. The one who had addressed Mr. Moffatt advanced quickly across the waiting room, taking a folded piece of paper from his shirt. "I've got a dispatch to be sent to Jackson. It's urgent. I'd appreciate it if you could get it on the wire right away."

Mr. Moffatt reached out for the paper and Callie moved back, her eyes riveted on the dispatch. *Urgent!* she thought, a shiver of excitement shooting up her spine.

"What is it, sir?" Mr. Moffatt inquired.

"The Yanks were spotted north of Philadelphia yesterday."

Mr. Moffatt gave a little start of disbelief. "Philadelphia?"

"That's right."

"But—good Lord, man! That's about—about thirty miles from *here!*"

"I thought you said our cavalry was drivin' the enemy back to La Grange!" Callie cried to Jim.

The mud-caked stranger laughed. "Not quite. Evidently there's been some confusion as to exactly where they were. But we've got them located now."

"But—" Mr. Moffatt said. "Do you think they're heading *here?*"

Impatiently the stranger shook his head. "The bridge north of Philadelphia's been destroyed. They can't get across the Pearl River. It's certain they'll head back to La Grange now. Come on, man! Get this dispatch on the wire! We've got cavalry hunting all along the Mobile and Ohio! We've got to turn them north!"

Mr. Moffatt opened the piece of paper and looked at it. "Directly to Pemberton's headquarters?"

"Yes. And hurry it up."

The other two men were still standing in the sunny doorway. Occasionally they turned to look behind them into the street.

"Whose command are you attached to?" Jim asked. "Gholson's state troops?"

The stranger shook his head. "We're scouts. Van Dorn's command. Out of Tennessee."

"Oh? Roaming pretty far afield, aren't you?"

"We were ordered down with dispatches for our troops along the Vicksburg Railroad. What the hell have you got here? I didn't even see any pickets when we were riding in."

"What company?" Jim said.

"You're damned lucky the bridge over Pearl River was destroyed. No infantry here either, is there? Expecting any to come over from Meridian? Or from Jackson? Today?"

"Who is your captain, sir?"

"Now look! I don't have time to stand here and chew the fat all day! Mister, are you going to get that wire out or aren't you? Every minute we stand here jawin' is another—"

Jim put his hand down across the telegraph key.

"Don't send it," he said.

Mr. Moffatt looked at him in surprise. The two men who had been standing in the doorway started across the room.

"What in the devil—" the scout began.

"You're not scouts from Van Dorn's command," Jim said. "I'm not sure what in the hell you are, but I think you're Federal spies."

Blair, still standing silently in the doorway to the loading platform, felt her stomach curl slowly, like a little animal, caught in a trap. *No*, she thought. *Not again—not today—*

The stranger unholstered his revolver and pointed it in Mr. Moffatt's startled face. "All right. Send any messages over that wire now and you're a dead man! Move back! *Back!* Dammit! Over there. Against the wall. You too, lady," he said to Blair. "Sit down on that bench. And you, you damned clever Johnny, you make a false move and I'll put a ball through you!"

"I'm not armed," Jim said.

"Move!"

Help! Callie thought wildly, glancing at the telegraph key. Could she make a mad dash for it and di-di-dit, di-dah it out before they shot her? Jim's hand gripped her arm, pulling her across the depot toward the bench. Mr. Moffatt, pale and trembling, climbed down from his stool. Blair had already sat down on the bench. Her blue-green eyes stared vacantly in front of her and her face had turned a chalky white.

Not a chance! Callie thought, looking over her shoulder at the telegraph key. The Yankee in butternut trousers and linsey shirt was ripping the instrument apart. Callie, Jim, and Mr. Moffatt sat down on the bench.

A train whistle sounded in the distance, tooting imperiously a few miles to the east. "What's that?" the Yankee said.

"A—a train!" Mr. Moffatt said in an awe-struck voice.

"Goddammit! I know that! What train, you fool?"

"The—the nine o'clock freight! From Meridian! Heading for—for Vicksburg!"

"It's not nine o'clock yet."

"Y-y-es," Mr. Moffatt said. "It's e-e-early! Today!"

The Yankee turned quickly to one of his companions. "Ride back and tell Colonel Blackburn if he wants that freight, he'd better get the battalion down here pretty damned quick!" Then he turned to the third Yankee. "What about those Johnnies we saw in front of that hospital down there? Any of 'em heading up here?"

The other two Yankees, who also had their revolvers in their hands, bolted through the waiting room door and clattered down the steps to the street. Callie, sitting on the bench between Jim and her sister, could hear one of them shouting.

"Remain inside! Remain inside! Don't come out on peril of your lives!"

Callie heard no resultant gunfire, so assumed all the convalescents were hobbling back inside.

There was a staccato drum of hoofbeats and she turned and quickly rubbed a spot clear on the dirty window behind her. She could see nothing except a cloud of dust rising in the street and the hotel across from it. The hotel veranda was empty. Did her mother and Mrs. Moffatt know what was happening?

WHOOO–WHOOO! the freight from Meridian tooted, approaching a crossing. How far was it from Newton Station now? A mile?

Turn back! Callie thought. *Turn back before the rest of the Yankees get here!* The butternut-clad spy was still in the waiting room with them, looking through the open doorway leading to the loading platform and tracks.

Blair's hand moved over from her lap and clasped Callie's. She began squeezing it so tightly Callie's fingers ached. "It's all right," Jim said from the other side of her. "They won't hurt you. Just sit still."

"I see it!" the Yankee shouted. "There's the smoke!"

Callie looked up at Jim.

"The freight," Mr. Moffatt whispered. "You can see

the smoke a long time before it gets here. Above the
trees."

Pitch pine, Callie thought.

Were they just going to keep on sitting here? She
reckoned they were. That Yankee would shoot Jim in a
minute, if *he* tried to leave—

Callie heard the drumming of hoofbeats approaching from the north. She whirled around to her observation hole in the grimy window. In a minute or two—
here they came, thundering down the street between
the depot and hotel. The dust swirled around them like
a regular tornado, obscuring the hotel. The colonel had
ridden in at the head of the column, standing up in his
stirrups and waving his hat in a circular motion above
his head. He was cheering loudly. Thought the freight
was as good as caught, Callie supposed. She had a
sinking feeling that it was.

In a twinkling the Yankees inundated Newton Station. All of them were so dirty and dust-covered she
found it hard to distinguish the officers from the men.
Ha! she thought with an angry sense of being taken.
Our cavalry is driving the enemy back to La Grange!

How could Jim have *told* them such a lie? Did he
really *believe* it? But that was the way they always
talked in front of ladies. They never wanted them to
know anything—

"Good Lord!" Mr. Moffatt said softly, rubbing a spot
on the window himself. "How many are out there, do
you suppose?"

"Enough," Jim said tightly.

In the street the Yankee officers were riding back
and forth yelling, "No bugles!" Gauntleted hands frantically wigwagged the signal to dismount. Swinging
down from their saddles, the soldiers led their horses
behind the hotel, behind the warehouse beside the depot, behind the depot itself. Callie, looking through the
window, saw a group of them heading right for her
peephole!

"What are they doing?" she asked.

"I believe they're hiding!" Mr. Moffatt said.

Two of the soldiers tossed their reins to someone else and went sprinting around the depot in the direction of the tracks.

"Where are *they* going?" Callie whispered to Mr. Moffatt.

WHOOO–WHOOO! the freight from Meridian whistled. It was almost *here!*

"The switches," Mr. Moffatt said. "They must be sending them around to throw the switches! In case the engineer tries to pull out!"

"Won't he *see* them?"

"I guess they'll hide in the grass. It's—pretty high."

One of the Yankees behind the depot reminded her of Captain Harwell. He had the same solid-looking build and the same curly hair. Only this one was so dirty and had such a beard, it was obviously someone else. They did look a lot alike, though.

Another Yankee suddenly stepped into the depot from the platform side, holding a revolver. He motioned to Jim and Mr. Moffatt. "All right, gentlemen," he said. "You're too close to the tracks. Time to step outside."

Mr. Moffatt popped up from the bench. Jim said, "What about the young ladies? Are you going to take them out in that mob?"

The Yankee looked at Blair and Callie. Mostly at Blair, Callie thought. "Oh, I guess not," he said agreeably. "They can stay in here. That is, if they promise to behave themselves."

"Where're you taking *them?*" Callie asked.

"Just outside, sis," the Yankee said. "Can't have them going through that door onto the platform before the train pulls in."

"Jim—" Blair said.

"It's better for you to stay inside. This won't go on much longer, Blair. The train's almost here."

As he was escorting Jim and Mr. Moffatt across the

waiting room the Yankee said, "We've got three men out by the platform, ladies. You'd best sit still."

Callie looked through the window, to see where he was taking Mr. Moffatt and Jim. They were being herded down the steps and over to the side of the building. There were Yankees packed all behind the depot now. The one who looked like Captain Harwell had taken off his cap. The resemblance was truly amazing. If it wasn't for the beard, Callie would have sworn it was him.

The Yankee suddenly rammed his gauntlets into his belt and looked impatiently up at the dirty window above him. Callie thought they were almost eyeball to eyeball. But he hadn't noticed her peeking at him through the dirt. He turned his head and looked off down the street.

Callie felt goosebumps popping out on her arms.

It *was* Captain Harwell!

The brown eyes were the same! She couldn't be mistaken about that! It was *him!*

"Blair," she whispered in delighted amazement, plucking at her sister's arm. "Blair! Captain *Harwell's* out there!"

There was a tiny silence.

"No," her sister said.

"Yes, he *is!* He's *right down there!* By the steps!"

WHOOO–WHOOO! The train was chugging nearer and nearer to the station. It must be within sight! They were going to see Captain Harwell capture the Meridian-to-Vicksburg freight! After it was over, she'd have to run out and talk to him. Find out what he'd been doing all these months—

It occurred to her that she should run across the waiting room and look out on the loading platform. See if there were really three Yankees out there.

Maybe there was still time to flag the engineer. *Stop! Reverse the engine! Yankees are all over Newton Station! They're waiting for you! Go tell General Pemberton! Boy! Was he dumb!*

Outside on the tracks in front of the station the train was puffing and steaming. Callie heard the rusty screeching of flanges and the clanking of couplers as the brakeman began applying his brakes. She couldn't stand the suspense. Scampering across the waiting room, she peeked around the door to the loading platform.

"Callie—" Blair said.

Out by the platform, in the shade of the trees, the three Yankees waited. Two of them were the butternut spies and the third, the mud-caked colonel. The brakeman, standing on a side step, jumped off and went loping over to a switch. He turned it and locked it. The engine, pulling twenty-five loaded freight cars, eased slowly onto a siding. The engineer, sitting high in his cab, looked down at the three waiting Yankees. He raised his hand in friendly salutation.

Callie heard him say, "Mornin', folks."

The colonel lifted his arm in a sweeping signal.

In the flick of an eyelash Yankees poured out from behind the depot, the warehouse, the hotel—all the buildings of Newton—and went whooping toward the train. One of the butternut spies jumped up onto the steps of the engine and shoved his revolver into the face of the engineer. The engineer scarcely had time to register any surprise. The freight and all of the twenty-five cars were captured. Callie realized that her mouth was open. She closed it. Her tongue felt dry.

WHOOO–WHOOO! She jumped at the sound of another train whistle, tooting from the west.

The colonel began shouting, ordering all the Yankees back to their hiding places. The engineer and crewmen were led away for safekeeping. The twenty-five cars of the freight sat secure on their siding. There was a brief confusion and milling about and then the loading platform and the front of the depot were once again clear of Yankees. Except for the colonel and the butternut spies, who took up their previous positions close by the tracks.

The Meridian passenger train was coming in from Jackson. It was eight forty-five.

"That's *our* train," Callie said to her sister, sitting across the waiting room behind her. "Now they're going to capture *it!*"

She turned to look at Blair. Her sister was gone.

The hotel, Blair thought. *It's just across the street. I've got to get out of here before he comes back. They're all around at the front now. I can run to the hotel.*

The sunlight bounced against her as she stepped through the door. For a moment she couldn't see. Bright spots of red and orange and glaring white danced in front of her. But she knew the hotel was there. It was just across the street.

The Yankees were coming back. Some of them were already behind the depot. In a minute, they would surround her again. She didn't care if they shot her in the back when she ran across the street. She couldn't stay in that waiting room. She couldn't stay there and wait until he came in and saw her.

Blair started down the steps.

But, of course, they weren't through with her yet. *Two more minutes,* she thought. *Two more minutes and I'd have been in the hotel. Two more minutes and I wouldn't have seen him. I can't stand this. Why does he have to be here now?*

He was almost directly below her, by the steps. She stopped, put her hand on the sooty railing, and stared past him, into the sunshine of the street.

For Matthew the world went dark around the edges. The grimy unpainted little station, the lingering swirls of steam from the captured engine, the soft nickerings of horses concealed behind the buildings—they all faded. There was only one thing now. Only one thing that he saw.

Blair had appeared out of nowhere and was so close he could almost reach out and touch her. He had no time to think of how she came to be here, or wonder where she was going. He thought only that she seemed to be a different person. She looked heavier, and years older, and as his eyes ran over her in a quick, oddly impersonal appraisal he saw that the old aura of airy, graceful seductiveness was gone. For a split second he allowed himself to remember and then immediately blanked it out. Because there was no way he could think of that now, if he wanted to keep functioning. Which, of course, he had to do.

"Get back inside," he said. "You can't leave until after we've taken the train."

She took a quick breath, lifted her chin and closed her eyes. Little drops of perspiration had come out along her upper lip. Yet in the pale blue dress she looked fresh and unwilted. A bonnet with blue ribbons was clutched tightly in her hand, the ribbons trembling against the flounces of her skirt. He had a terrible, brutal impulse to drag her away from the railing and sling her down into the dirt.

Blair's hand tightened on the railing and she opened her eyes. "I have to get on that train, damn you! Can't you at least let me do that? Or are you going to burn it like everything else?"

Matthew felt sick. Why was he standing here? Why was he talking to her? He should have let somebody who didn't know her stand here and look at her.

"Yes," he said. "We're going to burn it. Now get back inside. Or I'll have one of my men carry you in."

And tie you up and gag you, he thought. *Because, by God, you're probably getting ready to run down the track and give the alarm!*

She made a small, strangled sound. "You weren't ever coming back! Were you?"

A strange pounding echoed inside his skull. *Don't answer!* something warned. *You're wiser now. And nobody could be that big a fool twice. If you answer her, she'll carve another piece out of you and when that happens, you'll be finished. Because there's nothing left to carve from. And may God help you if you ever listen to her again!*

He turned to his gawking troopers, who had been watching the exchange in silence. "Clark?" he said.

The pounding in his head was almost blinding him. But there was no need for Sergeant Clark. She had already gone back into the depot.

Blair sat in the waiting room with her hand gripping the arm of the bench. At measured intervals an invisible broadax swung down across the small of her back. She was being chopped in half, while outside, pandemonium reigned. The passenger train from Jackson had been captured and was steaming in front of the depot. It contained twelve freight cars as well as the passenger car. Both trains were loaded with Confederate commissary and quartermaster supplies, artillery shells, railroad ties, bridge timbers, and planking. One boxcar on the passenger train was full of furniture belonging to families refugeeing from Vicksburg.

The Yankees had already smashed in the doors of the freight cars and now were smashing in the windows of the passenger car. Shouts, shrieks, and the squalling of infants rang out from the tracks. Callie said they had taken the passengers off. Blair's other hand rested on her stomach. The new hat with blue ribbons lay on the floor at her feet. Callie was in a frenzy of excitement, running from the waiting room to the loading platform and then running back again. Blair hadn't moved.

You were still hoping, weren't you? she thought. *You hadn't ever given up. Why did you go out there? Were you hoping you'd see him? Is that why you went?*

A strange little pain gnawed at the pit of her stomach. What did it mean? She felt sick all over now. A terrible, cold sickness that attacked her in waves. She held on to the arm of the bench. If she could only lie down. She took a deep breath and closed her eyes. Something was wrong inside her. She didn't know what. It felt as if something were crushed and mangled, dying in there.

Callie ran back into the waiting room and said some of the passengers had thrown their things out the train windows when they saw the Yankees all over the station. They'd thrown out wallets and pistols and packages, all out the windows on the opposite side from the station! Everything had landed in the ditch by the tracks! People had thrown their *money* out there! The Yankees were around in the ditch picking it up!

Blair pressed her hand over her stomach. *David*, she thought. *There's something wrong with my baby . . .*

Some of the passengers were coming into the waiting room. Blair sat and watched as they flooded around her: women in hoopskirts and bonnets, flushed, incoherent men, disheveled, crying children. One woman had five. Five hysterical children. Everything he owned was on that boxcar, a man was saying. And the Yankees were getting ready to burn the train!

The Yankees would burn the depot, too. And the Moffatts' hotel. The square piano would be burned. Why had she played it last night?

The Tylers' trunks were still in the waiting room, close by the bench, but they wouldn't be there long. In a minute, the Yankees would come in and smash them. All the dresses Callie had saved would be stolen. Everything they owned—all they had left—gone.

The greenbacks would be discovered. She and her mother would be stripped and searched. Sweat trickled down Blair's ribs and in the cleft between her breasts. *They're killing my baby*, she thought. *My back shouldn't be hurting like this. He's too little—they're killing David before he's had a chance to be born.*

She heard the trains' engines starting up again. Callie ran through the mob of people in the waiting room and sat down on the bench. She said the Yankees had brought the engineers back and were making them move the trains farther down the tracks. They were getting ready to set fire to the cars. Some of the Vicksburg refugees were pleading with the officers to take their furniture off before they burned the train.

They won't do it, Blair thought. *They're going to burn it all.* She took her hand off the arm of the bench and put it over her stomach. *I'm sorry,* she said to David. *I thought I was taking you where you'd be safe.*

"You look kind of funny," Callie said. "Maybe we ought to go back to the hotel."

Callie didn't want to leave. She was having a good time.

"I'm all right," Blair said automatically. She couldn't move. If Callie tried to make her get up, she would die. She needed to lie down. She felt as if she might be going to faint.

"That dumb colonel's makin' 'em line up out there," Callie said. "They've been runnin' all over the place! They've already been in the *hotel!* He's makin' the officers assign details to burn up the trains."

Matthew was out there. A Yankee, Blair thought. They took everything you loved and then when you found something else to love, they came back and took that.

"Where is Jim?" she whispered.

"He's still out there. They've got the men all separated. Civilians and prisoners of war. They're not lettin' the soldiers go to the hotel with everybody else."

Some of the Yankees came into the waiting room and went over to the Southern Railroad's safe. Blair knew they were getting ready to break it open. They were getting ready to burn the depot, too. The crowd of passengers was being herded outside.

After a while the smell of smoke began drifting in. Callie jumped up from the bench and ran to the door. "They're setting the cars on fire!" she cried.

Blair saw to her surprise that her mother was kneeling in front of her.

"Blair," Anna Mary said, "I couldn't find you. I've been looking all over the hotel. Darling—"

"We came over to see the telegraph," she said through clenched teeth.

"Blair, I didn't know you were here. They wouldn't let us cross the street—"

"Mama—I can't—move."

"What is it, Blair?"

"I can't walk."

"Yes, you can. You must."

"No, I can't."

"Then I'll find someone to carry you."

"No. I don't want—anybody."

The fire in the freight cars reached the artillery shells. The depot rocked to the explosions. Great, booming volleys that jarred Blair's teeth and vibrated down into her spine. She stared at her mother, who had jumped in surprise.

"Get up, Blair! You've got to get out of here!"

Callie came running back, shrieking with excitement, trying to be heard above the sound of the explosions. "Listen, Mama! Listen to that *noise!*"

Blair stood up from the bench. Her head swam and flashes of light shot in front of her eyes. The depot windows rattled in their frames. But the Yankees squatting by the safe paid no attention. They had broken it open and were taking the money out.

"Our trunks!" Callie screeched to her mother.

"Leave them," Anna Mary said, putting her arm around Blair as they crossed the waiting room. Outside, refugees from the passenger train huddled in terror on the hotel veranda, and the street swarmed with Yankees, some of them already carrying their personal loot. Anna Mary guided her daughter down the steps.

The smell of smoke and horses and sweaty soldiers swirled around them and the sun blinded her again. Somehow Blair made it down the steps.

"The hotel, darling," her mother said. "You can lie down—"

As they were crossing the street, a sudden pounding of hoofbeats rolled against Blair's eardrums, and she looked up to see a tidal wave of Yankees approaching from the north, thundering toward her relentlessly. More of them—more of them were coming—they were never through with her—there were always more. It was every Yankee on earth this time, galloping into Newton Station, bearing down on her in the street.

A huge black curtain fell around her, smothering her in its folds. She saw the dirt of the street coming up to meet her and heard her mother screaming. *Mama, I'm sorry*, she thought.

27

Callie huddled on the hotel veranda steps, shaking with delayed reaction. Her teeth chattered so noisily she had to grind her jaws together to make them stop. Every so often, one of her knees knocked against the other one, even though she was sitting down.

She could still hear her mother screaming and see Blair lying in the middle of the street, with all those horses coming. Her sister would be dead by now, if it hadn't been for Jim. He had come running out from the group of prisoners beside the depot with the Yankee guards hollering at him to stop. Callie had been afraid they would shoot him.

Jim went down on one knee and picked Blair up, and for a heart-stopping moment Callie thought he was going to drop her. His face turned so white when he stood up. But he went on across the street, and it seemed to take forever, because Jim's leg was dragging the way it always did.

Jim carried Blair all the way up the veranda steps and into the hotel. The ladies on the veranda were all screaming, too, while the artillery shells exploding on the trains were making such horrendous booms they almost deafened them. Then the new horde of Yankees came thundering past the veranda.

Where had all those new Yankees come from? She'd thought they were all already here. But the battalion that captured the train hadn't been a fifth of them, not a tenth. They were just the advance, or something. Now the whole caboodle was here.

The Yankee guards had come into the hotel and made Jim go back with the rest of the prisoners. Later they'd taken them down to the hospital. She supposed all the convalescents were prisoners, including the Kentuckian with the guitar. Would that mean Jim wouldn't be able to report to his new assignment at Meridian? Wouldn't be able to go with them the rest of the way?

The artillery shells were no longer exploding, but the freight cars were still burning. Although the two trains had been moved all the way past the hospital, the heavy black smoke rolling back along the tracks made Callie's eyes water and her nose itch. Across the street smoke-blackened cavalrymen moved crates and barrels from the warehouse beside the depot. She supposed they had got sooty from setting the boxcars on fire. How could the Confederates have *been* so careless? All the stores from the supply base at Meridian had been gobbled up before they got halfway to Vicksburg.

It was those butternut spies, she decided. Sending false dispatches to throw General Pemberton off their trail.

Callie sat glumly, watching the Yankees lug crates out of the warehouse. Then her heart gave a pleased little jump. There was Captain Harwell! In all the excitement she had forgotten to look for him!

Jumping up from the steps, she started toward the warehouse, being careful to look both ways before she crossed the street. Another torrent of Yankees might be coming. This might not be all of them, yet. However, except for the mob that was already in it, the street proved navigable. Callie snaked her way through and ran over to the warehouse, thinking that things would be better now. Captain Harwell was as good as Mr. Weems!

It took her a while to get his attention. The other Yankees kept getting in the way. One wiry, pleased-looking Yankee with a fuzzy blond stubble on his face was talking to him about what all he'd had to do today.

"I might as well be in the infantry," he was saying. "First I had to unload all that furniture out of that boxcar, and now I've got to unload thirteen tons of liniment out of here."

"Captain Har—" Callie said, dodging a couple of Yankees carrying a crate.

"I might as well be a pack mule," the wiry Yankee went on. "What am I going to have to unload next? This isn't much of a town, is it? Not exactly the charm spot of the sunny South."

"A little fire would help purify it," another Yankee said.

"Yeah," another Yankee agreed. "Why the hell can't we set it off without moving all this crap?"

"Hey!" Callie said loudly, trying to get around the sweaty soldiers. "Cap—"

"It's medical supplies for the hospital down there," a man with sergeant's stripes said.

"Grierson's going to hang around this damned place too long," Captain Harwell said.

"Captain Harwell!" Callie screeched.

He stopped looking at two men carrying a medical crate and looked at her.

"I saw you!" she cried. "I saw you out behind the depot! Before the trai—"

"What are you doing here?" he said. "Get over to that hotel."

Callie stopped her excited prancing and stared. He hadn't even said "Hello!"

"Huh?" she said.

"We're getting ready to fire this building. Go over to that hotel."

Captain Harwell turned back to the medical crates. "How much more of this?"

She stared at him in disbelief. Now he wasn't even *looking* at her!

A new Yankee came trotting up to Captain Harwell, his uniform soaked to the knees. "Where in the hell have you been, Miller?" Captain Harwell said, frowning at him.

The wet Yankee moved over confidentially and showed Captain Harwell something. Callie, craning to see, realized he was holding a thick wad of Confederate bills.

Callie mentally hung a big board across the wet Yankee's back and wrote on it in big, black letters: THIEF.

"Look what I found, Cap'n," he said in a low voice, thumbing through the bills.

"Whose is it?"

"Ahhh—no way to tell, sir. It was just floatin' in that ditch around there."

"Anybody claimed it?"

"No, sir. Believe they chunked it out."

"Then we'll assume they didn't want it."

"Yes, sir!" The cavalryman peeled off several of the bills and offered them to Captain Harwell. "Souvenir, sir?" he inquired.

To Callie's unbounded amazement Captain Harwell accepted! He put the money in his pocket! If she hadn't been looking right at him, she wouldn't have believed he'd done it! It couldn't *be!*

Then, to top it all off, he turned around and went into the warehouse. He left!

"How you doing, Red?" the fuzzy-bearded Yankee said, grinning at Callie through the fuzz. He put down his crate. "You come in on the train? Enjoy the big surprise we had waiting for you?"

"I knew you were there," she said. "I was in the station." She paused. "I was in the waiting room when that *spy* came in."

"Spy?"

"Uh-huh," she said disdainfully. "Trying to send General Pemberton a wire. But Mr. Moffatt didn't send it. That dumb *spy* couldn't tell Jim who his captain was."

"Must have been one of the scouts," the Yankee said. "My name's Phipps. What's yours?"

"Miss Tyler," Callie said, putting her nose in the air.

"I hear the brigade came in on the double," another Yankee said. "The colonel heard them shells going off and thought we'd walked into an artillery trap."

So that's what those last Yankees were, Callie thought. *The brigade. How many in a brigade?*

Captain Harwell emerged from the warehouse. "Get to work, Phipps," he said.

"Captain Harwell!" she cried, beginning to bob up and down in frustration. "Capt—"

He looked at her and scowled. "Jesus Christ! Are you still here? Now this is the last time I'm going to tell you! Get over to that hotel! We're about to fire this building! Do you want to get burnt up?"

Callie gaped at him. What was the *matter* with him? He didn't act like himself and he didn't talk like himself—she almost thought for a minute she had the wrong man!

"Don't you know me?" she cried.

He looked at her in surprise. "Of course I know you."

"Well, then, *listen* to me!" If he didn't quit snarling at her like that, she might start bawling! His face was grimy and smoke-blackened, and above his beard his forehead and nose were sunburned. There was a tight, forbidding look around his eyes.

"All right," he said. "I'm listening. What is it you want to say?"

"I can't say it here!"

Captain Harwell turned to the sergeant. "Make the men stay at it until they finish it, Clark. If Blackburn wants those medical supplies out, then out they come.

And hurry it up. The sooner we get it done, the sooner we leave."

He took Callie by the arm and led her over to the shade of a tree beside the depot. "Is this better?"

"Why are you acting so funny?" she said.

After a short silence he said, "Am I acting funny, Callie? Well, maybe it's because I've been—fairly busy."

"We were pretty worried about you!" she said accusingly.

Why hadn't he ever come back by the house? Even if he wasn't sorry to leave, it'd been pretty rude not to even tell them good-bye. And the awful part was, she'd thought he *did* like them! She'd even thought he and Blair might get married! She'd sat there and planned to write a letter to his sister!

"Why didn't you ever come back by the house?" she demanded.

Captain Harwell took a handkerchief out of his pocket and began to wipe some of the soot off his face. "Why? Did you want to see me again?"

"I reckon we did! You might have said something! I know you had time to come out!"

He looked at the soot on his handkerchief. "Well, how's the rest of the family? Is your mother all right?"

"Pretty good. We're refugeeing to Alabama. It's been sort of hard to find something to eat around Holly Springs. And"—she suddenly decided to tell him about this—"they came in after Van Dorn's raid and busted up the piano." Callie nursed a faint hope this would make Captain Harwell feel guilty. "And they threw Mama's china out in the yard."

She didn't tell him about Grandpa. That wound was too raw.

"Mr. Weems came by Christmas and brought us some peas." Callie felt compelled to add this small reassurance, because she didn't want Captain Harwell to think the *only* reason they'd missed him was because of the piano.

He wiped his handkerchief over his face and didn't say anything. His face was reassuming that tight, forbidding attitude.

Twisting around, Callie scuffed her toe in the dirt. "I wish you'd come over to the hotel. Blair fainted in the middle of the street. I reckon she's sick again." She felt the stupid tears rising. "I thought she was well."

Captain Harwell lowered his handkerchief and looked at her in a queer kind of way. "When?"

"When the brigade came in. Jim ran over and picked her up, and those soldiers guarding him yelled at him to stop. But then I reckon they decided we couldn't leave her out there in the street. With the horses coming and all."

"Where is she now?" he said in a strange, twisted voice.

Callie blinked rapidly, to keep from bawling right here by the depot. "Jim carried her on into the hotel. I —I wish you'd go on over there."

"Why? She doesn't want to see me."

Callie looked up in surprise. "Yes, she *does!*"

He rammed his sooty handkerchief back into his pocket. "No. You're wrong about that."

Callie had a feeling of panic. He acted like he wasn't going to come!

"Blair might die!" she cried ominously. Although she didn't really believe the situation was that drastic. And yet on the other hand, it had been terribly close! How could he ignore her like this? Blair had almost been killed!

Captain Harwell's face had turned pallid beneath its sunburn. He had gotten most of the soot off it now. "What's wrong with her? How do you mean, she's been sick? She didn't look sick to me."

"I don't know!" Callie said, feeling desperate. "She couldn't eat! And—and—" This was a delicate subject and she ground to a halt. She didn't think it would sound nice to say Blair was always throwing up. Her sister would kill her if she found out she'd told such a thing to a man!

"Callie," he said. "I'm—sorry. But you're asking me to do something that—I can't do."

"Why?"

"I can't explain it to you," he said, and turned and actually started walking away.

Callie ran after him and grabbed at his arm.

"You've *got* to!" she pleaded, all but groveling in supplication. "At least come over and see Mama! She's over there, too!"

He kept on walking.

"Captain Har—well!" Callie knew she was blubbering and hated herself for it. She couldn't seem to keep hold of his arm, he was going so fast. "They're—they're gettin' into the whiskey over there! They're gettin' *drunk!*"

This was a flat-out lie, but she didn't feel any guilt about telling it. Because there *were* whiskey barrels in front of the hotel, and the Yankees *were* going to get into them!

Captain Harwell stopped.

He turned around and headed toward the street. He seemed to be going in the direction of the hotel. Callie panted behind him, dashing tears from her face and feeling smoke from the burning freight cars stinging her eyes.

Matthew walked up the steps and into the hotel. He was aware that officers were on the veranda, probably members of Colonel Grierson's staff. They looked at him in mild surprise when he passed. Inside was a large room full of civilians. Men, women, and children from the passenger train. As soon as he entered, there was a faint scattering of gasps and some of the children started to cry. One of the women in the back of the room, sitting beside a large potted fern, suddenly stood up and pointed at him.

"Murderer!" she cried.

Matthew looked down at Callie, who was trotting beside him. "Where?"

Callie pointed toward a door at the left of the room. "Out there," she said breathlessly.

"Hessian! How many women have you tried to kill before today? How many—"

"For God's sake, Sara!" a man's voice pleaded in terror. "Be quiet!"

Matthew walked through the door, which led to a narrow, carpeted hall. Mrs. Tyler stood in the hallway, looking into a room. When she saw them, a faint ghost of a smile tugged at her mouth. "Hello, Matthew," she said. "I'm glad that you're here." Closing the door quietly, she came forward in a rustle of skirts. She clasped her hands tightly in front of her. "Callie, go into the lobby, dear."

"Mama—"

"Now, dear."

"Yes, ma'am," Callie said, and Matthew heard her scuffling away.

"Mrs. Tyler," he said noncommittally. "I don't believe I ever thanked you for saving my life."

"Yes," Anna Mary said. "I think you did." She was studying his face intently, as though trying to make a decision, the outcome of which would be determined by what she found there.

"Where is she?" he said.

The gentle blue eyes appraising him had an almost quizzical look. With a slight turn of her head Anna Mary gestured toward the closed door behind her. "The Moffatts were very kind. They insisted we take Blair in there. The stairs are quite steep, and Jim— well, Jim is not very strong."

Who was Jim? Matthew's numbness attested that it didn't matter.

"Is she all right?"

"I think you should go in and see her," Anna Mary replied.

Why did she think so?

Matthew wondered how much this pale, composed woman knew.

He shook his head. "No, I don't imagine she wants to see me."

"Matthew," Anna Mary said gently. "Blair is going to have a child."

Only the slight whitening of her clenched knuckles indicated the effort it must have cost her to make such a statement. Her eyes did not waver, but now they seemed to be pleading for something.

And whatever it was, Matthew did not know whether he was capable of giving it. The emotional jolt of the information just rendered him was so enormous that for a moment he could not grasp it. It was hideous and at the same time meaningless. He looked at her dumbly and felt the blood leaving his face. In the periphery of his consciousness the shouts of excited men outside blended with the buzz of voices from the lobby. They had nothing to do with him, or the quiet little world of the carpeted hall. He had a brief sensation of unreality. He and Anna Mary were wrapped in a cocoon.

He had to go in there now. Even if she didn't want to see him. Without stopping to say anything else to Anna Mary—there was nothing to say—he took a few irretraceable steps and opened the door.

The room was some kind of combination sitting room and bedroom and was on the west side of the building and pleasantly cool. Blinds were drawn halfway down the windows and no sun was streaming in. He was vaguely aware of velvet upholstery, an empty fireplace, a brass bedstead with a maroon coverlet, and flowered wallpaper bearing down on him from the walls.

He closed the door and walked silently across the room. Blair was lying on her back, with one arm thrown over her face. Her other hand was working a fold in the bedspread, which she had twisted into a small knot and was turning around and then turning back again.

Matthew stood and looked down at her. Below the upthrown arm her lips were slightly parted, and her breath came through them with a shallow, uneven sound. They had taken the hoops off, and the rumpled dimity skirts were powdered with dust. He wondered what he would have done if nobody had picked her up out of the street and he had come back and found her there, crushed beneath the hooves of the main column of cavalry.

"Are you awake?" he said.

The question was rhetorical. He knew that she was.

The arm moved a little, but Blair didn't answer.

He somehow found a chair, pulled it over by the side of the bed and sat down. Leaning forward, he put his elbows on his knees and clasped his hands. He looked down at them intently. They looked strange, as if he had never seen them before.

"Why didn't you tell me?" he said.

She stirred slightly on the bed. Eventually a faint voice drifted over from beneath the upraised arm.

"Tell you what?"

"Blair," he said, still staring at his hands. "I know you don't want me in here. And God knows, I didn't want to come. But I had to. Your mother just told me you're going to have a baby. Do you think anything could have kept me away? If I'd known that?"

There was a long silence, broken only by the sporadic shouts of the troopers outside. Blair continued to twist the little knot in the spread.

"Listen to me." Matthew heard the strain in his voice. "Callie says you've been sick. Have you been getting enough to eat?"

She suddenly sat upright, put her hand to the small of her back and took a deep breath. Carefully she looked at some distant point across the room. "You don't care about me. It bothered me for a while. But it doesn't anymore. They all thought I'd get over it, and

they were right. Why did you have to come here today,
Matthew? Do you hate me so much you want to kill my
baby, too?'' Putting her hands over her face, she
rocked back and forth on the bed.

Matthew sat hunched in his chair with a hollow feeling inside. Something had completely gutted him. It
had taken him, and stripped him, and turned him inside out. He had thought, *God help me if I ever listen to
her again.* Yet here he was, sitting here and listening.
And it was the way he had known it would be. She had
carved that last vital viscera out of him. And now—
there was nothing left.

Blair was gasping in dry, heaving sobs, as if she
were trying to cry and had no tears to be shed. He
knew it must be bad for her to be making sounds like
that, following right on the heels of her falling down in
the street. *God knows,* he thought numbly, *it'll be a mir-
acle if she ever has that baby at all!*

He got up from his chair, sat down on the bed and
took her in his arms. The gesture was vaguely familiar.
Somewhere—sometime—he had done it before. And
the consequences had been unbearable. He remembered that, too. But what was the use of thinking about
it. He had already done it again.

*"Damned Texan!" Eaton had said. "Showed her off to
the whole damned troop! Said, 'This is my girl! Ain't she
—pretty!' Laughing about how they—"*

"Shhh," he said. "You've got to stop crying. You'll
make yourself sick if you keep on like this."

Her shoulders were heaving with those struggling,
gasping sounds and she kept her hands pressed over
her face. "Blair," he said, "why are you doing this?
Don't you know it's not good for you? What do you
want from me? Tell me, and I'll do it." He took her by
the shoulders. *"Tell me!"* He gave her a little shake.

She took her hands away from her face, clenched
her fists, and cried, "Oh, why, why why? *Why* did you
leave like that?" Wildly she turned her head from side

to side and her hair whipped about her face. "I looked and looked for you, and I ran and I ran—"

"Stop it!" Matthew said sharply. She seemed to be on the verge of hysteria, and he gave her a harder shake. But good Lord! He couldn't keep shaking her like this—she suddenly went limp and sagged forward against his chest.

"I looked for you so hard! I was afraid you'd get killed!"

"Where, sweetheart?"

"Out at the—the fairgrounds. And then Preston looked for you, and he told me you'd gotten away. And then I didn't hear anything for s-s-such a long time! Matthew, how could you go away and not say anything? You said you loved me. Didn't you mean anything you said?"

A strange mist distorted his vision. The room seemed to be floating and the only tangible thing in it was what he held in his arms. "Yes," he said. "I meant it. I loved you. I never stopped."

"Why? *Why* did you leave?"

Why indeed?

"Because you didn't love me."

She didn't know what love was. She was sick and frightened now, because she was going to have a baby. It didn't matter. He loved her whether she loved him or not. He couldn't let her go. He couldn't live through it again . . .

Blair started to cry.

"Don't do that," he said, burying his face in her hair. He put his lips lightly on her temple, feeling the pulsing of blood through a vein. Almost gone, he thought. He'd almost lost it. Everything that mattered to him. Gone forever. Trampled out there in the street . . .

"I did love you," she said.

"It doesn't matter. I'm not going to let anything hurt you. We're together now."

Her arms went around his waist. "There was nobody to tell me! I didn't—I didn't know whether you were dead or alive! Nobody cared! They didn't want me to love you! Papa—''

She stopped.

"Are you all right?" he said. "Are you all right now? Lie back down, sweetheart. I'm filthy. Don't put your face on me. I'm too dirty to touch you—"

"No! No, you're not—I don't care! Matthew, they were out on the road that night! I couldn't let you come back home in the dark! I was so scared! I did it because I loved you—"

"I know," he said against her hair. He couldn't think clearly; he could scarcely see. No sleep at all last night, and how many hours the night before? Two? Three? When had they ridden out to the Rebel tannery? He couldn't remember. The days and nights ran together in a blur.

He stood up. He didn't trust himself to touch her. If he touched her, he would fall down on that bed and hold on to her until he blanked out. There was something important he had to do first.

"You won't get away from me again," he said. "Not this time. We've waited too long."

Blair sat up.

"Matthew—"

"Wait in here. Don't move."

"Where are you going?"

Should he tell her or not? *No*, he thought blearily. *Better not*. She would think of another reason why they couldn't do it. *Just sit still*, he thought. *Sit still.*

"I'll be back," he said. "Stay here."

When he closed the door behind him and stepped into the hall, an elderly, white-haired gentleman was coming rapidly down the stairs. He looked as if he belonged there, so Matthew intercepted him. "Listen," he said, stepping in front of him and blocking his path. "I'm getting married. There must be a preacher in this damned town. Find one. Get him here. Right now. I don't have much time."

The man opened his mouth and closed it again.

"Sir?" he said.

"It doesn't have to be a preacher. A judge—anything. Just get him here. Anybody that can perform a marriage ceremony. Hurry up!"

He realized Mrs. Tyler was still in the hall, close by the door leading into the lobby. He turned to her reassuringly. "Everything's fine now. Don't worry. I believe she'll be all right. Don't you?"

Anna Mary's face was drawn. "Yes, I think so."

"Mrs. Tyler—do you *know* this man?" the elderly gentleman said.

"Wait," Matthew said, remembering something. He reached in his pocket. "I can pay. I've got some money—" Damn! He couldn't find it! "Somewhere. He'll want some money, I suppose."

"I shall call an officer!" the elderly gentleman suddenly cried. "Surely, there is some limit to what we are expected to endure! This is a civilized country! I'll have you removed from this hotel!"

"Mr. Moffatt—" Anna Mary said.

Matthew found the Confederate bills in his other pocket. "Here!" he said, thrusting them toward the old man. "That ought to be enough. I don't know how much is there—you count the blasted stuff. And get a move on! Find a justice of the peace. I know you've got one."

Mr. Moffatt stepped back. "This man is insane!" he said to Mrs. Tyler. "You know him? You can't possibly—"

"Matthew," Anna Mary said, twisting her hands in front of her. "I'm not sure we're doing the right thing."

"I am," he said. "Don't worry." She did look worried, and he didn't blame her. After the way he'd behaved, she had no reason to trust him with Blair. "I'm sorry," he said. "You were very kind. I do love her. I can't lose her again. You understand that, don't you?"

"I suppose so," Anna Mary said with uncertainty in her eyes.

Blair opened the door behind them. "Matthew—"

He turned to her, thinking that she hadn't sat still. He had expressly told her to sit still. She was going to give him trouble again. No, not this time.

"We're getting married," he said.

She held on to the doorknob watching him. Her hair was mussed and her eyelashes matted with tears. Without the hoops she looked limp and bedraggled. Her waistline was gone. Matthew had never loved her so much in his life. He loved her so much it hurt. His love stabbed through him like a sharp pain.

"Yes," she whispered.

"Where is Colonel Grierson?" Mr. Moffatt said loudly. "I'll get protection from him!"

Jesus Christ! Matthew thought. Would he have to pull his revolver on him? "Here's the money! If it's not enough, I can get more." If necessary, he'd find Miller and take the whole roll. Maybe they preferred greenbacks. No? Yes?

Mr. Moffatt was staring at him in horror. He knew what he wanted him to do now. And he wasn't about to hand over that delicate flower of Southern womanhood to this stinking, bearded invader—ahhh, the Devil take him!

"Look," Matthew said. "Would it help if I took a bath? Just tell me where the soap and water is—dammit!—what do you expect me to look like? It's been eight days since I left La Grange!"

Anna Mary moved toward them. "This isn't accomplishing anything. Mr. Moffatt, you must let me explain. This is Captain Harwell—"

Somebody else had come into the hall. Matthew was aware of a plump, white-bunned old lady in a voluminous apron and starched skirts. "Ira?" she said. "What are you standing here for?"

"This—this *man*," Mr. Moffatt said, "wants me to secure a minister!"

"Mrs. Moffatt," Blair said from the doorway. "Matthew and I are getting married."

The old lady gave Matthew a piercing look. "Is this him?"

"Yes," Blair said.

"He's a Yankee."

"Madam—" Matthew began.

"That is a precious, brave girl," she said sternly. "You haven't treated her right."

"Mrs. Moffatt," Blair said. "He's—"

"My dear child," the old lady said. "Are you sure you want to do this?"

She was still looking at him. "Are you addressing me?" Matthew said.

"No, I'm asking that brave little girl. You don't have to marry him if you don't want to, dear."

Blair's hand was on his arm. "Why can't you leave him alone! Mrs. Moffatt—yes! I do want to! Please do what he says!"

Matthew looked down at her. "You shouldn't be standing up. I told you to wait."

"They don't know you," she said softly. "Don't pay any attention to them."

"Get Judge Baxley, Ira," Mrs. Moffatt ordered. "I saw him outside not five minutes ago."

Blair smiled a wobbly little smile against Matthew's sleeve. There was a short silence and then Mr. Moffatt turned and looked inquiringly at Anna Mary. She nodded. "Yes. Please do."

Mrs. Moffatt beamed at Matthew and Blair. "I'm sure you're a fine young man."

"Thank you," Matthew said.

Blair squeezed his arm, a gentle, conspiratorial squeeze. He saw that Callie had come in from the lobby and was watching them with interest.

"Callie," he said, "you're going to have me in the family."

She seemed unequivocally pleased. "You're gettin' *married*?"

"Are you surprised?"

"I knew you would," she said.

R

eckless abandon. Intrigue. And spirited love. A magnificent array of tempestuous, passionate historical romances to capture your heart.

Virginia Henley
- [ ] 17161-X The Raven and the Rose $4.99
- [ ] 20144-6 The Hawk and the Dove $4.99
- [ ] 20429-1 The Falcon and the Flower $4.99

Joanne Redd
- [ ] 20825-4 Steal The Flame $4.50
- [ ] 18982-9 To Love an Eagle $4.50
- [ ] 20114-4 Chasing a Dream $4.50
- [ ] 20224-8 Desert Bride $3.95

Lori Copeland
- [ ] 10374-6 Avenging Angel $4.50
- [ ] 20134-9 Passion's Captive $4.50
- [ ] 20325-2 Sweet Talkin' Stranger $4.99
- [ ] 20842-4 Sweet Hannah Rose $4.95

Elaine Coffman
- [ ] 20529-8 Escape Not My Love $4.99
- [ ] 20262-0 If My Love Could Hold You $4.99
- [ ] 20198-5 My Enemy, My Love $4.99